FORT
MISERY

FORT MISERY

A Fort Misery Western

WILLIAM W. JOHNSTONE

AND J.A. JOHNSTONE

PINNACLE BOOKS
Kensington Publishing Corp.

www.kensingtonbooks.com

PINNACLE BOOKS are published by

Kensington Publishing Corp.
119 West 40th Street
New York, NY 10018

First Printing: February 2023
ISBN-13: 978-0-7860-4961-5
ISBN-13: 978-0-7860-4966-0 (eBook)

10 9 8 7 6 5 4 3 2 1

Printed in the United States of America

CHAPTER 1

West of the Arizona Territory's Tinajas Altas Mountains, west of Vopoki Ridge, west of anywhere, Fort Benjamin Grierson, better known to its sweating, suffering garrison as Fort Misery, sprawled like a suppurating sore on the arid edge of the Yuma Desert, a barren, scorching wilderness of sandy plains and dunes relieved here and there by outcroppings of creosote bush, bur oak, and sage . . . and white skeletons of the dead, both animal and human.

The dawning sun came up like a flaming Catherine wheel, adding its heat to the furnace of the morning and to the airless prison cell that masqueraded as Captain Peter Joseph Kellerman's office. Already half drunk, he glanced at the clock on the wall. Twenty minutes until seven.

Twenty minutes before he'd mount the scaffold and hang a man.

A rap-rap-rap on the door.

"Come in," Kellerman said.

Sergeant Major Saul Olinger slammed to attention and snapped off the palm forward salute of the old Union cavalry. "The prisoner is ready, Captain."

Kellerman nodded and said, "Stand easy, Saul, for

God's sake. There's nobody here but us, and you know where it is."

Olinger, a burly man with muttonchop whiskers and the florid, broken-veined cheeks of a heavy drinker, opened the top drawer of the captain's desk and fished out a bottle of whiskey and two glasses. He poured generous shots for himself and his commanding officer.

"How is he taking it?" Kellerman said.

"Not well. He knows he's dying."

Kellerman, tall, wide-shouldered, handsome in a rugged way, his features enhanced by a large dragoon mustache, nodded and said, "Dying. I guess he started to die the moment we found him guilty three days ago."

Olinger downed his drink, poured another. He looked around as though making sure there was no one within earshot and said, "Joe, you don't have to do this. I can see it done."

"I'm his commanding officer. It's my duty to be there."

The sergeant major's gaze moved to the window, and he briefly looked through dusty panes into the sunbaked parade ground. His eyes returned to Kellerman. "Private Patrick McCarthy did the crime and now he's paying for it. That's how it goes."

The captain drank his whiskey. "He's eighteen years old, for God's sake. Just a boy."

"When we were with the First Maryland, how many eighteen-year-old boys did we kill at Brandy Station and Gettysburg, Joe? At least they died honorably."

"Hanging is a dishonorable death."

"Rape and murder is a dishonorable crime. The Lipan girl was only sixteen."

Kellerman sighed. "How are the men?"

"Angry. Most of them say murdering an Apache girl is not a hanging offense."

"That doesn't surprise me. How many rapists and murderers do we have?"

Olinger's smile was bitter. "Maybe half the troop."

"And the rest are deserters, thieves, malingerers, and mutineers, commanded by a drunk." Kellerman shook his head. "Why don't you ask for a transfer out of this hellhole, Saul? You have the Medal of Honor. Hell, man, you can choose your posting."

"Joe, we've been together since Bull Run. I'm not quitting you now." The sergeant major glanced at the clock and slammed to attention. "Almost time, sir."

"Go ahead. I'll be right there."

Olinger saluted and left.

Captain Kellerman donned his campaign hat, buckled on his saber, a weapon useless against Apache but effective enough in a close fight with Comancheros, and returned the whiskey bottle to his desk. His old, forgotten rosary caught his eye. He picked up the beads and stared at them for a long moment and then tossed them back in the drawer. God had stopped listening to his prayers long ago . . . and right now he had a soldier to hang.

CHAPTER 2

No other frontier army post had gallows, but in Fort Misery they were a permanent fixture, lovingly cared for by Tobias Zimmermann, the civilian carpenter, a severe man of high intelligence who also acted as hangman. So far, in the fort's year of existence, he'd pulled the lever on two soldiers and at night he slept like a baby.

Zimmermann, Sergeant Major Olinger, and a Slavic Catholic priest with a name nobody could pronounce, stood on the platform along with the condemned man, a thin young towhead with vicious green eyes. Fort Misery's only other officer, Lieutenant James Hall, was thirty years old and some questionable bookkeeping of regimental funds had earned him a one-way ticket from Fort Grant to the wastelands. A beautiful officer with shoulder-length black hair and a full beard that hung halfway down his chest, Hall stood, saber drawn, in front of the dismounted troop: thirty-seven hard-bitten, shabby men standing more or less to attention. The troop had no designation, was not part of a regiment, and did not appear in army rolls. Wages and supplies were the responsibility of a corporal and a civilian clerk in Yuma, and deliveries of both were hit or miss. As one old soldier told a reporter in 1923, "The army sent us to hell for our sins, and our only chance of redemption was to lay low and die under the guidon like heroes."

A murmur buzzed like a crazed bee through the troop as Captain Kellerman mounted the steps to the gallows platform. Private McCarthy's arms and legs were bound with rope and Sergeant Major Olinger had to lift him onto the trapdoor. Zimmermann slipped a black hood over the young man's head, then the hemp noose. He then returned to the lever that would drop the door and plunge the young soldier into eternity.

The army considered their castoffs less than human, and McCarthy lived up to that opinion. He died like a dog, howling for mercy, his cries muffled by the hood. Despite the efforts of Lieutenant Hall, the flat of his saber wielded with force, the soldiers broke ranks and crowded around the scaffold. Horrified upturned faces revealed the strain of the execution, soldiers pushed to the limit of their endurance.

"Let him go!" a man yelled, and the rest took it up as a chant . . . .

Let him go! Let him go!

A few soldiers tried to climb onto the gallows, but Sergeant Major Olinger drew his revolver and stepped forward. "I'll kill any man who sets foot on these gallows!" he roared. "Get back, you damned scum, or you'll join McCarthy in the grave."

That morning Saul Olinger was a fearsome figure, and there wasn't a man present who doubted he'd shoot to kill. One by one they stepped away, muttering as the condemned man's spiking shrieks shattered their already shredded nerves.

The priest's prayer for the dead rose above the din. Sent by his superiors to convert the heathen Comanche, he'd attended six firing squads, but this was his first hanging, and it showed on him, his face the color of wood ash.

Captain Joe Kellerman—he used his middle name because Peter had been the handle of his abusive father—said, loud enough that all could hear, "This man had a fair court-martial, was found guilty of rape and murder, and sentenced to hang. There's nothing more to be said."

He turned his head. "Mr. Zimmermann, carry out the sentence."

The carpenter nodded and yanked on the lever. The trap opened, and Private Patrick McCarthy plunged to his death. His neck broke clean, and his screeches stopped abruptly, like water when a faucet is shut off.

But the ensuing silence was clamorous, as though a thousand phantom alarm bells rang in the still, thick air.

And then Private Dewey Bullard took things a step further.

As Lieutenant Hall ushered the men toward the mess for breakfast, Bullard, thirty years old and a known thief and mutineer, turned and yelled, "Kellerman, you're a damned murderer!"

"Lieutenant Hall, arrest that man," the captain said, pointing. "I'll deal with him later."

Sergeant Major Olinger stepped closer to Kellerman and said, "His name is Bullard. A troublemaker."

"I know who he is. He won't trouble us for much longer."

"Insubordination, plain and simple," Olinger said.

"Yes, it was, and I won't allow him to infect the rest of the men with it," Captain Kellerman said, his mouth set in a grim line.

CHAPTER 3

After breakfast, the troop was assembled on the western edge of the post that looked out over the harsh wasteland of the Yuma Desert. A few blanket Apache, mostly Lipan, camped nearby, close to a boarded-up sutler's store that had never opened and a few storage shacks. The parade ground, headquarters building, enlisted men's barracks, latrines, and stables lay behind Captain Joe Kellerman as he walked in front of his ranked men. Dewey Bullard, under guard, stood a distance away, facing a stark sea of sand and distant dunes ranked among the most brutal deserts on earth.

"You men know why we're here," the captain said. "Under any circumstances I will not have insubordination at Fort Benjamin Grierson. I will not tolerate it. Deserters, thieves, malingerers, murderers, and rapists some of you; you're the soldiers no one wants. Damn your eyes, you're all condemned men, but the army is stretched thin on the frontier, and you were given a choice: death by firing squad or hanging, or the joys of Fort Misery. Well, you chose this hell on earth and now you're stuck with it."

Kellerman needed a drink, the effect of his morning bourbons wearing thin.

"Look around you," he said. "There were eighty of you

when this post opened and now there's thirty-six, since Private Bullard will not be rejoining us. Forty-four dead. Nine of them were deserters whose bones are no doubt out there bleaching in the desert. I executed three of you by firing squad and two by hanging, as you just witnessed. The other twenty-nine were killed by bronco Comanche and Comancheros. I know because I saw most of them die. And why did they die? I'll tell you why. It's because they were poor soldiers, coming to us half-trained and barely able to ride a horse. As a result the Comanche gunned them down like ducks in a shooting gallery. That will now change. By God, I'll make fighting men of you or kill you all in the process. In the meantime, I will not have an insubordinate piece of dirt like Dewey Bullard undermining my authority, especially now, when this post is under siege." Kellerman paused for effect and then said, "In an alliance from hell, the Comanche and the Mexican slaver Santiago Lozado and his Comancheros vow to wipe us off the map by executing every man in the garrison. Well I say, let them try!"

To the captain's surprise, that last drew a ragged cheer, and Lieutenant Hall whispered, "There's hope for them yet, Captain."

"Yes, be hopeful, Lieutenant, Just don't bet the farm on it," Kellerman said. Then, "Canteen!"

Sergeant Major Olinger formally presented a filled canteen to Kellerman, who hung it around Bullard's neck and then said, "Youngest soldier, step forward!"

A fresh-faced seventeen-year-old with a penchant for desertion took a step from the ranks, saluted, and said, "Private Reid reporting for duty, sir."

"You know what you have to do?"

"Yes, sir."

"Don't stint, Private Reid."

"No, sir."

"Then stand by." Kellerman directed his attention to Bullard. "Private Dewey Bullard, for the offense of rank insubordination to the detriment of military discipline and other past transgressions, I banish you from this post in perpetuity. If you make any attempt to return, you will be shot on sight. Do you understand?" Bullard said nothing and the captain repeated, "Do you understand?"

Bullard's black eyes blazed dark fire. "You're sending me to my death."

"You have water, make good use of it," Kellerman said. "Now begone from here and let us never see your face again. Youngest soldier Reid, get ready." Then to the pair of troopers holding Bullard: "Bend him over. No, right over." Bullard cursed and struggled but the captain had chosen the two strongest men in the troop to hold him. His arms elevated in vice-like grips, chest parallel to the ground, he ceased to battle his captors, and Kellerman said, "Youngest soldier Reid, carry out your order."

Private Reid grinned, relishing the task at hand. In the past he'd been bulled by Bullard, and now it was payback time. Reid took a few steps running and slammed the toe of his riding boot into the man's butt. The kick was so furious, so powerful, that the two soldiers holding Bullard lost their grip, and the man tumbled headfirst into hot sand.

"About . . . face!" Lieutenant Hall immediately ordered, and the troop turned its back on the stunned and hurting Bullard, as did Captain Kellerman and Sergeant Major Olinger.

"Forward march!"

The soldiers stepped away, and not an eye turned in Bullard's direction. The man was banished and was now invisible . . . as though he never existed.

CHAPTER 4

"Rider came in under a white flag, Captain," Sergeant Major Olinger said. "Comanchero by the look of him."

"You figure he's here to negotiate a truce?"

"I have my doubts about that, sir. He looks arrogant; like a man with an ultimatum."

Joe Kellerman rose from his desk and swayed slightly, his morning bourbon taking effect. "I'll talk to him,'" he said. "By the way, my breakfast bacon had green spots, the beans tasted stale, and the coffee was weak."

"Supplies are low, sir."

"Send a patrol to Devil's Rock, see if Yuma got up off its ass long enough to send us a supply wagon."

"Yes, sir."

"Have the Navajo ride scout for the patrol."

"Do you trust him?"

"No, but he's all we've got. I reckon Ahiga doesn't like eating rotten bacon any more than I do."

"I'll send out Corporal Hawes and six men right away."

The captain shook his head. "Hawes! Damn it, I know Hawes. When he was at Fort Griffin everybody knew he murdered and robbed that whiskey drummer for the ten dollars and five cents in his pocket."

"And that's the truth, but Dave Hawes is a good soldier, and we don't have many of them," Olinger said.

Kellerman buckled on his recently issued .45 Colt Single Action Army revolver and grabbed his hat from the rack. "Right now I'd forgive a hundred mortal sins for a hundred good soldiers. Now let's talk with the Comanchero. This should be interesting."

The Comanchero was a smallish man who wore the white shirt and pants of the Mexican peon, his chest crossed by bandoliers, a wide sombrero tipped back on his head, rope sandals on his feet revealing callused, gnarled toes. He sat a paint pony, probably of Comanche origin, and had a Colt in an open holster buckled around his waist. He carried a white sheet tied to a 10th Cavalry guidon, a deliberate insult.

When the man saw the shoulder straps on Captain Kellerman's shirt, he saluted and said, "Buenos días, mi Capitan."

"Buenos días. What can I do for you?"

"For me, nothing," the Comanchero said. He had quick, black eyes, and the mouth under his mustache was a straight, tough line that now relaxed in a smile. "But I bring you greetings and a wish for good health from the hidalgo, don Santiago Miguel Lozado."

"So, the raggedy-assed bandido is calling himself a hidalgo now. He's come up in the world."

The Mexican's smile slipped. "Oh, señor, I cannot tell mi general that. He would be very hurt. He is a man of a sensitive nature who longs for peace, not war."

"And what does he want from me? War or peace?"

"Don Santiago wants very little."

"And that's what he'll get . . . very little."

The Comanchero smiled, his hand waving. "It is but a small request."

"Name it."

"The general and hidalgo desires that you and your soldiers immediately pack up, leave this stinking fort, and never return." The man smiled. "Don Santiago is being generous. He wants only what is best for you and your soldados."

"And if I don't leave?"

The Comanchero chewed on the corner of his mustache, then said, "Then it will be very bad for you, I think."

"I have a message for Lozado," Kellerman said.

"Ah, then you've come to your senses at last."

"Tell Lozado he must immediately put a halt to his bandit activities, including running guns to the Apache and slaves to the Comanche. If he complies, I will allow him and his rabble to return peaceably to Sonora. Tell him I can't offer the same generous terms to the Comanche."

"And if he refuses?" The Comanchero's voice was tight, hardened by anger.

"Then I will kill Santiago Lozado and all with him."

"You already killed his son. Isn't that enough for you?"

"I killed Comancheros. I didn't know his son was among them."

The Mexican fell silent. He pulled down the brim of his sombrero like a monk's cowl, his shaded eyes glittering. The heat had bleached the sky into faded blue and the morning was heavy and oppressive, lying mercilessly on the suffering land like a smallpox blanket. A few idling soldiers crowded close, listening to every word, their faces carved from stone.

Finally, the Comanchero spoke. "Capitán, though grieving for his son, the hidalgo don Santiago Miguel Lozado extended the hand of friendship and you knocked it away.

The result will be the death of every man on this post, and for you, a terrible fate. Mi general has made it clear that if you refuse his offer, he will nail you to the wall of a building and skin you alive. I beg you to reconsider and pack your bags and leave. Leave now, before it's too late. This will not be the first time that mi general has extended mercy to the undeserving."

"You heard my terms. I will not change them," Kellerman said.

The Mexican leaned from his horse and spat into the dirt. "Pah! Your terms are worthless, the bluff of a frightened man. Do as the general says and save your lives." Then, talking to the soldiers, "Time is running out for all of you. You're all dead men. Surrender now while you still can."

Concern and some fear showed on the faces of the surrounding soldiers as Kellerman said, "I made a mistake. Perhaps I didn't put my refusal in strong enough terms."

He unbuttoned his holster flap, drew his Colt, and fired. His bullet hit the middle of the X made by the Comanchero's bandoliers, crashed through leather, bone, and flesh, and tore into the man's heart. The Comanchero shrieked, tumbled off his horse, and was as dead as hell in a parson's parlor when he thudded to the ground.

"Perhaps that answer was strong enough," Kellerman said as smoke trickled from the muzzle of his revolver. "One of you men, bring me Mr. Zimmermann. I have a job for him."

It was a measure of Sergeant Major Olinger's shocked surprise that he momentarily forgot his military discipline and addressed his commanding officer by name. "Joe, what the hell?"

"Lozado wanted an answer to his ultimatum. Well, I gave him one," Kellerman said.

"But . . . but he was under a flag of truce."

Captain Kellerman holstered his revolver. "A flag of truce means nothing to Santiago Lozado and his kind. All they understand is force."

"He'll come at us," Olinger said.

"No doubt he will. We burned him the last time."

"And it cost us three dead and a couple close to it, Captain. That was a month ago, and the Navajo says Lozado's numbers have grown since then. He says twelve more Comancheros came up from Sonora with the latest slave train and six cases of Henry rifles, and there are at least fifty Comanche in camp."

"If the Navajo isn't lying, we figure Lozado now has about a hundred fighting men," Kellerman said.

"And maybe more."

"Yeah, and maybe more." Kellerman smiled. "And that's why we're here at Fort Misery, Sergeant Major."

"'You are requested and required, with all expedition, to abolish slave and gun running from Mexico into the Arizona Territory and bring the perpetrators to swift justice.' I recollect that part of General Sherman's letter."

"So do I. Easy for him to say from his cozy berth in Washington." Kellerman thought for a moment and then said, "I don't want us to meet him in the open field again, so we'll let Lozado come to us. As before, station the pickets and we'll fortify the headquarters building and the infirmary. My compliments to Lieutenant Hall and ask him to report to my office in an hour."

"Yes, sir, and I'll give Corporal Hawes his orders."

"Yes, tell him to take the wagon and woe betide him if he doesn't come back with supplies."

Sergeant Major Olinger saluted and left, just as Tobias Zimmermann elbowed his way through a crowd of gawking soldiers and said, "You wanted to see me, Cap'n." He glanced at the body. "I heard the shot. A coffin?"

"No, I have other plans for this man. I think very soon we'll come under attack from Comancheros, so tell your wife not to leave headquarters. If she needs water, tell her to ask a soldier to take a bucket to the seep."

Mary Zimmermann was a tall, thin woman, straitlaced, much given to prayer, good works, lectures on the evils of demon drink and fornication and the power of prune juice to keep a person regular. She was the camp washerwoman and cook and the soldiers referred to her as the Virgin Mary.

Tobias Zimmermann listened to Captain Kellerman's instructions for the Comanchero's corpse and said, "Cap'n, I've never done the like before."

"There's a first time for everything, Mr. Zimmermann, so get it done."

"He brought a guidon."

"Yes, and he's taking it back. Nail the pole to his hand if you have to, but I want him carrying the guidon when he leaves here."

"It's a strange order, Cap'n Kellerman."

"And one you'll carry out. Just get it done. Tell me when you're finished."

The carpenter shook his head. "Fought in the war, didn't you?"

"Yes."

"It hardened you."

"How very perceptive you are, Mr. Zimmermann. Life hardened me. And now just surviving in this hellhole is finishing the job."

Zimmermann nodded. "Your dead man will be all ready to go in an hour."

CHAPTER 5

C aptain Peter Joseph Kellerman was a conflicted man. The army expected him to seek out and destroy the enemy with his ragtag bunch of rejects, at least half of them under a suspended death sentence or thirty years to be served in the Yuma Territorial Prison pending the opening of Fort Leavenworth. Given the assets he had, thirty-six calvary troopers of varying quality mounted on grade horses that had come to the end of their service and had narrowly escaped the knacker's yard, it was an impossible task. Facing them were at least fifty well-mounted Comanche, superb fighting men and fearless, and an equal number of Comancheros, ostensibly honest traders, but Santiago Lozado's ruffians, both American and Mexican, were slave traders and gunrunners, a bunch of hard cases whose only qualifications were that they were good with guns and would kill a man, woman, or child without a second thought.

Together, Lozado's Comanche and Comancheros made a formidable fighting force and a bitter enemy, and Kellerman was aware that the odds were stacked against him and his motley crew.

The battle was coming . . . and it would be a desperate fight for survival.

* * *

Sergeant Major Olinger's office was tacked on to the western end of the enlisted men's barracks and as always, the door was open. Captain Kellerman stepped inside and Olinger immediately sprang to attention. The rest of the headquarters building, including the commanding officer's cramped space, was covered in dust and smelled of dung from the stables, man-sweat, leather, and gun oil, but the sergeant major's office was swept clean, the top of his desk waxed, compliments of the Virgin Mary, and for some reason the odor from the stables never intruded. Without a second thought, Kellerman would've eaten his beans and bacon off the NCO's floor and happily slept on it if the occasion demanded.

"At ease, Saul," Kellerman said. "And get out the jug."

"Soldiers' whiskey, Joe."

"I know, army-issue rotgut, but if it's all we have it's all we have. But give Commanding General of the Army Sherman his due, he knows the only way a garrison can survive this posting is to stay half-drunk most of the time."

"All of the time." Olinger took two glasses and an earthenware jug from his desk drawer, poured the whiskey and said, "If Corporal Hawes doesn't bring in supplies from Devil's Rock, within a month this fort will be dry as dust in a mummy's pocket."

"Within a month we might all be dead," Kellerman said.

Olinger smiled, "Eat, drink and be merry, for tomorrow we die."

"And now it's all up to Corporal Hawes."

"Bless his heart."

That last brought a smile to Kellerman's face, and he downed his whiskey at a gulp. He slammed his glass on the desk and said, "You know something, Saul, thinking back, it wasn't worth it. All I went through was for nothing."

"They were too hard on you, Joe. Even General Sherman thought that."

"The decision of the court-martial was a foregone conclusion."

"It could be no other way. Joe, you were caught bare-assed in bed with your commanding officer's wife. That didn't give your defending officer much leeway and his insanity defense was a dud."

"Dropped two grades and sent to this hellhole. Why the hell didn't they just shoot me?"

"William Tecumseh Sherman, that's why. You covered his left flank on his March to the Sea and he considered you a fine soldier, and still does."

Kellerman sighed. "Well, it's all spilled milk now, isn't it?"

The sergeant major smiled. "Was pretty Ella Moore worth it?"

"In bed and out of it, she was a wooden Indian," Kellerman said.

"Did I hear something about Indians?"

Lieutenant John Hall, stood in the doorway smiling, his impeccable uniform brushed, long hair ringleted and perfumed, splendid beard combed and smoothed, the very model of the model cavalry officer.

"The sergeant major and I were discussing wooden Indians," Kellerman said. "What brings you here, Lieutenant? I ordered you to report in an hour."

"Yes, sir, but Mr. Zimmermann was most anxious to inform you that your carpentry work is finished. He said he used only discarded pieces of timber."

"Well, let's see his handiwork. Is it as I told him?"

Hall's face revealed little, but perhaps concealed a professional soldier's hint of disapproval. "It seems to be what the captain ordered."

"Then lead on, lieutenant. It's time to open the ball."

* * *

The soldiers of Fort Misery were a hard-bitten crew and as they crowded around the horror on a horse their expressions ran the gamut from amusement to disgust.

The sun was high in the hazy sky, burning like a white-hot coin and in the distance to the east, bookended by the Gila Mountains and the Davis Plain, Vopoki Ridge was a purple smear on the horizon. To the west of the ridge the earth was cleaved by rocky Spook Canyon where three weeks before Lieutenant Hall suffered casualties of three men killed and two wounded in a Comanche ambush. The two wounded men were still in the infirmary, attended, spreading herself thin, by Mrs. Zimmermann. It was confidently expected by the garrison, Captain Kellerman included, that the Virgin Mary would perform miracles.

"He's a sight to see," Sergeant Major Olinger said to no one but himself.

Captain Kellerman stared at the dead Comanchero and nodded. "Santiago Lozado sent me a message from his camp. I sent him a reply from hell."

His eyes wide open but unseeing, the dead man sat atop his paint pony, his body held upright in the saddle by a T-shaped, timber framework. In his right hand, the fingers broken and tied in place, he held the guidon, the pole over his right shoulder. But the white sheet was removed, one corner stuffed into his mouth so that the rest spread over his chest like a shroud. Kellerman noted with approval that Tobias Zimmermann had liberated the dead man's bandoliers, knife, and sidearm.

"The horse will find its way back to Lozado's camp," Kellerman said. "I want this man to be sitting upright when he gets there."

"My rig will hold him, Cap'n." Zimmermann drew the

Remington he carried on his hip, took a step back, and hammered five fast shots into the chest of the corpse. The body didn't flinch, and the man's eyes still stared into infinity.

The soldiers cheered and laughed, but Olinger said, "My God, Captain, how many times are we gonna kill that man?

Kellerman smiled. "I'd say now he's as dead as he's ever going to be."

"Wilson, Taggert," the sergeant major said, naming a couple of privates. "Take our guest to the edge of the post and let him go. He's outworn his welcome." He looked at Zimmermann. "Good shooting."

"I wasn't always a carpenter."

"No, you wasn't."

Zimmermann nodded, smiled, and walked away.

CHAPTER 6

D evil's Rock was a granite monolith abandoned millennia before by retreating ice caps. It was about ten foot tall, shaped like a deformed, crouching human, and it was Sergeant Major Saul Olinger who'd given the thing its name. The boulder stood about two miles north of Fort Misery in flat desert country, and it was a dumping off place for army supplies from Yuma. The civilian teamsters would come no closer to the fort and its evil reputation than the rock and wasted no time throwing off their load before scampering.

Mounted on a buckskin pony, the Navajo scout, a young man naked to the waist, wore a muslin loincloth, a Colt holstered in a canvas gun belt and knee-high moccasins. His only concession to a uniform was the yellow headband of an army scout that bound his shoulder-length black hair. The Indian seemed confused, his rifle trained on the man that sat among the pile of supplies.

Corporal Hawes was glad to see the grub, but his eyebrows raised in amazement at the young fellow with officer shoulder straps on his sweat-stained blouse who sat on an upturned barrel, Colt in hand, his eyes fixed warily on the Indian.

Hawes dismounted his men and ordered them to fill the

post's wagon. His practiced eye immediately determined that this time they'd not been shorted and had their full allotment of salt beef, salt pork, beans, bacon, coffee, and hardtack. There would also be salt, vinegar, brown sugar, molasses, bonded bourbon in bottles packed in straw for the officers and jugs of whiskey for other ranks, General Sherman well aware that Fort Misery had no sutler's store.

Hawes stepped to the lost-looking officer, saluted, and said, "Begging the lieutenant's pardon, but what the hell are you doing here?" He waved a hand. "This damned heathen goes by the name Ahiga, and you're lucky you still got your hair."

The officer rose to his feet, a tall, slender young man with earnest brown eyes and red hair showing under the brim of his kepi. His top lip was covered in the hopeful beginnings of the cavalryman's mustache, and from head to toe his uniform, still an unfaded dark blue, was covered in dust. He wore a revolver and a saber.

"Corporal, in answer to your question, I don't quite know what the hell I'm doing here. After I graduated from the Point it was my understanding that I was to be posted to Fort Concho, but when my orders came through I was assigned to Fort Benjamin Grierson."

"And the lieutenant arrived in Yuma . . ."

". . . and was then dumped here. I had the feeling the quartermaster sergeant in Yuma couldn't get rid of me fast enough."

"Why, sir?"

"I don't know why, sir. The civilians with the supply wagon gave me a canteen and some hardtack and said a patrol from the fort would be here directly. That was two days ago." The young man managed a smile. "I'm glad to see you, Corporal . . ."

"Hawes, sir."

"And I'm Second Lieutenant Atticus Cranston of the Philadelphia Cranstons—shipping and railroads, you know."

"No, sir, I don't know anything about that."

"Well, of course you don't. Why would you?"

"And you're fresh from West Point, sir?"

"Yes. I graduated a month ago."

Hawes smiled. "You're going to love Fort Misery, Lieutenant."

"Fort Misery? But I thought . . ."

"Just a soldiers' joke, sir." Hawes spotted Cranston's carpetbags and said, "Let's get your luggage into the wagon."

Second Lieutenant Atticus Cranston tried to hide his feelings, but frankly he was horrified. Meeting a real-life savage for the first time was shock enough, but after the spit and polish of West Point, where he'd graduated second in his class, the appearance of Corporal Hawes and his men astonished him. They looked like . . . not soldiers . . . but a band of brigands. None wore what even came close to the regulation uniform of field blouse and campaign hat but had stripped down to the top half of their union suits, originally red in color but now faded to washed-out pink, and a variety of hats, including one rogue sporting a straw boater. Untrimmed beards and uncut hair were everywhere in evidence, boots were unpolished and scuffed, and only the canvas belts and leather holsters seemed well cared for, as did the horses. Sabers were not worn on the belt but were strapped to the left side of the saddles, a .45-70 Sharps carbine in a non-regulation, commercial scabbard under their right legs.

Cranston called Hawes over after the corporal had loaded a barrel of salt beef into the wagon. "I was told Lieutenant Colonel Kellerman is in command at Fort Benjamin Grierson."

"You heard correctly, sir, but now he's Captain Kellerman."

"Ah, he was stripped of his brevet rank?"

"I wouldn't know, sir."

The young officer's eyes swept the troopers again. "What can you tell me about him?"

"What would you like to know, sir?"

"Is he a stickler for discipline?"

"You could say that, sir."

"But it seems to me he doesn't much care about the army's uniform rules and regulations."

"Sir, Captain Kellerman demands that pistols and carbines be clean and oiled and sabers sharp. The proper care of our horses is another of his . . . what is the word, sir?"

"Priorities."

"Just so, sir. His priorities. Captain Kellerman can be stern about those things, especially since we're surrounded by enemies. Oh, and just this morning he hung a soldier for committing rape and murder."

Cranston was shocked. "He hanged a soldier on his own authority?"

"Yes, sir. And later this very same day he threw another soldier off the post for insubordination. A man named Dewey Bullard."

"He sent him alone into the desert?"

"Yes, sir, into the desert never to return. And for good measure Bullard got his ass kicked."

The lieutenant looked for the lie in Corporal Hawes's eyes, found none, and said, "Who was the executed soldier?"

"Private Patrick McCarthy, sir." Then, "Be careful with those salt pork barrels, you louts! You'll burst the damned things!" Hawes's eyes returned to the officer. "Does the lieutenant have any other questions?"

"Yes, I have. Did McCarthy have a defending officer?"

"He didn't need one, sir. He was as guilty as sin."

"He had a court martial?" Sweat beaded on Cranston's forehead under the brim of his kepi, and his boyish young face was flushed.

"Yes, sir. Captain Kellerman and Lieutenant Hall presiding."

"And they found him guilty?"

"Of raping and murdering a sixteen-year-old Lipan girl, yes, sir."

"Lipan?"

"Blanket Indians, distant kin to the Apache. They camped near the fort, but they've all gone now that the Comanche have moved closer."

"How do your comrades feel about all this?"

"Does the lieutenant mean the hanging and the butt-kicking?"

"Yes, that's what the lieutenant means."

"They don't feel anything, sir."

"Surely those acts had a bad effect on morale."

"I don't believe so, sir. It sure didn't trouble me none. Hey, how do you boys feel about McCarthy getting hung and Dewey Bullard getting his ass kicked off the post?"

There was no collective shrug, but the indifferent silence was expressive enough.

Hawes said, "There you go, Lieutenant, nobody cares. McCarthy wasn't much and neither was Bullard. Good riddance, I say."

"Who are those enemies you speak of?" Cranston said.

"Sir, the post is under siege by Comancheros and their Comanche pardners. Add them both together and they outnumber us about three to one. Their leader is a man called Santiago Lozado, and he's the worst of them all."

"I've heard of the Comanche, but who are these Comancheros you speak of?"

"They're a mixed bunch of mostly honest whites and Mexicans who trade with Comanche and other tribes. But the Comanche are their best customers, and they exchange tools, cloth, flour, and tobacco for hides and horses. But some of them, like Lozado, go bad and trade slaves and guns in exchange for the gold and silver the Comanche take on raids into the New Mexico Territory and West Texas. But Fort . . . Benjamin Grierson stands in Lozado's way, hurting his business, and has to be destroyed."

"And Captain Kellerman's orders?"

"Are to wipe out Lozado and his bunch."

"And his strength in both infantry and cavalry?"

"Thirty-six cavalry and a Navajo scout."

"That's all?"

"Yes, sir."

Cranston looked like he'd just been slapped. "Thin on the ground, Corporal."

"Indeed, sir."

"Hey, Hawes, the wagon is loaded," the private in the driver's seat said.

Corporal Hawes said, "Begging the lieutenant's pardon, but since you don't have a horse, I suggest you ride the wagon with Private John Smith." He smiled. "Nobody knows Private Smith's real name, except maybe himself and the Texas Rangers. Ain't that right, Johnny boy?"

Smith, a hard case rumored to have killed seven men in his outlaw days, raised his shoulders and said, "The army gave me that name when I enlisted."

"And Johnny thanked them by helping to rob a payroll wagon out of Fort Grant. Six Buffalo soldiers of the escort were killed in that scrape, and Johnny and his cohorts made off with twenty-eight thousand dollars in gold and silver coin that's never been recovered."

"The army couldn't prove I was in on that robbery," Smith said, his tough face surly.

"But you know where the money is hidden, don't you, Johnny boy?" Hawes said.

"Maybe somebody told me, but I don't remember."

"And that's why he was posted to Fort Misery, Lieutenant: to improve his memory," Hawes said. "Ain't I correct, Private Smith?"

"The army can't break me. I can take anything they throw at me."

"Sure, you can," Hawes said. "Until the day you figure out how to desert and head to the place where the money is hid under a rock. You'll be a rich man, Johnny boy. That is, if the Comanche let you live that long."

"I'll take my chances, and maybe there will be a time when I come looking for you, Hawes."

The corporal smiled. "Johnny, you couldn't shade me on your best day."

Second Lieutenant Cranston had heard enough. "Stop the bickering," he said. "I want to reach Fort Benjamin Grierson before nightfall."

"We will, sir," Hawes said, dragging his eyes away from Smith. His grin was not particularly pleasant. "Captain Kellerman will welcome you with open arms."

CHAPTER 7

The Comanchero camp was wedged against a bedrock outcropping some six miles northeast of Fort Misery. Blankets and a single pup tent were spread across sandy ground, shaded here and there by bur oak, sage, and creosote bush. To the west lay mile after mile of flat sand and dunes,. and to the east Vopoki Ridge marked the outer edge of civilization. A dozen cooking fires burned throughout the camp, black smoke rising straight as a string into the stagnant air. The Mexican slaves, thirty in number, huddled together silent, scared, and watchful.

But all was not well in the Comanchero encampment.

The girl had displeased Santiago Lozado. He dragged her from his tent by the hair and threw her back among the slaves, tossing her tattered dress after her. She stood naked, tearful, and yelled Mexican obscenities at the Comanchero. She was lucky that Lozado had other things on his mind. On another day he might have shot her.

Tosawi, the Comanche war chief, sat by the campfire drinking coffee under the red dawn sky, watching. He grinned. "Santiago, my friend, Mexican women are always a disappointment. They don't have the passion of Comanche girls."

"Not so, White Knife," Lozado said, using the English

version of the young man's name. "The Sonora whores have fire."

"If you pay them enough."

"I pay them well." Lozado spat. "They haven't been spoiled by chanting priests, whispering nuns, and incense." He nodded at the girl who'd put on her dress and now cried on another woman's shoulder. "Look at her. She hates me."

"She weeps for the loss of her maidenhood."

"Pah! What is virginity to a slave?"

The Comanche smiled. "Among slave women it does not exist."

A call from the edge of the camp.

"Rider coming in!" Kyle Swan's voice.

"My emissary returns," Lozado said, rising to his feet.

"Something's wrong," Swan said.

Lozado hurriedly walked to him and peered shortsightedly into distance.

"Who is that man?" he said.

"He's the man you sent to threaten Kellerman," Swan said.

"Why does he look so strange?"

"Because Kellerman crucified him," Swan said.

As the dead man came closer, Lozado's eyes almost popped out of his head with shock, soon replaced by a raging anger. "He killed my man under a flag of truce."

"Looks like Kellerman made him eat your flag," Swan said. He stared at the body on the horse. "Looks like he shot him all to pieces, trussed him up, and then stuffed the flag into his mouth." He smiled grimly. "It seems Kellerman is a man of imagination."

Lozado shook his head slowly, very slowly, and then, his teeth gleaming in a feral snarl, he said, I . . . Will . . . Kill . . . Him . . . With . . . My . . . Bare . . . Hands."

He looked around and yelled, "Juan Ramirez!"

Ramirez, one of Lozado's captains, hurried to his side.

The man looked at the corpse on the horse and blanched. "What happened to him, don Santiago?"

"Kellerman crucified him," Lozado said, echoing Swan.

"But he was on a mission of peace," said Ramirez, a tall, well-built man wearing vaquero finery and a handsome, ivory-handled Colt in a tooled holster and gun belt.

"And this is Kellerman's answer. Juan, I won't quietly accept this insult. To do so would be to show weakness. I want you to take fifteen of our best men and attack the fort."

"When, don Santiago?"

"Now."

"But . . ."

"It will not be a full attack. Juan. You will fire on the fort and count how many rifles answer. I must know Kellerman's strength. When you've done that, retreat. Don't linger. Go now, get it done."

"Yes, don Santiago."

After the man left, Lozado beckoned to a couple of his men, pointed to the dead man, and said, "Take that into the desert. Bring back the saddle and horse." The two Comancheros hesitated, and Lozado said, "He failed me and needs no better burial."

"Why did you send only fifteen Comancheros to attack the fort and no Comanche?" White Knife said.

"I'm a cautious man, that's why I've lived this long. It is a probing attack to test Kellerman's defenses. I told Juan Ramirez not to take unnecessary casualties but to count rifles and then retreat pronto."

"Pronto," the Comanche said. "It is a good word. Alas, I cannot stay much longer, my friend. Now we have our slaves and rifles for the Apache, we must go north where our people are. Pronto. My warriors long for their wives and the buffalo herds."

White Knife was not an imposing figure. He was a small man, slender of build, but renowned as a brave warrior and a wise war chief. He wore a deerskin shirt and the mark of a fighting man, soft, pale blue boots that came up to his hips. His hair was combed back from his forehead and woven into one long braid. A calm, cool, and collected man of few passions, he was nonetheless driven by a hatred for the white settlers he considered a pestilence on the land, created by evil spirits. He considered bluecoat soldiers poor warriors and baby killers.

Lozado was a burly, unshaven man of medium height and coarse features who affected the white shirt and pants of the poorest peon. But he wore Texas-made boots with large-roweled spurs and his holstered Colt and gun belt were of the highest quality. He spoke again in Spanish, the lingua franca of the Southwest. "My friend, por favor, remain a few days until the damnation fort is no more and the man called Kellerman is dead or wishes he was."

"You can defeat him with the men you have."

"But how many would I lose?"

"I don't know. Kellerman is a beast."

"I sent a man to him with my peace terms and Kellerman killed him. If I can avoid it, I don't wish to make a direct attack. My plan has always been to lure him out of the fort. I can catch him in the open desert. With your warriors and my Comancheros riding together, we can overwhelm Kellerman quickly and our casualties will be small."

"And what do the Comanche receive in return?"

"All Kellerman's horses, arms, and ammunition, and whatever else you can find. The Apache will pay for guns and horses in gold."

"I already bring them such things."

"But there are many Apache, Chiricahua, Mescalero, Jicarilla, and they always need more guns and horses. You know they flog a horse until it drops dead under them and then they eat it."

"You say some true things about the Apache, friend Santiago."

"Will you stay, join me in the attack on the hated Kellerman?"

"Let us hear what Juan Ramirez has to say about the strength of the soldiers. My friend, there are few Comanche, and our numbers grow less every year."

"The Americans are devils."

"I do not wish to see more women's tears among the tipis."

"Your warriors are brave."

"Even brave men fear to die."

"Then you will have my men do all the fighting while the Comanche stand aside like frightened women?"

White Knife's face hardened. "Your angry words sting like hornets."

"Then I apologize, my friend. And you are correct, my cross words were ill-spoken. But where there is anger, there is pain, and it pains me that your warriors will not join in the attack on our bitterest enemies."

"My friend, what would you have us do?" White Knife said. "We are few in number, and the Comanche are in peril of being no more. The white soldiers have already herded most of my people like cattle onto reservations where there are no buffalo—just starvation, disease, and the death of hope."

Voices had been raised and both Comancheros and Comanche edged closer to their chiefs, faces concerned.

"White Knife, I am a compassionate man," Lozado said in a lower tone. "Look at me, I weep for the Comanche and what you are suffering. That is why it is so difficult to ask such a favor of you."

"I have no favors to give."

"Grant me this, my friend. Be present at the battle but do not join unless you see my men waver and the attack falter."

"Then ride to your rescue."

"Yes. Your numbers will turn the tide."

"This I will do, Santiago. But only if I see that the battle can be won. I will not litter the ground with Comanche dead by joining in a fight already lost."

"Then I will ask no more of you. You have spoken bravely."

White Knife's smile was without humor. "The time for the Comanche to be brave ended with the Red River War. We will go north and sell our slaves where we can and our guns to the Apache and by and by learn the ways of the white man and no longer make war on him. Then perhaps the numbers of the Comanche will increase."

"And if there are no Comanche, what then for the Comancheros?" Lozado said.

Again, the Indian smiled. "My friend, you will find a way."

"I think I will return to Mexico. I will be a hidalgo and live in a hacienda and the peons on my estate will call me don Santiago and I will flog the men and rape their women."

"You will be a great man, Santiago," White Knife said. "And perhaps you will find a rich bride."

"Yes, rich, but not old."

"Then why make war on the soldiers? Take your gold and silver and leave now."

Lozado shook his head. "Times have been hard, and I have little silver and no gold. My friend, I will not quit this ground until the shadow of the beast Captain Kellerman no longer pollutes the earth."

"I know he killed your son."

"My only son, born of a peasant woman who died birthing him. He was on his way to being a fine man when Kellerman shot him down like a dog. Damn his eyes, he will pay."

"My friend, the Comanche have ways to make a man beg for death. I have heard prisoners scream for many days."

"Then you will guide me when Kellerman is nailed to a door."

"Or staked out on an anthill."

"My mouth waters at the thought."

"Now we wait on the return of your men. Hah! Maybe Kellerman is already leaving the fort."

"I hope this is so," Lozado said. "I want him alive. He'll end his life suffering the torments of hell."

CHAPTER 8

Corporal Dave Hawes urged his horse alongside the wagon.

"Do you hear it, Lieutenant?" he said.

"I hear it. It seems to come from the fort."

"That's a heap of shooting. I guess I'll take the patrol and see what's happening."

"No, Corporal, not yet," Second Lieutenant Atticus Cranston said.

"Begging the lieutenant's pardon, but we can't waste time."

"We won't." Cranston's face settled in thought, then he said, "How much dust can we raise?"

"Sir?"

"We place the wagon in the middle of the detail and then charge at a gallop. How much dust can we raise?"

"Seven riders and a wagon . . . that's a fair amount of dust."

"We can't let the attackers see how few we are. We'll swing around and attack from the rear of the fort."

"And come out of a dust cloud."

"Exactly, Corporal." Cranston grinned. "My guess is the

enemy attack will be directed at the front of the headquarters building. We can surprise them."

"Will it work, sir?"

"Maybe. It depends on the dust."

"And if the dust doesn't do the trick?"

"Then my up-until-recently promising army career may come to a sudden halt."

"Very reassuring, sir," Hawes said.

Led by Corporal Hawes, Second Lieutenant Cranston and his small group swung wide to the northwest and then halted when they were about half a mile from the rear of the headquarters building.

The firing was sporadic, as though the Mescalero were testing the defenses prior to an all-out attack. The day was waning, the sun dropping like a coin into a slot, and the lemon sky was tinged with red.

"Corporal Hawes, gallop forward a hundred yards or so and then come back," Cranston said.

"Sir?"

"Carry out the order, Corporal."

Hawes shrugged and then urged his mount into a gallop. He rode the ordered distance and then swung around and came back.

Cranston grinned. "Dust, Corporal Hawes. Dust!"

Hawes turned his horse and studied his back trail, where a yellow haze hung in the still air, and smiled. "Yes, sir, that's a guaranteed fact."

"Right. You and three troopers on my left, the other three on my right. Let's stay close and make the dust cloud thicker. Private Smith, on my command make the nag in the shafts gallop, probably for the first and last time in its life."

Smith nodded and gathered up the reins.

The lieutenant drew his Colt and said, "Troopers, rifles at the ready. Shoot at anything that isn't wearing a blue coat. And I want to hear plenty of whooping and hollering. Let's sound like an army."

Cranston glanced at the sky, took a deep breath, raised his revolver, and yelled, "Charge!"

And what later became known to the denizens of Fort Misery as the Great Dust Dash began.

Juan Ramirez saw riders in a dust cloud coming at a gallop, a wagon that he figured must hold infantry in the middle of them. It was only a glimpse, but he'd seen enough. His order from don Santiago was to probe the fort's defenses, not to engage in a battle.

"Vamoose, muchachos!" he yelled, waving his rifle toward the tethered horses. Then, to the Americans with him, "Get the hell out of here!"

The Comancheros ran for their mounts, but Ramirez stopped and looked over his shoulder. The wagon had halted, probably to unload the infantry, and soldiers fired, their rifles winking red as the following dust cloud rolled over them.

"We'll be back!" Ramirez hollered. "We'll kill you all!"

A bullet kicked up an exclamation point of sand at his feet, and then he too ran for his horse.

Now soldiers piled out of the headquarters building and kept up a steady fire at the retreating Comancheros. Bullets split the air around Ramirez and his men, but no one was hit. A quick tally of empty saddles told Lozado's second-in-command that he'd lost three men in the day's action, and all for nothing. How many soldiers had arrived to reinforce the fort's garrison? Because of the fading light and infernal swirling dust, he'd no way of knowing, but it seemed like a full troop of cavalry and some infantry in wagons.

The news would not please don Santiago or the Comanche.

CHAPTER 9

C orporal Dave Hawes saluted Captain Joe Kellerman and said, "Sir, we brought in the supplies . . . and this officer."

Atticus Cranston stepped away from the wagon and came to attention. "Second Lieutenant Cranston reporting for duty, sir."

Kellerman slowly looked the young man up and down, his expression less than impressed. Cranston was covered in dust from head to toe, his face a yellowish mask. Only his brown eyes were free of the stuff—white circles, as though he'd fallen facedown in mud while wearing round spectacles.

"Hawes, what in God's holy name did you bring me?" Kellerman said. "What do I see before my misbelieving eyes?"

"A mislaid officer, sir."

"Who lost him?"

"I don't know, sir. He was dumped at Devil's Rock with the supplies."

"Then speak to me, thou dire apparition," Kellerman said. "What the hell are you doing here, wandering around, lost in the desert, inconveniencing my corporal?"

To Cranston's eyes his new commanding officer, badly

needing both a haircut and shave, looked more pirate than soldier. Kellerman wore a faded blue blouse without shoulder straps, canvas suspenders, and a red bandana hanging loosely around his neck. His boots that should've been varnished to a sheen were scuffed, strangers to a polishing cloth.

"Sir, I wasn't lost," the young man said. "I was obeying my order to report to Fort Benjamin Grierson."

Kellerman was suspicious. "In God's name, why?"

"Sir?"

"What did you do that was heinous enough to send you here among the barbarians? This outpost is teetering at the very edge of Western civilization. Did you know that?"

"No, sir, I did not know that, and I did nothing wrong except to graduate from West Point a month ago."

"A West Pointer, and they sent you here? Surely you must've murdered somebody, or at least robbed a bank?"

"No, I did neither of those things, sir. After I graduated, I was told I was being posted to Fort Concho. But somebody in Washington made a mistake, and I was ordered here."

"Only the army could make a mistake like that," Kellerman said. He called over Sergeant Major Olinger. "What's the butcher's bill?"

"Three Mescalero dead. On our side, Private Burke was cut on the cheek by flying glass, but we have no other casualties."

"Excellent," Kellerman said. "See that the men get an extra whiskey ration tonight."

"Yes, sir."

"Now, let me introduce Mister . . . what's your name?"

"Atticus Cranston, sir."

"Sergeant Major, under all that desert dust is a shiny new second lieutenant. See that he's allotted quarters."

"I'd like to bathe, Captain. I was in the desert for two days."

"Sergeant Major, introduce this officer to Mrs. Zimmermann and see what she can do for him, washing wise. Lieutenant, we draw our water from a seep and there's not very much of it at that, so no one at Fort Misery bathes. But I'm sure Mrs. Zimmermann can fill a canteen and scrub you down with lye soap and make you look all nice and shiny again."

"Sir, I think I can manage that task by myself," Cranston said.

"Very well, but Mrs. Zimmermann will be very hurt. She's never scrubbed a second lieutenant before, especially one from West Point."

Sergeant Major Olinger said, "Corporal Hawes, get the officer's bags." Then, "Follow me, sir."

"Before you go, Lieutenant Cranston, was the action you undertook today your own idea?" Kellerman said.

"It was my plan, yes, sir."

"Coming out of the dust to disguise your numbers was an excellent strategy and you sent the Comancheros running. Well done."

"Thank you, sir," Cranston said, smiling slightly.

"Then I'll see you in the officers' mess for dinner. Dress uniform is not required or expected, but a clean face and hands are, and add to that a pleasant countenance. You can talk about anything you like except politics. Tales of encounters with loose women always go down well."

"I've never met any, sir," Cranston said, his voice stiff.

"Too bad," Kellerman said.

CHAPTER 10

"Be damned to you, Juan Ramirez," Santiago Lozado said. "How many?"

"My guess is as I told you, don Santiago. I believe a troop of cavalry and some infantry."

"Kellerman, that black-hearted scoundrel, has the luck of the devil."

Ramirez's gaze moved beyond the camp. "The Comanche are leaving," he said. "They ride into the darkness."

"White Knife will ride through the fires of hell to get away from here," Lozado said, his eyes angry. "The news you brought disturbed him. Now that Kellerman is reinforced, he will not expose his band to a battle with him."

"The Comanche are no longer great lords."

"Pah! The Red River War turned their warriors into squaws. Now they follow the coward's road that Quanah Parker made for them."

"They left the slaves behind."

"I told White Knife to leave them, that they'd only slow him down and need to be fed."

"Why, don Santiago?"

"Because maybe I can use them as a bargaining chip.

I'll tell Kellerman that I'll kill them all if he doesn't do what I want."

"And that is?"

"Surrender himself to me."

"Do you really think he'd do such a thing?"

"I don't know. But when the word spreads that he allowed forty people to be killed to save his own skin, what might happen to him then?"

"He would be punished by the army, perhaps?"

"Perhaps. Drink coffee, Juan. I do not blame you for today. See how the sparks rise from the fire. A wise man might be able to tell the future by reading the path of the sparks."

Ramirez smiled. "I see no message there."

"And do you know why, my friend?"

The man's smile widened as he shook his head.

"It is because you have no tomorrows."

Lozado drew his Colt and fired.

Hit in the center of his chest, coffee spilled from the cup in Ramirez's hand, and he slumped forward, dead by the time his face thudded into the flames, throwing up a shower of sparks.

"Ah, the sparks, they tell me never to accept failure," Lozado said, as the skin of Ramirez's face bubbled. Alarmed men crowded around him, and he said, "Take that into the desert away from camp where you left the other body and let the buzzards dine tomorrow."

As the body was dragged away, a young Comanchero said, his face puzzled, "Don Santiago, why did you shoot that man?"

"Because Juan Ramirez failed me. When he saw that all was lost, the dog should've died, gun in hand, on Kellerman's doorstep."

"What has happened, patrón?" a tall, thin-faced man with green, reptilian eyes said. Kyle Swan was a knife-fighter out of Bisbee who'd done his best work in dark alleys, rolling drunken miners. The law made him a marked man, but when he gutted the pistolero and all-round nuisance Johnny Gusto in the Union saloon, the city fathers had given him a pass and offered him a hemp noose or a ticket out of town. Swan wisely chose the latter. Now a Comanchero, he was one of the few men Santiago Lozado trusted.

"My friend, I am saddened by the betrayal of Juan Ramirez," Lozado said. "I speak in English because I am pleased by your courtesy and concern."

"His attack on the soldiers failed?"

"It was meant to fail. I ordered him to launch a probing assault and count the rifles that answered."

"And this he did not do?"

Swan smiled inwardly. In common with the six other Americanos in this outfit he adopted a formal tone of speech when talking to Lozado, giving due respect to a smelly, jumped-up Mexican peasant. One day he'd probably shove a blade into the greaser's guts, but until then, he paid well.

"During the battle, Kellerman was reinforced. But Ramirez did not wait to count their numbers. Instead, like the coward he was, he fled the field. He thought perhaps a troop of cavalry and a number of infantry in wagons, but he was not sure."

"He should have made sure," Lozado said.

"Ramirez said a dust cloud made that impossible," Swan said.

"Damn him, patrón, he deserved to be shot."

"He could have read his fate in the sparks from the fire. I gave him the chance to run away."

"But he did not."

"No, and I shot him."

"And now what of Kellerman?"

Lozado shrugged. "The man who murdered my son still lives."

"And how do we deal with him and the others with him?"

"I have not yet decided on a course of action, my friend. But Kellerman will die soon, be assured of that."

CHAPTER 11

"Just move Major Mouser off your chair, Mr. Cranston," Captain Joe Kellerman said. "He knows he shouldn't be in the mess."

"By tipping the chair, Lieutenant," Sergeant Major Olinger said quickly. "Put a hand on him and you could lose a finger or two."

"The major is the meanest cat in the United States Army and probably Navy," Kellerman said. "That's why he's right at home in Fort Misery."

Second Lieutenant Cranston tipped the chair and the huge orange cat hissed like a baby dragon under a rock before he landed on all fours on the floor. "Looks like I've made an enemy," the young officer said.

"No, you haven't," Kellerman said. "Major Mouser hates everybody equally. He'll just add you to his list."

Cranston sat, picked up his napkin, and smiled. "Yet you saw fit to make him an officer, Captain."

"All cats are officers, Lieutenant. You don't commission a dog; too scatterbrained." Kellerman smiled as the Virgin Mary laid several large serving platters on the table. "Ah, Mrs. Zimmermann, you've done us proud."

"Braised salt beef, potatoes, and beans," the woman

said. "And for after, suet plum duff." She scowled. "Made with raisins, not plums. I don't have any plums."

"A veritable feast in your honor, Mr. Cranston," Kellerman said.

"Yes, you did well today, Atticus," Lieutenant James Hall said. "I couldn't have done much better myself."

"Thank you, sir," Cranston said, "Please pass the beef."

Thanks to the arrival of the supplies, the officers' mess was lit—an unheard-of luxury at Fort Misery—by not one, but two oil lamps that cast a guttering light in the room while never reaching the shadowed corners where the spiders spun and at night, pocket mice scuttled and squeaked.

Someone knocked on the door.

"Enter," Kellerman said.

The Navajo scout, a .44-40 Henry cradled in his arms, stepped inside. The tall Indian was never seen without his rifle, as though it was a part of him, like an extra appendage. "Captain, I have a report to make," he said.

"Damn it all, Ahiga, can't it wait, or are you hell bent on spoiling my dinner?" Kellerman said.

"Good news, Captain."

"Then let's have it. I need some good news."

"The Comanche have left Lozado's campground."

"And gone where?"

"North."

"You cut their trail?"

"Yes. Fifty warriors, riding north."

"By God, sir, that will weaken Lozado," Lieutenant Hall said, chewing on beef.

"If it's not a ruse to put us off guard," Kellerman said. "They might double back on us."

"For what purpose, sir?" Sergeant Major Olinger said.

"To hit us front and rear, Sergeant Major."

"Ah, a classic pincer attack," Hall said.

"Yes, I know what it is," Kellerman said, edgy.

Nonplussed, Hall said, "First used in 216 BC by Hannibal at the Battle of Cannae during the Second Punic War."

"I know that too, Lieutenant," Kellerman said. "We've all studied military history."

"Hannibal's envelopment killed forty-eight thousand Romans that day, maybe more," Hall said.

Kellerman caught Olinger's amused grin and said, "Mr. Hall, since you are such an expert on such things, at first light tomorrow you will take out a patrol and ascertain if the Comanche are still heading north."

"Nineteen thousand three hundred Romans captured," Hall said.

Kellerman's forkful of beans hovered between his plate and mouth. "Acknowledge my order, Mr. Hall," he said.

"Yes, sir, at first light I'll ride out with a reconnaissance patrol. According to Livy, only fourteen thousand Roman legionaries escaped the pincer's slaughter."

"Lieutenant Hall, I forbid you to talk on that subject any longer," Kellerman said.

"But . . . but why, sir?" Hall said.

"Because it makes me think of death and judgment day. Ahiga, you will scout for Lieutenant Hall's patrol tomorrow."

"Yes, Captain."

"You're dismissed. And tell Mrs. Zimmermann I said to give you a tot of whiskey and water. Well done."

The Navajo nodded and left.

Everyone ate the remainder of the meal in silence, then Kellerman sat back in his chair and said, "An excellent dinner, don't you think, Mr. Cranston?"

"It was indeed, sir."

But Second Lieutenant Atticus Cranston was lying

through his teeth. He'd found the beef tough and over-salty, the beans musty, and the plum duff was just all right but needed custard. When he looked around the table, the others seemed satisfied with the fare, and Lieutenant Hall ventured to say that it was the best repast he'd ever eaten in Fort Misery, a comment that made young Cranston, used to a more refined diet, shudder.

Kellerman poured large whiskeys all round to go with the coffee and cigars the Virgin Mary had brought, and said, "And now Mr. Hall, a song with you, if you please."

"Certainly, sir," the officer said. He sniffed, snapped shut his snuffbox, and in a fine, tenor voice sang "Good-bye Liza Jane" and then "Silver Threads Among the Gold," loudly cheered by all present. As the whiskey took effect, Sergeant Major Olinger made a brave attempt at "The Alabama Blossoms" and Mrs. Zimmermann obliged with her rendition of "Pass Me Not, O Gentle Savior," which Lieutenant Hall confessed brought a tear to his eye.

When pressed to sing, Lieutenant Cranston said he had no voice for a song and would leave that to others.

"And I see you don't smoke," Hall said.

"No, I don't."

The lieutenant retrieved his snuffbox, opened the lid, and said, "This snuff is of the very best quality and will ward off a host of miasmas. Try a pinch."

"Sir, I'd rather not."

"A wise choice, Mr. Cranston," Captain Kellerman said, grinning, his face flushed from whiskey. "Lieutenant Hall's snuff will blow your brains out."

"Captain, you malign Garrett's Best, made with care in the great city of Philadelphia," Hall said. "Such a potent snuff is for the strong at heart and not for weaklings."

"Sir, I do admire your snuffbox though," Cranston said. "Ivory, isn't it?"

"Bone, dear boy. Ox bone, given to me by a British observer on the eve of the Battle of Seven Pines. The officer in question said it was made by a French prisoner of war after the Battle of Waterloo." Hall pointed a finger at Cranston. "What date was that?"

"May thirty-first, 1862."

"No, Waterloo, not Seven Pines."

"June eighteen, 1815, sir."

Hall applauded. "Oh, well done, Mr. Cranston. I'm glad to hear that West Point taught you something."

"Did you attend the Point, Lieutenant Hall?"

"Yes, I did, class of '59."

"Captain Kellerman?"

"No, I didn't attend West Point. I rose through the ranks. It took a battlefield commission to make me a gentleman."

"And a fine officer," Sergeant Major Olinger said.

Kellerman smiled. "Well said, my faithful Saul." He splashed whiskey into everyone's glass. "Let's drink to my commission and your Medal of Honor, both won on the same day."

More than slightly tipsy, Lieutenant Cranston stood, raised his glass, and said, "To you, Sergeant Major. It's indeed a great privilege to be in your company."

"And I in yours, sir," Olinger said. "You played the man's part today."

"I'll drink to that," Captain Joe Kellerman said. "Well done, indeed."

CHAPTER 12

Come rooster time next day, the officers of Fort Misery were a hungover trio as Lieutenants James Hall and Atticus Cranston mounted their horses under a cobalt sky bannered with ribbons of scarlet and jade. The new aborning day was coming in chaste, smelling of horses, men, and saddle leather.

"This will be your first patrol, Lieutenant Cranston," Captain Kellerman said. "Learn all you can from Lieutenant Hall. He's a fine officer."

"Yes, sir," Cranston said. He had a pounding headache and even the pale morning light hurt his eyes. With every beat of his thumping heart, he profoundly regretted last night's whiskey.

The patrol consisted of eight men including Corporal Hawes and the surly John Smith. Since the Fort Misery garrison was not attached to any army unit there was no guidon.

Lieutenant Hall stood in the stirrups and waved his small command forward. Looking fresh, groomed, and rested, his ringleted hair and magnificent beard impeccable, he grinned at Cranston and said, "How do we feel this fine morning, Lieutenant?"

Deciding that honesty was the best policy, Cranston

said, "Sir, we feel awful, like someone has turned our head into a snare drum."

"I thought as much. I'll have Mrs. Zimmermann fix you up with some prune juice and lecture you on the evils of demon drink. She's told me many times that there's a serpent in every bottle and he biteth like the viper." Hall slapped the younger man's shoulder and said, "The Virgin Mary will soon put you to rights and set your feet back on the straight and narrow, Lieutenant. It's a beautiful day to be sober, is it not?"

As a reply, Second Lieutenant Cranston figured a groan would suffice.

An hour later, the sky now denim blue, the patrol rode through a stretch of brush-scattered desert, sand dunes just visible on the horizon to the west. The clambering sun stoked the furnace of the day and both men and horses sweated. The only sounds were the creak of leather and the soft thuds of hooves.

Lieutenant Hall broke the silence.

"Mr. Cranston, a few miles to the southwest of here is the encampment of Santiago Lozado and his rogues," he said. "Now bear that in mind. How's your head?"

"Somewhat better, sir."

"Glad to hear it; now watch your drinking."

Cranston ignored that and said, "If Captain Kellerman knows where he is, why doesn't he attack?"

"That would be suicidal, Lieutenant. Oh dear, yes. Suicidal."

"But why not take it to them under a black flag? Show them we intend to take no prisoners and they might as well surrender."

"They won't."

"It's worth a try, don't you think, sir?"

"At last count we had thirty-six effectives. That's not much of a force." Beads of sweat budded on Hall's forehead and the armpits and back of his blouse were black. Lieutenant Cranston looked the same. Only the troopers, stripped to their undershirts, seemed cooler. "Even if the Comanche are gone, Lozado still outnumbers us."

"A surprise attack might work."

Hall's eyes swept the desert. "See the sand? An ocean of sand . . . and dust. The same dust that was your ally yesterday would be your bitterest enemy if you tried a surprise cavalry attack. The Comancheros would see us coming when we were still miles away, and they'd be good and ready." Hall shook his head. "Lieutenant Cranston, during the Late War, one lesson the generals learned very quickly was the folly of using cavalry to attack steady, entrenched infantry."

"Then how do we get the better of this man, Lozado?"

Hall smiled. "Go on doing what we've been doing, Lieutenant. Hit and run mostly. Ambushes—what the wise Duke of Wellington called guerrilla tactics. Unfortunately, every brush with the enemy costs us casualties—one, two, three, or four dead at a time. A few more months of this war of attrition and every man in Fort Misery will be dead." The officer's smile hardened into a grimace. "And maybe, in its wisdom, that's what the army wants . . . get rid of all their miscreants in one fell swoop." Then a moment of uncharacteristic gloom. "Second Lieutenant Cranston, at Fort Misery you'll find plenty of gore, but no glory."

The younger man was spared commenting on that last as the Navajo scout rejoined the patrol at a canter. He drew rein and without any preamble pointed east and said, "Comanche attacking two wagons. Big fight."

"Army wagons, by God," Hall said.

"Maybe so," the Navajo said. "But . . ."

The lieutenant didn't wait for the but. He barked out a series of orders. "Draw pistols. Ahiga, lead the way. Forward at the gallop!"

His belly tying itself in knots, Atticus Cranston kicked his mount into motion, his long-barreled Colt held high alongside his head. In the distance he heard rifle shots and saw a pall of dust rise above the fight. To his left, Lieutenant Hall, ringlets and beard in place, looked like a gallant knight in dirty-shirt blue riding into battle for the honor of his ladylove. By contrast, Lieutenant Cranston felt himself scared, sweaty, a quivering lump on a horse. What did West Point teach him about such occasions? He couldn't remember a damned word.

"Shoot straight and hit 'em hard, boys!" Hall yelled. "Lieutenant Cranston, stay by me!"

The young officer was confused, everything around him was happening so fast. This wasn't an orderly charge; it was a reckless stampede. His mount had the bit in its teeth, its neck stretched, a wild, uncontrollable force of nature running as though the devil himself had a grip on its tail.

The Comanche, about two dozen in number, drew back from the wagons when they saw the patrol and Hall's men crashed headlong into their flank.

Cranston's memory of the action later returned to him in a series of fleeting flashes, like the flickering images of a magic lantern show . . . the bronze face of a war-bonneted warrior registering shock a split second before his face erupted in blood and bone as a bullet smashed into his forehead . . . a brave who looked no older than a half-grown boy, slashing at him with an iron-bladed ax . . . Hall putting a bullet into the boy's skull . . . riders lost in dust . . .

screams . . . yells . . . shots racketing like firecrackers . . . his horse stumbling over a body on the ground . . .

And then Cranston was through, nothing but flat sand ahead of him. He fought his battle-crazed mount to a halt and swung around in time to see a man step out from between the wagons, a huge Walker Colt in each hand. The man got his work in, hammering shots at the now milling, unsure Comanche, wounding a few, killing several.

It was enough.

The Indians broke and streamed north, riderless ponies galloping alongside the fleeing warriors.

Cranston saw Lieutenant Hall draw rein and talk to the pistolero, a tall man made taller by the gray top hat he wore.

The young officer urged his horse forward, holstering his Colt, only now aware that he hadn't fired a single shot.

Hall said, "Ah, Lieutenant Cranston, allow me to introduce the right honorable Mr. Roscoe Wolfe, a scalper by profession who's scratched his name on more jailhouse walls than he can count."

Cranston nodded at the man, a gaunt giant wearing a Confederate greatcoat over a stained ditto suit and collarless shirt, his pants shoved into mule ear boots. Wolfe rammed his dragoons into the twin holsters he wore around his waist and said, "Right pleased to meet you, Lieutenant. I can't say the same about your fellow officer." His blue eyes moved to Hall. "Meeting you again was an unpleasant surprise."

Hall smiled. "Roscoe, Roscoe, Roscoe, how could you say such a thing, after I just saved your worthless life?"

"Maybe you did, maybe you didn't. Why do you hate me, Hall?"

The lieutenant's smile widened. "Roscoe, you know why I hate you. It's because you're scum."

"Men like you made me scum."

"Roscoe, you're a peach, always blaming others for your own atrocities. Why do you murder Mexican peons and sell their scalps to the Díaz government as gen-u-ine Apache?"

"That's a lie."

"No, it isn't." Hall smiled. "Lieutenant Cranston, look at this man. He has the face of a Renaissance saint, but under that handsome exterior lurks a creature of pure evil. Man, woman, or child, no one is safe from his scalping knife. Who's the female with you, Roscoe? Is she yours?"

The woman in question hung back with the wagons. She was slender, with long blond hair and wore a cheap, flower-patterned dress that made her look like a prairie wife. As far as Hall could tell, she'd been pretty at one time, but her features had hardened, from whiskey and a tough life he guessed.

"Her name is Sara Lark," Wolfe said. "She's a whore we picked up on the road. She's nothing."

"Lieutenant." The Navajo rode up to Hall. "Nine Comanche killed, one man with the wagons dead, and one of our own men wounded and likely to die."

"Who is he, Ahiga?"

"Private Smith. Corporal Hawes is with him."

"No Comanche wounded?" Cranston said.

Hall and the Navajo looked at the young man as though he'd just grown another head. "Lieutenant, wounded enemies recover and come back to fight another day," Hall said. "There were no wounded on this field. Do you understand, me?"

Cranston took that like a punch to the gut but said, "Yes, sir. I understand."

"Good. I'm glad you do. Now go see how Private Smith is faring. I'll converse with our friend Roscoe a while longer. It's been such a pleasure to meet with him again."

"You've nothing to say to me, Hall," Wolfe said.

"You'll be surprised at the number of things I have to say to you," the lieutenant said. "One of them is that the last time we met . . . where and when was it?"

"A year ago, on the Sonoran border near the village of Santa María de Álamos." Wolfe removed his top hat and waggled a finger through each of two in-and-out holes in the crown. "You tried to put a bullet in me, Hall."

"No, that was Captain Kellerman. He shot up your hat while you and your scoundrels were flapping chaps out of there. It was a bad miss on the captain's part. He was aiming for your head."

"You and Kellerman are tarred with the same brush. I despise you both."

Hall smiled. "Roscoe, the feeling is mutual, I assure you."

Corporal Hawes kneeled beside the body of Private John Smith but rose to his feet when Lieutenant Cranston drew rein beside him.

"He's dead, damn him," Hawes said.

"Some respect for our honored dead, Corporal," Cranston said.

"He died before he told me where he'd stashed the army payroll. He pulled me closer and then tried to spit in my eye."

The dead soldier's chest was soaked in blood, obviously a hit from a rifle bullet.

"Put Private Smith over his horse," Cranston said. "We'll bury him at the post."

Hawes, his face a twisted mask of hate, kicked the body.

"You son of a dog, why did you have to die so fast? You could've made me a rich man."

"Corporal!" Cranston said, his voice rising. "Carry out my order."

Hawes shambled to attention and saluted. "Yes, sir. Go to hell, sir."

The man didn't know what hit him.

Lieutenant Hall's horse slammed into Hawes at a gallop and sent him sprawling on his back. Hawes got to his feet, staggering, but Hall left the saddle and was right on top of him. His gloved fist crashed into the corporal's face and again the man fell. Groggy, when he looked up, he was staring into the muzzle of Hall's revolver.

The other members of the patrol gathered around, as did Roscoe Wolfe and his men, stunned by this turn of events.

"Hawes, you sorry piece of trash, you have a choice to make," Hall said. His normally placid, good-natured face transformed into features sculpted from granite. "You either apologize to Lieutenant Cranston or I'll shoot you right now for gross insubordination."

Atticus Cranston was horrified. "Sir, you can't do that," he said.

"What do you think, Hawes?" Hall said. "Can I do that?"

Blood trickling from the corner of his mouth, Hawes said. "You can do that."

"Now apologize."

Hawes stiffened to attention. "I'm sorry, Lieutenant Cranston," he said. "I misspoke myself."

Cranston said, "Apology accepted. Carry on, Corporal Hawes."

"Private Hawes," Hall said. "Cut off those stripes as soon as we get back to Fort Misery. And another question: Private Hawes, have you learned a lesson? Will you soldier?"

Chastened, the man said, "Yes, sir. I'll soldier."

"If you slack, I'll have the hide off your back. Do you understand?"

"Yes, sir. I understand."

Hall turned to one of the gaping troopers. "Scott, get my horse. Make sure Hawes didn't hurt him."

CHAPTER 13

"You did well, Lieutenant," Captain Joe Kellerman said.

"Thank you, sir," Lieutenant Hall said.

"Roscoe Wolfe worries me. What's he doing this far west? He always stays around the Rio Bravo country in the New Mexico Territory."

"After the Corporal Hawes incident, I spoke to him at some length. He says he's headed south again, into Sonora."

"Scalp hunting?"

"He denies it."

"He's a swine. He once lynched three lawmen at a bordello in White Oaks, and that same day outdrew and killed a couple of miners playing vigilante. And those are the least of his crimes. I heard he boasts that he's killed a dozen men and sold more than a thousand scalps to the Mexican government, most of them Mexican peons, both men and women."

"And he denies that too," Kellerman said.

Hall said, "Of course he denies it. He'll tell you it's an old story the Texas Rangers made up to justify killing him. He claims the peons love him because he plays Robin Hood and gives them money he takes from rich hidalgos. But the Comanche know him. I reckon they scouted his wagons, and then the young warriors broke off from the rest and attacked."

"That top hat of his is easy to spot," Kellerman said. "I don't want him linking up with Lozado."

"I thought about that, Captain."

"And what's your decision?"

"I think it's more than a probability."

"A probability I can well do without. We'll need to discourage that alliance. How many men does Wolfe have with him?"

"He had four. Now he has three."

Kellerman refilled Hall's whiskey glass and his own and said, "How did young Lieutenant Cranston do today?"

"It was his first cavalry charge, at least on a horse and not a wagon. He did well enough, ran through the Comanche on a runaway mount and didn't get a chance to fire his pistol."

"He'll learn."

"If he lives that long."

"What about former Corporal Hawes?"

"He was insolent to Lieutenant Cranston, and I punished him."

"Near broke his jaw, I heard."

"He's lucky I didn't shoot him. I understand he was angry because Private Smith died without telling him the whereabouts of the army payroll he'd stashed somewhere."

"Lieutenant Cranston spoke to me earlier. He said your behavior could get you court-martialed."

"He's a treasure, isn't he?"

Kellerman smiled. "James, he could be right."

"Lieutenant Cranston doesn't understand how things are on the frontier."

"I can see that. And he hasn't been here long enough to realize that more than anything else, the army wants every man on this post conveniently dead."

"Well, when you think about it, we're a major embarrassment to king and country."

"You're talking about the wrong army."

"I know, but it sounds better than the Senate and people of the United States of America. Pithier, I daresay."

"Well, Lieutenant Hall, you shouldn't have cleaned Hawes's clock, so consider yourself reprimanded. Let's drink to that."

Hall raised his glass and smiled. "To my reprimand." He drained his glass. "How many does that make?"

"An even dozen I'd say."

"One day when I'm a general I'll look back on all this and laugh."

"Will that be before or after you bust me to private, Lieutenant Hall?"

"Hmm . . . I'll have to think about that, Captain Kellerman."

"Well, until then, let's have another drink."

Second Lieutenant Atticus Cranston rapped on the door of Sergeant Major Saul Olinger's office and was told to enter.

Olinger snapped to attention when the young officer stepped inside. "At ease, Sergeant Major. I'd like to have a few words with you, if I may."

"Of course, sir," Olinger said. He indicated the chair in front of his desk. "Please be seated." After Cranston sat, he said, "What can I do for you, sir?"

"Sergeant Major, can we keep this confidential?"

" 'That depends' is my answer to that question."

"It's a matter of military discipline."

"I know something about that."

"Lieutenant Hall struck an enlisted man this morning and threatened to shoot him."

"Yes, sir, I heard. And he took Corporal Hawes's stripes."

"Lieutenant Hall should not have struck an enlisted man."

"I wasn't there, sir."

"I was. And Lieutenant Hall had the Comanche wounded killed."

"As they would do to our soldiers. Only it would not be as quick a death."

"I believe Lieutenant Hall should be court-martialed."

"Sir, James Hall fought in eight engagements during the Late War, was wounded twice, and each time returned to duty, the second time on crutches."

"I don't doubt Lieutenant Hall's bravery. I do question his judgment."

"You were not in command, sir."

"Nonetheless, his disciplinary actions were excessive."

"In your opinion, sir."

"Yes. I haven't yet spoken to Captain Kellerman."

"Lieutenant, on the eve of the Battle of Waterloo, the Duke of Wellington referred to his soldiers as, 'the scum of the earth recruited for drink.'"

"I am aware of that."

"But the rest of his quote was, 'It's wonderful then, that we have made of them the fine fellows they are.'"

"And your point is, Sergeant Major?"

"My point is that at Fort Misery you're dealing with the scum of the earth, but you haven't a hope in hell of turning them into fine fellows. Begging the lieutenant's pardon, but Mr. Hall speaks our soldiers' language, a tongue you haven't learned yet."

Cranston took that last in silence.

"I've disappointed you, sir," Olinger said.

"Disillusioned me, maybe. But then, after this morning's action, I was already disillusioned."

Hanging on the wall behind the sergeant major was a

framed and glassed Confederate flag, all torn by shot and shell, a trophy from a forgotten skirmish in a desperate war.

Cranston's eyes moved from the flag to the sergeant major's face. "Where do I go from here?"

"It's not my place to give an officer advice."

"Make a stab at it, Sergeant Major, just man to man."

"Then my suggestion is to soldier on, Lieutenant Cranston. Fort Misery is a monstrosity, a leper's stain on the army's bright banner, and it can't last much longer."

"You mean soldier on until we're all dead?"

"Let's hope it doesn't come to that, sir," Olinger said. "Is there anything else I can do for the lieutenant?"

"No, I guess we covered it. Well, there is one more question: You won the Medal of Honor, so why are you still here?"

"Lieutenant Colonel Kellerman saved my life on several occasions, so I guess you could call it gratitude."

"Or loyalty."

"That too, sir."

Cranston rose to his feet, as did the sergeant major.

"You've been in two successful engagements, Lieutenant," he said. "You've done well."

The younger man smiled. "I didn't fire a shot this morning."

Olinger returned the smile. "At Chancellorsville, under heavy fire, I once panicked and loaded three .58-caliber balls into a Springfield Model 1861 rifle. Needless to say, I couldn't shoot any of them."

Cranston's smile widened. "Thank you, Sergeant Major Olinger."

CHAPTER 14

"How long has it been, my old friend?" Santiago Lozado said.

"Too long, mi amigo," Roscoe Wolfe said, returning Lozado's embrace.

"You haven't changed, Roscoe. Still as handsome as ever."

"And your belly gets bigger every time I see it."

"Eating well, my friend. The Comanche and Apache pay for my food."

"I had a fight with Comanche this morning," Wolfe said.

"Then you must tell me about it. Come to the fire and have coffee, you and your men. Ah, and you have a woman with you I see."

"She's a whore and for sale. I'll take a hundred dollars for her."

"She's skinny and looks sour."

"Seventy-five."

"Fifty."

"Done and done, my friend. She's yours."

"Good, I'll try her out tonight. Now be seated, Roscoe, and tell me why you visit the camp of the hidalgo don Santiago."

A crescent moon had risen in the sky and horned aside

the stars, and the surrounding desert drew darkness over its stark nakedness like a cobalt-blue counterpane. At a distance the Comancheros sat around fires and ate tortillas and frijoles with peppers. The slaves, less fortunate, made do with corn cakes and a watery, wilted vegetable stew.

"I didn't know you were in camp, Santiago. The soldiers who helped me fend off the Comanche told me you were here."

"Soldiers? From the fort?"

"I don't know. I suppose they were. James Hall, curse him, was in command."

"I know of him. Ha, I've tried to kill him myself a few times."

"He's a pig. A year ago, he and Kellerman chased me back into Sonora, and before that, when he was at Fort Bowie, he ran me all the way to the Dos Cabezas Mountains. Damn his eyes, I escaped, but his troopers killed five of my men and burned my wagons with all my scalps inside. I watched a year's hard work go up in smoke because of that villain."

"Pah, may he and Kellerman both burn in hell, my friend," Lozado said.

One of Wolfe's men stepped to the fire and dropped a bottle of mescal into his boss's lap. Wolfe acknowledged the man with a nod and then offered the bottle to Lozado, but the Comanchero shook his head and said, "I do not drink. But I enjoy many other vices."

"I know you enjoy whores and opium."

"No, I enjoy opium and whores, in that order. When I can, I stock up on laudanum."

"My friend, if I'd but known, I would've brought you some as a gift."

"Perhaps the next time."

"I won't forget."

Lozado waited until Wolfe took a swig of mescal and then said, "Out there in the darkness, bound hand and foot, I have slaves. They were for the Comanche, but now the great lords are impoverished and no longer want them."

Wolfe's interest was piqued. "How many?"

"Forty. Mostly men, but a few women, and all Mexican." Lozado smiled. "My friend, there is no profit to be had in slaves, except for a few women I could perhaps sell in mining towns. But I'm running out of food for all those mouths, and I plan to turn them out into the desert tomorrow."

Wolfe smiled. "There is no profit to be made from live slaves, but good money is to be made from dead ones."

"Explain how that can be, mi amigo. I've never before profited from dead men except by emptying their pockets."

"Then listen and learn, my friend. The Porfirio Díaz government will pay a hundred dollars for an Apache scalp, or anything that looks like an Apache scalp. You have forty slaves on the hoof, and that amounts to four thousand dollars just for their hair."

"But, Roscoe, my dear comrade, we can't march slaves all the way to Mexico. How do we feed and water them?"

"We don't."

"Then what . . . I mean . . . I don't understand."

"It's simple, don Santiago, we kill and scalp them here." Lozado was horrified. "Roscoe, so much blood."

"Not so much. Just kill them and then move camp."

"Forty people . . ."

"Peons. Who cares? I don't, do you? Think about four thousand dollars. How many whores and how much laudanum will that buy? And that's only the beginning. When we cross the big river into Sonora we can add to our scalps and double our money. Santiago, General Porfirio Díaz will kiss you on the cheek and treat you like a hero."

"Alas, Díaz might do neither of those things. He knows

me well, and he could hang me for stealing his peons and running guns to the Apache."

"Water under the bridge, my friend. Give Díaz the scalps and he will forgive much. But if you are afraid, then you can remain on the American side of the river, and I will take the scalps to the general. We go back years, and he is my amigo."

"And bring me back my share?"

"Of course, don Santiago," Wolfe said. "And the sum will be correct to the last red cent."

"You are a dear friend, Roscoe, but alas, I do not trust you that far."

"Then I am hurt, don Santiago, that you have so little faith in me."

"Yes, we are close friends separated by a lack of trust. But that lack is"—Lozado formed a tiny space between his thumb and the tip of his forefinger—"pequeñito."

"Then it is settled. We must cross into Sonora together and I will deal with Díaz."

"That is fine with me, my friend. But first I have a task to perform."

"Name it. I will help all I can."

"I must destroy the garrison at Fort Misery and nail Captain Joe Kellerman's hide to a wall."

Wolfe smiled. "My men are at your disposal. What is your plan, don Santiago?"

"I have not made a plan yet, but I think on it day and night. Soon I'll be ready to attack and wipe the fort and its accursed commander off the face of the earth."

"Then when do we slaughter the livestock?"

"After the fort is destroyed."

"I'm not a patient man."

"Roscoe, my friend, the booty in guns and horses from the Americans will be reward enough for your patience.

In the future, a partnership between us will bring us both wealth. The scalps of the peons and the destruction of the fort are only the beginning."

Wolfe was eager. "My friend, what do you see in your crystal ball?"

"Scalp hunting and gunrunning will soon be a thing of the past. What we do is take our profits and follow the American rails."

"I do not understand."

"Then listen to me. Railroads are now being laid all over the nation, and the pace is increasing day by day. From ocean to ocean, the tracks will soon cover the entire country, and we will be a part of it."

"What you say is true, don Santiago. I myself, have seen the rails, mile after mile until they vanish into distance."

"And when a frontier town welcomes the rails, what happens? That town prospers like never before, and so will we."

"Tell me how, mi amigo."

"One town at a time, we use our funds to open saloons, brothels, and dance halls, and we use our men to enforce the law . . . our law."

"I see a picture forming in my mind. Our town, our laws." Wolfe laughed and slapped his thigh. "Mexican hair will be the foundation of our fortunes."

"Yes, my friend. You make a good joke but speak the truth," Lozado said. "The possibilities are endless, and the future bright with gold. Share my dream, friend Roscoe, and help make it a reality."

"With all my heart, dear friend. I am at your command."

Lozado smiled and stretched. "Now the hour is late, and I grow weary. Send the woman I bought to my tent."

* * *

Lozado rose to his feet and walked toward his tent but made a detour.

Kyle Swan stood when his boss stepped up to his fire. "How are you faring, friend Kyle?"

"I am well, patrón," the American said. Firelight highlighted his reptiloid features and made of them more predatory animal than human.

"Listen to me, mi amigo," Lozado said. "And this must be our little secret."

"Say what you have to say, patrón. I will tell no one."

"After the bluecoat soldiers are all dead and their fort burned, we will ride into Sonora with the scalp hunter Roscoe Wolfe."

Lozado paused and Swan said, "And . . ."

"And before we recross the Rio Grande, I will have need of your knife and fast pistol."

"Killings?"

"Yes. After he has outlived his usefulness, I want Wolfe dead."

Swan nodded. "He is a pistolero, is Wolfe. Fast with the Colt."

"I know, and so are you."

Swan grinned. His teeth were small and pointed like a snake's. "When the time comes, I'll take care of him."

"You are a loyal friend."

"I watch your back, patrón," Swan said. "That's why you pay me."

CHAPTER 15

"Lieutenant Cranston, I want no heroics. Just have the Navajo ascertain if Roscoe Wolfe joined up with Lozado, and then get him the hell out of there. Do I make myself clear?"

"Perfectly clear, sir."

"You and newly promoted Corporal Scott have one purpose: you are there to protect the Navajo. I can replace second lieutenants and corporals, but I can't replace a first-rate scout."

"I understand, sir," Cranston said, suddenly aware of his worth to Fort Misery and its commanding officer.

To the east, the sun had just announced its rise over the horizon with a fanfare of burnished gold set in an amber sky. The morning was cool and tasted like raw iron.

"How can we get him close enough, sir?"

"Who? The Indian?"

"Yes, sir."

"He's a shape-shifter. He says he rolls in the sand and becomes a coyote. So let him handle it."

Atticus Cranston smiled. "Why a coyote?"

"Because the Indians say the coyote is a trickster and a sneak."

"I see, sir."

"Do you? I don't," Kellerman said. "Maybe he really is a shape-shifter, who knows?" He patted the neck of the lieutenant's horse. "Move out now and take care."

Cranston nodded and he and Scott, freckle-faced and ten years too young to be a corporal, kneed their mounts forward, the Navajo taking the point.

Ahead of them lay the desert and an Indian who might be a coyote, and beyond him deadly enemies who could also rapidly shape-shift . . . into wolves.

Cranston and the corporal rode in silence for an hour, their eyes constantly scanning the desert around them and the now-distant Navajo.

"Sir," Corporal Billy Bob Scott, said, "do you think Captain Kellerman was funning us about the Indian?"

"About him being a shape-shifter?"

"That's the word the captain used, sir."

"I think Ahiga covers himself in sand and believes himself to be invisible against the desert."

"But he doesn't really become a coyote?"

"No, Corporal, I don't think he really does."

"It's spooky, sir. Like ha'ants and stuff."

Cranston smiled. "I reckon Santiago Lozado is a lot spookier." Then, "Why were you posted to Fort Benjamin Grierson, Corporal?"

"I'd rather not talk about it, sir."

"Suit yourself. I won't order you to tell me."

A long silence passed, and then Scott said, "I'm an Alabama boy, from Tuscaloosa County, Lieutenant."

"Ah, you were a Johnny Reb."

"Yes, sir. In 1862, when I was fourteen, I joined the Fifth Cavalry Regiment. They took me because I brung my own horse. I stayed with the regiment until what was left of us surrendered at Danville, Alabama, on May sixth 18 and 65."

"Seems that you have an honorable service record."

"Yes, sir, I did. Then, knowing nothing else but soldiering, I joined the US Second Cavalry and was posted to Fort Laramie. It was there that it happened."

"What happened?"

Scott swallowed hard, as though gulping down words he didn't want to speak. Then, after an effort, "I struck an officer. Second Lieutenant Lang."

"Corporal Scott, it occurs to me that it's always open season on second lieutenants." Cranston settled his restive mount, and then said, "Why did you strike the officer?"

"Well, sir . . ."

"Go ahead. I won't bite you. Second lieutenants have no teeth."

"He called Robert E. Lee a secessionist traitor to his country and a piece of white trash. And then he said, "Like you, Scott.""

"And that's when you hit him."

"No, not just then, but it was when he said, "Like the parents who spawned you.""

"Had the officer bullied you before?"

"Yes, sir. He hated Southerners, and I pulled constant latrine and stable duties."

"So when he cast aspersions on your folks . . ."

"I socked him. Gave him a black eye, and he had me arrested and marched to the guard house. Later the army offered me a choice: loss of pay and ten years in Leavenworth or a transfer to Fort Benjamin Grierson. If I'd known then what that meant, I'd gladly have taken the ten years."

Cranston smiled and said, "Come now, is Fort Misery that bad?"

"It's worse than I ever expected. Lieutenant. I'm not yet thirty years old and I'm already losing my teeth and my hair. I get rashes and sores all over my body, especially my legs, and the constant salt beef and bacon, usually half-rotten, plays hell with my stomach. Dysentery, the army calls it. Add to that the desert heat, the lack of fresh water for bathing, and the constant battle against head lice, and Fort Misery is a terrible place. If it wasn't for whiskey, I'd go mad. We'd all go mad if we aren't already."

"Is Captain Kellerman aware of all this?"

"Of course he is, sir. He eats what the soldiers eat"—a sidelong glance then—"and drinks . . ."

"What the soldiers drink."

"Yes, sir." Scott looked straight ahead of him and said, "Why were you posted to Fort Misery, sir?"

"A clerical error, Corporal. A slip of the pen."

"Oh my God," Corporal Scott said.

"Yes indeed, Corporal. Oh my God."

The Navajo came back at a walk, keeping the dust down. The sun was now higher in the eastern sky, and the morning grew warmer.

He drew rein and said, "Lieutenant, you wait here. Comanchero camp very close."

"Be careful," Cranston said. "On order from Captain Kellerman, I'm here to look after your welfare."

It was the first time he'd seen the Navajo smile. "Then I am in safe hands," he said.

Whether or not that last was an Indian joke, the young officer couldn't tell.

As the morning yielded to afternoon, Second Lieutenant Atticus Cranston and Corporal Billy Bob Scott dismounted and sought the meager shade of their mounts' shadows. Both were sweat-drenched, rationing frugal sips from their brackish canteens. Cranston's eyes closed, seeing in his mind's eye a fern-shaded mountain pond where lime-green frogs jumped into the cool, dark water with a soft . . . plop!

Scott's alarmed voice dragged him back to sweltering reality.

The corporal stood, legs apart, revolver in hand, staring to his left.

Cranston joined him, saw what he saw and said, "What the hell?"

"Three men, Lieutenant," Scott said.

"Yes, I can count, Corporal."

"Walking out of the desert," Scott said.

"Yes, I can see that too," Cranston said. He unbuttoned the flap of his holster and drew his revolver. "Comancheros?"

"I don't think so, sir. More like walking dead men."

"Hold your fire. Let them come in."

"Two of them are armed."

"Revolvers stuck in their pants." Cranston smiled. "Desperate characters."

"Sir, do you think they can walk this far? The small, fat one keeps stumbling."

"All right, let's go help them. Bring the canteens."

The soldiers, guns at the ready, walked warily toward the three men. When they were about ten yards apart, Cranston said, "Two-finger the weapons and let them drop. Slowly."

The armed men did as they were told, both young, unshaven, with hard, tight-lipped faces. One wore a broad-brimmed hat and typical range clothes, the other the stained and tattered remnants of gambler's attire that still showed traces of its original fine tailoring. The plump one sported a brown bowler that matched his shabby ditto suit.

The little man dropped to his knees, clasped his hands together, gazed heavenward, and in a dry croak said, "Oh, dear Lord thank you. I'm saved."

"Are you boys thirsty?" Corporal Scott said.

"What do you think, soldier boy?" the man in the gambler's frock coat said. He had pale blue eyes, the kind that Frank James would years later famously call "gunfighter eyes." In the young man's case that was one hundred percent correct. "Our canteen ran dry yesterday."

As the trio drank, Corporal Scott holding the canteen so that they didn't gulp and injure shrunken stomachs, Cranston said, his voice officer-sharp, "And what did you do with it?"

"Do with what?" Scott asked.

"Your canteen." Cranston said.

"I threw it away. It was empty."

"Never throw away an empty canteen, mister," Cranston said. "Suppose you found water? How would you carry it?"

"I never in my life depended on a canteen," the man said, wiping off his mustache with the back of his hand. "If I wanted water, I called over a waiter and told him to bring it in a clean glass."

"What's your name, mister?" Scott said.

"What's it to you, soldier boy?"

"Answer the corporal," Cranston said.

"Bertrand, Jim Bertrand."

Scott's face lit up. "Wait a minute. Wait just a doggone minute. Ain't you the Jim Bertrand that killed Platte River Tom Wakeman in El Paso that time?"

"Yes, that Jim Bertrand was me."

"They say Tom was fast on the draw."

"They say right, soldier. He was fast on the draw and shoot."

"But not as fast as you."

"Sometimes a gambler gets lucky."

It was then that Lieutenant Cranston decided Bertrand was not to be trusted. He saw the man's eyes lift to the horses and then drop to the gun at his feet. The young officer didn't frame it mentally in these terms, but his instinct was correct . . . the gambler was about to make a play.

It was the Navajo who dissuaded him.

The Indian's instincts were honed as sharp as those of a lobo wolf. He saw Bertrand's right shoulder drop, no more than half an inch, but the *click-clack* of a Henry lever stopped the man cold.

"I don't mind shooting white men in the back," Ahiga said. "Want to try me, white man?"

Bertrand didn't move a muscle; he didn't so much as twitch.

"Corporal, pick up those revolvers," Cranston said. Then, smiling, "I don't mind shooting white men in the front." His questioning eyes moved to the Navajo.

"The scalp hunters are with Lozado," the Indian said.

"I thought as much," Cranston said. "Right, let's get these men back to the fort."

"Ain't you gonna talk to me?" the man in range clothes said.

"Not here," Cranston said. "You can do all your talking at Fort Benjamin Grierson."

"We left three dead men behind us. You should know that."

"Did you kill them?"

"No, we didn't. Apoplexy killed one and the other two got shot, but not by us. And there's a prison wagon, but the mule took off with it."

Bertrand shook his head and said, "You're a talking man, Bill Worley."

"Jim, they'll know eventually." Then to Cranston. "Yuma prison sent the wagon to the railroad station to collect us. They know we were in it when the guard up and died and Jake Kelly and the other guard got killed, so they might come looking for us."

"By the look of you, Worley, you're a cattle drover. Why were you sent to Yuma?" Cranston said.

"The judge found me guilty of cattle rustling, petty theft, and for being a damned annoyance to everybody. He gave me five years."

Cranston said to the plump man, "And what about you?"

"I'm a physician. And I was in the wagon with these two."

"Not a prisoner?"

Bertrand said, smiling, "His name is Isaac Stanton, and he caught his wife in bed with another man, cut loose with a pepperpot revolver and killed them both. He was sentenced to twenty years hard labor."

"I didn't mean to kill my dear wife. It was an accident."

"And a damn poor aim, huh, Doc?" Bertrand said.

Lieutenant Cranston said, "It's a long walk to the fort, so Bertrand, you'll get up behind me. Worley with Corporal Scott, and Ahiga, the doc behind you. If any of these three even think about escaping, shoot him."

"So the Indian can read minds?" Bertrand said.

"Yes, he can," Cranston said. "And he's a shape-shifter. Move the wrong muscle on the way to Fort Benjamin Grierson, and you could find a timber wolf at your throat."

The Navajo threw back his head and emitted a spine-chilling howl.

The doctor and Worley exchanged a frightened glance, and even Bertrand looked uneasy.

Second Lieutenant Cranston was pleased. The ride back to Fort Misery should prove to be uneventful.

CHAPTER 16

"The Navajo says the scalp hunters have joined up with Lozado and his bunch," Captain Joe Kellerman said.

"That seems to be the case, sir," Second Lieutenant Atticus Cranston said.

"It's all we needed."

"Indeed, sir."

Kellerman sighed. "All right, bring in the . . . what the hell do we call them? Prisoners?"

"Escaped prisoners will cover it, sir."

"Well, whatever they are, bring them in."

"I've placed them under guard, sir."

"A wise precaution."

"And, sir, one of them claims to be a doctor."

"We need one of those. Does he have a medical bag?"

"No, sir. Just the doctor."

"Well, I'm sure Mrs. Zimmermann has one lying around somewhere. Show our guests in."

Lieutenant Cranston, in an excess of zeal, had manacled the three men hand and foot, and their chains clanked when they stepped into Kellerman's office and shambled to a halt in front of his desk. They were flanked by two scowling troopers.

The captain picked up the piece of paper that Cranston had handed him earlier and then read, "Jim Bertrand."

"Right here," the man answered.

"Why were you sent to Yuma Territorial Prison?"

"I killed a man."

"Sir," Cranston said, "Corporal Scott says this man is a pistolero, but it may only be soldiers' scuttlebutt."

"Are you what the officer says, one of those Texas draw fighters they're all talking about?"

"I can draw and shoot quickly, but I'm not a Texan, I was born and raised in the Montana Territory."

"Where did you kill this man?"

"At the Oriental Saloon in Tombstone."

"Why?"

"He was a card cheat, and he'd already been notified."

"How long did you get?"

"Three years. He was the judge's brother-in-law."

"Killing a card sharp should've been a ten-dollar fine for disturbing the peace."

"I know, but the judge didn't see it that way."

Kellerman consulted his paper again and then said, "Bill Worley."

"Here."

"You look like a drover."

"I am. Or at least I was."

"Who did you kill?"

"Nobody. I got five years for cattle rustling."

"You ever use a gun?"

"I am a Texan, and I can shoot."

The captain nodded and said, "And you must be Isaac Stanton."

"Yes, sir. I'm a physician by profession."

"Who did you kill? Not a patient, I hope."

"Sir, it wounds my heart to speak of it."

"He plugged his old lady and her lover," Bertrand said.

"Alas, I did, I surely did, and it grieves me to this day. Curse the pepperpot pistol that took my dear Euphemia from me."

"How long did you get, Doc?" Kellerman said.

"Twenty years at hard labor."

"Where did the shooting happen?"

"In my bedroom."

"I mean in what city."

"Prescott, right here in the Arizona Territory." Stanton's hands fled to his face, and he sobbed. "Curse the thrice-damned pepperpot, that heartless killer."

"Amen," Kellerman said. "Now listen up, you three. This post is currently under siege by a bandido named Santiago Lozado and his Comancheros. He outnumbers my garrison by almost two to one, and I expect an all-out attack on Fort Misery soon. I need every man I can muster to man the walls. Any questions?"

Only Stanton spoke. "Captain, is my life in danger?"

"Imminent danger, Doc."

"Then I'd rather return to Yuma where it's safe from bandits."

"What about you two? Do you want to go back to Yuma or remain here and help me defend this post?"

"That isn't much of a choice," Jim Bertrand said.

"It's the only one I've got," Kellerman said.

"And if we agree, what then?" Worley said.

"If you survive, I'll give you a horse and canteen of water and point you east. Your crimes are a civil matter, no concern of the United States Army."

"Give me some time to think about it," Bertrand said.

The captain pointed to the clock on the wall. "In two minutes, the clock will strike one. Then your time is up."

Bertrand smiled. "And if we say no?"

"Then you can leave."

"With water and a horse?"

"With the clothes on your back, nothing else. Just pick a direction and leave."

DING!

The clock struck one.

"I'll stick," Bertrand said.

"That goes for me, too," Worley said.

"A wise choice," Kellerman said. "Doc, you stay. This post needs a physician."

"But my dear sir, that's . . . that's kidnapping."

"You stay. That's an order."

"And if I refuse?"

Kellerman turned his attention to one of the guards. "Private Hamer, if this man disobeys my order, take him out and shoot him."

"Yes, sir," the soldier said.

"You wouldn't dare . . ."

"Private Hamer, shoot him."

Hamer, a tough-faced man with a granite rock of a chin, grabbed Stanton's arm and said, "Right away, sir."

The plump little man squawked like a startled chicken. "Desist! I'll stay! Don't shoot me!"

Kellerman nodded. "An excellent choice, Doctor. We have a couple of wounded men in the infirmary, so you can get started right away."

"And what about us?" Bertrand said.

"There's spare bunks in the enlisted men's quarters. You can take your pick and make yourself comfy. Lieutenant Cranston will show you the way."

The exchange between Tobias Zimmermann and Jim Bertrand took place at the edge of the never-used parade ground where a flag never flew.

It was a strange encounter, not friendly, and Lieutenant Cranston wondered at it later.

Both men saw the other at the same time and stopped in their tracks. Zimmermann, carrying a wood saw, shifted it from his right to his left hand and said, "What the hell are you doing here?"

"I could ask you the same thing, Tobias."

"It's a long story."

"Then we've both got long stories to tell."

"No, we haven't. I don't know why you're here, Bertrand, and I don't want to know. Just stay the hell away from me." Zimmermann's eyes hardened. "You look like you shrunk since the last time I saw you, maybe a couple of feet. Not wearing a gun sure cuts you down to size."

"You just can't get over Heck Renfrew. Can you?"

"He was just a kid, and I liked him."

"He was an eighteen-year-old with a gun looking for a rep at the bitter end of a range war. I told him not to go for the iron."

"He didn't have a hope in hell against you, Bertrand."

"Are you listening? I gave him a chance to walk away from it."

"Heck Renfrew was in the company of belted men."

"I knew most of those men, Wes Hardin and the others. They would've understood."

"Yeah, understood that you put the crawl on him."

"I'm talking to a brick wall."

"I came looking for you that day, Bertrand."

"The war was long over. Thirty-seven men dead. There had been enough killing."

"You rode out."

"Of course I did. The fighting was done. I drew my gun wages, rode out, got drunk, and lost the whole roll to a high-yeller whore in Cuero."

"You skedaddled because you knew I could shade you."

Bertrand's smile was thin. "Tobias, I saw you on the draw and shoot in the Gates saloon in Indianola. Mister, you couldn't shade me on your best day."

"Big talk from a man who ain't heeled," Zimmermann said.

"All right, you two, that's enough," Lieutenant Cranston said. "If Captain Kellerman is right, you'll soon have a bellyful of fighting."

Zimmermann restored the saw to his right hand. "Bertrand, from now until you leave this post, walk clear of me."

"That doesn't present a problem, Tobias. I was never fond of your company at any time."

After a fuming Zimmermann stalked away, Bill Worley, the young cowboy said, "Geez, Jim, did you really know John Wesley Hardin?"

"The only person who knew Wes was himself," Bertrand said. Then, seeing the disappointment on the young cowboy's face, he said, "Yes, I knew him."

"Was he as fast as folks say?"

"He was mighty sudden, that's for sure," Bertrand said. Then, as an afterthought, "And so is Tobias Zimmermann."

CHAPTER 17

The night after Lieutenant Cranston's patrol, Sara Lark made her escape.

She lay in the dark tent beside the snoring Santiago Lozado. He lay on his back, smelling like a wallowing hog, the great mound of his belly just another mountain to climb in Sara's harsh world. She rose silently and dressed quickly, then picked up the pointed, broad-bladed knife she'd removed from the sheath on the man's belt. She wanted to cut his throat with it, feel his hot blood splash over her hand, but he might struggle and cry out, and she couldn't take that chance. The soldiers' fort was to the east, a few hours' ride; that much she'd wormed out of Lozado before he beat her as a prelude to having her. The man was a disgusting animal.

There would be night guards. But where? She needed a mount, but undoubtedly there would be a man patrolling the horse lines. Moonlight glinted on the knife blade, her only hope of escape. No, not her only hope. During his rough handling of her, Lozado had torn apart the front of her cheap dress, exposing her breasts. Those were the lure that would land her a fish . . . or so she hoped.

Sara Lark stepped out of the tent and then stood beside the flap unmoving, and her lovely hazel eyes, alluring remnants of a once-beautiful face, searched the darkness. At a distance, campfires glittered like sparks fallen from a passing shooting star, and she froze as a man coughed, groaned, and then became silent. A profound silence followed as the disturbed night settled and closed in on her again.

The horse lines were close, no more than thirty yards away, and she moved from the tent and walked slowly, carefully, in that direction, her unlaced ankle boots making soft sounds in the sand.

The sentry—a Mexican dressed in white shirt and pants, a Winchester in his arms—and Sara Lark saw each other at the same time. She walked to the horse line, her hips swaying, breasts visible, smiled, and patted the neck of a paint mare. The guard knew who she was: the whore who'd come into camp with Roscoe Wolfe and his men. The man grinned. The slut already had don Santiago and obviously wanted more. Well, he would oblige. He laid down his rifle and walked toward her, grinning, his teeth gleaming in the darkness. Sara smiled in return, a coy smile, that nonetheless said, "Come and get me."

The Comanchero had raped before, many times, and his hungry hands grabbed the woman and roughly pulled her toward him, his mouth seeking hers. Sara Lark went limp in his arms, signaling her surrender, and the man tried to force her to the ground, his mouth still pressed against hers. Then she resisted.

Sara felt the man's mouth open in surprise, then stretch wide, his eyes popping as the broad, clipped blade of her knife plunged to the hilt into his belly. As he staggered back a step, the woman followed up quickly. She quickly withdrew the bloody knife and then rammed the blade into the man's throat, stifling the scream that died on his lips. He fell, taking the knife with him. Sara dropped to a knee beside the Mexican and whispered, "Estas muerta todavia?" *Are you dead yet?* The Mescalero made no answer. He was as dead as he was ever going to be.

Sara Lark rose to her feet and stood still as a marble statue. Her heart pounded in her chest as she scanned the campground. All seemed as before: fires glimmered, nothing moved, and shadows covered the ground like black tarps. The moon remained aloof, indifferent to the affairs of men, and the horses had ignored the commotion. Even the paint mare who'd witnessed it all up close seemed unconcerned.

The horse's saddle and bridle lay on the ground. The woman bridled the unprotesting mare and led her away from the horse line. Only when she'd walked a hundred yards into the darkness did she mount and knee the paint into a walk. Half an hour later, when she was well free of the camp, she headed east at a canter.

The daughter of a prostitute and an unknown father, Sara Lark had spent her childhood slaving on Kansas farms. Often hungry and subjected to the leather belt and sexual abuse, she'd grown to adulthood hard and tough and took up the only profession available to her: whoring in the frontier cattle towns. By the time she escaped Lozado's clutches she had ten harsh, degrading, and sometimes violent years behind her and expected nothing better in the future.

In the opalescent moonlight, Fort Misery looked like a flotilla of little boats adrift on a mother-of-pearl sea. Sara Lark saw only one light, an oil lamp guttering above the door of the biggest structure, which she guessed correctly was the soldiers' headquarters building.

She slowed the mare and came in at a walk.

A voice to her left, coming from darkness.

"Stop right there or I'll blow you right out off'n that hoss."

"Don't shoot," Sara said. Then, using the timeless words as a shield, "I'm a lady in distress."

"Don't get many of them around these parts."

The voice came from a young throat, a heavily accented Southern drawl. A soldier stepped out of the gloom, a Winchester across his chest. "Hell, you are a woman, but no lady as far as I can see."

Sara reached up and held her dress together over her breasts. "I was attacked and managed to escape."

"Who attacked you?" the soldier said. He was a young towhead with a bad haircut, courtesy of Tobias Zimmermann. Since the man was a carpenter, Captain Kellerman considered him eminently qualified to be the post barber, since someone who cut wood could also cut hair.

"A bandit."

"What bandit?"

"Santiago Lozado."

That gave the young trooper pause. He thought for a moment and then said, "That bronc has come a ways. We'll put her up in the stables, and then you follow me."

"Where are we going?"

"There's another lady at the post. She'll take care of you tonight, and you can talk with Captain Kellerman in the morning."

Sara Lark managed a smile. "Thank you. You're very kind."

The young man shook his head. "No, I'm not."

Since she'd resumed her virginity, Mary Zimmermann no longer shared a bed with her husband but occupied a small room off the kitchen. The soldier tapped on her door and sleepless, in the midst of reading the Bible, she answered immediately.

"Who is it?"

"Private Reilly. I've got a woman with me needs attending to."

"Who is she?"

"What's your name?"

"Sara Lark."

"She calls herself Sara Lark."

The door opened a crack, and Mary's eye appeared at the opening. "It's late."

"I know it is," Private Reilly said. "I can bed her down in the stables until morning."

"No. Go away and leave the lady there. I'm in my night attire."

"I wouldn't want to see you in your night attire," Reilly said, grinning.

"You're impudent and immodest, Private. Right now, Our Lady is shedding a tear. Please, go away."

"All right, I'll get back to my post," the soldier said. Then to Sara, "She's all yours."

The door opened wider, and Mary Zimmermann stuck her head out, looked around and then said, "Come in."

She struck a match and lit the oil lamp on her dresser. Outside, a pair of scrawny desert coyotes yipped back and forth, hunting close to the fort.

Mary took in Sara Lark's appearance at a glance and said, "What in God's holy name happened to you?"

"I was attacked."

"Who attacked you?"

"A man named Lozado."

"Santiago Lozado?"

"That's him."

"He's a terrible, godless man."

"Yeah, sister, he's all of that."

"I'm not your sister."

"I need a friend."

"You have a friend in Jesus. That's quite enough for anyone. Did you come here with an immigrant wagon? Are you some stalwart's wife?"

"No, I came in a scalper's wagon, and I'm a whore."

Mary Zimmermann swayed, as though she were about to faint, and then sat on the corner of her bed. "Forgive me. But just before you came here, I was reading the book of Revelation 17 about the Whore of Babylon, the great mother of prostitutes and of earth's abominations, a woman drunk with the blood of the saints and martyrs of Jesus."

Sara Lark shrugged. "I plead not guilty on all counts."

"Is it a sign?" Mary said.

"A sign of what?"

"Did the Lord send me a sign to cast you out? No, in his infinite wisdom He wouldn't do that. It's a sign that I must save you."

"Save me from what?"

"From yourself, from your own sin and iniquity."

"Then get started," Sara said. "I'll take just about anything over the life I've got."

Mary Zimmermann rose to her feet. "First we'll attend to your body, and then your soul."

"My body?"

"Yes, my dear. You don't smell very nice."

The woman stepped into the kitchen and returned with a small bowl of water and a sponge. "The water for this post comes from a seep and is in short supply. But remove that ragged dress and do what you can." Then, her voice chiding, "Lawdy, lawdy, but you're thin, child."

"I haven't been eating well."

"Yes, I can see that. Now I'll find one of my old dresses and some undergarments to fit you. You must look your best when you meet Captain Kellerman in the morning before he sends out the morning patrol."

"Is he nice?"

"Nice? No, he isn't nice. No one on this post is nice. One way or another, they're all rogues. The boy who brought you here, Private Reilly, murdered his own father with a pitchfork, escaped to the army, and then shot a man in a house of ill repute at a settlement near Fort Union in the New Mexico Territory. He was given the same choice as most of the men here got: the gallows or Fort Misery."

"Is that what they call this place? Fort Misery?"

"It's what the soldiers call it. Its real name is Fort Benjamin Grierson."

"I like the real name better," Sara Lark said.

"I wanted to call it Fort Salvation, but Captain Kellerman wouldn't hear of it."

Sara Lark bathed as best she could, and Mrs. Zimmermann provided a frayed, moth-holed nightgown. "You can share my bed for tonight and see what Captain Kellerman says about your accommodations in the morning." She smiled. "And now a little treat before retiring, good for both body and soul." She opened a cupboard and produced a bottle of Gordon's gin and two glasses. "Lieutenant Hall gave me this. It seems he has doting parents somewhere who manage to supply him with gin, cigars, and snuff." She sighed. "I've no idea how he does it, but he does it." Mary Zimmermann poured three fingers into each glass. "Well, here's to your future, you poor thing."

"I don't have a future," Sara said. "Only a past and a present. Mainly a past."

"Your future is in God's hands. I am but His beacon to illuminate your path."

"God, I need this," Sara said. She downed her drink in one gulp, sighed, and said, "Good gin, Mrs. Zimmermann."

CHAPTER 18

"You stole a horse and escaped?" Captain Joe Kellerman said.

"Yes, that's what I did," Sara Lark said. She thought it best not to mention the man she killed.

"Oh, well done," Lieutenant James Hall said. He took out his box. "Do you take snuff?"

"No, only gin," Sara said.

"I noticed you with Roscoe Wolfe's men after we fought off the Comanches," Hall said. "Is he now with Lozado?"

"I sent out Lieutenant Cranston with the Navajo to answer that question yesterday," Kellerman said.

"Well, I can answer it too. Yes, he is."

"I wish I had spoken to you earlier."

"I wasn't here earlier, Captain," Sara said. "I spent two days and nights in Lozado's tent. The man is not human. He's a kind of wild animal. And Lieutenant Hall, I noticed you too, when you fought off the Comanche. You were very brave—and of course your hair and beard are hard to miss."

Hall hesitated, analyzing that remark, and then said, his voice tentative, "Did you like them?"

Years of training as a man-pleaser came to Sara's rescue. "Yes, I thought you a fine-looking officer."

"Kind words to be sure," Hall said. He dipped snuff, inhaled a pinch into each nostril, and then said, "And all perfectly true, of course."

"You're no blushing violet, are you, Lieutenant?" Kellerman said, slightly irritated.

"Sir, I always like to hear what the ladies have to say about my appearance. They are always very impressed."

"Did the Virgin Mary give you those clothes, Miss Lark?" Kellerman said.

"The Virgin . . . oh, you mean Mrs. Zimmermann? Yes, she did."

"You look very nice, Miss Lark," Hall said, returning compliment for compliment.

"Thank you, Lieutenant. You are most gallant."

"The question is, what are we going to do with you?" Kellerman said. "I can hardly throw you out into the desert."

"I'd rather you didn't, Captain. Perhaps I can catch a stage."

"No stages stop at Fort Benjamin Grierson, madam. Though recently so many people have arrived here, it would be a good idea." He turned to look at Sergeant Major Saul Olinger. "You've been quiet, Sergeant Major. Any suggestions?"

"The young lady could assist Mrs. Zimmermann and Dr. Stanton in the kitchen and infirmary until we can find a safe way to get her off the post."

"Once again your sound common sense has set us to rights, Sergeant Major," Kellerman said.

"It's the best offer I've had today," Sara said.

"Oh, well said, Miss Lark. Bully!" Hall said.

Kellerman gave a hint of a smile. "It seems my second-in-command is quite enamored of you, Miss Lark."

"Captain, please," Hall said. "I admire all the ladies equally."

"And I'm sure they're most taken with you, Lieutenant," Sara said. "That magnificent beard would make any woman go weak at the knees."

"And once again you hit the nail right on the head, dear lady. Indeed, it does," Hall said. "Ah yes, weak at the knees indeed. You were traveling with that rogue, Wolfe, but I take you for a teacher of some kind."

"No, I'm a whore of some kind."

"Ah," Hall said, suddenly feeling the need for more snuff.

"I'm sure Mrs. Zimmermann will put you back on the straight and narrow," Kellerman said, suppressing a smile.

"She already has. In one day, I've gone from the Whore of Babylon to the whore on the path to redemption."

"Well, I'll say it again, Miss Lark," Hall said. "Bully for you!"

"And I'll say thank you again," Sara said, smiling.

Outside, wielded by Tobias Zimmermann, a jack-of-all-trades, a rhythmic hammer clanged in the blacksmith's shop, and a restless horse neighed in the stables. The morning sun spread its light over Fort Misery and promised the blistering day to come.

"Captain, there is something I should tell you," Sara said.

"Then tell away? More coffee?"

"No thank you. It's about Wolfe and Santiago Lozado."

"Now I'm all ears," Kellerman said. "Tell me more and put the spurs to it."

"Lozado has Mexican slaves in his camp, maybe around forty, I really don't know. They were for the Comanche, who no longer want them."

"The Comanche are gone."

"Yes, they are, and they left the slaves behind."

"And now Wolfe and Lozado plan on selling them somewhere else."

"Yes, but only their scalps. It was Wolfe's idea."

Kellerman shook his head. "Miss Lark, I'm not catching your drift."

"There is no market for slaves in the United States or in Mexico either, but there is a market for Apache scalps in Mexico. The government will pay a hundred dollars bounty."

"Miss Lark, how do you know all this?" Hall said.

"I overheard Wolfe and Lozado talking about it. When bandits talk business, who notices a skinny whore in the darkness?"

Captain Kellerman said, "Let me get this right. Wolfe plans to kill the slaves, take their scalps, and sell them in Mexico?"

"Yes. He calls the Mexicans livestock, and that's what he thinks of them, and so does Lozado."

"Then we must free the slaves, poor creatures that they are," Lieutenant Hall said.

"How, Mr. Hall?" Kellerman said.

"Why, sir, we charge the camp and give the Comancheros the edge of the saber."

"And lose half my command with no guarantee of freeing anybody. Damn, I need a drink."

Hall hesitated and then said, "A night action, perhaps?"

Kellerman shook his head. "Lieutenant, you know better than that. It would be impossible to disengage while trying to herd forty frightened people in pitch darkness. I agree that the advantage in a night action lies with the attacker, but not in this case. Sergeant Major Olinger, do the necessary. My glass is gathering dust."

"Yes, sir. Coming right up."

Second Lieutenant Cranston spoke for the first time. "Captain, if we did rescue the slaves, how would we feed and water them?"

Kellerman smiled. "Lieutenant Hall would forgo his dinner."

"Sir, I'll make any sacrifice but that one," Hall said. "Of course, my sacrifice would not include my cigars, snuff, and whiskey. Oh, and Mrs. Zimmermann's plum duff, and perhaps my breakfast bacon."

"Of course not, sir," Olinger said, straight-faced, as he poured whiskey into the lieutenant's glass.

"And coffee," Hall said. "I can't live without my coffee."

"Lieutenant, you're a living saint and a martyr for the cause," Kellerman said.

"Yes, sir, it's always been my nature to willingly sacrifice for the welfare of others."

Cranston said, "Miss Lark, did you notice if the Mexicans were shackled with irons?"

"No. I think their hands and feet were tied with rope. But I can't be sure. No, wait . . . yes definitely ropes."

"You're sure?"

"Yes . . . pretty sure."

"Enlighten us, Mr. Cranston," Kellerman said.

"Sir, where the entire troop might fail, a couple of men might succeed."

"At night, you mean?"

"Yes, sir, at night. With the troop standing-to outside the camp ready to intervene in support of the extraction."

"Extraction, Lieutenant? You mean the withdrawal of the slaves?"

"Yes, sir."

"Mighty thin, if you ask me," Hall said. "Give them the point of the saber, I say. The Comancheros can't take it in the guts."

Kellerman sat in silence for a while, staring into the amber depths of his glass, then said, "The Navajo and one other man. It's risky, but it might work."

"With the troop standing by, sabers drawn," Lieutenant Hall said.

"Half the troop." Kellerman said. "I'm not putting all my eggs in that basket."

"Yes, sir, you're right of course," Hall said. "Too many holes in the wicker, all right."

"Sir, I volunteer to take command of the rescue," Cranston said.

"And you've got it, Lieutenant," Kellerman said. "But I will lead the troop myself."

Disappointment showed in the faces of two men.

Cranston said nothing.

Hall spoke out. "But, sir, if you are . . ."

"Killed, Lieutenant? You are perfectly capable of taking command of this post until another miscreant arrives to take my place."

"Miscreant," Hall said. "One who behaves badly and breaks the law. Yes, sir, I am eminently qualified for the position myself."

"With the exception of Second Lieutenant Cranston we're all eminently qualified," Kellerman said.

"As miscreants or commanding officers?" Hall said.

"Both," Kellerman said.

"Ah, one word says it all: both," Hall said. "As Sergeant Major Olinger says on occasion, a truer word was never spoke."

"Thank you, sir," Olinger said.

"Think nothing of it. Have a pinch of snuff."

"Don't mind if I do, Lieutenant."

"Sergeant Major, after you stop sneezing, stay behind. Miss Lark, my officers will escort you to your quarters."

* * *

"Before you say a word, Saul, you're not taking part in this action," Captain Kellerman said. "You're needed here."

"Then send Lieutenant Hall in your place, Joe. He's capable enough."

"No, I need to be there when the slaves are freed. I don't want a massacre on my hands. Two hours before sundown, mount up fifteen of our best."

"Our best are our worst, Joe."

"I know, but mean soldiers are good soldiers. Dave Hawes was a rattlesnake and the best corporal we ever had."

"Yes he was, the best and the worst," Olinger said. He waited until Kellerman filled his glass and then said, "Do you think Lieutenant Cranston is up to the task?"

"I don't know, but I'm willing to let him prove himself. Even the army is bound to realize its mistake eventually, and I want Fort Misery to send them back a good soldier, by God."

"I'll talk to the Navajo."

"Tell him to keep an eye on Cranston."

"He will. If he doesn't cut his throat."

"Why would he do that?"

"It's an Indian thing. The Navajo won't let an officer be captured alive. He knows Lozado would have a lot of fun killing him."

"Saul, I feel like a Roman legionary fighting barbarians."

"From what I know, the Romans were pretty barbaric themselves."

Kellerman smiled. "And so are we."

"Damn right, Joe," Olinger said. "We learned the killing trade in a barbaric war, and so did half the garrison."

"And after the war, most of them indulged in further study of that particular profession."

The sergeant major shook his head. "Joe, we're a tough outfit."

"Yes, we are. Pity that there's just not enough of us."

"Well, we can do the best we can with what we have."

"Starting tonight," Kellerman said.

"As Tiny Tim said in Mr. Dickens's Christmas book: 'God bless us, every one.'"

Kellerman smiled and shook his head. "Mr. Dickens? Tiny Tim? Sergeant Major, you never cease to amaze me."

CHAPTER 19

"Lieutenant Cranston, hold tight on to the handle of your weapon and use the front sight. That's the best way to shoot a Colt revolver."

"Sir, it will be dark. How do I see the front sight?"

"My dear fellow, I've already taken care of that. I borrowed some white paint from Mr. Zimmermann and put a blob on your front sight. Ha—you'll see it in pitch darkness all right, trust me. A pinch of snuff before you ride out?"

Cranston very much wanted to look at his desecrated Colt, but he resisted the temptation. "No thank you, sir," he said.

Captain Kellerman turned in the saddle and said, "Lieutenant Hall, did you just confess to Mr. Cranston that you painted his Colt white?"

"Only the front sight, sir. Um, how did you know?"

"I have spies everywhere."

"The paint will aid his marksmanship, sir. Though I must confess that Lieutenant Cranston has the odd habit of carrying a gun but never actually shooting it. So who knows."

"I guarantee he'll shoot on this detail, Mr. Hall," Kellerman said. He turned to the Navajo. "Ahiga, take the point. We're moving out."

The Indian glanced at the lemon sky that imparted a strange tawny light to the waning afternoon. He shook his head and said, "Not a good day, Captain."

"What does it portend, Ahiga?" Kellerman said.

"I do not know," the Indian said. "Cougar light."

He swung his horse around and took up his position ahead of the column.

"What did he mean, Captain?" Cranston said.

"Who knows what an Indian means," Kellerman said. He stood in the stirrups and waved his arm. "Forward, ho."

Sixteen men fell in behind him in column of twos, Corporal Billy Bob Scott riding next to Patrick Reilly. Dressed in regulation blouse and campaign hat, both men had overheard the Navajo and didn't look particularly happy, either from what Ahiga had uttered or an awareness of their own insignificance as they rode under a vast and strange sky on a desert that had a beginning but did not end until it reached the sandy beaches of the Pacific.

The column was two hours out of Fort Misery when Captain Joe Kellerman called a halt, close enough to Santiago Lozado's camp that he smelled woodsmoke and heard the laugh of a man sitting at a fire.

"Dismount," he ordered. "Corporal Scott, take the horses to the rear and detail a couple of men to hold them there." As the horses were rounded up and led into the darkness behind him, Kellerman said, "Now it's up to you and the Navajo, Lieutenant Cranston. Do you have your knife?"

"I have a Barlow folder, sir."

"Is it sharp?"

"Sharp enough to cut rope."

"Then it will do."

The Navajo emerged from the darkness, and Kellerman said, "What can you tell me?"

"Comancheros sitting around fires." He waved a hand behind him. "The slaves are back that way. They have no fires."

"Bad for them, good for us. Mr. Cranston, herd the slaves this way, and we'll be waiting."

"In the dark, will I be able to see what way is this way?"

"Probably not. But the Navajo can see in the dark."

"If he shape-shifts into an owl."

Kellerman's smile was quickly there, quickly gone, but sincere enough. "Good, you haven't lost your sense of humor. Get it done, Lieutenant. Bring those people out of there."

Cranston saluted, followed the Navajo, and was swallowed by darkness. Kellerman shook his head and sighed. The lieutenant looked like an overgrown schoolboy. Then, unbidden, a crippled child's voice sounded in his head . . . *God help us, every one.*

The Navajo moved through the darkness like a ghost but was painfully aware that Lieutenant Cranston wore thumping riding boots. At least he'd the good sense to remove his spurs.

When they were a few yards from the huddled slaves, the Indian stopped Cranston with an outstretched arm, strong, like a bar of wrought iron. Both men stood still, watching, listening, their breaths coming in tight gasps. Cranston thought he could hear the beat of his own heart.

The Comancheros, and there seemed to be a lot of them, sat around flickering fires in the middle distance. There was a parked wagon, and a single tent glowed amber in the glossy moonlight.

Ahiga grabbed Lieutenant Cranston's arm. He was aware that a knife-wielding Navajo who looked like an Apache appearing in their midst could scare the Mexicans and set up an alarmed tumult. A blue-shirted soldier might have a calming effect. "You go," he whispered. "Let them see you first." He held a forefinger to his lips and then said, "Hush them."

Cranston nodded, and the Navajo said, "Knife?"

The lieutenant showed the opened Barlow, and Ahiga shook his head and said, "Aiii . . ." Then, "Go now. Cut them free."

Cranston looked at the squatting slaves and to the broad area where wide-awake and armed, dangerous men sat around campfires.

Then suddenly, to himself, his courage faltering, "This, isn't going to work."

A push in the back from the impatient Navajo propelled him forward, and suddenly he was among the slaves, weather-beaten, work-seamed faces turned in his direction. With hope? No, the lieutenant decided, with utter resignation, a willingness to accept each new horror as it presented itself.

As the Navajo had done, Cranston held a finger to his lips and then took a knee beside a captive and cut his bonds. He pointed out a direction in the darkness and whispered, "*Vamos.*" The man caught on quickly. On all fours he scuttled into the gloom. Cranston didn't watch him go. He was already cutting free another. Then the Navajo was beside him, his finger to his lips, quickly cutting ropes with one slash of his knife. One by one the Mexicans fled into the night, the women with shawls over their heads as though hurrying into a bell-ringing chapel.

All but one . . .

She was young, with a beautifully boned face and a voluptuous figure. In the dim light, Cranston figured her to be about eighteen, maybe a couple of years older or younger. Of all the slaves he and the Navajo had freed, she was the only one who was not bound with ropes. When he tried to raise her to her feet, she stubbornly refused to budge but turned dark eyes, dead as coals, to the young officer.

"Get up, ma'am," Cranston said, his whispering voice urgent. "We need to get out of here."

The girl either didn't understand English or her mouth was as closed as her face. She sat unmoving and stared straight ahead, unseeing, like a blind person.

Then two events happened that Lieutenant Cranston would remember for the rest of his life.

The first was that the Navajo pushed him aside, grunted, then lifted the girl bodily and threw her over his shoulder.

The second was that the girl shrieked . . . and suddenly the encampment came to life, her scream hitting like a rock thrown into an ant colony.

Men scrambled to their feet and yells fractured the night. Guns flashed and bullets split the air like angry hornets.

"Get her out of here!" Cranston yelled to the Navajo above the sudden din of gunfire. "Take her to Captain Kellerman with the others."

The Indian didn't hesitate and strode into the night, the kicking white bundle of the girl still over his shoulder.

Lieutenant Cranston pocketed his knife and drew his Colt. The white-painted sight didn't help much. Blinded by the flare of each shot he fired, he cut loose at shadows, constantly shifting position as he retreated after the Navajo. He didn't believe he scored any hits, but unaware of the force they faced, the Comancheros stayed back. For now.

Damn, it was a long way back to the troop.

Cranston took time to reload his revolver, pleased that his hands didn't tremble, and resumed his retreat. Then a figure suddenly loomed out of the murk, a gun in each hand, very close. The Comanchero fired, and a bullet tugged at the left arm of the officer's blouse, followed by a second that burned across his cheek, drawing blood. As he'd been taught at the Point, Cranston extended his gun arm and fired. This time the white outlined sight helped. As far as he could tell, his bullet hit the man center mass. He heard a stifled groan and then the thud! of the Comanchero hitting the sand. The lieutenant snapped off two more shots, firing blindly into a wall of darkness, and hotfooted it out of there. He felt blood run down his cheek and throat and for a panicked moment thought he might be mortally wounded. But no, that wasn't likely. He was still on his feet, running, and there was little pain. Ahead of him, he saw a glint of metal and realized that Kellerman and his troopers were close. Then another moment of panic spiked at him. Suppose they mistook him for the enemy?

"It's me, Cranston!" he yelled.

A jeering voice answered that he suspected came from Corporal Billy Bob Scott.

"And who else?"

"Just me, damn it!"

"Come in with your hands up."

Cranston cursed under his breath. *Billy Bob, I plan to make your life a misery at Fort Misery*. But he stuck his hands in the air and stumbled forward, almost falling into the arms of Captain Kellerman.

"Are you hurt bad?" Kellerman said.

"I don't think so," Cranston said.

"Then take a place in the line."

"Sir, you only have ten men."

"Two with the horses, the others herding the Mexicans. What's left are the very best and very worst of them, every mother's son a villain and cutthroat."

"What do you want me to do, Captain?"

"Stand in the line and shoot when you see the white of

their eyes. We'll retreat step by step until we remount and get the hell out of here, a recoil retreat as the artillery call it. Now get ready, Lieutenant. They're coming."

Cranston reckoned that odds were four to one, consoled himself with the thought that it could be worse, then shifted back to reality . . . no it damn well couldn't.

But confused by the darkness, the attack when it came was tentative, almost timid. Crouched men emerged warily from the darkness and walked into a withering fire from Sharps carbines. Men dropped, tried to turn back, and collided with others. Shrieks of pain and fear emerged from several throats, providing a background symphony from hell.

Cranston fired steadily, falling back as Kellerman paced off the retreat, then he saw the captain involved in the only mano a mano combat of the fight.

Kellerman shot his Colt dry, stopped to reload, and then saw a Mescalero, big and tall enough to be an American, levering a Henry as he ran at the firing line from the right flank. Kellerman dropped his revolver, drew the bowie from his belt, and flung himself at the Comanchero. Startled, the man got off a quick shot that whined through the night but went nowhere. Kellerman slammed the knife into the man's belly to the hilt and then kicked him off the blade. The Comanchero dropped the Henry and fell on his back, babbling in pain and fear, his right hand raised in a gesture of surrender like a Roman gladiator, begging for mercy. His blood up, Kellerman had none. He picked up the rifle and levered two .44-40 bullets into the man's face and saw his features erupt like a ripe watermelon.

Captain Kellerman waved the bloody bowie in the air and yelled, "Back! Ten paces. Keep firing, you damned ruffians."

The line retreated—all but one man who lay facedown

and unmoving on the sand. Cranston recognized him by his bad haircut: Private Patrick Reilly, one of the worst of them, who'd never need a haircut again.

A few rifles fired from Lozado's camp, bullets split the night, and men yelled at each other in several different languages. But the battle was over. Lozado had no taste for night fighting, and the attack had cost him three men dead, four wounded, and a couple missing. The butcher's bill was too high, the scalps were gone, and both Lozado and Roscoe Wolfe were enraged, a fortune lost in a single night.

As the battle faded into silence, Captain Kellerman picked up the dead trooper as though he were a child and carried him to the rear. His men might be scum, but by God they were fighting scum, and he would not leave one of his dead on the field. Reilly was slung across his saddle, and Corporal Scott took up the reins.

A couple of the older slaves who'd slowed down the march were mounted behind troopers, and Kellerman ordered Lieutenant Cranston to take the troublesome younger woman up with him. "If she gives you any trouble, dump her," he said.

But the girl went limp in Cranston's arms as he sat her in front of him, and she leaned back, her head on his shoulder.

"Are you comfortable?" he said as he followed the others at a fast canter.

The girl made no answer.

"What's your name?"

"I have no name."

Cranston smiled. "Everyone has a name. You're very pretty."

"I had a name once, a name I no longer deserve."

"Tell me your name and let me decide."

"Maria. After the Madonna."

"Maria is a real nice name."

"The Madonna is a virgin. I am no longer a virgin. I am nothing."

The girl made the lieutenant uneasy, taking him down a road he wasn't qualified to travel. He hugged her a little closer. "Now you're safe and we'll take care of you."

"Would you marry me?"

"I beg your pardon."

"Officer, would you make me your wife?"

"Ah . . ." He sighed. "No, I don't want to get married, not yet."

"You said I'm pretty, but you wouldn't marry me. It's because you wouldn't stand at the altar with a bride who is not a virgin."

Cranston swallowed hard then smiled, like a magician pulling a rabbit out of a hat. "You speak English very well, Maria."

"The holy nuns taught me. If they knew I was not a virgin they'd beat me with willow canes."

Desperate now, the lieutenant pulled a second rabbit out of the same hat. "There are two other women at the fort. You'll like them."

The girl made no answer, and high above her and Cranston a silver-edged black cloud glided across the face of the moon and for a moment brought more darkness to the night.

The always-watchful Navajo took up the drag as the slaves were herded forward. Some prayed, some sobbed, others clasped their hands and wailed their relief, rejoicing at the liberation.

As he rode, Kellerman worried. The Mexicans numbered

around two score . . . forty mouths to feed . . . a seemingly impossible task at Fort Misery, where rations were already cut to bare minimum, or cut to the marrow bone, as Lieutenant Hall ofttimes said. Maybe Mrs. Zimmermann would come up with a solution, but he doubted it.

CHAPTER 20

Private John Wall, exiled to Fort Misery for gross insubordination, drunkenness, and bigamy, nonetheless took his guard duty seriously, and the moving white mist emerging from the darkness puzzled and unsettled him. His hands tightened on his Sharps as he peered into the murk, and he took half a dozen steps forward to get a closer look.

Was it a ha'ant? The Navajo scout once told him that Fort Misery was full of restless spirits. Then his training took over and, a young man with a painfully bad speech impediment, he called out, "H-h-halt. Who g-g-goes there?"

An answering yell from the white-streaked gloom. "Wall, you stuttering halfwit, it's Corporal Scott and the troop!"

"A-a-advance, f-f-friend, a-a-and be r-recognized."

As Wall watched, the mist resolved itself into a bunch of Mexicans wearing white shirts and pants, and then the mounted troopers came into view, Captain Kellerman in the lead. As he passed Wall, he said, "Well done, soldier. Very alert."

"Th-thank you, sir."

Sergeant Major Saul Olinger stood outside the headquarters building where Kellerman drew rein, halted the troop, and dismounted.

"You brought them in, Joe," Olinger said.

"We got all of them," Kellerman said. "I call that a miracle."

Olinger cast his eyes over the troopers and lingered on the empty saddle.

"Private Reilly," Kellerman said. "Lieutenant Cranston slightly wounded, no other casualties."

"Did Reilly do his duty?"

"He stood in the firing line, steady as a rock."

"I'm glad to hear it, a poor boy with a bad haircut."

"We'll bury him at first light. I want a four-man honor guard." Kellerman saw the doubt in the sergeant major's eyes and said, "One round each." He smiled. "Saul, we can afford four cartridges."

"As you say, sir."

Kellerman said to Lieutenant Cranston, "Mr. Cranston, once you finish molesting that young woman, you can dismiss the troop."

"Sir, I didn't . . . I mean . . ." The young officer was flustered, more so when he heard the troopers giggle.

"Then take Private Reilly's body to Mrs. Zimmermann. She knows what's expected of her. And do the same with the girl. Oh, and whiskey and water for the troop and the Navajo. Lieutenant Hall is officer of the guard, so I'll leave it to him to find accommodation for the Mexicans. And last but not least, get the doctor to look at your face wound. Any questions, mister?"

Resigned to his fate, Cranston said, "No questions, sir."

Kellerman nodded and said, "You did well tonight, Lieutenant. Did you fire your pistol?"

"Yes, sir."

"Good. You're learning. That's why Sam Colt made the damned things . . . to be shot."

* * *

"Sir, I've quartered the Mexicans in the sutler's store," Lieutenant James Hall said. "It's a tight squeeze, but they'll manage." He watched as Sergeant Major Olinger filled his glass, nodded his thanks, and then said, "They'll need to be fed, of course."

"I'll deal with that problem tomorrow," Captain Joe Kellerman said.

"Sir, may I add my congratulations to those of the sergeant major. Tonight's action was brilliant."

"Thank you, Mr. Hall. I killed a man tonight, hand to hand. It was not a clean kill at a distance, but up close with a knife. The noise he made when my blade entered his belly . . ." Kellerman shook his head. "I don't want to think about it."

"During the war we all heard that sound, Captain," Hall said. "Those of us who used the saber. It's a cry a man never forgets." He took a pinch of snuff. "Still, better him than you."

"Very profound, Lieutenant Hall," Kellerman said. He was almost drunk.

"Tortillas and bean paste," Hall said.

"What are you talking about, Lieutenant?" Kellerman said.

"Tortillas and bean paste. That's what Mexican peons eat, sir."

"We don't have any of that stuff."

"No, we don't. More's the pity. Squash, now that's another traditional food."

"We don't have any of that either."

Hall sipped his whiskey and then said. "Salt pork, maybe?"

"That would kill them," Kellerman said.

"Salt beef too, I suppose?"

"That would kill them quicker."

Olinger coughed and said to Hall, "Sir, we don't have enough meat to feed the garrison plus another forty people."

Hall smiled. "Once again, Sergeant Major, you have put us to rights. Our supplies would be quickly used up." He snapped his fingers. "I've got it. Hardtack! We can feed them hardtack."

Kellerman, irritated, said, "Lieutenant, I forbid you to say another word on the subject of food, grub, vittles, or eatables. May I suggest you go check on your Mexican charges and see if you can find Lieutenant Cranston? I hope he's not somewhere sparking that young Mexican gal."

"Right away, sir." Hall drained his glass, stood, and smoothed his magnificent beard. He stopped at the door and turned. "Hardtack fried in bacon fat, sir."

Before Kellerman could reply he was gone.

Olinger smiled. "He means well, Joe. For all his faults, he's a good officer."

"Hardtack fried in bacon fat," Kellerman said. "Hmm . . . it might just work."

"That's a pile of hardtack, and a lot of bacon fat," Olinger said.

"Yeah, it is, isn't it?' Kellerman said. "And I doubt the Mexicans will eat it. Damn it, Saul, I need another drink."

CHAPTER 21

The post infirmary, an adobe structure connected to the west side of the headquarters building by a short timber passageway, contained a twelve-patient ward, the post surgeon's office, dispensary, linen closet, and store-room. It had a tin roof and wood floor, and there had never been a post surgeon at Fort Misery. Mrs. Zimmermann took that role on the condition she could heal with prayer, and the penurious army, unwilling to send a real doctor to what was the most expendable of their forts, gladly agreed.

Second Lieutenant Atticus Cranston, the Mexican girl in tow, found Mrs. Zimmermann in the ward with Dr. Isaac Stanton, standing between the iron beds of the two wounded soldiers, their faces grim, the woman's hands joined, lips moving in prayer.

Stanton's blazing eyes found Cranston's face, and he said, "Before you ask, the answer is no, they're not fit for duty, and they'll never be fit for duty. They'll both die within the next forty-eight hours."

Shocked, taken by surprise, the young officer managed, "Why . . ."

"Why?" the little physician said. "You ask me why? Neglect, dysentery caused by bad food and contaminated water, lack of fresh air, and the fact that a competent doctor was not assigned to this fort. Look, you damned bluecoat butcher . . ." Stanton pulled the sheet from one of the patient's legs, a man with gray in his hair. Cranston's sharp intake of breath revealed that he'd never seen or smelled such a foul atrocity before. West Point hadn't prepared him for a leg rotted by gangrene.

"I could amputate, but it would do no good. The gangrene has spread to the rest of his body, and he's already in shock. He'll die soon." Stanton replaced the sheet and laid his hand on the chest of the other soldier, young but skeletal. "He was shot through the lungs, and he was already a dead man when they brought him in here. Another death hastened by neglect."

Stanton saw Cranston's eyes move to Mrs. Zimmermann and said, "Don't blame her. She did her best with what little she had. When it's a contest between prayer and gas gangrene, I'm afraid gangrene wins every time."

"Mrs. Zimmermann . . ." Cranston said.

The woman's eyes were shut, her lips moving.

"Mrs. Zimmermann . . ."

The woman's head turned slowly, reptilian, like a basilisk.

"This girl's name is Maria," Cranston said. "She's had a terrible time as a slave and needs to be cared for. I thought you . . . I mean . . ."

"I know what you mean," the woman said. She crossed the floor, took the girl's unprotesting hand, and said, "Come with me."

Maria showed no emotion, no interest, an automaton going through the motions, and allowed herself to be led out of the ward.

Stanton said, "Lifeless, but a pretty girl."

"She was raped."

"By whom?"

"Santiago Lozado."

"The bandit?"

"Yes. He's a Comanchero."

The doctor shook his head. "I'm in the midst of barbarians. I wish to God I was in Yuma."

Cranston was suddenly defensive. "As far as I know, there are barbarians in Yuma."

"Yes, Lieutenant, the world has no shortage of them."

"I was ordered to ask Mrs. Zimmermann to prepare Private Reilly's body for burial."

"Just a boy, but he'll be ready for his final journey. I had Mr. Zimmermann build two coffins; now I'll need a third."

Cranston, struggling to say something, settled on, "Doctor, I'm sorry."

"Yes, Lieutenant, you're sorry, I'm sorry, Mrs. Zimmermann is sorry, and her husband is sorry that he has to knock together another coffin. The girl you brought in is sorry she was raped. We're all sorry. And there's not a thing we can do about it."

"I'll report to Captain Kellerman that his orders are being carried out. Good evening to you." Almost by instinct, Cranston's hand came up in a salute, but Isaac Stanton's hand knocked it down again. "Lieutenant, don't salute me. I murdered my wife and her lover and then rejoiced that I had ended their lives. You don't pay respects to a monster like me."

"For a moment I forgot . . ."

"Don't forget. Don't ever forget. I'm here at Fort Misery and do you know what that means?"

Cranston was confused. "I . . . I don't . . ."

"It means I'm in hell, already numbered among the

damned. Now let me take a look at that facial wound of yours."

"You and your bandaged face bring me bad tidings indeed, Lieutenant Cranston," Captain Joe Kellerman said.

"It's a small bandage for a slight wound, sir. The iodine hurt worse. Sir, the doctor says the two soldiers in the infirmary will both be dead within the next forty-eight hours."

"Privates Dick Bly and Gustave Charpieaux," Kellerman said, shaking his head. "Bly was a habitual deserter, and Charpieaux, well, we only know he was a lieutenant colonel in Lee's Army of Northern Virginia. But why he landed himself in Fort Misery is a mystery."

As he adjusted a smoking oil lamp in Kellerman's office, Sergeant Major Olinger said, "I spoke to him once. He said it was a fight over the affections of a lady, but he'd go no further than that."

"He was my oldest soldier," Kellerman said. "He must've been forty when he was posted here."

Cranston said, "Gangrene, sir. Doctor Stanton . . ."

Kellerman smiled. "Are we calling the little man Dr. Stanton now?"

"Captain, he's the only medical man we've got," Olinger said.

"Yes, I guess that's the case. All right, Dr. Stanton it is. Lieutenant, you mentioned gangrene?"

"Yes, sir, that's what's killing Charpieaux."

"And Private Reilly?"

"His body will be ready for burial soon." Cranston stood to attention in front of Kellerman's desk and said, "Captain, can I make so bold as to ask for a drink?"

"Can he make so bold, Sergeant Major?"

"I don't see why not. I'd say the lieutenant has earned it."

"Then another glass for Mr. Cranston." Kellerman poured

the whiskey and handed the glass to Cranston. "There you go, Lieutenant. You've now joined the Fort Misery drinking fraternity."

Atticus Cranston downed the raw whiskey in one shuddering gulp and then gasped, "Thank you, sir. I needed that."

"Watch your drinking, Lieutenant," Kellerman said, waving a forefinger.

CHAPTER 22

"Both my women gone," Santiago Lozado said, whining. "And I planned to try that young Mexican slut again."

"Don Santiago, our scalps are gone, we lost men, and you concern yourself with women?" Roscoe Wolfe said.

"The patrón has his needs," Kyle Swan, the green-eyed knife fighter said, smiling slightly.

"Our need is to recover our scalps," Wolfe said.

"Damn him," Lozado said. "Kellerman brought a full troop of cavalry and a company of infantry to free the slaves. The gringo pig has been reinforced."

"Are you saying he's now too strong for us?" Wolfe said.

"No. I'm not saying that. But to defeat him we'll need to use every ounce of our cunning."

"Don Santiago, we need to recover the scalps, not defeat Kellerman. One can be done without the necessity of the other."

"But I want Kellerman dead. When he is no more, the others will fall apart. The soldiers will mutiny."

"Yes, it's Kellerman who holds them together."

"The sooner he's dead, the better. Dead, hear me? Dead, dead, dead."

"Patrón, what do your men crave most?" Swan said.

"My Comancheros? They desire what all men want."

"And that is?"

"Gold, tequila, and whores, the wilder the better."

"What's your drift, Swan?" Wolfe said.

"How much risk to his life would a man accept to be assured of enough gold to keep him in tequila and frisky whores until he turns gray?"

"Who knows? There are men who might risk their lives for such an opportunity," Lozado said.

"Any of them your men, patrón?" Swan said. "Two, three, or four who'll trade a hard life in rope sandals for wine, women, and song?"

"And what would these men do to earn such a reward?" Lozado said.

"Why, assassinate Kellerman of course," Swan said. "We send them to the fort one by one. If an assassin fails, another takes his place."

"And we give gold to the executioner who succeeds," Lozado said.

"Of course not," Swan said. "When he comes to collect his gold, we pay him in lead."

The air was cool, dark, and smelled of mesquite wood-smoke.

"Ah, Kyle, my dearest friend, you are truly a remarkable man," Lozado said. He shifted his attention to Wolfe. "Is he not, my friend Roscoe?"

"Remarkable," Wolfe said without much enthusiasm. He pegged Swan as a gun, and that made him wary.

"Here is what you must do, my friend Kyle," Lozado said. "Talk to the men, those who will risk all for a life of pleasure. Be persuasive, give them much respect, remind them how tequila smells when the bottle is opened and the soapy fragrance of a young whore when she steps out of the bathtub and drips water on the floor. Paint them pictures, my friend—exciting, colorful pictures—and find me the men I need."

Swan nodded. "I'll see what I can do. By the way, patrón, do we have gold?"

Lozado shook his head. "No, my friend. They think me rich, but the gold is an illusion. Never fear, I'll show them a double eagle and tell them there are thousands more where it came from. They won't believe you, but they will me." He waved a hand. "Now go, get your scheme to kill Kellerman started."

After Swan left, Wolfe lit his pipe and then said across the firelight, "We'll have to kill that man someday."

"I know, but we must be careful. He's good with a gun and the blade."

"A gun and the blade. A bullet in the back takes care of his kind. A dose of lead, and then the carrion birds."

"When the time comes, you will rid me of him, my friend. Until then, he is useful."

"Will he find an assassin?"

"I don't know." Lozado smiled. "If he doesn't, will you volunteer?"

"Wear a cloak and carry a dagger? I think not."

"The blade is silent."

"And it must be the assassin's weapon if he has any hope of escaping after he kills Kellerman."

Lozado pressed his palms against the sides of his head. "Aii . . . it is an easy task that's not easy at all."

"Unless the assassin is willing to die for you, don Santiago."

"I'm surrounded by dogs. Who among them is willing to give his life for poor Lozado? The answer is none, my friend."

"Then let us hope that where love and loyalty fail, the promise of gold will triumph."

CHAPTER 23

Two soldiers were buried at first light in the Fort Misery cemetery, Private Patrick Reilly and Private, formerly Lieutenant Colonel, Gustave Charpieaux, who'd died a few minutes after midnight. The Slavic priest said the words, and on Captain Joe Kellerman's order, the four-soldier honor guard fired a one-volley salute.

Mary Zimmermann, who'd been praying at the graveside, waylaid Kellerman on his way back to the headquarters building. "Captain, can we talk?" she said.

"Of course. Here or in my office?"

"Here is fine, Captain. It's about the young girl you brought in with the Mexicans."

"Yes, she was Lieutenant Cranston's responsibility."

"My responsibility now," Mrs. Zimmermann said.

She and Kellerman stood under a rose-tinted sky, and a rising wind slapped the woman's dress against her legs and blew strands of graying, unbound hair across her face.

"What seems to be the trouble?" Kellerman said.

"Frankly, I'm worried about her. She won't talk and refuses to eat. She just sits and stares, looking at no one and listening to no one. Sara Lark, poor thing, tries to engage her in conversation, but Maria just sits, not looking at her, but looking right through her. And she does the same with me and Dr. Stanton."

"The girl is Catholic. Have your asked Father Stas . . . Stasz . . ."

"Father Staszczyk."

"Yes, indeed. Have you asked him to talk with her?"

Mrs. Zimmermann made a face. "I did, and he said she may be possessed by a demonic force."

"And . . ."

"There is no *and*, Captain. He left it right there, and I haven't talked to him since."

Kellerman thought for a moment and then said, "Lieutenant Hall! If he can't get the girl to talk, no one can. And he can probably banish demons with his snuff."

"I'm at the end of my tether, Captain. "I'm willing to try anything." A pause, then, "Even Lieutenant Hall."

"Good, then I'll send him to the infirmary."

Lieutenant James Hall palmed his beard smooth to his chest, set his kepi at a jaunty angle, and then said, "My dear young lady, I am here to help you regain your senses and set you back on the road to health and happiness. Now, what do you think of that?"

The girl called Maria stared through him with eyes as expressive as smears of matte brown paint.

"Do you see what I mean?" Mrs. Zimmermann said.

"Hmm . . . I saw such cases as this during the war— among men, of course, not the weaker sex. Minds gone, you understand, from the stress of battle." He shook his head. "A truly terrible state of affairs." Then, after studying Maria for long moments, "I understand that this poor creature was quite recently undone."

"She was raped," Mrs. Zimmermann said.

"Ah, yes, such a terrible word."

"And such a terrible experience."

"Yes, indeed. Mrs. Zimmermann. What is needed here is firmness but not severity. Oh, dear no, never harshness in these cases." He produced his snuff box and offered it to the woman. "Would you care for a pinch, dear lady?"

Mrs. Zimmermann shook her head no. The morning sunlight angled through the window of the doctor's office and made dust motes dance. In the ward, Private Bly's breathing was shallow and irregular. Isaac Stanton was there, watching the boy die.

Lieutenant Hall helped himself to snuff, sniffed heartily, and said, "Now, Maria, that's your name, isn't it?"

No answer. Expressionless eyes in a vacuous face.

"Maria. Such a pretty name," Hall said. "Who gave you that name? Your dear mama?"

"Probably nuns," Mrs. Zimmermann said.

"I see we must use our wits, dear lady, as did the bold Odysseus during the Trojan War. Like that hero, we face a powerful enemy who can only be overcome by guile."

"What enemy?" Mrs. Zimmermann said.

"The girl's own mind, of course. She has built a high wall between us that can only be overcome by a Trojan horse of our own making. Now, does that make sense to you?"

"No."

"It will. Just give me time. Ah, dear lady, could I trouble you for a cup of coffee? This is a difficult case. and I must be sharp—sharp as a thorn."

When Mary Zimmermann brought the coffee, Lieutenant Hall held the cup in one hand, laid the other on the girl's shoulder. She didn't flinch or move but stared blankly into space as before. "You had a terrible experience, young lady, and now you must tell me all about it. Get it off your chest. I'm listening."

No answer. No reaction. Something inside the girl was as dead as stone.

Hall shook his head. "A challenging case as ever was, Mrs. Zimmermann. But we must persevere. There's a light at the end of every tunnel."

The woman said, "Asking Maria to describe her rape isn't really helpful, Lieutenant. That's a soldier's question."

"It is? I didn't mean it in any offensive way."

"You're a soldier. You have the ways of a soldier. Why don't you just order her to stand to attention?"

Hall's face brightened. "Would that help?"

"No, it wouldn't help!" This from Sara Lark who'd just stepped into the room. "Mrs. Zimmermann was making a good joke," she said.

"This is not a joking matter, Miss Lark." Hall said. "The girl is far gone."

"Yes, she is—in a dark place from where she might never return," Sara said. Then, no change in her expression, she added, "Private Bly just died."

To his credit, Lieutenant Hall looked shocked. "I'm sorry to hear that. Private Bly always did his duty."

Sara Lark said, "I'm sure he's saying that to St. Peter right now, 'Let me in, I always did my duty.' "

Hall nodded. "I'm certain that will be the case, but I rather think there is a separate Valhalla for soldiers."

"And one for whores," Sara Lark said.

"With Aphrodite at the gates," Hall said. Sara looked like she'd drawn a blank, and he added, "The Greek goddess of love and beauty."

"Then let's hope she's waiting up there for me and my kind," Sara said. "Why don't you take her for a walk?"

"Who, Aphrodite?"

"Lieutenant, you're a peach. No, Maria. I think she'll walk with you."

"She ignores me."

"I think I can talk her into it."

Sara kneeled beside the seated girl and took her hand. "Maria, why don't you take a stroll with the lieutenant?"

The girl blinked.

"Get some fresh air," Sara said.

"Fresh air," Maria said. Her voice flat, disinterested.

"Si, aire fresco."

The girl rose to her feet.

"Lieutenant, take her hand, walk with her for a while, see if she takes an interest in anything," Sara Lark said.

Hall smiled at the girl. "It's a fine morning, señorita. Will you take a promenade with me under the linden trees, and perhaps stop for ice cream and cake at a little café I know?" He turned his smile on Sara. "A soldier's joke."

"Well, if you find such a place, take me with you." Sara said. She smiled in return and suddenly looked years younger.

"It will be my pleasure, dear lady," Hall said, always a gentleman. "Now Miss Maria, take my hand and let us go for a walk."

The girl took his hand and together they left the infirmary and stepped into the sunlight of the aborning day.

CHAPTER 24

Lieutenant James Hall thought things were going well . . . until they didn't.

Holding Mrs. Zimmermann's yellow parasol above her head, Maria took his arm and they strolled into the desert for a ways, stopping at a nine-foot-tall, candy barrel cactus. He invited the girl to admire its pretty bloom, but her expression didn't change; she said nothing and showed no interest, as though she stared at a brick wall.

Disappointed, Hall said, "And now, dear lady, we'll walk this way and perhaps catch a glimpse of a roadrunner bird. The roadrunner can outrace a human, and it can kill a rattlesnake. Did you know that?"

If Maria did or didn't, Hall never found out, because she said nothing.

The hunt for the roadrunner was unsuccessful and so was Lieutenant Hall. After an hour, the morning grew hot, and he returned to the fort . . . and for the first time the girl took an interest in something and seemed almost animated.

"No, dear lady, that is not a sight for the gently raised," Hall said. "Avert your eyes." He grabbed the parasol from Maria's hand and held it horizontally, blocking her gaze. "I'm sure Mrs. Zimmermann has coffee ready." But the girl knocked down the parasol and stared, open-mouthed, eyes shining . . . at the gallows.

"Come, let us away from here, out of the heat," Hall said.

God forbid that Lieutenant James Hall would ever lay a rough hand on a woman, but he did that day, dragging the girl by the arm toward the infirmary. Maria resisted every step of the way, her eyes fixed on the gallows until she was finally hauled inside.

"You took the girl off the post to admire a candy barrel cactus?" Captain Joe Kellerman said, morning drunk and irritated.

"Only one, sir. And we looked for a roadrunner."

Kellerman sighed. "You looked for a roadrunner . . . Mister, the sentries reported seeing two Comancheros with field glasses reconnoitering the fort. Suppose you and the woman had run into them? Especially since Mrs. Zimmermann said you left your sidearm in the infirmary, and the same Mrs. Zimmermann also says that the girl is hysterical. Did you threaten to hang her?"

"No, sir, I did not," Hall said.

"Did not what?"

"Threaten to hang her."

"And your sidearm?"

"Sir, I left it behind because I didn't wish its presence to alarm the young lady."

"She'd have been a sight more alarmed if you'd been attacked by Comancheros."

"Yes, sir. As you say, sir."

Kellerman, deep in thought for a few moments, then said, "What's wrong with that girl?"

"Sir, she was raped by Lozado, and perhaps others, and lost her maidenhood. She can't get over it. She seems to think that no man would ever want her. At least that's Lieutenant Cranston's opinion."

"And the lieutenant is an expert on women?"

"I don't know, sir. I doubt it."

"She was taken by a man once. Suppose she wants it again?"

"Sir?"

"Perhaps that's why she went with you into the desert?"

"Sir, that was not the young lady's intention. Or mine."

"Certain questions needed to be asked."

"I understand, sir. And certain questions were answered."

"What do we do with her?"

"Leave her with Mrs. Zimmermann."

"What about the priest, Father Stasz . . ."

"He's useless, sir. He says Maria could be possessed by a demon. Does the captain mind if I take snuff?"

"Go right ahead and stand at ease for God's sake. You look like a wooden Indian with a beard. A glass of whiskey with you?"

"Yes, sir. I've had quite a trying morning."

Kellerman handed the drink to Hall and said, "Consider yourself reprimanded."

"Yes sir." Hall raised his glass. "To your good health, sir."

Kellerman did the same and said, "And yours." Then, "Why were the Comancheros scouting the fort?"

"For another attack?"

"Hell, they know the layout of this place only too well."

"Counting heads?"

"Possibly. Lozado thinks we have infantry here."

"Then that's what he was looking for, sir."

"Field glasses. A close-up view."

"I guarantee he saw only pants with yellow stripes," Hall said. "No infantrymen."

"I know, and that worries me."

"Should I double the guard, sir?"

"Yes, do that. Lieutenant Cranston will be the new guard commander."

"Good experience for the youngster," Hall said. "There's a limit to what I can teach him, though he's eager to learn." He drained his glass. "I must attend to my duties, sir."

"Yes, you're dismissed. And by the way, Lieutenant—for the next five days you will wear your sidearm at all times, in bed and out of it."

CHAPTER 25

"Roscoe, my dear friend, two of my most trusted men scouted the fort and they assure me they saw no infantry," Santiago Lozado said. "I'm sure that Kellerman has only his cavalry troop."

"What's left of it," Roscoe Wolfe said.

"This is true. We engaged in several fights, he and I, and when the Comanches were here we took a toll of his men."

"Then how many men does Kellerman have?"

"No more than half a troop, say around thirty."

Wolfe's eyes searched the camp all the way back to the rock shelf and then he said, "With my men, you have nearly twice that number."

"Yes, and a few stragglers recently came up from Sonora. Good men who rode on raids with both Comanche and Apache. Fighting men who will make short work of Kellerman's rabble."

"We need the slaves back."

"When the battle is won we can scalp the peons at the fort, my friend. Why herd them like hogs?" Lozado slapped Wolfe on the arm. "Use the blade, eh?"

"How clever you are, my friend," Wolfe said. "Over

there at the big rock I see another wagon parked. Why did I not see it before?"

"A few of my men brought it in last night. Later you will laugh to see what I've planned for your amusement."

"Does it involve the wagon?"

"Not directly, but it involves the driver. He is a peddler, one of the People of the Book. His wagon is loaded with pots and pans, clothing, and jugs of whiskey. My men will celebrate tonight and have ringing heads tomorrow."

"Why would such a man be here in the desert?"

"Peddlers wander far and wide. He says he was headed for Sonora, but who knows?" Lozado grinned. "Later we'll run him. That is, when my men are good and drunk. It will make for better sport."

Wolfe let his smile die and said, "My friend, when do we attack the fort?"

"When the time is right."

"And when will that be?"

"Soon, my friend."

"Why wait?"

"When it's a good time for Kellerman to die."

"Don Santiago, there are times when you talk in riddles."

"Roscoe, if one thing happens as planned, we need not try another."

"Again, I don't understand."

"I have a volunteer, the man who will assassinate Kellerman."

Roscoe's bearded face brightened. "Who is this man?"

"Ahh . . . I will show you."

Lozado poured himself coffee. The morning was hot, sweaty, dusty. The sun burned like melted bronze in the sky, and a single white cloud drifted, a soon-to-be-wilted lily in a blue pond. He turned his head and called out to the nearest man, "Send me Silverio Borja."

Wolfe watched the man come and whispered, "He's a runt."

"He is what we need, my friend. And he speaks English."

Silverio Borja was small, just four inches over five feet, but muscular, with huge hands. On his left wrist he wore a thick silver bracelet, perhaps a vanity because of his name, and he was dressed like a gringo, boots, black pants and shirt, a red bandana, and a wide-brimmed, low-crowned hat. As all Lozado's Comancheros did, he wore a holstered Colt around his waist and sported a bandolier of .44-40 ammunition. Like the young Bill Bonney, who would soon make a name for himself in the New Mexico Territory, he had a choirboy's face and the murderous instincts of a rabid wolf. A fast-draw artist, later historians would claim that Borja had killed eight white men, but only two of those were named shootists; the others, settlers, drovers, and wannabes. But he was the man who'd assassinate Joe Kellerman—or so Santiago Lozado fervently wanted to believe.

"Amigo, sit down and have coffee," Lozado said, grinning from ear to ear. "It is a pleasure and an honor to have such a famous pistolero in my company of heroes."

Kyle Swan arrived just in time to hear that last and said, "Patrón, Borja is an hombre to be reckoned with." A thin smile, then, "Kellerman is already as good as dead."

Lozada splashed coffee into the little gunman's cup. "Silverio, my dear friend, what our amigo Kyle says is sweet music to my ears. He has already told you what has to be done, now we all depend on you."

Borja tested his coffee and scanned the men around the fire. His black eyes were seldom still, and the half-smile on his lips never changed. He carefully set the cup on the sand beside him and said, "Gold."

"Ah, my friend, you come right to the point," Lozado said. "I like that in a man."

"Silverio, you will have gold aplenty," Swan said. "All you can carry."

"Buy mucho whiskey and whores, eh, my friend?" Wolfe said. "Make yourself a big man in the railroad towns."

"When?" Borja said.

"Why, when the deed is done and Kellerman is dead," Lozado said.

"Look at me, don Santiago," Borja said. "I said look at me!"

"I am doing so now, mi amigo," Lozado said. His tone was mild, but his eyes glittered.

"How much gold?"

"As friend Kyle says, all you can carry."

"Swan gave me a twenty-dollar gold piece."

"And there are many more where that one came from," Roscoe Wolfe said.

"Does he speak the truth, don Santiago?"

"Roscoe always speaks the truth," Lozado said.

Slowly, deliberately, Borja drank coffee and then said, talking over the rim of his cup, "I will kill Kellerman to-morrow."

Lozado clapped his hands and yelled, "Bravo! A man to be reckoned with indeed."

"Borja, have you decided on a way to do this thing?" Wolfe said.

"Am I stupid?"

"No, I don't think that."

"I don't like men who think I'm stupid."

"Then tell us how you will find Kellerman, kill him, and make your escape."

Borja said to Lozado, "Do I speak with this man? Who is he?"

"He is a dear friend. He is Roscoe Wolfe, the famous scalp hunter."

"Mexican scalps."

"Yes, but we are not here to talk about a man's profession. Roscoe asked you a fair question and, por favor, you will answer it."

"Then I will answer you, don Santiago. Even in the dark, I cannot search the fort for Kellerman. I would not live long."

"Then how, dear friend, Silverio?"

"I will make him come to me."

"Ah, you have a plan. Then I will ask you no more questions. You must do as you see fit. Only you must kill him."

"I'll do away with him." Borja tossed away the dregs of his coffee and stood. "The fire stinks like burning hair." He looked hard at Wolfe and then said, "Make sure the gold is waiting for me on my return."

"It will be, my friend," Lozado said. "It will be."

"And then I leave to spend it all."

"A wise man, a practical man, a man of great intensity," Lozado said. "I know I can place my trust in you, and you can place yours in me."

"I trust no one."

"You can trust me, my dear friend."

"Then only you, Lozado. My trust will go that far."

"A prudent man indeed, whose faith in me will not go unrewarded, and that is my word of honor. But, Silverio, one request, if I can make so bold."

"Name it."

"Ha, this makes me smile to say it, but if you can, shoot Kellerman in the belly. He'll die, but take a long time doing it."

Borja nodded. "It will be my pleasure, don Lozado."

"Then go with God, my friend. Rid this land of Keller-man's shadow."

After the gunman walked away. Later Wolfe would say he swaggered away, but now he spat into the fire and said, "If we didn't need him so badly, I'd gun that runt."

"Agreed, he's a most unpleasant person," Lozado said.

"All the gold he can carry. He doesn't want much."

"Oh, be assured we'll give him all the gold he can carry, dear friend. We'll melt a few double eagles and pour them down his throat."

When he and his men ran the peddler, Santiago Lozado's dark mood much improved. In fact, he laughed so loud and so often that his Comancheros slapped one another on the back and told themselves it was good that the don had re-turned to his old mirthful self.

The game itself was quite simple.

As daylight faded, adding to the excitement, they dragged the peddler—small, bearded, and terrified—to the edge of the camp and faced him into the desert. Then they gave the man, he called himself Solomon Adler, the Comancheros called him Jack Rabbit, a choice, a gun to his head: *Run for your life into the desert or die where you stand.*

The little man chose the run and guaranteed some good sport.

A dozen riflemen lined up, Lozado with a Sharps .50-90 in the middle.

When everyone was in place, and wagers were made on how far Jack would run, the game was ready to begin.

Lozado was the starter. "Run, Jack!" he yelled, head back, laughing.

Solomon Adler, father of five children, ran for his life.

A couple of bullets straddled him, kicked up Vs of sand, and he ran on. Another round hit a foot to his left, and he jogged right, only to be halted by a round hitting in front of him. He ran straight again, stumbled and fell, and behind him men jeered. The peddler sprang to his feet, again, zigzagging as bullets tracked him and forced him to constantly change direction. He ran, stumbled, ran, stumbled again, and then a round grazed his left arm, staggering him. Running in soft, clinging sand, Solomon Adler showed signs of exhaustion. Clutching his wounded arm, he staggered forward, his chest heaving. A bullet hit him a second time, on his right hip, and to everyone's amusement he bowled over like a shotgunned rabbit. The game was almost done. The peddler got to his feet, but he could barely move, weaving forward on wobbly knees as bullets kicked up sand around him . . .

And now Lozado grew bored.

He shouldered the Big Fifty, aimed and fired. His bullet smashed into the fleeing man's spine, between his shoulder blades.

It was a killing shot.

Solomon Adler fell facedown in the hot sand and didn't move.

The Comancheros cheered Lozado's marksmanship and a couple of them paced off the distance Adler had run. There were bets to be settled. As it turned out, the little man had not run very far: a little over fifty yards, and everyone was a little disappointed. They'd thought the man might have covered a hundred yards and provided more sport before Lozado's rifle cut him down.

Still, it was a fairly exciting distraction, and men cheered Lozado when he ordered them to break out the peddler's whiskey and share the rest of the spoils among them.

Lozado stood among his bustling men, spread his arms,

looked up at the sky, and yelled, "I give and give. I am a great torrent to my people."

That drew many huzzahs, and there were men that day who declared that don Santiago Lozado was the finest man and finest master who ever lived.

Fifty yards away, Solomon Adler died with his face in the sand.

CHAPTER 26

"Mrs. Zimmermann is complaining," Lieutenant James Hall said.

"Now what?" Captain Joe Kellerman said, morning sunlight glinting amber in his glass.

"All those extra mouths to feed, sir. She made a soup out of Abigail."

"Abigail? Who's she? The Mexicans aren't cannibals, are they?"

"She's a chicken, sir. Well, a hen actually, who stopped laying eggs about three months ago. The Mexicans don't like the soup, and Mrs. Zimmermann says we have a culinary crisis on our hands."

"Lieutenant, have you any other bad news?"

"Not right at the moment, sir. But I'm sure there is some pending."

"What happened to your beard?"

"Why do you ask, sir?"

"It's . . . scraggly."

"Lying in bed fully armed is not conducive to a good night's sleep. One tosses and turns and the hammer of a sidearm digs into the body in the most painful places."

"Walking in the desert without your weapon is not conducive to a long and happy life either, mister."

"Just as you say, sir."

"Ah, hell, take your revolver off at night. Just make sure you wear it at all times during the day."

"The captain is most understanding."

"The captain is not understanding. The captain understands nothing, including why Mexicans don't like chicken soup."

"Abigail was a tough old bird, sir, and made for a thin stock."

Kellerman sighed. "Orderly!" A young private appeared at the office door. "My compliments to Sergeant Major Olinger and ask him to join me. If he asks you what's it's about, tell him it's all about soup or broth or whatever the hell he wants to call it."

"Yes, sir," the orderly said, looking puzzled.

"Indeed, Mrs. Zimmermann's creation was more a thin broth than a soup," Lieutenant Hall said.

Kellerman stared at his subordinate, then, "Thank you for that information."

"Not very appetizing."

"I'm sure it wasn't."

"Lacked salt, I thought. And proper vegetables, of course."

"You sampled it?"

"Just a soupçon in a spoon, sir."

"Did you like it?"

"No, sir. As a soup, it left much to be desired. Very thin and watery. Now vichyssoise uses chicken stock and can be served cold. But Mrs. Zimmermann would need to have added pureed leeks, onions, potatoes, and cream."

"And she has none of that," Kellerman said, irritation creeping into his voice.

"No, sir, more's the pity, though I do believe we still have some potatoes—sprouted of course."

"Then let's drop the soup discussion until the sergeant major gets here."

"Of course, sir," Lieutenant Hall said. He was quiet for a while and then said, "The Scots make a fine chicken soup they call cock-a-leekie, but again, it calls for leeks and barley. And prunes too, for garnish."

A sharp retort that he didn't want to hear another damned word about soup, Scots or otherwise, died on Kellerman's lips as the sergeant major stepped inside and slammed to attention. "Sergeant Major Olinger reporting as ordered, sir."

"At ease," Kellerman said.

"We were just talking about soup, Sergeant Major," Hall said.

"You were talking about soup, Lieutenant, I wasn't," Kellerman said.

Olinger smiled. "Ah, Mrs. Zimmermann's witch's brew, eye of newt and all that stuff. Apparently it was thin and watery and a great disappointment."

"I know. The Mexicans don't like it," Kellerman said.

"To say the least," Olinger said.

"Probably just as well," Hall said. "Pretty soon we'd run out of hens for the soup pot."

"Thank you for that acute observation, Lieutenant," Kellerman said. "I'm sure the chickens are relieved."

The sergeant major beckoned to someone waiting outside the door. "Come in, Marco. Talk to the captain."

Hat in hand, a Mexican peon stepped inside accompanied by a boy who looked to be around ten or eleven. Both wore white shirts and pants, much stained, and rope sandals. Because of their confinement their hair was long, almost shoulder length. Both looked too thin, too ragged, and too frightened.

"This is Marco Camacho and his son Carlos," Olinger said.

"And why are they here?" Kellerman said.

"Señor Camacho says he can end our food problem."

"I'll entertain any suggestions except cannibalism."

"Marco doesn't speak English, but his son does. Carlos, tell el capitán what you told me."

The boy swallowed hard and then in a high, unbroken voice said, "There is food to be gathered in the desert that will feed us. This says my father."

"There's nothing in the desert except sand and cactus," Kellerman said.

"There is much food to be gathered in the desert. This says my father," the boy repeated.

"I've never seen it."

"You must know where to look. This says my father."

"What do you think, Saul?"

"I think Marco knows what he's talking about."

"Or his son knows what he's talking about," Kellerman said.

The boy said, "Send us into the desert with baskets and we will find food. This says my father."

"What do you think, Lieutenant Hall?" Kellerman said.

"Sir, we can't feed all those Mexicans, so I think it's worth a try."

Kellerman sat in thought for a few moments, drained his whiskey glass, and then said, "All right then, we'll try it. Who knows, maybe when they're wandering the desert God will send down manna to feed us all."

Hall said, "Now the house of Israel called its name manna. It was like coriander seed and the taste of it was like wafers made with honey." He smiled. "My father read the Bible to my brother and I every night before bedtime."

"Then you're my expert on food gathering, Lieutenant," Kellerman said. "You and a six-man detail will wander in the desert with the Mexicans and collect food. Wear your sidearm."

"Yes, sir, as you say, sir," Hall said. He turned his attention to Carlos. "Boy, tell your father to get his gatherers ready. We'll ask Mrs. Zimmermann for baskets, sacks, and whatever else she has that will hold . . ."

"Manna," Kellerman said.

"Or its equivalent," Hall said.

The boy translated this to his father, and the man beamed and bowed.

"And one more thing," the lieutenant said, turning his attention to Carlos. "I dislike small boys intensely—grubby, prancing, mischievous creatures that they are—so don't get underfoot."

"Si, mi capitán." Carlos giggled, standing to attention, and saluting.

Lieutenant Hall groaned, and Captain Kellerman hid a grin behind his empty glass.

CHAPTER 27

With the help of Corporal Billy Bob Scott and five amused troopers, Lieutenant James Hall lined up his twenty Mexican volunteers: twelve men, including Marco Camacho; four older women and four children; Carlos, another boy his age; and two wide-eyed girls, both about ten.

"Corporal, have the gatherers present their containers," Hall said.

It took a deal of cussing, shoving, and fractured Spanish to get the Mexicans to show their receptacles to the lieutenant's satisfaction. "The women and girls will be the basketeers," Hall said. When this was done, he said, "The men and boys can carry the sacks, pots, and boxes."

When the switches were made, Hall waved his gleaners forward into the vastness of the unsuspecting desert.

Before they'd set out, Captain Kellerman had ordered Hall to remain within arrow shot of the fort and said that if any of Lozado's Comancheros came in sight he should round up the gatherers and run like hell.

The lieutenant dutifully relayed this order to Corporal Scott who said, "What kind of grub do they expect to find, sir?"

"Manna."

"What the hell is that, sir?"

"Read your Bible, you damned heathen soldier," Hall said.

To the east of the fort were patches of scrub vegetation the lieutenant could identify: prickly pear, mesquite, desert chia, agave, and a few piñons, among others . . . including the candy barrel cactus that had cost him an uncomfortable night. But he saw the Mexicans—especially the women and girls—dive like hawks on mice upon low-growing plants and cactus that were a mystery to him.

The sun-scorched morning air was still and hard to breathe, and Lieutenant Hall's normally impeccable blue blouse was stained with sweat. Three canteens filled with precious but brackish water from the seep lay in the shade of a projecting rock, and at noon he determined to call in the gatherers for a drink. Perhaps then he would smoke a cigar, a much-pondered indulgence given his dwindling supply.

Hall knew what Corporal Scott was about to say before he said it. "I see him," he said. "He's been watching us for quite a while."

"Keeping his distance, sir," Scott said. "One of Lozado's men?"

"Undoubtably. He probably wonders what the hell we're doing."

"Sir, he could put two and two together and figure the fort is low on grub."

"That we're reduced to eating grass?"

"From where he is, it might look like it, sir."

"Hell, from where I am, it looks like it, Corporal. Why should he be any different?"

Scott unshouldered his rifle. "Want me to dust him, sir? Send him on his way?"

"No, he's leaving. Let's not detain him."

"Why was he here, sir?" Scott said, blinking against the sun glare.

"A good question, Corporal. Lozado knows where we are. Why send a scout?"

"Maybe just a saddle tramp passin' through. He wore a white man's duds."

"Passing through from where to where, Corporal? There's hundreds of miles of desert behind and hundreds ahead of him." Hall shook his head. "No, he's not passing through. He's one of Lozado's men, and he's up to something, but what, I do not know. I'll drop it on Captain Kellerman's desk and let him decide."

Scott's gaze swept the distance. "He's gone now, sir, damn him."

"Right, Corporal, call in the gatherers," Lieutenant Hall said. "Time for a water break."

"Captain Kellerman, they've completely taken over my kitchen," Mrs. Zimmermann said, her voice bordering on hysteria. "I'm at my wits' end."

Startled, Joe Kellerman said, "Who?"

"The Mexicans. They've filled every pot with stuff."

"What kind of stuff?"

"Plants, pieces of cactus, and beans. Odd-looking beans. Lieutenant Cranston says they're making Mexican soups and vegetable stews."

"Lieutenant Hall is an expert on these matters. What does he say?"

"Oh, the temerity. The sheer nerve . . ."

"What did the officer say, Mrs. Zimmermann?"

The woman swallowed hard. "He said . . ."

"Tell me."

"He stood in my kitchen and said, 'It smells good in

here.' And then, I'm so upset I can hardly get out the words . . ."

"Say them, Mrs. Zimmermann."

"And then he said, 'Smells a sight better than your salt pork.'"

Kellerman battled hard to suppress a smile as he said, "This is very serious, a very serious matter indeed. I'll look into it."

The woman drew herself up to her full height and said, "What does Lieutenant Hall say about the smell of my plum duff, I wonder?"

"Oh, the lieutenant loves your plum duff, Mrs. Zimmermann." Then, making it up as he spoke, "He calls its smell . . . the . . . the fragrance of the gods."

"Well, at least Mr. Hall shows a glimmer of common sense. My salt pork smells bad indeed. The gall of the man."

"I'll speak to him instanter, Mrs. Zimmermann."

"Quite harshly, I hope."

"Oh, depend on it, dear lady. I will," Joe Kellerman said.

"Damn, that's good," Captain Kellerman said.

"Isn't it, though, sir?" Lieutenant Hall said. "I knew you'd like to try it."

"What's in it?"

"The basic stock is a mesquite broth, but after that, I don't know."

Kellerman dipped into the earthenware bowl on his desk and sampled the soup again, a strand of some kind of green plant hanging off the rim of his spoon.

"Is there enough for the men?"

"Sadly, no. Officers only. And Sergeant Major Olinger, of course."

"What does he think about it?"

"He said with lots of salt and pepper, it's fair to middling. Lieutenant Cranston declined to sample the soup. He said it should be reserved for the hungry Mexicans."

"He'll make general one day, that young man. Mrs. Zimmermann says you told her . . . what was it? Oh yeah, that her salt pork stinks. She's very upset. And she says the Mexicans have taken over her kitchen."

"Only briefly. The women cook quite quickly."

Kellerman spooned soup into his mouth. "Mmm . . . this is really good. Why did you tell Mrs. Zimmermann that her salt pork stinks?"

"Well, sir, it does."

"I know, but you didn't have to tell her that. She's the only cook we've got."

"Sir, I'll apologize."

"Here's a tip: Tell her how fond you are of her plum duff."

"I am fond of it."

"Then telling her so won't be much of a stretch. Say you love its taste and smell. Tell her its aroma is the fragrance of the gods."

"Begging the captain's pardon, but isn't that a bit of an exaggeration?"

"Lieutenant Hall, when you're complimenting a woman there's no such thing as exaggeration."

"Yes, sir. Then fragrance of the gods it is. I'll talk to her right away. Have you finished your soup?"

"Yes. And my compliments to the chef."

CHAPTER 28

Tobias Zimmermann's hands, once soft, supple, and well-cared for, were now work-hardened and callused, the knuckles big and knobby, the mitts of a laboring man. Once a paid-up member of the Texas gambler/fraternity, he'd left all that behind him when he wed Mary. In his time, he'd killed seven white men, all but one in saloon and street fights, the other man a deputy sheriff by the name of Hugo Roberts he'd gunned on the roof of a Virginia City brothel in the middle of a blizzard. The passing years and lack of practice had slowed Zimmermann's draw, but his honed, gunman's instincts were sharp as ever, and as he stood outside the Fort Misery headquarters building smoking his evening cigar, he sensed there was something wrong with the night, something off-kilter, something ominous. Blood stained the moon, always a sinister sign, and he heard the bad luck keening of Maria, the raped Mexican girl, who seemed never to sleep. Out in the desert the lone, lost call of a coyote lanced the darkness, and crawling things squeaked and scurried and scuttled under the building.

But none of these explained Zimmermann's unease.

Suddenly he was grateful for the reassuring weight of the Colt on his hip.

* * *

Thirty yards from where Zimmermann stood on the headquarters-building porch, nineteen-year-old Private Mark Tweed, quickly exiled to Fort Misery for "utter stupidity and constant petty theft," shouldered his rifle and watched the rider emerge from the darkness. The man drew rein, swung out of the saddle, and walked his horse forward.

"Halt, who goes there?" Tweed said.

"A friend."

"Advance, friend, and be recognized."

The soldier studied the man as he walked closer. He was small, dressed in black except for a red bandana. He appeared to be unarmed.

"What do you want?" Tweed said.

"I'm here to see Captain Kellerman."

"What do you want to see him about?"

"I have news of don Santiago Lozado that he will want to hear."

The man looked Mexican but spoke English well, and Tweed lowered his rifle. "Tell me and I'll tell him," he said.

"No. I will speak only to Captain Kellerman, and he must come alone. The lives of every man in this fort are at stake. Lozado plans to attack very soon."

The man was unarmed, as far as Tweed could see, and his dim brain grappled with the implications of his visit. Borja helped him. "Hurry. If Lozado finds me here, he will kill me."

The soldier scratched his head and then made up his mind. "Wait here. I'll tell Sergeant Major Olinger that you're here."

"Captain Kellerman must come alone, with no minions. What I have to say is for his ears only. My life is at stake, and I trust no one."

Tweed nodded and hurried toward the headquarters building.

"He . . . he says he wants to talk to you alone, sir," Private Mark Tweed said. After being marched in by the terrifying Sergeant Major Olinger, he was visibly uneasy at being in his commanding officer's bedroom.

Captain Kellerman, sitting up in bed, a pillow at his back, laid down his book, *A Tale of the New Forest* by R. D. Blackmore, one of the most boring novels ever written, but well-thumbed, since it represented ten percent of Fort Misery's library.

"It could be a trap, Joe," Olinger said. "I don't like the sound of it."

Kellerman thought for a while, then, "Suppose the man is telling the truth? Maybe we can have a serious talk about Lozado's planned attack."

"Or maybe you'll get a knife in your back," Olinger said.

"The man wasn't armed," Tweed said.

"Are you sure about that?"

"No, Sergeant Major, sir."

"I'll be armed," Kellerman said. "All right, I go talk with him. If he's on the level, perhaps he can give me information I can use."

"Joe, I still don't like it," Olinger said.

"He can tell me all I need to know in five minutes. If I'm not back by then, you and Private Tweed come looking for me." Kellerman smiled. "On the double."

"Let me go," Olinger said.

"The man said he'd only speak to Captain Kellerman," Tweed said.

"And so he will."

Kellerman rose from the bed, dressed quickly, and buckled on his Colt.

"Five minutes mind, Saul," he said.

"We'll be ready, sir."

"Sergeant Major, you look as though you're planning to visit my funeral."

"As I said, I don't like it."

"I'm taking a risk, I know, but if this man blabs it may be our best chance yet to get rid of Lozado and his rabble."

"Five minutes, Joe, and then I'm coming after you."

"Good man," Kellerman said. He adjusted the lie of his gun belt. "Now I'll go hear some war talk."

When Tobias Zimmermann heard the headquarters door open, he stepped back and faded into shadow. Captain Kellerman walked outside and hurried into the darkness.

Zimmermann followed.

Apart from a feeling of unease and a gunman's inherent sense of danger, he had no real idea of what impelled him to go after the officer. There was nothing concrete on which to build his fears. But Zimmerman could be taking cards in a dangerous game. That much he did know.

The man was small, with Mexican features, eyes shadowed under his hat brim. Dressed like a vaquero rather than one of Lozado's Comancheros, he wore no gun belt, and his rifle was with his horse. On his left wrist he wore a wide silver bracelet.

"You are Captain Kellerman?" The man had a low, whispering voice.

"Si, I am Kellerman. You have something to tell me?"

The little man smiled. "I have much to tell you, señor. Es muy importante."

"I'm listening," Kellerman said.

Damn, he couldn't see the man's eyes. They were shuttered in shade and revealed nothing.

"No, maybe I won't tell you too much, eh? Just enough."

"Then tell it," Kellerman said.

"Ah, yes, that I will do."

"All right, get it over."

"Get it over! An excellent choice of words. Captain, it's all over for you, I think." Silverio Borja reached behind him and drew a Colt from his waistband.

Tobias Zimmermann had little time and the angles were all wrong. As the little man drew, Kellerman went for his unhandy butt-forward Colt and inadvertently stepped into Zimmermann's line of fire. The captain was a big man, the Mexican small, and all Zimmermann saw was a left shoulder and arm. He drew with blinding speed and fired. The Peacemaker's bullet crashed into the gunman's shoulder a split second before the hammer of Borja's revolver fell. But the impact of Zimmermann's round turned the gunman slightly, and he shot wider than he intended. His bullet burned across the right side of Kellerman's chest, drawing blood but doing no major harm.

Then mistakes were made.

Borja's whole attention was fixed on Kellerman, his intended victim, and he ignored Zimmermann, the greater danger. As the captain finally completed his awkward butt-forward draw from the leather, the little gunman, slowed by his grievous shoulder wound, thumbed back the hammer, and shoved out his gun hand, aiming for a sure kill. He was slow—way too slow. Zimmermann took a step to his right and had a clear shot. He fired, fired again, and Borja, hit in the chest and belly, dropped to his knees like a man in prayer. Kellerman finally got his work in and thumbed off a round that scored a hit, but by then the little gunman was already dead. He stayed in his kneeling position, his eyes wide, staring into eternity, until Kellerman kicked him over onto his back.

"Not one to hold a grudge, are you, Captain?" Tobias Zimmermann said, smiling in the direction of the dead man.

"Tobias, if it wasn't for you showing up, he would've killed me," Kellerman said.

"Yeah, I got that impression."

Lieutenant Atticus Cranston, Sergeant Major Olinger, and a dozen armed soldiers arrived.

"Another of Santiago Lozado's calling cards," Kellerman said.

Olinger looked at the body and said, "Who punched the holes in him?"

Kellerman nodded at Zimmermann and said, "He did. He saved my life."

Jim Bertrand, wearing only long johns, like the soldiers, said, "Good shooting."

Zimmermann gave him a frosty thank you and then said, "But Captain Kellerman got off a shot . . . eventually."

If Kellerman took offense, it didn't show.

"Joe, you're wounded," Olinger said, alarmed.

Kellerman looked down at his bloodstained blouse. "It's not serious. I got burned by a bullet."

"Let Doc Stanton take a look at that."

"Sure I will. He's a great healer."

"Well, he's better than no doctor at all."

"Now that's a natural fact, Sergeant Major." Then to Cranston, "Lieutenant, have that horse taken to the stables, and put the dead man's guns into the armory."

"Wait a minute," Zimmermann said. "I want that silver bracelet."

"To the victor belong the spoils," Kellerman said. "Take it."

"What about the body, sir?" Cranston said.

"Order a couple of troopers to drag it a mile or so into the desert. The buzzards will take it from there." He read the disapproving expression on Cranston's face and said, "He was an assassin. He's not fit to lie in hallowed ground."

"Sir, I didn't know Fort Benjamin Grierson had hallowed ground."

"It does, Lieutenant. Father Stas . . . Stasc . . ."

"Staszczyk," Cranston supplied.

"Well, anyway, the priest blessed the cemetery, and as far as I'm concerned that makes it hallowed ground."

Zimmermann finally wrenched the silver bracelet from the dead man's wrist and held it up for everyone to see. "Got it," he said. In the wan moonlight the bloodstained cuff looked like a fresh bone.

"Better see to that wound, Captain," Olinger said.

"Right away. Lieutenant Cranston, carry on."

The young office saluted. "Yes, sir."

Zimmermann studied the bracelet, holding it close to his eyes. "Looks like Pueblo work," he said.

It would be pleasant in this chronicle to report that after the rigors of the night the Fort Misery garrison slept soundly and woke early to their breakfast of coffee, fried salt pork, and hardtack. But fate had another less tasty dish to offer, and horror piled on horror.

CHAPTER 29

Mary Zimmermann was an early riser, up before first light to feed the stoves, boil the coffee, and fry the morning salt pork. Her work was made less onerous by Sara Lark, who insisted on helping with the chores. She was a hardworking whore, Mrs. Zimmermann always said, giving credit where credit was due. And she sang as she toiled, that morning giving voice to "Eileen Alannah." which Mrs. Zimmermann thought singularly pleasant . . .

Eileen Alanna, Eileen Asthore
The ocean's blue waters wash by the shore
Of that dear land of shamrock, where thou doth
  abide
Waiting the day when I'll call thee my bride

The song was sweet to Mrs. Zimmermann's ears as she opened the door of the kitchen to throw out a pan of peelings from the potatoes destined for the officer's dinner that evening. As was her habit she looked out across the desert, still cloaked in darkness and full of mystery. Closer, where the gallows, that terrible instrument of justice, stood, she thought she saw something white, like a sheet hung out to dry. That was strange.

"Miss Lark, come here a moment," she said. "I want you to look at something."

Sara Lark came and stood at her side, wiping her hands on her apron.

"Your eyes are younger than mine," Mrs. Zimmermann said. "What is that white thing over by the gallows? Is it a sheet?"

Sara peered into the gloom. "I don't know."

"Go take a closer look, my dear."

"Is it a ghost?"

"There is no ghost but the Holy Ghost, Miss Lark. Now do as you're told."

Sara walked slowly toward the gallows, her head turning constantly as she scanned the darkness around her.

Then a scream of surprise and fear. "Oh, my God!"

She turned on her heel and ran for the kitchen door.

"What is it, you silly girl?" Mrs. Zimmermann said, alarmed.

"It's Maria!"

"Maria is in bed."

"No. She's hanged herself. A rope. She got a rope . . ."

"She's in bed, I tell you."

"She's not. She's hanging from a rope around her neck on the gallows. She's dead . . . dead . . . dead . . . oh my God, oh my God . . ."

Crack!

Mrs. Zimmermann slapped Sara hard across the face. "Control yourself, girl. Go see if Maria's in bed."

"She's not in bed! She's hanging from a noose out here on the gallows!"

"What's going on here?"

Isaac Stanton rushed into the kitchen, still in his underwear.

"Maria hanged herself!" Sara shrieked.

"Where?"

"The gallows! The gallows!"

"Get me my coat, girl," Stanton said. Sara Lark hesitated, and he yelled, "Get it now!"

When Sara retuned with the coat, Stanton rushed outside, pulling on the threadbare garment as he ran. Mrs. Zimmermann and Sara Lark followed.

Stanton stood on the gallows and called out, "You women up here!" Then, to a sentry who'd arrived after hearing the commotion, "Quick, bring your officer!"

The soldier left at a run and Stanton said to the women. "She opened the trapdoor and jumped."

Sara said, "Is she . . ."

"Yes, she'd dead. Her neck is broken."

Mrs. Zimmermann buried her face in her apron and sobbed, and Sara looked stunned.

"It's a mercy," Stanton said. "She could've strangled to death."

"How . . . I mean how . . . did she . . . ?"

"She tied the rope to the crossbeam, made a loop, put the noose around her neck, and jumped. That took a great deal of determination. Maria very much wanted to kill herself."

Lieutenant Atticus Cranston, a half dozen troopers in tow, arrived, took the situation in at a glance, and said, "Corporal Scott, get her down from there." The soldier hesitated, his open-mouthed gaze fixed on the hanging female body with its contorted neck, and Cranston yelled, "Instanter!"

"Lieutenant . . . her face," Scott said. "She's looking at us."

"She's looking but not seeing, Corporal. Now cut her down."

Scott and a couple of soldiers freed the dead girl from the noose and laid her on the gallows platform. Stanton knelt beside her and put his ear to her chest. "No heartbeat," he said. "She's gone."

"Where the hell did she get the rope?" Captain Kellerman said.

"From the armory," Lieutenant Cranston said. "By mistake, the door was not locked."

"Mistake? Whose mistake?"

"Since I was the officer in command, the mistake was mine, sir."

Kellerman scowled. "The armory door has to be locked at all times, Lieutenant."

"I'm aware of that, sir."

"More aware of it now I imagine?"

"Indeed, sir."

"Where is the girl now?"

"In the infirmary. Mrs. Zimmermann and Miss Lark are very upset."

"We're all upset, Lieutenant."

"How could this happen without anyone seeing her?"

"There was no moon, sir. It was very dark."

"Sergeant Major Olinger, don't hover," Kellerman snapped. "You know where it is."

"Yes, sir."

Olinger got the bourbon bottle from the desk and said, "Lieutenant Cranston?"

"Lieutenant, do you want a drink?" Kellerman said.

"I could use one, sir," Cranston said.

"Good, and we'll drink to what?" the captain said. "The poor girl's death?"

"No, sir," Cranston said.

"Then what?"

"Just another day at Fort Misery," Cranston said.

Kellerman picked up his glass. "You're learning, Lieutenant. Well, here's to just another day at Fort Misery. An assassin shot dead, and a young girl hanged." He and the others drank, and the captain said, "Let's do that again. My ribs hurt like hell."

A suicide was surely damned, and Father Staszczyk could not in all conscience say the prayers for the dead. His place was taken by Mrs. Zimmermann, who read from the book, her words punctuated by much sobbing.

Sara Lark was at the graveside, as were Isaac Stanton and Lieutenant Hall.

After the prayers were read and four grim-faced soldiers stood by with shovels to cover Maria's shroud-covered body, Hall said, "She never spoke a polite word to me, but she was a nice lady and very pretty. May God give her rest."

"Amen," Mrs. Zimmermann said. Her eyes were red from crying.

CHAPTER 30

"Damn his eyes, he's not coming back," Santiago Lozado said. "This is more of Kellerman's doing."

"Silverio Borja wasn't much," Kyle Swan said.

"You've changed your tune since yesterday," Roscoe Wolfe said. "You said it was a sure-thing kill."

"I overestimated the man."

"Or underestimated Kellerman," Wolfe said.

"He's a devil that one," Lozado said. "I will enjoy watching him die."

"Any more volunteers, Swan?" Wolfe said.

"None. The men know Borja failed."

"They fear Kellerman?" Lozado said.

"Now we have only thirty Comancheros in camp," Swan said. "We've had desertions and casualties. Wolfe and his men make four more."

"Still enough to destroy Kellerman," Lozado said.

"If we attack soon," Swan said. "Before there are more desertions."

"Then I will plan for a day within the next week," Lozado said. "We will attack suddenly and crush Kellerman like the hammer of God."

"Why not tomorrow or the next day?" Roscoe Wolfe said.

"Perhaps. I await a sign that the time is right. Then we will strike."

Historians have long debated why Santiago Lozado hesitated. Was it out of fear? Did he dread the wrath of the legendary Kellerman, who'd become his bogeyman? Or had his scouts already told Lozado that twenty well-mounted and well-armed Apache warriors were headed for his camp, on their way to slaughter Mexicans in Sonora? Most Mexican experts, including the famous journalist and writer Gregorio Lopez, agree that Lozado was aware that the Apache were on their way and hoped to make them allies by dangling the carrot of the spoils to be had at Fort Misery. That is the most likely explanation.

The Apache, mostly Chiricahua with a few Mescalero, rode into camp at dusk, into a ring of armed and alert Co-mancheros. But their leader, a young and ambitious war chief named Alchesay, made it clear by his raised right hand that he came with no hostile intent.

Santiago Lozado had no Apache, but in good Spanish the chief said, "My name is Alchesay, and we come in peace to drink coffee and rest our horses."

"Then you are most welcome, my friend," Lozado said, smiling. "We have coffee aplenty and are proud to play host to the Apache. Come, come sit by the fire and we will talk." Then, in English to Kyle Swan. "Give our guests coffee and be friendly. Make them feel welcome."

"Don Santiago, we're sitting on a powder keg here," Swan said. The man looked worried.

Then, a surprise, Alchesay said in English, "The name Lozado is known to us from the Comanche. You are not our enemies. Our fight is with the Mexicans, the ones who slaughtered my family on the San Pedro."

"Then a hundred thousand welcomes, my dear friend," Lozado said.

The Apache dismounted. A man of medium height dressed like his warriors, he wore a white tunic and pants, knee-high moccasins, and a red headband. All had crossed bandoliers with ammunition for the rifles they carried, and a few had holstered revolvers. The Apache were short, wiry, and muscular, desert warriors with the endurance and courage of timber wolves. They were, on any given day, both notional and dangerous, and the concept of mercy was foreign to them.

Lozado knew he was holding a nest of rattlesnakes to his breast, but he needed fighting men, and the Apache were numbered among the best.

"You have a taste for coffee, dear friend," Lozado said as he watched Alchesay drain his cup.

The Apache nodded. "The only good thing the white man ever gave us."

Lozado smiled. "That and the Winchester rifle."

Alchesay slapped the brass receiver of the rifle on his lap. "And the Henry."

"Now where will you go, my friend?"

"Sonora. To the San Pedro."

"You still have people there?"

"No. My people are all gone, but there are others to kill. The wailing of Mexican widows will be pleasant to my ears."

Lozado refilled Alchesay's cup and said, "There is a mist coming down."

"The spirits of ancient warriors."

"I never thought of it like that."

"You don't think like the Apache."

"Then you must be patient with me as I try."

"Alchesay is not a patient man."

"Then I will say it straight out: I know something, my friend. Something that might interest you."

"What is this something?"

"You could be a big man in your village."

"What something? Your talk goes around and around, like the white men with the big bellies and long beards who come from Washington to convince us that what is good for them will be good for the Apache."

"But I will not lie to you, my trusted friend."

"Then speak, Lozado. What do you know? I am listening."

"There is a fort, an army fort, a few miles to the east of where we sit."

The Apache's knuckles whitened on his rifle. "And what about this fort?"

"It is weak. And there are many horses and guns to be had there."

"How many soldiers at this fort?"

"Few. No more than a half troop of cavalry."

"And it is your wish that I attack this fort?"

"Yes. I want you to join with my men, Alchesay, and together we'll destroy that place."

"Guns and horses for me. And what for you?"

"There are Mexican slaves there that were stolen from me. I want them back."

"And that is all?"

"Everything else is yours, my dear friend."

Alchesay fell silent, thinking.

The mist had grown thicker, the fires like cinders glowing behind a white lace curtain. The camp, usually full of loud talk, was strangely quiet, Comancheros and Apache sitting silent and watchful in mutual distrust.

Lozado, his brutal face sweaty, added an additional lure to his hook. "There are women at the fort for your amusement, my friend."

"Perhaps," Alchesay said. "But often white men shoot their women when the Apache are victorious. Still, what you say interests me, Lozado."

"I'm happy that it does. You will not regret it, my friend."

"But an Apache does not charge into a thicket until he knows the size of the bear. Half a troop? How many men?"

"No more than thirty."

"I will send a scout to find out if that is the case. Now I have something else to say."

"Then say it, friend. I'll listen to your every word."

Alchesay's face hardened. "You keep filthy company."

Lozado was taken aback. "Great chief, who has offended you?"

"When I entered your camp, I saw the man Roscoe Wolfe. He is an evil dog who trades in Apache scalps. He offended me."

"My friend, we need every man who can fight. But after the fort is destroyed, I will give Wolfe to you as a gift."

"His death will not be pleasant and will take many days."

"And a man named Kellerman will die beside him."

"Who is this man?"

"He is the commander of the fort. His death will also be slow and painful." Lozado smiled. "Are we not a pair, you and I? Such a short time together and already fast friends."

"No, Lozado, we are not friends, and if we meet again, it will be as enemies."

"Then my heart is wounded, but when the fort is taken, we will go our separate ways and never meet again."

Alchesay rose to his feet. "So be it. At dawn I will send

out a scout. We will decide on our plan of attack after he returns."

"Stay away from Wolfe until then," Lozado said. "Unlike me, he is not to be trusted by the Apache."

"Very well, for now. The scalp-taker's time will come."

As Lozado watched the Apache walk into the mist, his brain was working. But not too hard, because it was all so simple. Let the Apache take the brunt of the attack and when the victory was won and their numbers had dwindled, his own men would cut them down. He wasn't about to allow a bunch of savages to ride away with dozens of horses and an armory of guns. There wasn't a hope in hell.

CHAPTER 31

At first light the Navajo began his daily swing around Fort Misery, first heading west in the direction of Lozado's camp. The desert was still cool under a lightening sky, and the distant sand dunes yet held onto their shadows. And as always in the Yuma, the day was coming in clean, the air clear and sweet.

Ahiga turned north and after a quarter mile spotted horse tracks headed toward the fort. One rider, at a fast walk, keeping down the dust. He followed the tracks for ten minutes and then dismounted and tested a pile of horse dung. It was still damp. The rider was close.

The Navajo swung into the saddle again and trailed east, his black eyes constantly scanning the terrain ahead: a vast land of sand with patches of scrub and cactus and profound silences.

After fifteen minutes, Ahiga drew rein. Ahead of him a paint pony, reins trailing, nosed among a clump of yellow cups, its rider nowhere in sight.

The Navajo sensed danger, his Henry up and ready. Too late. Suddenly the sand shifted, erupting into an Apache warrior who sprang at Ahiga with incredible speed, like an attacking cougar. The Apache hit the Navajo hard on his left side and drove him from the saddle. His rifle cartwheeling away from him, Ahiga landed on his back, and an instant later the Apache was on top of him, a knife raised in his right hand. Ahiga grabbed the man's wiry wrist and the two wrestled on the ground and rolled under the Navajo's horse. Alarmed, the animal reared and kicked, and Ahiga and the Apache separated, both men instantly on their feet. His face twisted in hate, the Apache came at Ahiga, his knife held low for a belly thrust. The Navajo carried a bowie in his belt, but he did not consider it a fighting weapon. He knew the Apache would close fast because the man didn't want a knife fight either; he wanted to kill quickly without danger to himself. Ahiga realized that if he got into a tussle with blades he'd get cut badly and end up covered in his own blood, a death sentence at Fort Misery, where even slightly wounded men died from gangrene. As the Apache closed, he had to defang him in a hurry. He drew his knife and threw it at his attacker. The blade missed by inches, but it was enough to make the Apache quickly move to his right. Ahiga now had a couple of seconds left to live, but he could draw his Colt and fire in half that time. The Apache was close enough that he could smell the man's rank sweat when his bullet hit, a killing shot to the belly. Shocked, the Apache staggered back and then fell, agony stretching his mouth into a grimace. The concept of mercy was unknown to the Apache, and the Navajo weren't real familiar with it either. Ahiga aimed and put a bullet between the warrior's eyes, killing the man and ending the fight.

The Navajo stood for a couple of minutes, breathing hard, listening, but hearing nothing. Sound doesn't travel well in a desert, and the chances were that the shot was not heard in Lozado's camp. He was certain that's where the Apache had come from. The chances were he was on his way to scout the fort when he spotted Ahiga on his back

trail and laid his ambush. The question now was . . . how
many Apache? It was something Captain Kellerman would
want to know.

The Navajo picked up his rifle and mounted his horse.

Now he must become *ma'ii*, the coyote trickster, and spy
on the enemy's camp.

There was much coming and going among the Apache
and the Comancheros, and from his hiding place behind
the sparse cover of a creosote bush. the Navajo had trouble
counting them. Finally, he settled for nineteen—when it
came to Apache, a force to be reckoned with. He watched
big-bellied Lozado talk with a young warrior who could be
their war chief. The Mexican smiled, gestured with his
hands, and seemed mighty pleased about something.
Probably that the Apache were joining his band and would
ride with him in the attack on the fort. Careful that the sun
did not block his view, Ahiga laid the sights on Lozado.
How easy it would be to kill him. Of course, it would be at
the cost of his own life, and no matter the reason, Lozado
was not worth dying for. "How close you came to death,
carrion dog," the Navajo whispered. "But there will be
another time."

Ahiga tensed. An Apache strolled to the edge of the
camp and stared into the desert . . . a predator sensing prey.
The man, squat, bowlegged, wearing a blue headband,
cradled a Winchester and stood still, only his head moving
as he scanned the terrain. The Navajo made of himself a
gopher and slowly burrowed into the sand. Long moments
passed, the Apache intent, suspicious, took a few steps forward and then stopped. His black eyes again probed the
sands, then lingered on the creosote bush. Ahiga froze and
his breathing slowed.

Damn the Apache. Can he hear my heartbeat?

A shout from the camp.

The Apache turned and saw Alchesay beckon to him. A last curious look at the creosote bush and then the man jogged away. And the Navajo breathed again.

CHAPTER 32

"Nineteen Apache in camp, Captain," the Navajo said. "There were twenty, but I had to kill one of them."

"Good man," Joe Kellerman said.

"I think he was on his way to scout the fort."

"Then Lozado is planning another attack very soon. The Apache are bad news, Ahiga."

The Navajo allowed himself a fleeting smile. "One Apache is bad news, Captain. Twenty Apache are . . ."

"Something else entirely."

"A calamity," Ahiga said.

"Yes, that's the word, all right. A calamity for Fort Misery. What think you, Lieutenant Hall?"

Hall looked around Kellerman's office as though trying to seek inspiration. Finally he said, "It does not bode well, Captain."

"Tell me something I don't know," Kellerman said. He refilled his glass with whiskey and then said, "Lieutenant Cranston, your thoughts?"

"Lozado will attack, and soon," Atticus Cranston said. "My feeling is that the Apache were either on their way to or coming from Sonora and bumped into Lozado. In either case, they will not want to linger, and that means an attack is imminent."

"Imminent. Do you hear that, Lieutenant Hall?" Kellerman said. "Imminent."

Hall dipped snuff, put a pinch in each nostril, and said, "Sir, there's only one way to fight Apache, and that's to stay drunk." He raised his glass. "And I'm making a start on that."

"Ahiga, do you think an attack is imminent?" Kellerman said.

"The Apache have made Santiago Lozado strong," the Navajo said. "Yes, he will strike soon."

"Then how do we defeat him?"

Ahiga shook his head. "Captain Kellerman, you won't defeat him. Not with what you have."

"Lieutenant Hall, speak words of comfort to me," Kellerman said.

"I wish I could, sir, but I can't find any. Unless . . ."

"Unless what?"

"Unless we pull up stakes and skedaddle."

"The army considers desertion in the face of the enemy a mortal sin, Lieutenant. If we survived, we'd all be hanged."

"Very likely, sir," Hall said. "The army is not very understanding about transgressions like that. In fact, it can be quite testy at times."

Kellerman said, "Lieutenant Cranston, you're fresh from West Point with a head full of military know-how. Lieutenant Hall suggests we all skedaddle forthwith. What do you suggest?"

"Sir, I suggest we fight them only from the headquarters building, and we should take steps to reinforce weak areas like windows and doors."

"What about the Mexicans?" Kellerman said.

"We bring them here."

"It's going to be crowded," Hall said.

"That can't be helped sir," Cranston said.

Kellerman sighed. "Then tell Sergeant Major Olinger to work on that right away, and get Mr. Zimmermann involved. He's handy with a saw and a hammer. Use some of the Mexican men as laborers. Let's turn Fort Misery into a fortress."

Cranston saluted. "Right away, sir."

"Good man. Now finish your whiskey as though you were a man with a big beard like Lieutenant Hall."

"Not much chance of that," Hall said. "It took me years of care and sacrifice to grow this beauty."

"And it's why all the ladies love you," Kellerman said.

"Indeed, sir. The beard enhances my manly features."

"A woman told you that, no doubt."

"Yes, sir. Well, she was a highly intelligent and beautiful whore in Baltimore by the name of Celestine Beaufort, and who am I to doubt her veracity?"

"Even a fallen woman will tell the truth sometimes," Cranston said, placing his drained glass on the captain's desk.

"Well said, my dear Atticus," Hall said. He smoothed his beard. "I'm happy to learn that the Point taught you common sense enough to recognize magnificence when you see it."

Kellerman turned his attention to the Navajo. "Ahiga, you did well this morning. Go tell Mrs. Zimmermann to give you whiskey and water. Lieutenant Cranston, see to our defenses."

After the others left, Kellerman poured Hall another drink and said, "Now, Lieutenant, tell me about the beautiful whore named Celestine Beaufort and how you met her."

"Certainly sir. Well, let me see. Ah yes . . . it was a dark and stormy night . . ."

CHAPTER 33

Second Lieutenant Atticus Cranston sat in a threadbare tapestry tub chair in his room in the officer's quarters. By the dim light of an oil lamp, he'd finally gotten down to reading a translation of *The Idiot* by Fyodor Dostoevsky, a graduation gift from his sister. So far, its Russian doom and gloom bored him, and when someone knocked on his door, he was glad of the distraction.

Expecting a soldier, he was surprised to come face-to-face with Sara Lark. The woman, who had obviously been at pains to improve her appearance, smiled and said, "I wondered if you could use a little company, Lieutenant."

"Well, I was reading," Cranston said.

Sara nodded. "Then I'll leave you alone."

"No, please come in," Cranston said. "Sorry, that was quite rude of me."

"I'm only a whore," Sara said. "Not very good company, I suppose."

"Please, come in."

Sara stepped inside, and Cranston directed her to the tub chair. But she said, "I'll sit here, on the corner of the bed."

She looked around his cramped quarters, and Cranston

said, "Second lieutenants don't rate bigger rooms, I'm afraid."

"It's cozy."

"It's hot, you mean."

"Yes, that too. What were you reading?"

Cranston picked up the book from the floor and let her see the cover.

"*The Idiot*. A strange name for a book."

"It's a strange book."

"Why are you here in Fort Misery, Lieutenant?"

"Call me Atticus. It was a mistake. My posting was supposed to be Fort Concho, but a clerical error landed me here."

"Can you leave?"

"Not now."

"Yes, I guess it's too late. I hear Santiago Lozado has Apache with him."

"So I believe."

"He raped Maria, you know."

"I know."

"She couldn't live with that. She wanted to be a virgin on her wedding night."

"It was a tragedy, and it was heartbreaking."

Sara's smile came and went. "I'm a whore, so he couldn't take my maidenhood. He beat me instead. He's a beast. A wild animal."

"One day soon I hope to end his career," Cranston said. He took a cigar from the table beside him and said, "May I crave your indulgence, ma'am?"

"Please do. I didn't know you smoked."

"Lieutenant Hall got me interested in the finer attributes of tobacco."

"Lieutenant Hall is a bad influence."

"Yes, he is. But doctors do say that smoking is very

good for the heart and lungs. My father is almost seventy and swears by his pipe."

Sara was silent for a few moments then said, "Will we all be alive for much longer?"

"You mean Lozado?"

"He will attack now he has Apache with him."

"I'm confident that we have the forces available to defeat him."

"No you're not, Atticus. I can see it in those beautiful brown eyes of yours."

"It will be a hard-won battle, but in the end the US Cavalry will prevail. We always do."

"Atticus, this is a starvation post manned by the dregs of the army. You're not the US cavalry, you're . . . something else."

"Yes, we're a unit the army doesn't care to define. But ragtag and bobtail as we may be, any man will fight for his life. Sara, are you afraid?

"Yes, afraid that I'll still be alive when Santiago Lozado and his Apache take this fort. You'll experience death, Atticus. But what I'll face is worse than death. Hey, do you remember Sara Lark? She was raped to death down Yuma way by a bunch of Comancheros and Apache.' I don't want that to be my epitaph."

"It won't because it's not going to happen," Cranston said from behind a haze of cigar smoke.

"You can guarantee that, soldier boy?"

"Yes, I can guarantee it. They'll get to you over my dead body."

"And that's exactly what Lozado will do. He'll step over you like you're a dead dog on the doorstep." Sara shook her head and smiled. "Atticus, I came to offer you some cheerful company and all I've done is depress you."

"I'm not depressed," Cranston said. "Because none of

that is going to happen. We'll send Lozado and his Apache running with their tails between their legs."

"You're right, it won't happen. Mrs. Zimmermann has a revolver. She says she'll shoot us both if the Apache get into this building."

"Miss Lark, did you come here to argue with me?"

"No. That thought didn't enter my head."

"Would you care for a drink?"

"What do you have?"

"Bourbon. More of Lieutenant Hall's contraband."

"How does he get it here?"

"His parents send whiskey, snuff, and cigars from Yuma with the supplies. How they manage that is Lieutenant Hall's secret. I assume that somewhere along the line money changes hands."

Cranston took a bottle and a couple of glasses from the bottom drawer of his dresser. "Old Crow," he said, holding up the bottle. "I hope it's to your taste."

"You bet," Sara said.

After they settled with the whiskey, the woman said, "Do you want to bed me, Atticus?"

"Um . . ."

"Cat got your tongue?"

"Yes, you surprised me."

"Well, do you? There's no charge."

Cranston recovered quite well. "No, and it's not because I don't find the offer tempting. It's that I'd be taking advantage of a vulnerable woman, and my honor as an officer does not allow such conduct."

"I take it that means, no?"

"Yes. I mean no. I mean . . ."

"I understand."

"You're an attractive woman, Miss Lark. I'm aware of that."

"That's nice to hear."

"If I was not an army officer then perhaps . . ."

"You'd bed me."

"Ah, yes . . . perhaps . . ."

"Do you know that you're blushing, Lieutenant?"

"It's the sun on my fair skin."

"You're blushing, Lieutenant." Sara smiled and drank from her glass. "Good whiskey."

Relieved, Cranston said, "Yes, isn't it?"

"Listen. It's thunder."

Cranston stepped to the door, walked a few yards outside and studied the ballooning sky. When he came back inside he said, "A thunderstorm without rain. The clouds are silvered by lightning."

"The storm will pass overhead in a few minutes and then travel to the edge of the world and rain on a jungle," Sara said.

"How do you know that?" Cranston said.

"It's what desert thunderstorms do."

Sara rose from the bed. "Thank you for the drink, Lieutenant."

"Atticus."

"And thank you for refusing my offer of mattress time, Atticus."

"Why?"

"Because it convinced me that there are still decent men in this world. And you were right: I am vulnerable and very afraid."

Cranston opened the door. "Don't worry, everything will be just fine," he said.

Sara Lark nodded. "I'll fall sleep tonight hearing those words in my mind."

Thunder roared, and the night air was as dry as bone.

CHAPTER 34

The first probing attack came at dawn, surprising and killing three of the pickets. Privates Dawson, McCann, and McDermott were shot down at their posts as a dozen Apache and an equal number of Mescaleros swept among the outbuildings and then dismounted and took up firing positions.

Glass shattered and timber splintered as rifle rounds rattled through the partly barricaded headquarters building, testing the progress made on the defenses by Lieutenant James Hall and Tobias Zimmermann.

Captain Joe Kellerman, wiping off his mouth with a white napkin after an interrupted breakfast, saw that his remaining troopers were shooting back and seemed steady enough as Hall strode back and forth along the firing line, dodging bullets, encouraging the men.

"Choose your targets and don't just spray shots, you damned villains," he yelled. "Prove to me that you shouldn't all be dangling from the end of a rope."

"The hell with you, Hall!" a voice from somewhere shouted above the rifle din.

"Who said that?" The lieutenant paced up and down the line. "By God, you scoundrel, reveal yourself. I'll have your guts for garters."

Kellerman took aim, fired his revolver, and then said, "Lieutenant Hall! How many?"

"I didn't count them, sir. But there's enough."

"What about the infirmary?"

"Lieutenant Cranston, the Navajo, and three men, one of them Sergeant Major Olinger. Oh, and Zimmermann. And I armed Jim Bertrand and the cowboy. They can both shoot."

A hailstorm of bullets slammed into the building and another soldier was struck, a head shot that killed him instantly. But the garrison's return fire remained steady, and now and then a man yelled when he scored a hit. A pall of gray gun smoke hung in the hallway, which ran the length of a structure that was poorly designed and badly constructed, built on the cheap to accommodate soldiers who didn't matter.

Both Kellerman and Hall fired steadily, and the captain dropped a Comanchero who came too close. "Did you hear the thunder last night, Lieutenant?" Kellerman said, shouting over the crashing rifles. He fired again and again, thumbing his Colt quickly and expertly.

"No rain, unfortunately," Hall said. "The Mexicans drink a lot of water."

"We could use rain," Kellerman said, as he fed fresh rounds into his revolver. And then, smiling, he added "This is hot work."

"Indeed, it is, sir." Suddenly Hall made a yelping sound and fell.

Kellerman took a knee beside him. "James, are you hit?" Then he saw blood glisten on the front of the lieutenant's blouse.

"Yes, sir. I don't know how badly."

"Bad enough." Kellerman looked around and then said to the young trooper next to him, "Get help and carry Lieutenant Hall to the infirmary."

Hall said, "No, sir. This could be an all-out attack. Please, don't weaken the firing line on my account." His head moved and he looked to his left and pointed. "Drag me into that room. I have some Mexicans stashed in there and they'll take care of me."

"You're badly wounded, Lieutenant."

"A little snuff and I'll survive. Now please, sir, do as I ask."

Kellerman nodded to the soldier. "Carry the lieutenant into the room."

After that was done, Kellerman went back to encouraging his men, patting a shoulder here and there. As brass shell casings littered the floor, he organized the supply of extra ammunition.

So far Lozado's men had made no sign of pressing closer, preferring to shoot at long range from cover. Kellerman doubted this was the main attack, but his small command couldn't survive too many more of these probing actions that constantly eroded his numbers.

Then a cry from one of his men farther down the firing line. "Cap'n, they're heading for the infirmary!"

Six of the Apache and three Comancheros had remounted, charging directly for the infirmary, firing their rifles as they came. As bullets shattered through the two large front windows and thudded into the adobe, Cranston and the others inside returned fire, with little effect. The Apache on their swift, agile ponies galloped up and down outside, fleeting targets that were hard to hit. A soldier was shot and dropped, and another's forehead was severely cut by a shard of flying glass, sudden blood blinding him, putting him out of the fight. Now the Apache were drawing rein at the windows, their glittering black eyes seeking targets inside. Bill Worley left the cover of an upturned mattress, brushed past Cranston, and ran to a window that framed the mounted Comanchero outside, and fired. The man at the window vanished, replaced by an Apache with streaks of blue paint on his cheeks who saw Worley and instantly cut loose from the shoulder. The .44-40 bullet slammed into the young man's chest and sent him staggering backward, his legs bucking, his Colt falling from his hand.

Jim Bertrand watched Worley die and through a mist of smoke yelled, "Zimmermann, the hell with this!" He picked up the dead man's revolver and beckoned. "Come with me!"

As more bullets swept the room, Zimmermann saw the writing on the wall. Like Bertrand, he yanked the Colt from the holster of the wounded soldier and rushed to the gambler's side.

"Are you ready?" Bertrand said.

"Let's get it done," Zimmermann said.

Bertrand raised his booted foot and with tremendous force kicked the door which splintered it off its fragile hinges and fell outward.

"Now!" Bertrand yelled, his face savage.

The two men clambered across the door, hit sand, and took wide-legged stances, shocking their attackers. Bertrand and Zimmermann commenced firing, expertly working the Colts that had made them named shootists. In ten seconds of hell-firing havoc they downed five men and broke the back of the entire attack. The remainder of Lozado's Comancheros saw what happened and shocked, ceased firing.

Joe Kellerman took advantage of the situation and counterattacked, leading his troopers out of the headquarters building, yelling at the run, firing from the hip. Badly burned, nearly half their number dead or wounded, Lozado's men mounted and got the hell out of there, pursued by bullets that split the air around them.

* * *

After the wounded were dispatched, eleven of Lozado's Comancheros and six Apache were heaped on a pile in the parade ground. But Captain Kellerman's butcher's bill was also high. He'd lost four troopers and the civilian Bill Worley was killed; he also had two wounded men, and Lieutenant Hall was also wounded. His command was reduced to twenty-three men fit for duty and no hope of reinforcements. Santiago Lozado had suffered a defeat, but he was still strong enough to launch a major assault. It was a grim prospect.

CHAPTER 35

"You did well enough, Lieutenant Cranston," Captain Joe Kellerman said. "You held the infirmary as you were ordered to do."

"The civilians saved us, sir," Atticus Cranston said. He shook his head as though trying to get rid of a thought he didn't want to put into words.

"I've already thanked both those gentlemen." Kellerman said. "Zimmermann claims he was only saving his wife, and Bertrand shrugged it off. He said he only did what seemed right at the time and that he may not do it again tomorrow."

Cranston said, "I've never seen men shoot like those two. It was as though their pistols were Gatling guns."

"Texas draw fighters are a breed apart. They say that John Wesley Hardin fellow is hell on wheels with a Colt's gun in each hand."

"So I've heard, sir."

Someone knocked on the office door and Kellerman said, "Enter."

Isaac Stanton, looking exhausted, the front of his white shirt bloodstained, stepped inside and said, "Corporal Scott just died. I couldn't save him."

"Doctor, you'd nothing to save him with," Cranston said.

"Perhaps I could've done better, but there were two bullets in him, both deep. He was only a boy."

"He was a soldier," Kellerman said. "For God's sake take a seat, man. You look dead on your feet. Have a drink."

"I don't normally imbibe, but I'll take you up on your kind offer," Stanton said. The doctor sipped his whiskey, shuddered, then said, "Captain, will they be back?"

"Yes, they'll be back, and soon."

"Will we prevail?"

"The odds are against us, but anything can happen in a war. I learned that at Gettysburg."

"A terrible slaughter."

"When a man's seen thousands of dead lying on the field it hardens him. It hardened me. It hardened Sergeant Major Olinger and Lieutenant Hall and in the end, it will harden you, Lieutenant Cranston."

"Sir, this wasn't Gettysburg."

"I know. But your hardening process has begun. Death and destruction, the hammer and the anvil. Soon you'll have so much tempered iron in you, you'll find it difficult to bend."

"Captain, today has affected you more than you pretend," Stanton said.

Kellerman poured himself more bourbon, splashed some into Cranston's glass and said, "Maybe you're right, Doc. Hell, everybody did well today. My soldiers may be the refuse of the army, but they gave me fighting men, each and every one of them, the living and the dead."

Cranston finished his whiskey and said, "Captain, may I have your permission to visit Lieutenant Hall?"

"You don't need my permission. What does the doctor think?"

"A visit will do him good," Stanton said. A pause, then, "Lieutenant Hall is a difficult patient."

Kellerman smiled. "So would I be if I'd just had a bullet dug out of my shoulder."

"The ball deflected off something solid before it hit the officer," Stanton said. "It wasn't a deep wound, and the extraction was quite straightforward, not difficult at all, though Lieutenant Hall does not share that opinion."

"Go hold his hand, Lieutenant Cranston. Tell him I'll visit him shortly."

But before the young officer could leave, Sergeant Major Olinger rapped on the door and stepped inside. "Begging the captain's pardon, but I have to report that Private Michael McDermott is missing."

"I thought he was dead along with the other pickets."

"That was the assumption, sir, but he may have only been wounded."

"You mean Lozado's men took him?"

"That would be my guess, sir."

"Did you search the post? He may have gotten hit and crawled somewhere."

"I conducted a search, sir, but he's nowhere to be found."

"McDermott . . . McDermott . . ."

"Sir, he's a tall, thin fellow, a transfer from Fort Duncan." Olinger read the question in the captain's eyes and said, "Cowardice in the face of the enemy, though at his court martial McDermott claimed his horse got stung by a bullet and bolted."

"Away from the enemy?" Kellerman said.

"Yes, sir. Comanches apparently."

Kellerman shrugged. "It could be true."

"Yes, sir. Or it could be false. Take your pick."

"Did McDermott soldier here at Fort Misery?"

"I had no complaints with his conduct. He did his duty."

"And now he's gone. With his horse?"

"Yes, sir."

"Maybe he ran away?"

"There is always that possibility, sir."

"Sergeant Major, the men are exhausted. I'm not sending out patrols to look for him. Let's hope he shows up."

Lieutenant Cranston said, "There's always the possibility that Lozado's men took Private McDermott."

"Why would they do that?" Kellerman said. "To hold him hostage?"

"It's a possibility, sir."

"Sergeant Major, what do you think?"

"Not as a hostage, but more likely revenge," Olinger said. "They lost a lot of men and might want to take out their anger on one of the soldiers responsible."

"Let's hope that's not the case," Kellerman said. "Or just about now Private McDermott could be very much wishing that he wasn't still alive."

Cranston slammed to attention. "Sir, I volunteer to attempt a rescue of Private McDermott."

"You're going nowhere, Lieutenant," Kellerman said. "We don't even know if he was taken. Hell, his horse could've been burned by a bullet, and he skedaddled. Either that or he's hiding out somewhere."

"I'll make another sweep of the fort," Olinger said. "As you say, Captain, he may be lying low."

"Do that, Sergeant Major. If he's alive, find him. If he's not, then Lozado has him and he's already a dead man."

"The man's a damn butcher, I tell you," Lieutenant James Hall said.

"Sir, he did get the bullet out," Lieutenant Cranston said.

"And left me with a haggled shoulder that hurts like hell." Hall swooned back on his pillow, covered his eyes with an arm and groaned, "I'm done for. I'll never survive this."

"How do you feel, sir?" Cranston said.

"How do I feel? Doctor's orders: no snuff, no whiskey, and no cigars. How do you think I feel? And the Virgin Mary and Sara Lark are his partners in crime." He shook his head and whispered, "Atticus, they're hard, conspiring women."

Cranston smiled. "You'll be up and about in no time, sir."

"And what time is no time?"

"Two or three days."

"Two or three days! Damn their eyes, they're trying to kill me. The wounded enlisted men were bandaged up and released. But I'm still being held prisoner."

"Your wound was the most serious, sir."

"Damn right it was, but that's no excuse to cage me here like a mad dog." Hall struggled upright, the fat bandage on his right shoulder hampering him. "Right, Lieutenant Cranston, clear the way there. I'm out of here. It's time to put wheels on the whorehouse."

Cranston didn't budge, and Hall yelled, "Step away, mister! That's an order!"

The lieutenant moved aside and Hall, wearing one of Zimmermann's old nightshirts, pushed away the sheet, sat up, and swung two hairy legs over the side of the cot. "Just hold on to me when I stand, Atticus. I might be a little dizzy. There's a good fellow."

Hall stood and immediately his knees buckled under him, and only a timely catch by Cranston saved the lieutenant from a nasty fall.

"Back into bed with you, sir," he said. He half lifted, half manhandled Hall into the cot and after he had the officer settled, his head on the pillow, bare feet sticking out from under the sheet, he said, "Sir, you've lost a lot of blood, and you're still very weak."

"Weak as a newborn kittlin'," Hall said. He sighed. "It's all up for me."

"You'll be back on your feet soon, sir," Cranston said.

"Perhaps . . . perhaps not. Do me one last favor, Lieutenant Cranston. No, delete that . . . I should've said obey one last order ere death overtakes me."

"Of course, sir."

"Bring me my snuffbox."

"Where is it?"

"I don't know. Ask Medusa, and if she says no, pry it from her cold fingers."

"Sir, you mean Mrs. Zimmermann?"

"I mean Medusa. Don't fail me, Lieutenant."

"The doctor said he wasn't to have snuff," Mrs. Zimmermann said. "It's bad for his wound."

"Not having it is bad for his mind," Lieutenant Cranston said. "I'll take full responsibility."

"Well, on your head be it, Lieutenant. The snuffbox is here with his beard comb, hair comb, eyebrow tweezers, nail file, toothpick, and a medal."

"What kind of medal, Mrs. Zimmermann?"

"British, I suppose. It's got Queen Vic's head on it."

"Probably a memento of a British army observer during the war. But all I need is the snuffbox."

"Then it's your responsibility, Lieutenant. Imbibing snuff won't replace the blood he's lost."

"Indeed not, Mrs. Zimmermann, but I believe it will make Lieutenant Hall a little more cheerful."

"Then let's hope so. He's the most difficult patient and cantankerous man I've ever nursed."

CHAPTER 36

"Listen to the white soldier, my dear Alchesay," Santiago Lozado said. "What beautiful music he makes."

"He screams like a woman in childbirth, but his torments have just begun. He will suffer for six days. My mourning warriors and the restless spirits of my six dead demand it."

Lozado smiled. "Then be careful you don't kill him too fast."

"That will not happen. The Apache know how to make an enemy die many times before the spirit leaves him. We were taught much by our fathers and grandfathers, but it was our mothers and grandmothers who taught us the ways of torture, how to inflict pain but make the screaming last over long days and nights."

"You will get your revenge soon, Alchesay." Lozado said. He poured coffee into the Apache's cup. "We will attack with all our force and smash the fort and its garrison into a million pieces."

"And this time we use fire, Lozado. Those buildings are as dry as tinder and will burn with the pony soldiers inside. We will watch them die in flames, Lozado, and laugh and slap our thighs at their agonies."

Santiago Lozado clapped his hands. "How well you

speak, Alchesay, my friend. One day you will be a great man among the Chiricahua and Mescalero, and all will honor you, as I do."

"You are a man of vision, Lozado. All great men possess such a gift."

Lozado bowed his head, acknowledging the praise, as Roscoe Wolfe and Kyle Swan stepped to Lozado's fire. Irritation showed on Alchesay's face. He looked up at Wolfe and then spat in the man's direction. "You were not at the fight, woman-killer," he said.

Wolfe's eyes hardened and his gun hand dropped to his holster. Lozado immediately sought to defuse the situation. "Welcome, my friends," he said. "Sit and have coffee with us."

But the Apache wasn't buying it.

He threw his coffee onto the fire, extinguishing flame, sending up smoke, then rose to his feet. "I will not drink coffee with this man. He is a filthy thing."

Angry now, his hand close to his gun, Wolfe said, "Don't push it, Indian."

A scream. Then a prolonged screech of mortal torment. Then another and another, fragmenting the morning into splinters of horror.

"Damn it, must we torture the soldier?" Swan said. "He's a white man for God's sake. Just shoot him."

"Friend Kyle, it's Kellerman's debt, but the soldier must pay the price," Lozado said. "That is the way of things."

"Get used to the racket, Swan," Wolfe said. "It will be a long time until the poor sidewinder dies."

"Just shut your ears, my friends," Lozado said. "Sit, drink coffee, and we will talk of many things."

"Then, I go," Alchesay said. "Pah, am I a child in the dark afraid of noise? My young warriors test the man's courage. If he passes the test, they will honor him."

"Hell, Indian, he don't sound too brave to me," Swan said.

"Only time will tell. Now I go."

"Roscoe, my friend, I know how you feel about the Apache," Santiago Lozado said. "You want to kill him and so do I, but we need his warriors for the attack on the fort."

Kyle Swan said, "I spoke to Louis Gonzalez."

"Yes, my friend Louis saw what happened at the adobe that joins the main building."

"He told me the high casualties were caused by a pair of pistoleros, not Kellerman's soldiers," Swan said. "Where the hell did they come from?"

"That I don't know," Lozado said. "What do you think, Roscoe?"

"I wasn't there, so I don't know either."

"During our attack, they must be eliminated," Lozado said. "Roscoe, that will be a task for you and Kyle."

"Sure, if we can single them out," Wolfe said. He shook his head. "God, listen to that man scream. I've never heard anything like that. He screams and screams . . ."

Swan smiled. "You must've heard it when you scalped a Mexican."

"The greasers were always dead or dying when they lost their hair," Wolfe said. He returned Swan's smile. "Call it a professional courtesy."

"As I said, close your ears to the noise," Lozado said.

"Patrón, a lot of your men are standing over there where the soldier is staked," Swan said.

"Right now, the Apache are sticking cactus spines into the man's body and then setting them alight," Lozado said. "No doubt my Comancheros who lost comrades are amused by that. But back to a more serious matter: When we attack,

I will depend on both of you to seek out and destroy the shootists. Do nothing else until they're dead. Do you understand me?"

"When will the attack be, patrón?" Swan said.

"In a couple of days. I want to give the Apache enough time to get worked up about it. Torturing the soldier will whet their appetites."

Wolfe looked up to where buzzards were quartering the sky, elegant as waltzing dancers in a blue ballroom. The man smiled. "Too early, my friends. Come back in a couple of days."

Lozado grinned. "Yes, return soon when there will be plenty of rotten meat at the fort for our feathered friends."

CHAPTER 37

Big Buck Bowman was twenty miles out of Yuma in desert country when he figured he was on a wild-goose chase. Three days before, an old desert rat of a prospector had walked into the city marshal's office to report that he'd come across a prison wagon and three dead men southeast of town.

"Buck, it sounds like the wagon that never arrived at the penitentiary," Marshal Tim Haddon said. "Three violent prisoners missing."

"I reckon so," United States Marshal Bowman said.

"Are you interested?"

"Some."

Bowman was forty-six years old that fall, a large man, well over six feet, wide in the shoulders, big in the chest, all supported by a round, well-nourished belly. He had heavy, florid features, broken-veined cheeks, and sported a huge mustache, the same shade of brown as his thick mop of hair. Rumored to have ridden with Quantrill's raiders during the war, Bowman later became a deputy sheriff and then a Texas Ranger. He'd been a US Marshal for four years. As a lawman he'd been in several gunfights and had been wounded twice. He liked bonded whiskey, good vittles, women, and hound dog puppies, in that order.

"Buck, you just got through telling me how bored you were, so why not go take a look-see," Haddon said. "By now the birds have flown, but they couldn't have gone far in the desert."

"Bring 'em in, you mean?"

"It would be a feather in your cap."

"I already have so many feathers in my cap I look like an Injun," Bowman said. He rose heavily to his feet. "But I'm willing to dance it around the floor. Get me out of Yuma for a spell."

"And away from Bobbie Jean Ransom for a spell."

Bowman shook his head. "She's a clinging woman, that's for damn sure."

"I'll tell her you had to leave town in a hurry." Hadden laid a pint of whiskey on his desk. "Drink before you saddle up, Buck?"

"No, I got to go, cover us much ground as I can before sundown."

"Then take the bottle with you. A man gets thirsty in the desert."

Bowman shoved the bottle into the pocket of his coat and touched his hat. "Much obliged, Tim."

"Two canteens, Buck. It's as dry as mummy dust down south of us."

"Tim, in my time I rode all over West Texas. I know how to survive in a desert."

"Then good luck. Bring them back alive if you can."

"I will . . . if I can," Buck Bowman said.

Now, as his eyes scanned a wasteland of sand that stretched to the horizon, Bowman thought about heading back to Yuma and the pink comforts of Bobbie Jean

Ransom's whorehouse. But his lawman's instinct nagged at him mercilessly . . . just a little bit farther . . .

He kneed his horse into motion, searching for anything that suggested tracks in the sand. Even if there had been no weather events, it was still an almost impossible task, since dry sand fills a track as soon as the foot leaves it. As he was taught in the Rangers, the solution was to identify the overall shape of a human impression and the trail pattern. It wasn't easy, and Bowman drew rein twice and took a swallow of whiskey each time to cut the dust and help him solve the puzzle.

He rode on. The sun was high and hot, and the marshal had a pounding headache, the blazing light spiking into his eyes. It was a common complaint of his, and he dug into an inside pocket of his coat and came up with a pair of round, dark eyeglasses that helped cut the glare. His vision improved, at least slightly, and it was then he spotted the abandoned prison wagon in the distance.

Bowman approached the wagon at a walk, a foul stench betraying the presence of the dead mule in the traces. There were no human bodies to be seen, and judging by its dim tracks, the wagon had traveled a fair piece before the mule succumbed to the bullet wound in its neck.

The tracks pointed in the direction where he'd likely find the escaped convicts, either dead or alive, and Bowman came to a decision: He'd come this far, so he'd continue his search, splitting headache be damned. It was his duty, he told himself. *Buck, old son, that's why you wear the badge.*

At sundown Buck Bowman made a cold camp. He unsaddled his horse, let the big American stud drink from his cupped hand, and then fed the animal oats from his saddlebag. He built a cigarette, since a doctor told him that smoking was a sovereign remedy for migraines, and afterward ate

some beef jerky. Yawning, he spread his blanket on the soft
sand and fell asleep in the moonglow, his eyes closing on
the star-flung sky. Come first light he saddled up and resumed his quest.

United States Marshal Buck Bowman had been riding
for two hours when he saw the tracks of three men heading
east, away from the disturbed area of sand and sprawled and
animal- and buzzard-torn bodies that marked the prisoners'
escape from the prison wagon.

Bowman was twice lucky that day. His search took him
well south of Santiago Lozado's camp, and he ran into
Captain Joe Kellerman's Navajo scout.

How it came up: Ahiga's sharp eyes spotted the rider
when he was still a ways off—a white man, but not one of
Lozado's rabble. He rode a good horse and by the stiff-
backed way he sat his saddle, as arrogant as a Union general
on parade, he was either an out-of-uniform army officer or
a lawman. Either way, his like was an unusual sight out here
in the wilderness. The Navajo drew rein, placed his Henry
across his horse's withers, and waited. He knew he was
taking a risk. Here in the territory, if a white man saw what
even looked like an Apache, he'd shoot first and identify his
target later. Well, let the man come. He wouldn't be here if
he didn't have a story to tell.

Apache!

Buck Bowman drew rein and slid his Winchester from
the scabbard under his knee. He swallowed hard and looked
around him. If you saw one Apache, more could be hiding
behind every patch of brush.

What the hell . . . the Indian had raised his right hand in
a peace gesture.

Bowman's headache had eased, but now it was returning.

He mimicked the Apache and raised his hand. He kneed his horse forward, and when he was within talking distance, drew rein. His Winchester lay across his saddle, but it was handy.

"Will you give me the road?" he yelled.

The Indian nodded.

"Name's Buck Bowman, I'm a United States Marshal out of Yuma."

"Ahiga. Army scout."

"Is the army close?"

"Fort Benjamin Grierson." The Navajo pointed northeast. "That way."

"I didn't know there was an army post this far south."

"Now you do."

"I'm looking for three escaped convicts. They came this way."

"Talk to commander of fort, Captain Joe Kellerman."

"Lead the way . . . what's your name again?"

"No matter. You will follow me."

CHAPTER 38

"One of them, Bill Worley, is dead, Marshal," Captain Joe Kellerman said. "He was a young drover who died bravely defending this fort."

"And the other two?"

"Isaac Stanton. He's now our camp doctor, and Jim Bertrand helped break up an Apache and Comanchero attack on the infirmary. I need his gun."

Buck Bowman took a paper from the inside of his coat. "Says here that your camp doctor shot his cheating wife and her lover and showed no remorse. Worley I can cross off my list, but I'll need to see proof of his death."

"He's in our cemetery. Dig him up."

"This is not a time for levity, Captain."

"No, it's not."

"Bertrand shot and killed a man in Tombstone."

"A card sharp who'd been notified," Kellerman said.

"Who killed the prison wagon guards? Bertrand?"

"A man named Jake Kelly. . . ." Kellerman said.

"Twenty years for rape and murder," Bowman said.

"Well, he won't serve his sentence—he's dead. He shot one of the guards, but before the man died, he returned the compliment and plugged Kelly."

And the other guard?" Bowman asked.

"Died of apoplexy. It seems the excitement was too much for his ticker."

"Who says?" Bowman asked.

"Bertrand and the doctor. Either one of them could've shot the other guard," Kellerman said. "Or Bill Worley. But I believe their story."

"When you're in my line of work you believe nothing without hard evidence."

"Then go back to that rotten corpse in the desert and see if it has a bullet in it," Kellerman said.

"Captain, you're not taking this seriously."

"On the contrary, Marshal, I'm taking it very seriously. Right now, I can't spare either the doctor or Bertrand, and I'll tell you why. You better have a drink for this."

"I could use one," Bowman said. He took out the makings and showed them to Kellerman. "Do you mind? Smoking is the only thing that stops my headaches."

"Go right ahead, I smoke myself."

Bowman built and then lit a cigarette and sampled his whiskey. His lips formed an O of surprise that he sucked air through and gasped, "Now that is gen-u-ine busthead. . . ."

"Army whiskey. After a year or two you get used to it," Kellerman said.

"God help you." The marshal sat back in his chair and said, "Now tell me why you're threatening to obstruct the duties of an officer of the law."

Buck Bowman was incredulous. "You mean this man . . ."

"Santiago Lozado."

"Is planning to attack the fort again?"

"Yes, he is."

"When?"

"It could be anytime . . . today, tomorrow, the day after," Captain Joe Kellerman said.

"And he and his Comancheros are running with Apache?"

"Yes, they are. Mescalero and Chiricahua mostly."

"A bad bunch, Captain."

Kellerman nodded. "They're a handful."

"And where are the Mexicans he took as slaves?"

"Right here in the headquarters building. I'm surprised you didn't see them."

"I was too busy keeping my eyes on that Navajo of yours. I don't trust him."

"Ahiga doesn't say much, but he's loyal."

Bowman shook his head. "I'm stunned. I never expected something like this in the territory."

Kellerman smiled. "Welcome to Fort Misery, Marshal."

"And your men are all . . . malefactors?"

"The scum of the army, but the rascals know how to fight."

Bowman sipped his whiskey, shuddered, and said, "It does grow on you, doesn't it?"

"Over time, like moss on a rock."

His head bent over the makings, Bowman said, "My duty is clear, Captain."

"So long as you know that I can't part with a doctor and a pistolero. I need every man I've got."

"You're outnumbered two or three to one."

"The odds are not good."

"Not in your favor, for sure, and that's why I see my duty clear."

"And that is . . . ?"

"I will speak to this Lozado fellow and tell him to cease and desist. I'll also warn him that charges will be leveled against him and his men and, if found guilty, death by hanging is not out of the question."

"And if he refuses?"

"I'll warn him that I can have a hundred marshals here in a few weeks, all well-armed and determined men."

Kellerman smiled. "Marshal, those would be the last words you'd ever say. If Lozado just shoots you, think yourself lucky. He has other ways to kill a man, all of them unpleasant."

"Yes, I'm sure the Comanche and Apache have taught him well."

"But you still want to talk with him?"

"Hell no! Captain, I'm not a particularly clever man, but I'm no fool. I know exactly what would happen if I rode into the camp of a man who's made several attempts to destroy this fort and is planning another."

"Then . . . I'm confused . . . what about the hundred tough marshals?"

"Could never happen. Right now, I don't think there are a hundred tough United States marshals and deputy marshals west of the Mississippi."

"So explain all that jawing about doing your duty?"

Bowman smiled. "If I'm ever called to account for the time I spent at Fort Benjamin Grierson, I'll call on you to witness the fact that I planned to defuse the situation but was overtaken by events—namely Lozado's surprise attack."

"You plan to stay, Marshal?"

"I won't ride away with two of your men at a time when every available man is needed." Bowman saw the confusion on Kellerman's face and said, "Captain, how could I ever again hold my head high in the company of men if I deserted you in your greatest time of need? Besides, it's my duty to safeguard my prisoners."

"Rationalize however you want, Marshal, but you're welcome to stay. As you said, I need every man I can get. We're stretched mighty thin."

Kellerman called for his orderly and ordered the man to

have Lieutenant Cranston bring the doctor and Jim Bertrand to his office.

When the two men were ushered into the office by Atticus Cranston, Kellerman waved a hand, "Gentlemen, this here is United States Marshal Buck Bowman. He's here to take you to the Yuma penitentiary when this present unpleasantness at Fort Misery is over."

"As of now, you boys can consider yourself under arrest," Bowman said. "Sorry, but that's how it is."

"You're taking me nowhere," Bertrand said. Just four matter-of-fact words uttered without emotion.

Bowman smiled, unfazed. "We'll see, won't we? How about you, Doc? Will you resist arrest?"

The little man looked to Kellerman for guidance. "No," the captain said. "Doctor Stanton is a desperate character, but he'll go quietly." Then to Cranston. "You can remove the prisoners, Lieutenant. And then find Marshal Bowman a cot in the infirmary. We have no guest quarters, Marshal, but I'm sure Lieutenant Cranston can make you comfortable. You may dine in the officers' mess."

Bowman rose to his feet, a big man whose presence filled the room. "I'm obliged to you, Captain," he said. "Lieutenant, lead the way. . . ."

CHAPTER 39

Kyle Swan was a hard case. Some might call him an evil man, but he'd reached a limit. It was the screams of the soldier taking forever to die that forced him to cross the line.

He pulled his gun and walked to where knelt four Apache working on the man with fire and knives. He kneed a warrior aside and looked down at what had once been Private Michael McDermott, the second son of a first son of the Emerald Isle. There was little left that was human about McDermott. He'd been burned, cut all over his body, gelded, and one eye had been gouged out, leaving the other one to see what was happening to him. Yet he refused to die, his screams and the arching agonies of his body two horrifying constants.

Swan had seen enough. He thumbed back the hammer of his Colt and shot McDermott in the head, instantly releasing the man's soul from his savaged body.

The Apache were incensed at being robbed of their sport. They surrounded Swan, yelling, their faces contorted in anger. Knives were drawn and pushing started, and Swan backed away, his gun coming up fast.

"Kyle, no!"

Santiago Lozado and Alchesay hurried to the scene.

"Kyle, put the gun away. Alchesay, call off your young men," Lozado said. "I'll have no fighting among us."

"My young men weren't done with the soldier," the Apache said. "He had still much to suffer, much to learn."

"You're a damned filthy savage," Swan said.

"And you are not?"

"Enough!" Lozado said. "Kyle, go somewhere and calm yourself. Later come to my fire and we will laugh and talk of women and drink whiskey."

The Apache had circled the three men and they were angry, muttering to one another. Lozado feared for his already fragile alliance.

"Whiskey for everybody!" he yelled. And to Alchesay, "Translate this to your warriors, my friend. Tell them I have reached a decision, and the day after tomorrow we attack the army fort and take their horses, guns, and women."

The Apache passed this news on to his men, and their boiling anger seemed to reduce to a simmer. The whiskey would also help, but Lozado knew he was taking a chance. Drunken Apache nursing a grudge could be a real danger. Well, they'd nurse their hangovers tomorrow and be ready for the attack the day after. Lozado felt a surge of relief. The full-scale attack on the fort was long overdue and the Kellerman murderer would soon be in his hands. Then an amusing thought . . . Kyle Swan complained that the soldier screamed too loud . . . just wait until he heard Kellerman's squawks. That made him laugh, and he was still laughing when he walked to his fire as whiskey was broken out for his men.

"An outright assault, dear friend Alchesay," Santiago Lozado said. "First fire, and then we attack in force and destroy the Kellerman rabble."

Around the two leaders the Apache were getting drunk

quickly, and their whoops and war cries created a bedlam of the gray quiet of the dying day.

"But we do not harm the Mexican slaves, is that not so?" Alchesay said.

"Yes, if possible, I want them spared. At least for a while."

"That could be difficult in the heat of battle."

"My friend, it's no matter. I want their scalps. Whether the livestock is alive or dead makes little difference."

"And you will sell them in Sonora as Apache scalps?"

"Yes, and then use the money to start up businesses here in the United States. My friend, on the frontier there is always a ready market for whiskey and whores."

"You will be a rich man, don Santiago, and when I return to my rancheria with guns, horses, and women I will be a big man among my people."

"Then the destruction of the soldier fort will serve us both well, my friend," Lozado said. He raised his tin cup. "Let us drink on that."

Rifles fired in the air as the Apache and Comancheros made merry, and there was much boasting and backslapping about how many soldiers they would kill the day after next.

Lozado smiled. "Hah, the young men are eager for the fight. The soldier fort will be laid waste, and the buzzards will feast with bloody beaks and talons."

"It warms my heart to see you smile, don Santiago," Alchesay said. "We will do great things, you and I."

"And the reason for that is simple, my friend," Lozado said. "It is because we are great men."

CHAPTER 40

"Lieutenant Cranston, this is not an order, but a favor I ask," Lieutenant James Hall said.

"Then ask it, sir," Atticus Cranston said.

"You see that chair over there?"

"Yes, sir, I see it."

"I plan to sit in it, and you will detail two strong soldiers to carry me to the officers' mess."

"When?"

"This evening."

"Sir, as I told you earlier, you've lost a lot of blood, and you're still very weak."

"I know I'm weak. That's why I need two strong men to carry me. Damn, even my voice is weak. I don't think I could sing a note of 'Rose of Killarney' if it was to save my life."

"And there's another reason to stay in bed. It will rest your vocal cords."

"I don't plan to sing tonight anyway. Now, about that favor . . . wait, here is Miss Lark right on time. Do you have the items I asked for?"

Sara Lark nodded. "Pomade, curling tongs, comb, brush, scissors, it's all here."

"The hair first—make sure the tongs are good and hot to keep the ringlets tight—and then the beard. Be extra careful with the beard, it's a masterpiece. Oh, and I think my eyebrows are a bit unruly. They need a trim."

Sara answered Cranston's unasked question. "Lieutenant Hall intends to eat dinner in the officers' mess."

"No, he doesn't," Cranston said.

"Yes, he does," Hall said.

"I'm afraid his mind is made up," Sara said.

"As is mine," Cranston said.

"Then it's come to this," Hall said. Blood stained the bandage on his shoulder, and his eyes were bright and feverish. "Very well then, Lieutenant Cranston, this is a direct order: Detail two strong soldiers to carry me to the mess this evening. There, it's done and done."

"Do you want your hair cut a little, Lieutenant?" Sara said.

"Perhaps just a little, but not too much, dear lady. Oh, and find my dress blouse, the one with the shoulder straps. I intend to look my best this evening."

"Why . . . sir?" Cranston said. "You can eat salt beef and beans in bed."

"The only thing I want to do in bed is sleep . . . well, and other things, but the presence of a lady prohibits me from mentioning them."

"I know all the things that go on in bed, Lieutenant," Sara said. "I'm a whore, not a lady, remember?"

"You were a whore, but no longer. I have seen to that. Now, are those tongs getting hot? Be very careful how you use them, Miss Lark. Tight ringlets is what we must strive for, dear lady. Tight ringlets."

"Sir, are you still determined to attend the mess?" Cranston said.

"Oh, for heaven's sake, mister, you haven't realized that already?"

"Then I feel I must report this matter to Captain Kellerman."

"Then report away. Joe won't give a damn. Miss Lark, while we're doing the hair we'll talk about my beard. Extra care must be taken with brushing and trimming."

"Sir, you're not attending an officer's ball." Cranston said, irritated.

"I know, more's the pity. Carry out your order, Lieutenant Cranston. Two strong men, mind. Miss Lark, the tongs must be warm enough by now and you are quite free to proceed."

Lieutenant Hall is a strong-minded man," Captain Joe Kellerman said.

"But sir, he's lost a lot of blood," Lieutenant Cranston said.

"He's lost a lot of blood before, Lieutenant. At First Bull Run and the siege of Vicksburg, if memory serves me right. Carry out your order; he'll be all right. Talk to Sergeant Major Olinger. He'll detail two stalwart chair carriers."

Kellerman rose from his chair and stepped to the window overlooking the weed-choked parade ground. After a few moments of contemplation he said, "On July first, 1863, my cavalry regiment engaged with some Confederate infantry headed into the town of Gettysburg to seize shoes and other supplies. At first the action was written off as a minor skirmish, but I had the strangest feeling that General Lee's entire army was right behind those barefooted Rebs. As we now know, I was right."

"And you have that feeling again, sir?" Cranston said.

"Yes. Just as strong."

"How do you explain it, sir?"

"I don't know how to explain it, but I do know by the pricking of my thumbs that something wicked this way comes."

"Not Macbeth, sir."

"No, someone just as bad, or worse . . . Santiago Lozado."

"He's on his way?"

"Soon. Very soon."

"Should I turn out the troop, sir?"

"No. The attack won't come today, but possibly tomorrow or the next day. We'll be ready."

Cranston took time to frame his next question. "What are our chances, sir?" he said.

"We'll fight with what we have, Lieutenant," Kellerman said.

"And we'll win, sir."

"Yes, Lieutenant, we'll win. Now see about Lieutenant Hall's chair carriers. How is he?"

"Sara Lark is doing his hair and beard, sir."

"He's a fine-looking officer is Lieutenant Hall. The ladies love him."

"Then maybe I need a beard, sir," Cranston said.

"Maybe we all need a beard. We should get Lieutenant Hall to teach us how to cultivate one."

That evening two sturdy troopers carried Lieutenant Hall to the officers' mess and deposited him, not too gently, at the table.

"Your turnout puts us all to shame, Lieutenant," Kellerman said. "When you were carried in on the sedan chair, I took you for a general."

"Thank you, sir, but Miss Lark was a little too enthusiastic with the scissors. I swear she took a quarter inch off my beard."

"Your whiskers are as splendid as ever. What think you, Lieutenant Cranston?"

"As you say sir, splendid. I envy them."

Marshal Buck Bowman nodded and said, "A magnificent display, sir. Your beard does you credit."

"Thank you," Hall said. "Coming from a civilian, that's a fine compliment. It does take a deal of dedication you know. Beards like this one don't grow on trees."

"Only on chins, I imagine," Bowman said.

"Well said, sir. It's a pleasure to meet someone who appreciates the hirsute arts."

"And how do you feel, Lieutenant?" Kellerman said.

"I'm starting to feel better, sir. My shoulder hurts, of course."

"Bullets always do," Kellerman said. "Ah, here is Mrs. Zimmermann with dinner."

The lady in question glared at Hall and said, "You should be in bed."

Hall smiled and extended his snuffbox. "Care for a pinch, Mrs. Zimmermann?"

The woman made a face. "Disgusting stuff." She laid out the plates and said, "Salt beef and beans and some green stuff the Mexicans gathered this morning. Miss Lark swears it's very nourishing, but how would she know?"

"I apologize for our short commons, Marshal Bowman," Kellerman said. "Food is always a problem at this fort."

"It looks just fine to me, Captain. But I think I'll have to pass on the green stuff."

"Mrs. Zimmermann will save the day with her plum duff," Hall said. "Is that not so, dear lady?" He was very pale, dark shadows under his eyes, but thanks to Sara Lark he was well-groomed as ever. If he hadn't been a disgraced reject exiled to Fort Misery, he would've been a credit to the cavalry.

"You don't deserve any, Lieutenant Hall, but yes, there's duff for dinner," Mrs. Zimmermann said. "I hope you don't choke on it."

"I won't, dear lady, depend on it."

After a dire warning from Mrs. Zimmermann that both flour and raisins were now in short supply, and the last of the plum duff was eaten and much appreciated, Kellerman's orderly informed him that the Navajo scout requested a meeting.

"Send him in," the captain said. "We all should hear what he has to say."

The Navajo stepped into the mess, cradling his Henry as always.

"Ahiga, you have a report to make?" Kellerman said.

"Santiago Lozado's men are very drunk. The Apache dance for war and have painted their horses." He spread his fingers. "Many red hands vow vengeance against a hated enemy."

"Ahiga, will they fight tomorrow?" Kellerman said.

"Not tomorrow. The Apache sleep off big drunk tomorrow. But the next day they will attack."

"Are you certain?" Lieutenant Cranston said.

"As certain as tomorrow's sunrise will wake me from sleep."

"Then it's coming—the final showdown," Kellerman said.

"It seems like it," Sergeant Major Saul Olinger said. "Lozado has the Apache all riled up."

"They don't need much riling," Bowman said.

"Then we have tomorrow to get ready," Kellerman said. "As we did before, we'll defend the headquarters building and the infirmary."

Lieutenant Hall said, "Sir, as before, I'll help defend headquarters."

"You're too weakened for that, Lieutenant," Kellerman said. "You'll remain in the infirmary and lie low."

Hall was outraged. "Sir, my shoulder rules out the use of a rifle, but I'll get those two rogues who so unceremoniously dumped me here in the mess to carry me to the firing line. By God, sir, with a brace of pistols I can wreak great execution among the enemy."

"Lieutenant Cranston, what do you think?"

"Me, sir?"

"You, sir."

"Ah . . . Lieutenant Hall is a determined man."

"Damn right," Hall said.

A smile played around Kellerman's lips. "Can he handle a brace of pistols in the fight?"

"He's lost a lot of blood."

"Answer the captain's question, young man," Hall said.

"Then, yes, sir. He can shoot pistols from a sitting position."

Hall thumped the table with his fist. "And that's the right answer," he yelled. Then, a withering look at Cranston and in a softer voice, "Lucky for you."

"Then it's settled, Lieutenant Hall, you stand . . . or rather sit . . . in the firing line."

"You're damn right it's settled," Hall whispered.

"What did you just say?" Kellerman said.

"Nothing, sir. Just talking to myself. Anyone for a pinch of snuff?"

CHAPTER 41

After the others left, Lieutenant Hall carried out amid much grinning from his chair bearers, Captain Kellerman lingered in the mess to have a nightcap and a word with Sergeant Major Olinger.

"What are our chances, Saul?" he said, pouring the drinks.

"That last time Lozado attacked us with less than half his force and it was a close-run thing," Olinger said. He shook his head. "Joe, it doesn't look good."

"What have we got, less than twenty-five effectives?"

"Around that and add Zimmermann and Jim Bertrand. Oh, and Buck Bowman the marshal. Does he have a gun rep?"

"Not that I know of, but I'd wager he's been in a gunfight or two in his time."

"Maybe having three pistoleros will tip the scales."

"If it was a saloon fight, maybe. But this will be a battle."

"Bertrand did all right the last time."

"I know. He took the Apache by surprise when he stepped outside and turned the battle into a close-range shootout. But Lozado will be expecting that kind of play, and Bertrand may not be so lucky next time."

"He does need it close. He's not a sharpshooter."

"Yes, and so does Zimmermann need it close, and probably Bowman. They're what the Texans now call draw fighters. They won't stand in a skirmish line and shoot like soldiers. How many men did John Wesley Hardin kill with a rifle?"

"None that I ever heard of."

"Probably Bertrand and Zimmermann never shot a man at distance either."

Saul Olinger smiled. "Suppose by some miracle we win, Joe?"

"If we do, it will be a Pyrrhic victory. How many of us will be left standing?"

"What does pir . . . pir . . . what you said, mean?"

"It's a battle that costs the victor such devastating casualties that it's the equivalent of a defeat. In other words, it means Fort Misery will cease to exist."

"That will please the army."

"Yeah, in one fell swoop it gets rid of a major embarrassment and all of its deadwood." Kellerman sipped his whiskey, smiled, and said, "Sorry, for so much doom and gloom, Saul. Old age is making me cranky, I guess."

"Joe, we hit Lozado's riffraff hard and fast and put the run on them. That way we keep our casualties low."

"And how are we going to do that?"

"I don't know."

"Me neither."

"We'll think of something. Young Lieutenant Cranston is fresh out of West Point. His head is probably crammed full of strategies and other notions."

"All right, Saul, I'll consult with Second Lieutenant

Cranston and ask him how I should conduct the upcoming battle."

"It doesn't sound like such a good idea the way you say it, Joe."

"Drink your whiskey, Saul. I'll come up with something."

"If the fight is set for the day after tomorrow you don't have much time."

"I'll sleep on it."

"I know you, Joe. You won't sleep until it's all over."

"Then I'll lie awake and study on it."

Olinger rose from his chair and stared out the window into the darkness.

"See anything interesting, Saul?" Kellerman said.

"Yes . . . Sara Lark is walking back and forth. She's wearing one of Mrs. Zimmermann's shawls."

"She's worried. I doubt she'll sleep either."

"She's afraid of Lozado. He abused her."

"I know. I feel sorry for Sara Lark. She's an innocent caught up in a war that's none of her making."

"Oh, Mrs. Zimmermann just came out and they're talking. Now Mary is taking her inside. She has her arm around Sara's shoulders." He shook his head. "This waiting is hard on women." He paused. "What am I talking about? It's hard on everybody, including our men."

"What do the soldiers think?"

"About what?"

"The big fight brewing."

"They've gone as silent as shadows. All the talk and backtalk and joshing that goes on in this fort has just about stopped. The soldiers know what's coming. They're very aware what they're facing."

"Fort Misery is misery piled on misery, Saul. You ever think that?"

"Joe, it's a punishment posting. We're here to suffer, repent of our many sins, and die like heroes."

"Not you, Saul. You volunteered."

"Because I owe you, Joe. You know that."

"That debt was paid many times over in another, more honorable war."

"My debt to you will never be paid, Joe." The sergeant major shook his head. "Damn, this waiting is getting to me, eating me up inside."

"It's doing that to all of us, Saul. You're not alone."

"Busy day tomorrow," Olinger said, turning from the window. "I better hit the hay."

Kellerman nodded. "Sleep well, old friend."

The sergeant major snapped to attention and saluted. "And you, sir."

CHAPTER 42

Captain Joe Kellerman took a sponge bath with a cupful of precious water, shaved a three-day growth of beard, and trimmed his splendid mustache. He smiled at himself in the dresser mirror and whispered, "Joe, God forbid you'd leave an unkempt corpse for others to bury." He recalled that Spartan warriors bathed, combed their long black hair, and oiled their bodies before battle for the same reason. He shook his head. "Vanity. All is vanity." And fear, of course. There was always some measure of that.

Sleep would not come.

After an hour Kellerman rose and shuffled on bare feet to his window at the rear of the headquarters building. He had a splendid view of the latrines, splashed in moonlight's white paint, and beyond them the dead of the desert's night darkness, where there was no sound and nothing moved, not even one grain of sand brushing against another.

He sat in a tub chair and thought about again courting fickle sleep. *Sleep that soothes away all our worries. Sleep that puts each day to rest. Sleep that relieves the weary laborer and heals hurt minds. Sleep the main course in life's feast, and the most nourishing.*

Shakespeare said that, and the old bard knew what the hell he was talking about.

Kellerman rose, blinking in the darkness, and stepped to his cot, where he pummeled his pillow into submission and then threw himself onto the unyielding army-issue mattress.

A hesitant, timid, knock-knock on the door.

"Enter, dread phantom," Kellerman said. Then, "Oh, it's only you. I expected a specter of some kind. This better be important, Lieutenant Cranston. You woke me up from a sound sleep."

"Sir, we have so little time, I thought you'd like to know this right away," Cranston said. He stood in the doorway fully dressed and wearing his sidearm.

"You're a man of mystery, Lieutenant. Enlighten me, you midnight oracle."

Cranston turned his head, beckoned, and said, "Juan, come."

A small, dark-skinned Mexican at his side, the lieutenant entered the room and said, "Sir, this is Jorge Valdez. He speaks English after a fashion and has something to say to you."

"Then speak, Mr. Valdez, I'm listening."

"Excellency, I wish to join in big fight against Santiago Lozado," the little man said.

"Can you shoot?"

"Yes. Me and twenty others."

Ramirez saw the doubt in the officer's face and said, "All of us can shoot a rifle, as we have since boyhood. And we can ride."

Now Kellerman was interested. "Who taught you to shoot?"

"Mi padre and mi abuelo."

"Sir, that means his father and grandfather," Cranston said.

Kellerman was silent for a few moments, thinking, and then said, "Mr. Ramirez, if you can ride and shoot, why were you and your people taken so easily by Lozado?"

The Mexican looked down at his rope sandals and said, "I am ashamed to speak of it."

"Don't be ashamed, just tell me why."

"We welcomed Lozado and his Comancheros with open arms because he gave us mescal and tobacco and called us his queridos amigos."

"Sir, that means dear friends," Cranston said.

"Thank you, Lieutenant. I caught his drift. And then what happened?"

"Then one morning without warning Lozado and his men turned on us like lobos. Before we could defend ourselves, they dragged us out of our homes and roped us together. They shot all the old men and women with gray hair and ignored the children. Thank the blessed Virgin, the young women were already out gathering food and firewood and only a few were captured. Maria, the girl who hanged herself, was one of them."

"And now you want to take revenge on Lozado and his men for the girl's death?"

"Maria and fifty-six others, my mother and father among them."

"I'm sorry about your parents, Jorge. But I must warn you that the battle against Lozado could be lost. You and all your men might die."

"Better to die than live as a slave, Capitán."

"Then I'll take a chance on you, Jorge."

"We will fight. We will not run. The time for running is over."

Kellerman nodded and said, "Lieutenant, you'll be in

command of the Mexicans. Tomorrow morning supply them with rifles and ammunition from the armory and see how they shoot. If they can't shoot, teach them. I'll also want them mounted. If they can't ride, teach them. And if they can't understand you, teach them English. I want them ready by the day after tomorrow. Is that clear?"

"Perfectly clear, sir," Cranston said. The only acceptable military answer to an impossible order.

"The Mexicans won't be in the firing line, Lieutenant," Kellerman said. "I want them mounted and ready to charge when I give the word. In the meantime, wake up Lieutenant Hall and ask him to teach to you how to manage a cavalry action."

"Yes, sir. Right away, sir."

Kellerman smiled. "Atticus, I'll boil down all that I said to you . . . do the best with what you have."

"Do you think the Mexicans can tip the balance, sir?"

"God, I hope so. I believe they're brave enough, but still an unknown quantity. I guess we'll find out soon enough."

"I'll have them ready, sir."

"Don't fail me, Lieutenant Cranston."

"A dip of snuff, Lieutenant Cranston?" Lieutenant James Hall said, extending his box. "Good for whatever ails you."

"No thank you, sir. I'd rather not."

A single candle burned on the table beside Hall's cot and reduced the officers' features to shifting patterns of light and shade. His eyes gleaming in the semidarkness, Hall said, "Repeat all I've told you, Lieutenant."

"I won't make mounted dragoons out of Mexican peasants in a single day."

"Correct. Continue."

"Go to the saber."

"Splendid. You're learning."

"The Mexicans know nothing about the .45-70 Sharps carbine, but they understand the blade."

"What blade?"

"The machete."

"Good, good . . . and?"

"The slashing motions of the machete are the same as the saber."

"The instinctive slashing motions, Lieutenant. Instinctive is very important."

"Yes, sir. And . . ."

"Tomorrow I spend the day training the Mexicans. . . ."

"To charge in line abreast."

"And to use the saber."

"Good, Lieutenant Cranston, very good. You learn quickly. It's no wonder you won all those prizes at West Point."

"Sir, I didn't win any prizes at West Point."

"Well, you should have. Care for a dip?"

"No thank you, sir. Ah, but I must warn you that Captain Kellerman wants rifles."

"Sometimes Joe doesn't know what he wants. We must teach him, you and me. What do you prefer, Lieutenant, sabers or rifles?"

"The saber, of course."

"Bully! Like knights of old and all that."

"Indeed, sir."

"Now listen to me," Hall said. "When the attack comes, and it will, form up your troop behind the stables. The enemy, especially the Apache, want horses and will not risk harming them. When you spy an opportunity for a flanking attack, emerge from your position, form a line, and have at it. Practice that maneuver tomorrow. Damn it all, I wish

I could be with you. The charge of Cranston's hussars will be a moment of glory."

"Or a complete disaster," Cranston said.

"Why so glum?"

"My troop is twenty Mexican peasants, not the Seventh Cavalry."

"They'll do just fine, Lieutenant. Just remember what I've told you: Charge and give Lozado and his rabble the edge of the saber. That will send them running. It's hussars we need, not dragoons. Now, are you sure I can't tempt you to a dip of snuff?"

"No thank you, sir."

Hall reached under his pillow and produced a bottle of Hennessy brandy. "Then take a swig of this. I've been saving it for a special occasion and getting all shot to pieces is a special occasion."

"Sir, where did you get this?"

"I got it from my fond mama."

"I mean who brought it to you?"

"Why, Sara Lark. She's so grateful for me saving her from a life of prostitution that she shifted sides, deserting Miss Zimmermann's strict regimen for my looser rules— or I should say rule, since I only have one."

"And it involves snuff, cigars, and brandy."

"Bully! You catch on quickly, Lieutenant Cranston."

Cranston shook his head. "Yes, sir, I'll take a swig. Right about now I need one."

CHAPTER 43

"Your warriors are quiet this morning, Alchesay, my friend," Santiago Lozado said.

"Too much whiskey last night."

"But they will recover for tomorrow's attack."

"My men have hurting heads, but they are eager for tomorrow."

"Many horses and guns. They will be big men among the Apache."

"Tomorrow will be a great day, don Santiago. Songs will be sung about us around the wickiups, and the young women will look on us with much favor."

"I want the man called Kellerman," Lozado said. "We must take him alive if we can."

"His death will come as a welcome thing, be assured of that."

"I'll savor his agonies like fine wine on my tongue. "

"Our attack must be swift and overpowering, don Santiago. We fire the outbuildings and attack from the smoke."

"Spare the slaves and the stables, my friend."

"We will not harm the slaves or the horses."

"Nor the women."

The Apache smiled. "Not in the attack, but later. . . ."

"Ha, we will all enjoy them later."

Kyle Swan stepped to the fire. "The Apache and most of our men pass the morning holding their heads and groaning."

"They will be well enough tomorrow," Lozado said. "Friend Kyle, do you look forward to the fight?"

Swan smiled. "Three more Comancheros came in last night, bringing our number to fifty, plus the Apache. It won't be a battle; it will be a massacre."

"These new men will fight for don Santiago?" Alchesay said. He had drunk little, and his black eyes shone like obsidian.

"They'll fight for money. And there must be plenty of money at the fort. Soldiers' pay with nowhere to spend it mounts up to a large sum over the years."

"My friend, Kyle, those mercenaries must be dealt with when the fight is over. The money must go into our coffers, not theirs."

"We'll take care of it," Swan said. "Me and Roscoe Wolfe."

"You are a fine friend, Kyle. You pick up and carry my heaviest burdens."

"Wolfe says he will herd away the livestock when the fight starts. We can't afford to sacrifice any. Scalps are money, and we can't lose sight of that fact."

"Roscoe is always concerned with my welfare," Lozado said. "He is a true friend. But be assured, our undertaking will not be harmed. After the fort is destroyed and Keller-man dealt with, we head for Sonora and lay the foundation of our future wealth."

"One of the Comancheros who recently joined us told me a scalper can just about name his price in Hermosillo," Swan said.

"Then we strike while the iron is hot," Lozado said. "Kyle, you bring only good news this morning and for that you have my thanks."

"Big day tomorrow, patrón," Swan said, grinning.

"Big day . . . joyful day. Alchesay, my friend, what say you?"

"The Apache will take the scalps of many white men."

Lozado shook his head, scowling. "And then throw them away, dear friend. Pah, they are worthless."

CHAPTER 44

"Green spots on the salt pork again, Mrs. Zimmermann," Captain Joe Kellerman said.

The woman sighed. "Yes, I know, and it smells. The soldiers are complaining enough, and Marshal Bowman says my coffee is pigswill. The nerve of the man."

"Maybe there are supplies at Devil's Rock," Sergeant Major Saul Olinger said.

"Miracles do happen, I guess," Kellerman said.

"After tomorrow we may not need any supplies," Mrs. Zimmermann said, her face grim.

Kellerman smiled. "That thought had occurred to me."

"'And the condemned men ate a hearty breakfast,'" Olinger said. He smiled. "I read that once in a newspaper during the war, after three Reb spies were hung. I recall that they ate fried eggs, bacon, and grits, and sopped up their plates with bread. I couldn't do that."

"Nor could I," Mrs. Zimmermann said. "But I'd spend the time in prayer."

"They should've fed them Mrs. Zimmermann's salt pork. Then they wouldn't have needed to hang 'em," Olinger said.

Kellerman smiled. "Kill those boys stone dead, huh, Sergeant Major?"

The woman sniffed. "I expect that kind of talk from the ill-bred troopers, but not from an officer and a sergeant major."

After Mrs. Zimmermann flounced out the door, Olinger said, "We hurt the lady's feelings."

"She'll get over it. She always does."

"Lieutenant Cranston didn't join us," Olinger said.

"No, he was up at dawn to train his Mexicans." Kellerman looked puzzled. "But that's strange . . . I haven't heard any rifle practice."

It seemed something was wrong, but he couldn't put his finger on what it might be.

"I better go and take a look," he said. "See to the positioning of your men, Saul. I've got a feeling that Lozado will surround the building and then attack. His frontal charge didn't do too much for him last time."

"The men will sleep at their posts tonight, Joe?"

"Yes. I expect a dawn assault."

"I'll see it done, and after that it's in the hands of the gods."

"And our Fort Misery ruffians. By the way, have you promoted a trooper to corporal yet?"

"Yes. Trooper John Lockhart, a member of the Fourth Cavalry and a Fort Clark reject. Apparently, he killed two drovers in a barfight over a woman and was to be hung. But the army claimed him as one of their own and gave him the option of a military hanging or a posting to Fort Misery. He foolishly chose the latter."

"Does he soldier?"

"Yes. And the men respect him."

"That's good because he obviously doesn't have a lick of common sense. You're right, a smart person would've chosen the noose."

* * *

All was confusion, chaos, and tumult.

Second Lieutenant Atticus Cranston, red in the face, yelled at his mounted Mexicans to face front and form line, but they wandered all over the parade ground, fighting their prancing horses, cursing each other every time there was an inevitable collision. Dust billowed saddle high, a rider was thrown by his irritated mount, another man's foot was caught up in the stirrup and he danced an odd little jig as he tried to remount his bucking sorrel. And here and there in the morning sunlight sabers gleamed like needles randomly stuck into a pin cushion.

"Form line! Form line!" Cranston hollered, riding among his men, pushing, tugging on reins, slapping human and horse rumps with the flat of his saber, in the dust-roiling turmoil acting like a madman at a devil's equestrian ball.

Order there was none. Dust, curses, yells, and shrieks there were aplenty.

And no one in that pandemonium bellowed louder than Captain Joe Kellerman.

"Lieutenant Cranston, what the hell are you doing?"

Then an unfortunate mishap.

A Mexican on an unruly horse T-boned Cranston's mount. Both the lieutenant and his horse went down in a wild, kicking heap, raising a huge cloud of dust. The young officer scrambled to his feet, dusted himself off and picked up his fallen saber. When his horse scrambled upright, he checked the animal over and only then did he salute and reply to Kellerman's question.

"Sorry about that, sir," he said. "The Mexicans haven't ridden for a while, and they're a little bit rusty."

Kellerman's face showed his horror. "A little bit rusty? Lieutenant, they're a disaster."

Then another unfortunate mishap, worse than the first.

A young Mexican on an unmanageable bay sideswiped

Captain Kellerman and sent him flying. Now it was the captain's turn to stagger to his feet and dust himself off. "Lieutenant Cranston, you better have a mighty good reason for this calamity," he said, his eyes blazing. "Where are their rifles?"

The young officer gathered up the reins of his mount and said, "Sir, for safety's sake, we'd better step out of the way."

Cranston led his horse a few yards from the bucking, yelling, saber-waving bedlam that were his Hispanic hussars, and Kellerman followed, limping a little, his back stiff with rage.

The lieutenant smiled. "Sir, what you see here is just the start of their training. I'll soon lick them into shape. They're a fine group of men and as keen as mustard to meet the enemy."

Kellerman took a deep breath, calming himself and then said, "I'll ask it again . . . where are their rifles?"

"Oh, well done, you men!" Cranston yelled. Then, smiling broadly, "Did you see that, sir? Three of them formed line."

"Where. Are. Their. Rifles, Second Lieutenant Cranston?" Kellerman said, spacing out the words, a sure sign of trouble.

The younger man nodded. "Ah, yes, sir, the rifles. Well, Lieutenant Hall and I decided that one day wasn't enough to make these men into dragoons, I mean mounted infantry trained to ride to the battle and then dismount and fight on foot."

"I know what dragoons are, Lieutenant."

"Yes, sir, quite so, sir. So, what we have are hussars, quick, light cavalry . . ."

"I also know what hussars are, Lieutenant. So, you and Lieutenant Hall put your great military minds together and came up with arming the Mexicans with sabers instead of the Sharps carbine. Why?"

"Ah, there's the crux of the matter, sir. These men are not familiar with the Sharps, but they all use machetes."

"Machetes? What the hell is a machete?"

"Sir, it's a broad, heavy knife used in Mexican agriculture. The slashing, sweep of the machete is very close to the action of the saber, and the men have taken to our cavalry weapon quite naturally."

"What are they doing with the sabers, apart from waving them over their heads and grinning."

"They're showing off for your benefit, sir. I'll soon teach them how to use the edge and the point."

Kellerman went silent for a few moments, staring at the Mexicans, who were lost in billowing dust, and then said, "I suppose there's some twisted logic to your and Lieutenant Hall's thinking. You know Apache won't let the Mexicans close enough to use the saber."

"Not if we take them by surprise, and that is my plan."

"That's your plan? Take battle-hardened Apache warriors by surprise and catch them with their guards down?"

"Bully! Sir, you've got it exactly."

"Bully? You've been listening to Lieutenant Hall again."

"Sorry, sir. But we will surprise them and give them the edge of the saber. Lieutenant Hall says an unexpected flank attack is guaranteed to send the rascals scampering."

Kellerman stared at the dusty, noisy turmoil of Cranston's command and after a while said, "You're correct, Lieutenant, arming these men with the Sharps carbine would endanger the lives of everybody on this post, mine included. The only safe place would be behind them, and I'm not too sure about that."

He saw Sergeant Major Olinger walk onto the parade ground, stare at the turmoil with the round eyes, and then turn and beat a hasty retreat. He obviously was unimpressed by the Mexican hussars. Only Major Mouser, the orange cat, sat on the headquarters' porch and gazed on the uproar with apparent satisfaction . . . he'd just found a new bunch of people to hate.

Captain Kellerman sighed and then said, "Lieutenant Cranston, God help us, I see no other option than your saber-armed cavalry. Just . . . just see what you can do with them."

"They'll be ready, sir. I guarantee it."

"All right. As soon as the rear windows and door of the headquarters building are barricaded, I'll send you Tobias Zimmermann, Jim Bertrand, and Marshal Bowman to stiffen your line with their guns. That is if you ever form a line."

"We'll form line, sir."

"Atticus, I have a feeling your . . . for want of a better word . . . hussars . . . could make the difference in this fight. The result of their charge might mean defeat or victory. Do you understand me?"

"Perfectly, sir."

Kellerman's smile was thin, without humor. "And needless to say, if, by some miracle, we survive this, your career depends on it."

"Yes, sir, I understand. But I do have another, formidable weapon that will spur us to victory."

"Really? What is that?"

"Hatred, sir."

"Explain."

"The Mexicans were abused by Santiago Lozado, their women raped, their worth as human beings reduced to the value of their scalps. They hate Lozado and his Comancheros and Apache with a passion. Don't doubt it, sir; they'll form line. And they'll use their sabers with a fire in their bellies, a desire to destroy a despised enemy. They want vengeance, and they'll fight and kill until their last gasps of breath."

"You have that much faith in them?" Kellerman said.

"Yes, sir, I have. That much and more."

"All right, then carry on, Lieutenant Cranston."

Kellerman looked at the Mexicans attempting, without much success, to push and shove one another into line abreast, the just-arrived Navajo giving them scowling pointers with the butt of his rifle.

"Atticus, give me my hussars," the captain said. "And may God help you."

CHAPTER 45

The young Apache bucks ate Santiago Lozado's meager breakfasts of fried cornmeal mush and told each other they would soon eat heartier when the fort was taken, with all its food supplies. The braves planned a great war dance for that evening that would bring them strength and such gallantry in battle that their very appearance would make the trembling white soldiers cry like women and wither and die from fear.

Alchesay, noted among the Apache as a fine dancer and singer, would lead the young warriors, his steps teaching them how to pound the enemy to dust under their feet as they thrilled to his war songs.

"It seems the Apache are ready for the big fight, friend Roscoe," Santiago Lozado said. "They already wear paint."

"There will be no sleep for them tonight," Roscoe Wolfe said. "They'll have worked themselves into a killing frenzy come dawn."

"And then we have to kill them. It's such a pity."

"Yeah, it's too bad, but they're in the way. We're not going to let a bunch of savages ride away with horses and guns and whatever other loot they can carry from the fort."

"How will it be done, dear friend?"

"Tomorrow night we'll give them whiskey and the

women, and when they're good and drunk me and Kyle Swan will take care of things." He made a gun of his hand. "Pop! Pop! Pop!"

"But I'll shoot Alchesay," Lozado said. "He doesn't like me very much. He speaks friendly words, but I see the disdain in his eyes."

Wolfe smiled. "Then we'll set him aside for you, don Santiago."

"Such warriors I have in my camp! We will do well in Sonora, friend Roscoe."

"The hell with Sonora and its mud-hut poverty. Our good times will come right here in the good ol' United States."

"Ah yes, whiskey, whores, and location will be the three pillars of our prosperity. One day you'll be a rich man, friend Roscoe." Lozado smiled. *No, one day you'll be a dead man, friend Roscoe.*

Santiago Lozado strolled around his camp, here and there giving a word of encouragement to a Comanchero and smiling at a non-smiling Apache. What strange war paint they wore; red and black stripes on their cheeks were the predominate colors. He recalled that the Comanche wore red because it symbolized strength and power; black, a living color, very aggressive, indicated that the wearer was a powerful warrior who was brave in battle. A black streak across the forehead under the headband also predicted victory, and that pleased Lozado immensely. The Apache were full of confidence that the next day they'd destroy their enemies.

The victory couldn't come soon enough. Feeding the slaves had reduced Lozado's supplies, and in a few days he and his men would've gone hungry. Well, the white soldiers fought with full bellies, so the fort was no doubt well stocked with food.

He walked to the horse lines and all the mounts, both Comanchero and Apache, looked strong and healthy—fine war horses that would carry his men to triumph. On his way back to his fire, he met Kyle Swan, who looked troubled.

"Friend Kyle, you have a problem?"

"Those damned savages," Swan said.

"What about them?"

"This morning one of them went out riding and came across a dead soldier."

"Plenty of those can be found in the desert between here and Yuma."

"He was wearing riding boots, a cavalry uniform, and an empty canteen lay under him, but he'd no weapons on him."

"Why should that disturb the Apache? They've seen dead soldiers in plenty before."

"Some of the young bucks say it's a bad omen, that a dead man has been spying on their camp. But others say the opposite, that it means the soldiers in the fort are doomed."

"The man was probably a deserter," Lozado said. "I'll talk to Alchesay."

The war chief was talking with a group of young men who immediately walked away when Lozado stepped to his side. "Alchesay, my friend, I hear one of your warriors found the body of a soldier."

The Apache nodded. "Some of my young men think it is bad omen and say they will not fight tomorrow."

That last was alarming, and Lozado had to put an end to it quickly.

"The man was a cowardly deserter who fled the fort rather than face tomorrow's big fight." Lozado smiled. "Now that is a good omen, a sign that the gods favor us."

Then, sealing the deal, "I saw him in a dream last night and he spoke to me. He told me we would soon ride our horses over the bodies of dead soldiers."

"I will tell that to my young men. They are very foolish and sometimes speak like frightened women. Your vision will cheer them."

Alchesay called his warriors back and told them what Lozado had said. That seemed to satisfy them and set their minds at ease.

As he walked back to his fire, Lozado was mighty pleased with himself. He had defused what could've been a bad situation.

But worse was to come.

His name was Denny Link, out of the Tennessee hill country, the spawn of a brother and sister union, a tall, thin man with a small head, long, stringy yellow hair and shifty, pale-blue eyes that never looked directly at a man. He was stupid, vicious, and had raped and then murdered several Mexican women. Inbreeding, going back generations, had produced a creature more brute beast than human. A coward at heart, Link had been with Lozado for a year, but he had no belly for the next day's fight. He wanted out, and he wanted paid.

"And that's how it is, Mr. Lozado," Link said. His teeth were rotten, and his breath stank. "I want what's owed to me."

"No, Denny, my friend, not now. Come to me after tomorrow's victory and we will talk."

Link shook his head. "I want paid now. I reckon two hunnerd ought to cover it."

"You'll get your share when we sell the scalps in Sonora, not before," Lozado said. "You can't quit me on the eve of battle."

"You're a big, important man, but I'm tired of you telling me what I cain and cain't do. Just pay me my money. I've earned it."

"Denny, friend, no one picks my pocket and then walks out on me. You'll get paid when I say you get paid."

"Two hunnerd. I need the money. I'm sick from the clap, and I need he'p."

"Then you should've chosen your partners more carefully, my friend. But that's no concern of mine."

"Are you gonna give me my money?" Louder, drawing an interested crowd.

"Come see me after the fight tomorrow and I'll see what I can do. Two hundred dollars, you say? Perhaps I can untie my purse strings that much."

"I want money now. I'm sick. I need a doctor."

"Maybe there's a doctor at the fort."

"I ain't goin' near any fort."

"Then I can't do anything for you at this present time. Perhaps tomorrow, my friend."

Link's hand dropped closer to his holstered gun.

"Denny, don't even think about that," Lozado said. "Poor fellow, I believe you were conceived from bad seed and that's why you're so . . . repulsively stupid. Now walk away from this and we'll talk later."

The man's blue eyes watered, and his voice took on a whining edge. "Two hunnerd. I tol' you . . . I have the clap real bad, and I need he'p."

"No, Denny. Come back and talk to me later."

Then Denny Link made the biggest and last mistake of his miserable, senseless life.

He went for his gun.

Santiago Lozado was forty years old, and he didn't live that long by being slow on the draw. But he didn't pull his gun, he went for the ivory-handled bowie knife on his belt and drove the blade with great force into Link's slack mouth. The clip point slammed into the back of the man's throat, and, his eyes popping, the pain and shock dropped him to his knees.

But he wasn't done.

Spitting blood and saliva, Link completed the draw, and his gun came up fast. Lozado immediately saw the danger and kicked at the Colt. His finger in the trigger guard, Denny got off a shot before the gun flew from his hand. The bullet went nowhere, and Lozado again used the blade, this time plunging it deep into the man's skinny throat.

It was a killing wound that snuffed out Denny Link's candle and sent him sprawling into the sand. He twitched a few times like a pinned insect and then lay still.

"Patrón, are you hurt?"

Kyle Swan rushed to Lozado's side.

"No, I am quite all right, my friend."

Swan looked at the body. "Denny Link. What happened?"

"He threatened to kill me unless I paid him money. I tried to talk him out of it, but he went for his gun, and I gave him the point of the bowie."

Swan kicked the still body. "Inbred Tennessee pig," he said. "He had the clap, you know."

"I know. He told me that at some length. I'm sorry he had to die, but he gave me no choice."

"He was nothing," Swan said. "His mother couldn't outrun her brother. He told me that once, as though he was proud of it. You men," Swan motioned to a couple of stunned onlookers, "drag that carcass away from camp. You can keep his gun and boots."

"His gun, maybe," a white man said. "Not those boots. It would be like walking in a stagnant swamp."

Denny Link was both distrusted and disliked by the other Comancheros, who considered him stupid and unstable. But his death and the manner of it spread a pall over the camp that Lozado was quick to recognize.

He spent the day with his men, encouraging them with promises of quick wealth after they destroyed the fort and returned with him to Sonora. The Apache were indifferent; the death of a white man at the hands of another white man of little importance to them. They were eager for war and ready for the next day's fight.

As the morning brightened into afternoon, Roscoe Wolfe took Lozado aside and with a worried look asked how the men were feeling.

"They are once again in good spirits my friend," Lozado said, smiling. "No one liked Denny Link; he was an animal."

"I didn't know the man," Wolfe said. "But I thought he was a strange-looking cuss. He had huge feet. Swan told me that no one would wear his boots."

"I'm surprised anyone would want to. I'd guess they smell like a rotting skunk," Lozado said.

"There's no accounting for what a barefooted man will wear," Wolfe said.

"Roscoe, my friend, none of my men are barefoot."

"I'm still surprised he went for his gun. Was he so stupid that he thought he'd get away with shooting you?"

Lozado said, "Roscoe, my friend, some dead men are worth talking about, but, Link is not one of them."

"Yeah, well, on a brighter note, I told my boys that the Apache will do most of the fighting."

"And that is true. I will only use my Comancheros if Alchesay and his warriors waver."

Wolfe smiled. "Apache ain't big on wavering."

"Good. The less there are left, the less we have to kill."

Wolfe nodded. "I look forward to tomorrow; it will be a good day for us. Then we collect our scalps and head back to Sonora."

"Let the Apache help with that task, friend Roscoe. Forty heads are a lot to scalp in one go, and there will be much struggling and screaming."

"There won't be. I know because I've handled situations like that before. The answer is to shoot the livestock first and then scalp them. It's quite a simple process really."

"Then make it so, my friend. I leave it in your capable hands."

"Consider it done, don Santiago."

"You are such a dear friend, Roscoe. You are my crutch. Without you I might stumble and fall."

"I'll always be on hand to support you. Here and in Sonora."

"Do you think Kellerman knows we're coming?"

"By now I'm sure he does. I'm sure he's scouted the camp."

"I wonder how he's feeling."

"Shaking in his boots, I imagine."

"He's a coward."

"Maybe, maybe not. We'll watch as the Apache work on him and soon be able to answer that question."

"That will be a glorious day."

"A glorious day that will come tomorrow at sunrise, don Santiago," Roscoe Wolfe said.

CHAPTER 46

"Lieutenant Cranston has those Mexicans pretty much licked into shape," Sergeant Major Saul Olinger said. "At least they can form line."

"And charge?" Captain Joe Kellerman said.

"Well, enough that they scared the hell out of Corporal Lockhart and a couple of troopers who were crossing the parade ground. Lockhart says all those waving sabers put the fear of God into him."

"Let's hope they do the same with Lozado's men."

"I'm sure they will, Joe. Those Mexican boys are rarin' to go."

"Tobias Zimmermann, Jim Bertrand, and Marshal Bowman will strengthen Lieutenant Cranston's line, give them some firearm support."

"I know. I spoke to them. Buck Bowman isn't real keen. He says he's too old for that death-or-glory stuff, but he understands the reason for his being there with the other pistoleros."

"To stiffen the line."

"Yes, that's what I told him."

"Saul, I spoke to Mrs. Zimmermann," Kellerman said, filling Olinger's whiskey glass. "She'll feed the soldiers at their posts tonight."

"Good for Mrs. Zimmermann," Olinger said. "She always comes through for us."

"She says she and Sara Lark plan to use the last of the raisins to make plum duff for everybody. Lieutenant Hall is very excited," Kellerman said.

"The lieutenant can barely stand. He shouldn't get overexcited."

"He's sitting. He'll be defending the rear of the building from the enlisted men's mess. Well, him and three others."

"Joe, how will Lieutenant Cranston know when to make his charge? Can you signal him?"

"No, I can't, Saul. It's up to him. He'll make the decision when he sees an opportunity."

"A big responsibility for a junior officer."

"I know. And if he fails me, and lives that long, he'll be a junior officer for the rest of his career."

Olinger smiled. "Did you tell him that?"

"I can't remember. But he knows that much already."

"I have faith in him. He has a head on his shoulders."

"Strangely enough, so do I have faith in him. I did tell him that his Mexicans, he calls them hussars, could be the difference between victory or defeat."

"Does he realize that? I'm sure he does, but I'll ask the question anyway."

"Yes, he realizes that. And he told me he has a secret weapon."

"What kind of secret weapon?"

"Hate. His men hate Lozado and his Comancheros so much that they'll be on them like the sword of God."

"He could be right."

"Of course he could be right. He could be very right. I admire hatred in a soldier, and I nurture it. Hate is made of clean iron tempered in a red-hot kiln: inflexible, heavy, unyielding, merciless, a powerful weapon to turn on the enemy. The opposite of hate is love—lacy around the edges, weak and soft and sweet and not for a fighting man."

"Damn, Joe, I never heard you talk like that before," Olinger said.

"I never felt like this before, as though fighting for Fort Misery is the single most important thing I've ever done in my life. And the strange thing is that it doesn't matter. To the army, to the government, and to the citizens of this republic, it's of no more importance than a hill of beans. We're the military's refuse fighting a raggedy-assed Mexican bandit, and who the hell cares?"

Sergeant Major Olinger thought about that and then said, "All of us, Joe. All of us care. From Mrs. Zimmermann to the lowliest private, to Lieutenants Cranston and Hall, to the Navajo scout—we all care. And we're depending on you, Joe. Every single damn one of us."

"So all of this is my responsibility?"

"You're the commanding officer, sir. There is nobody else."

Kellerman was silent for long moments then said, "You are right to chide me, Saul. It does matter. It matters to a lot of people right here at this post."

"Yes. Fort Benjamin Grierson, a place with some mighty brave men and women. Look out at the desert, Joe, and the blue sky that stretches forever in all directions. Smell Mrs. Zimmermann's plum duff cooking in the kitchen and listen to Sara Lark singing as she does laundry, happier than she's ever been in her life. Imagine Lieutenant Hall forever offering his snuff that few people ever accept. Damn it all, there are worse places to die."

Captain Kellerman looked at the sergeant major, opened his mouth to speak and then closed it again, as though he'd forgotten what he wanted to say. He smiled. "All right, have another drink, Saul, and then we'll check our defenses and listen to Lieutenant Cranston yell at his hussars. Sometimes I think he's the army's noisiest second lieutenant."

"He'll be a fine officer one day," Olinger said. "I've met a lot of second lieutenants in my time, and he's one of the best."

Kellerman's orderly tapped on the door and then stepped into the office. "Sir, a message from Mrs. Zimmermann. She begs to report that she had enough raisins to make plum duff for everyone, and if the captain cares to sample it, now would be a good time."

"Tell her I'll be there in a few minutes," Kellerman said.

Olinger said, "Mrs. Zimmermann once again rises to the occasion."

"She must be in a fine mood. She never gives samples of her cooking to anybody."

"Who needs samples of salt beef and beans?" Olinger said, making a face.

Captain Kellerman laughed for the first time in a long time, and it felt good.

CHAPTER 47

As the sun dropped, Second Lieutenant Atticus Cranston's Mexican hussars formed rank and charged. They did it seventeen times before the young officer was satisfied. The line was a little ragged, the charge on the haphazard side, but it would do. The Mexicans understood that when the shooting started their position would be behind the stables, an adobe-and-timber structure about two-thirds of the length of the headquarters building. Someone had cared enough about the construction to provide a slatted ventilating tower in the middle of the roof, disguised to look like a low steeple. The weather vane on top featured a creaking brass rooster that now and again pointed the correct direction of the wind. The bird had a bullet hole in it, put there months before by an inebriated Lieutenant Hall, who took a potshot at it with his revolver. His indiscretion had earned him a reprimand and, as a reluctant aside, Captain Kellerman's praise for his shooting.

Cranston crossed the parade ground and reported to Kellerman, who stood behind a barricaded window, a Sharps propped against the timber boards.

"Sir, I'm pleased to report that my command is now trained and ready for action," Cranston said.

The captain nodded. "I watched your last few charges, and I'm afraid the Seventh Cavalry has nothing to fear."

"Sir, I expect my Mexicans to distinguish themselves in the coming battle," Cranston said. "They're eager for the fight, every man jack of them."

"Every man jack of them, huh? Where did that come from?"

"Sir, it was current at West Point when I was there."

"It's got a ring to it. Well, every man jack of us here got our plum duff. Did you get yours?"

"Yes, sir. Miss Lark brought it to me. I tried to share it with one of my more competent men, but he wanted nothing to do with it."

"More fool him. A drink with you?"

Cranston looked around, and Kellerman said. "There's a bottle at my feet. Take a swig, Lieutenant. You've earned it."

The young officer did as he was told, and the raw whiskey hit the spot.

"Feel better?" Kellerman said.

His throat husky from its scorching, Cranston managed, "Yes, sir."

"Watch your drinking, Lieutenant."

"Yes, sir."

"Now go speak to Lieutenant Hall. He wishes to reassure himself that his sound military advice didn't fall on deaf ears. Don't linger, and then return to your post."

"Yes, sir."

"Bully! I didn't lead you astray, did I?" Lieutenant Hall said.

"No, sir, you didn't." Cranston said.

"I turned a Mexican rabble into a fine body of men, did I not?"

"You most certainly did, sir."

"Give them the edge of the saber. I said that, didn't I?"

"Yes, sir, you did"

"Bully! Now what did you think of Mrs. Zimmermann's plum duff?"

"I enjoyed it."

Hall shook his head. "Not one of her better efforts. It badly needed more raisins." He nudged the soldier beside him with his barefoot toe. "What do you think, you rascal?"

"About what, sir?"

"The Virgin Mary's plum duff."

"It was very good, sir."

Hall mimicked the man's voice. "It was very good, sir. It was substandard. That's what it was."

"Substandard. Yes, sir."

"How would you know, you villain?"

"I wouldn't, sir."

"Then in future leave the criticism of Mrs. Zimmermann's food to your betters, you hear?"

"Yes, sir."

"Damned ungrateful reprobate."

"Sir, I should return to my post," Cranston said.

"Hold just a moment, Atticus, my able student. A drink with you."

Hall produced the Hennessy brandy from under his chair and said, "Here, take a swig."

"Yes, sir."

The lieutenant drank and Hall passed the bottle to the soldier. "Take a swig, you ruffian, and don't complain."

The soldier took a swig, and Hall held the bottle up to a hanging oil lamp. "Look, it's half gone. I didn't want you to take that big of a swig, you stinker."

"Sorry, sir."

"Damned scalawag."

"Sir, I should return to my post," Cranston said.

"Yes, yes, of course," Hall said. He took a long swallow from the bottle. "Make us both proud, Lieutenant."

"Yes, sir."

"As for me, I have a brace of pistols and intend to do great execution on the morrow."

"I'm sure you will, sir," Cranston said as he backed toward the enlisted men's mess door.

"And Atticus, watch your drinking. You're hitting it pretty hard."

"I'll be careful, sir."

"Bully! Then good luck, Lieutenant."

"And you, sir. Good luck."

All the Mexican chatter of the day was stilled when Lieutenant Cranston returned to his men. Brave as they were, eager as they were, each man knew what he faced come morning. The Apache had a fearsome reputation as fighting men, merciless desert warriors, hardy and enduring. After years of warfare they still ran rings around the United States Army, as the graves of hundreds of soldiers attested. The coming fight would not be a walk in the park. It would be hard won, and some of their number would die. If the battle was lost, all of them would die.

Each man squatted beside his mount, the trailing reins in one hand, the saber in the other. They looked up when Cranston approached them, and a few smiled, but most were stone-faced, each busy with his own thoughts. The lieutenant let them be. To disturb them now would be like walking into a church and playing a fiddle among a praying congregation.

Cranston walked to the front of the barn and stood in darkness. He was on edge, restless and concerned. Captain Kellerman told him that his hussars could be the difference between victory or defeat. Now the young lieutenant asked himself if he was up to the task. Might his courage flee him at the last minute? Would his half-trained Mexicans cut and run? Were the Comancheros and their Apache allies just too strong, too warlike? He looked at the starry sky and the sublimely indifferent moon and found no comfort.

Dear God, would this night never end?

The soundless Navajo appeared at his side and jarred Cranston out of his funk. "Woman want talk with you," he said. "Tonight, of all nights, she should not walk alone." He shook his head. "Very foolish woman."

Sara Lark emerged from the gloom and the scout left.

"Ahiga is right, Miss Lark. You should not be out alone."

In the darkness she looked almost pretty, the lines and muddy skin of her hard life already leaving her. Her lips were open, teeth visible, as though she found it hard to breathe.

"Atticus," she said, "I am very afraid. I fear what tomorrow will bring."

Cranston smiled and took her hand in his, surprised by how small and delicate it was. "Don't be. I won't let any harm come to you."

"You say it with sincerity, but you don't really mean it. You will be here, fighting with your men."

"Stay close to Mrs. Zimmermann. She'll take care of you."

"Mrs. Zimmermann is terrified. She says she's not, but I can see the fear in her eyes. She told me she hopes that God will not fail her and let the Apache have her. She's never said anything like that before."

"We'll send the Apache and the Comancheros running, Sara. Don't ask me why, but I know we will."

"I am asking you why. How do you know, Atticus? Tell me. Take my fear away."

Lieutenant Cranston shook his helpless head. "Sara, I

can't do that. I can't perform miracles and make everything right again."

"Then hold me. For a few minutes hold me close and let me share your strength."

"That I can do."

Cranston took the woman's slender body in his arms and hugged her close. Through the thin stuff of her borrowed nightgown he felt her heartbeat, fluttering like a frightened bird in a cage. "It's going to be all right," he said, his lips moving on her hair. "Everything is going to be just fine."

CHAPTER 48

"They're crushing the white men's skulls underfoot and splitting open their bellies with the lance; those are the pictures the war dance of my young men paint," Alchesay said, smiling.

Lit by a central fire, flames glowed on the copper skins of the prancing warriors, highlighted the red and black streaks on their faces, and glinted on the steel of lances and axes. An older man sat to the side and chanted as he pounded on a hand drum. It was a savage and frightening scene but strangely beautiful in the flickering firelight, and don Santiago Lozado was mightily pleased.

"Your young men dance well, friend Alchesay," Lozado said.

"Hear how hard the moccasins strike the ground, pounding the bones of the white men to dust."

"Ahh . . . it is wonderful to see and hear, and it fills me with joy that the soldiers will all die tomorrow," Lozado said.

"Like a pack of ravenous wolves, we will tear them apart and bathe in their blood," Alchesay said.

"Well spoken, my dear friend. My heart beats faster in anticipation."

"It will be a day long remembered by the Chiricahua and Mescalero. We will sing of it."

"And remembered by me, my friend."

"Now I will dance," Alchesay said.

Without another word the Apache joined the dancers, and Lozado watched for a while and then returned to his fire, where Kyle Swan and Roscoe Wolfe were waiting.

"I don't know what the Apache will do to Kellerman's men, but they scare the hell out of me," Swan said.

"It's a dance of death for the fort, not for us," Lozado said. "Is all ready for tomorrow?"

"As long as we have no more desertions, we have a force of thirty-five Comancheros and thirteen Apache," Swan said.

"Thirteen is an unlucky number," Wolfe said.

Lozado grinned. "For the Apache, not for us."

"So how do we play it tomorrow?" Swan said.

"The initial attack will be made at dawn by my Comancheros, perhaps when the soldiers are still asleep. We'll surround the headquarters building, and when Kellerman's numbers are whittled down, unleash the Apache. You two will not be in the initial attack. As I said before, you must make yourselves ready to take care of the pistoleros."

"We'll find them," Wolfe said.

"And kill them," Swan said.

"Then it is decided. And, of course, I want Kellerman alive."

"There's a real possibility that when his fort is taken, he'll blow his brains out," Wolfe said.

"Then, my friends, get to him before he pulls the trigger."

"It's a tall order, patrón, but we'll see what we can do."

"And once again, do not harm the slaves," Lozado said. "I want none of my livestock lost."

"Hell, we can scalp any dead Mexicans we find," Wolfe said. "You won't lose any."

"That is true. See, I worry constantly about trivialities. It is well I have you strong men at my side."

"Patrón, do you think Kellerman knows we are coming?" Swan said.

"He knows we are coming for him, but he doesn't know when. We will have the element of surprise on our side."

"We'll shoot them in their bunks, maybe," Wolfe said.

"That is a probability, dear friend. Kellerman's men will never wake from their last sleep." Lozado smiled. "It is an exquisite thought. Oh, and as I talk about exquisite thoughts it reminds me: There is a young girl among the slaves who calls herself Maria. I want her."

"We'll find her, patrón," Swan said.

"After I have finished with the fair Maria and the Apache have had her, you can scalp her and add her hair to the rest. Ahh, listen to the drum."

"It's getting louder," Wolfe said. "Those boys are getting worked up."

"They'll be ready to fight in the morning," Swan said.

"Pity poor Kellerman," Wolfe said, grinning.

"I don't pity him. I want to kill him," Lozado said.

CHAPTER 49

The Navajo once again made of himself an owl, the death bird who can see in the darkness. The Apache danced wildly, and around Lozado's camp men saw to their weapons. Then it was so that the attack on Fort Misery would come in the morning, probably with the dawn. His eyes glittering, he made of himself a snake and slithered away from the camp toward his waiting horse. The full moon beamed down on him as he rode away, and the desert night flowers danced in its honor.

"We're ready for him, Ahiga," Captain Kellerman said. "You did well to confirm that Lozado's attack will come in the morning."

"Probably at dawn," the Navajo said. "Lozado wants to catch you asleep."

"He'll find us wide awake, full of fighting spirit and Mrs. Zimmermann's plum duff."

If Ahiga thought that even remotely funny, he didn't let it show.

He stood with Kellerman in the hallway of the head-quarters building, the soldiers on either side of them alert at their posts, staring out into the moonlit night.

"The Apache dance," he said. "They expect a great victory."

"The last time they tried to best my scoundrels it didn't go too well for them," Kellerman said.

"Lozado will have learned his lesson, Captain. He will try something different."

"He'll surround us with riflemen, I'm sure of that, and then try to pile up my casualties. I hope the Apache charge us head-on. I have a surprise waiting for them."

"Lieutenant Cranston's Mexicans?"

"Yes. He has them trained to fight as cavalry."

The Navajo shook his head. "Mexicans can't fight. They're afraid of Apache."

"They hate the Apache, but most of all the Comancheros for what they did to their village. They'll fight."

"Lieutenant Cranston has that opinion."

"Yes. He's a wise man."

"It's a time for warriors, not wise men."

"I believe him to be a warrior, Ahiga."

"Time will tell."

"Tomorrow will tell."

"Where do I fight, Captain?"

"Choose a position. Make it yours."

"I'll fight with Cranston. He's a young man and needs guidance."

"Then fight with the lieutenant. Bertrand, Zimmermann, and Marshal Bowman will also be part of his command."

"Pistoleros."

"Yes, Bertrand and Zimmermann are. I don't know about Bowman."

"He has pains in his head, sees strange lights, not good for a fighting man."

"Then let's hope he has no pains tomorrow."

"I will go now, Captain. Speak with Lieutenant Cranston and put his Mexicans in order."

"Don't be too hard on them, Ahiga. They are not soldiers."

"There is a full moon tonight and it will shine on the Mexicans and give them strength. Many good spirits ride the moonlight to earth and search for those they can best help. It is my belief the spirits will help the Mexicans and whisper words of encouragement into their ears. This I leaned from my father and his father."

"Then let's hope that it's so," Kellerman said.

"It will be so, Captain. Feel them around you; the good spirits are already here."

"I'm glad of your help, Ahiga," Lieutenant Atticus Cranston said.

"You had a woman in your arms," the Navajo said.

"It was Sara Lark. She's very afraid."

"Then it is good that you shared your courage with her."

Cranston managed a smile. "I have little courage to share."

"You are afraid?"

"Afraid? Yes, I suppose I am. Afraid of failure most of all."

"Any warrior, even great heroes, can be afraid. But when he swallows his fear, mounts his horse, and rides into the fight, he once again reveals his bravery."

"Thank you for the words of encouragement, Ahiga. If I could, I'd give you whiskey and water as Captain Kellerman does."

Then the rarest of the rare: a smile on the Navajo's lips. "I don't drink whiskey. I tried it once and it made my head spin. I vowed never again to taste its fire."

"I won't tell Captain Kellerman if you don't," Cranston said, returning the Indian's smile.

"Now let us inspect the Mexicans, Lieutenant."

The Navajo was angry and used the butt of his rifle to bully the Mexicans to their feet. "Stand to attention when your officer comes," he said.

Ahiga's voice was edged like sharpened steel, and he'd no need to shout. His savage, warlike appearance, so like an Apache, was enough to quell any rebelliousness the Mexicans might have felt, and, to a man, they quickly stood.

The Navajo inspected each man's saber, testing the edge, and then examined their mounts, angrily shoving on a chest or pounding a shoulder when he found something amiss. He then ordered the men to sit . . . and they sat.

When he returned to Lieutenant Cranston, he made a face and said, "They are not Navajo."

"Ahiga, we do the best with what we have," Cranston said. "The soldiers in the headquarters building are not the cream of the crop either."

"Cream of the crop? What is this?"

"It means they're not the best the army has."

"Maybe so, but they know how to fight. But Mexican peons . . . pah!"

"Come tomorrow, they'll fight and fight well."

"You have confidence in your . . ." then using a term he'd heard from Captain Kellerman, ". . . raggedy-asses."

Cranston bristled. "Yes, I have confidence in them, and watch your tongue, army scout. They are my command."

"Hah!" The Navajo nodded. "You are loyal and respectful to your men, and this is good."

"You're testing me, Ahiga."

"A test you passed, Lieutenant Cranston. I will be honored to fight beside you tomorrow."

"And I, you."

The Navajo stood to attention, his rifle sloped on his left shoulder. "Army scout reporting for inspection, sir."

Cranston played along. He closely studied Ahiga, examined his rifle and sheathed knife, and then nodded, "You pass inspection, army scout Ahiga. Well done."

"Thank you, sir," the Navajo said. He seemed pleased.

"I thought I heard a war drum beating in the distance of the night," Sara Lark said.

"It was your imagination, my dear," Mary Zimmermann said. "We're too far from the Lozado camp to hear a drum." The woman thumbed fat cartridges into a .44-caliber British Bull Dog revolver. "You were with Lieutenant Cranston tonight."

"Yes. I told him I was afraid."

"That was all?"

"Then I asked him to hold me, and he did. I told him you were afraid."

"The Virgin Mary afraid? Never."

"Why did you load the pistol?"

"To defend myself and you."

"Suppose they get in here to the infirmary?"

"Sara, I won't see you get raped by dozens of men. Or me."

"You'll shoot me and then yourself."

"That is my intention, and you already know that."

"I'm a coward, Mrs. Zimmermann."

"Tonight, there are no cowards here in Fort Misery. Every man . . . and woman . . . will do his or her duty, and you know yours."

"Help Dr. Stanton with the wounded and pretend to be brave. That's easy; whores know how to put on airs."

Mrs. Zimmermann placed the revolver in a desk drawer and then produced a bottle of whiskey from another. "How drunk do you want to get, Sara?"

"Pretty drunk."

"But not so drunk that you can't stand."

"No, not that drunk."

"All right then, let's work on it. It's going to be a long night."

CHAPTER 50

Santiago Lozado rode beside war chief Alchesay in the predawn darkness, his Comancheros and the Apache behind him, raising dust. The full moon had started its descent in the star-studded sky, and the desert air was cool in his mouth.

"A great day begins, Alchesay, my friend," Lozado said. "My dream of revenge will soon become reality."

"Today, you will wake from your dream, don Santiago, and see the red blood of your enemies," the Apache said.

"Oh, how their women will weep tonight when we drag them to our beds by the hair, trampling over the bodies of dead white men."

Alchesay laughed. "You are indeed a storyteller. I can see pictures in your words."

"Remember, my friend, my Comancheros will lead the assault, and when the enemy is weakened, you will attack. Spare no one except the women and Kellerman."

"Yes, that is how it will be. I understand you, don Lozado."

"Our numbers will overwhelm Kellerman. I have two or three times as many fighting men as he has." Lozado smiled. "How his knees will tremble when he sees us coming at him."

Behind the two leaders, the Comancheros and Apache talked among themselves, smiling, laughing, eager to take part in what would be an easy victory, a massacre guaranteed by the full moon that was now dropping in the sky among the fading stars.

Captain Joe Kellerman's pickets saw the coming dust cloud as a ghostly mist in the darkness and high-tailed it back to the headquarters building to report.

Kellerman quickly spread the word that the enemy was in sight and the drowsy soldiers stood to their weapons, all at once wide awake.

"Take your time and choose your targets," he said as he walked along the hallway. "They'll come on strong and almighty sudden."

"We're ready for them, Joe," a man called out.

"Who said that?" Kellerman said.

Another voice said, "It was Private Spiers, sir."

"Was that you, Spiers?" Kellerman said.

"Yes, sir, it was me."

"An extra ration of whiskey for you when this is over, Spiers, you villain," Kellerman said. "Don't let me forget."

"Don't worry, sir, I won't," Spiers said.

That brought a laugh from the soldiers, and it pleased Kellerman. He heard amusement, but no fear.

Santiago Lozado dismounted his Comancheros, but he and Kyle Swan and Roscoe Wolfe remained on horseback. As Lozado had ordered them, his men advanced in line through the gloom and then split into a V-shaped formation to encircle the headquarters building.

Kellerman heard muttering from his men that they couldn't see a damn thing, and the yet unborn morning remained stubbornly dark.

"Hold your fire," the captain said. "Don't shoot until you have a target."

Kellerman stared out into the murk, but it was like looking at a black-painted wall. He shook his head. What was Lozado up to?

Slow minutes ticked past without a shot fired. There was now a sense of unease around Kellerman. His soldiers couldn't shoot at an enemy they were unable to see. And then it came to him . . . Lozado's men couldn't see either. They were waiting for first light.

"Steady, men, steady," he said. "It will be dawn soon."

Time dragged on, unnerving, scraping nerves raw like fingernails drawn across a chalkboard. Kellerman realized he was breathing heavily and did his best to control himself. Damn it, would this darkness never leave? Somewhere close a bird sang, greeting the coming day, and a soldier coughed and coughed, a victim of one of the many lung diseases that afflicted every army post west of the Mississippi. Kellerman dropped a hand to his holstered Colt, a gesture that comforted him, at least momentarily. He badly needed a drink.

"Soon, my friends," Santiago Lozado said to Kyle Swan and Roscoe Wolfe. "When the shooting from the building falters and my Comancheros storm inside, you will go seek out Kellerman and bring him here to me."

"Depend on it," Swan said. "We'll bring him here."

"Kicking his ass all the way," Wolfe said, grinning.

"Hah, my friends, you always know how to amuse me," Lozado said.

"Look to the east, patrón," Swan said. "The dawn comes."

On the horizon a fan of light rose over the Altas Mountains, heralding the new morning.

"Then it begins," Lozado said. "And its beginning is the end of Captain high-and-mighty Kellerman." He drew his revolver and waited. Let the dawning grow a little brighter.

The night surrendered to the day and the light changed from black to gray. Lozado grinned, raised his Colt, and fired a shot in the direction of the headquarters building.

A split second later all hell broke loose.

Lozado had opened the festivities but it was Lieutenant James Hall who fired the shots that began the battle. A Comanchero, dressed in a vaquero's finery, let his curiosity get the better of him and, his rifle at the ready, he advanced too close to the window of the enlisted men's mess. Hall cut loose with both pistols, his bullets shattering glass before they slammed into the Comanchero's chest. The man fell away from the window and Hall yelled to the soldier beside him, "They're headed this way, you scoundrel! Get ready!"

Hall and his two troopers waited for the onslaught, but none came. The Comancheros seemed to be holding back, only now and then taking potshots at the building.

"Why don't they come in a rush?" Hall said to no one but himself.

"You shoot too good, sir," Corporal John Lockhart said. "They don't want the same medicine."

"Of course, they do, you ruffian. Before this day is out, they'll fear the name James Hall." He fired again at a fleeting figure in the distance and missed. "I winged that one," he said.

"I think you missed, sir," Lockhart said.

"No, I didn't miss. I never miss, you scalawag."

The corporal shouldered his rifle and fired, as did the other trooper. Bullets crashed into the mess, and outside men yelled bloodcurdling threats, shooting as they advanced on the mess window.

Hall unraveled a bullet, then another, and outside the Comancheros flattened to the ground and shot from a prone position. Corporal Lockhart got burned from a round and yelped, but to Hall's left a soldier's head erupted in blood and brain when a bullet smashed into his skull.

Hall, splashed by the man's blood, roared above the snare-drum rattle of gunfire, "Hot work, Corporal. Keep shooting, you damned scoundrel."

Lozado had blundered. By surrounding the building with his men, he'd stretched himself thin, and the volume of fire was not as great as he'd hoped. The return fire from Kellerman's men was steady, and he'd seen two of his Comancheros drop. Beside him Swan looked worried, and even Roscoe Wolfe seemed uneasy. The Apache were in line and moved forward a few yards, ready to charge when Alchesay gave the word. They were now just south of the stables.

A quick tour of his defenses told Kellerman that two soldiers had been killed defending the infirmary and another in the hallway. In addition, he had two men wounded and out of the fight. He immediately pulled Sergeant Major Olinger and his remaining men from the infirmary along with Mrs. Zimmermann, Sara Lark, and Dr. Stanton, and ushered the civilians into a windowless storeroom.

"Stay there until I tell you to come out," Kellerman said.

"I should be with the wounded," Stanton said.

"I've abandoned the infirmary, so there's nothing you can do."

"I can try," Stanton said. He dodged around Kellerman into the hallway and died instantly when a bullet caromed off the head of a board nail and crashed, tumbling, into his temple. He dropped at Kellerman's feet, and Mrs. Zimmermann screamed as she was splashed by the little man's blood and brain.

"Don't just stand there, girl, see to her," Kellerman said to the horrified Sara Lark.

He turned and hurried back to his position in the hallway, stepping over the bodies of dead men. The Comancheros' fire was beginning to take its toll, and already they'd used oil lamps to set the abandoned infirmary ablaze.

Kellerman shot at a man who was down on one knee in a firing position. A miss. He shot again, and the man threw up his arms and fell on his side.

"Good shooting Joe," Olinger said between thumbing off shots.

"Now we only have to kill a couple of dozen more," Kellerman said as bullets whined across the hallway and rattled into the timber-framed rooms behind.

The thrown-away soldiers performed well. Not a man left his post and they fired continuously, taking down attackers. But Comanchero bullets crashed into the building relentlessly, splintering wood and human bone, taking their toll.

"Joe, the noose is tightening around us," Sergeant Major Olinger said. "We can't afford many more losses. We're down to maybe fifteen men."

"Then we'll retreat out of this hallway. Saul, get the women into the enlisted men's mess with our remaining effectives. We can cover the mess window and doors and make a stand there."

"You men!" Olinger yelled above the firing din. "To the enlisted men's mess, all of you! Joe, are you coming?"

"Yes." Kellerman fired and then, wreathed in gun smoke, yelled, "Go! I'll follow."

THUD!

Something heavy slammed into the headquarters building's front double doors.

THUD!

The doors shivered on their hinges, the space between them growing to several inches. Kellerman stepped back. Lozado's men had found a battering ram, probably one of the hardwood logs from Tobias Zimmermann's workshop.

THUD!

The right door shattered, and its top hinge gave way, and Kellerman heard yells of triumph from the throats of the men outside. He snapped off two quick shots then beat a hasty retreat in the direction of the mess, one question uppermost in his mind . . . where the hell was Cranston?

CHAPTER 51

"Kellerman's door is down, and his defenses breached," Santiago Lozado said. "Now, my friends, it's time to find him and bring him to me."

"We'll find him, patrón," Kyle Swan said.

"Then let's have at it," Wolfe said, grinning. He was much pleased, his top hat at a jaunty angle. The firing from the building had suddenly lessened, and the man called Kellerman was done.

Lozado watched his two men ride to the building, dismount, and enter through the splintered opening left by the demolished door.

"Now friend Alchesay, the battle is won, and the spoils are yours," Lozado said.

The Apache smiled and nodded and rejoined his warriors. They did not charge but advanced at a walk, line abreast, wary of drawing gunfire from hidden soldiers. Then, when he was about twenty feet beyond the stables, Alchesay, a wary man, halted his men and studied the building. His young men yipped and held their rifles aloft, anxious for the attack. But still Alchesay hesitated. A stealth warrior by nature, he determined to wait until the defensive firing was reduced to a few rifles.

It was a tactical decision that would cost the Apache his life and Santiago Lozado the battle.

From the shadow of a horse stall, Lieutenant Atticus Cranston watched the Apache ride past in line and then draw rein, the man who appeared to be their leader riding a few yards ahead to study the headquarters building.

The realization hit Cranston like a thunderbolt . . . now was the time!

Cranston returned to his Mexicans, ordered them to mount, and Zimmermann, Bertrand, and Marshal Bowman did the same. There would be no opportunity to form a line. He would have to lead his men from behind the stables and attack the Apache in the rear like a spearhead. There was no time to lose, it had to be done that moment, and a lot was riding on the skill and bravery of his three pistoleros, the men who'd provide the firepower.

Cranston drew his saber and silently motioned his hussars forward. The only sound the fall of hooves and the creak of saddle leather, they rode at a walk around the gable end of the stable and then Cranston's resounding yell . . .

"CHARGE!"

The young lieutenant led the Mexicans at a gallop, their souls burning for vengeance. They formed a wedge without an order and crashed into the Apache, their sabers glittering in the morning light.

From his safe distance, Lozado saw what was happening and horrified, called out, "Nooo!"

His cry went unheard, but he had a ringside seat as he watched the slaughter of the Apache.

The Mexicans, driven by their intense desire to destroy a hated enemy, tore into the startled Apache, their sabers rising and falling, splitting heads open, gutting with the point, slashing with the edge, scarlet fans of bloodied dust erupting above the heads of the battling horsemen. Cranston slashed at an Apache, opening his face like a ripe melon, and then swung his horse around and saw a Mexican holding a slender warrior close, his teeth ripping into the man's throat. And above the din of the battle, came the steady, measured, hammering of Colts, his gunmen killing effortlessly, masters of their trade.

The Apache, trapped, with nowhere to run, fought back with savage ferocity, but the odds were stacked against them, and they knew they were fighting a losing battle. Warrior after warrior went down, sprawling in the dust, the screams of the wounded ringing in their dying ears.

The fight was over in a few minutes.

Alchesay was the last to die. He dispatched a Mexican with his lance and then rode into a bullet fired by Jim Bertrand that took him in the center of his chest, blew apart his heart, and toppled him dead from his horse.

Cranston quickly looked over the carnage but didn't hesitate.

"Headquarters!" he yelled, pointing to the building with his bloody saber. "At the charge!"

Five of his Mexicans lay dead in the dust, tangled in Apache bodies, and Buck Bowman stood aside, out of it, nursing a bloody gun hand, gazing at the wound with banjo eyes. The remainder galloped to the building and dismounted, except for three hussars who stayed mounted and rode through the shattered doorway, screaming like demons.

Inside was a scene of bloody chaos.

Lieutenant Cranston led his men into the hallway, avoiding his three mounted men who rode up and down at a canter, slashing at Lozado's Comancheros wherever they found them. Men shrieked and went down as sabers rose and fell, guns blazed, and the hurting dead were trampled underfoot, pools of blood slick on the wood floor. This was Zimmermann and Bertrand's kind of fight—up close and personal—and that morning their hammering revolvers beat out a legend, as man after man fell to their deadly expertise.

Kellerman led his men out of the enlisted men's mess and joined in the fray, charging into a charnel house. Even Lieutenant Hall got to his feet and staggered out of the mess, a gun in each hand as he looked for a target. But he found none. The fight was over, the battle won.

The surviving Comancheros fled for their lives, pursued by frenzied, blood-spattered Mexican peons who hacked at them mercilessly.

As Roscoe Wolfe and Kyle Swan made for the door, panicked, Swan recognized Jim Bertrand and stopped in his tracks, the surprised and scared Wolfe running past him.

Up until that moment, Swan had no idea that Jim Bertrand was one of the pistoleros Lozado ordered him to kill. He decided there and then to settle an old score that had festered like a cancer inside him for years.

After Swan killed Johnny Gusto in the Union saloon in Bisbee, Bertrand, then a young deputy marshal, had buffaloed him and dragged him by the scruff of his neck through a crowd of jeering townsfolk to the jailhouse. It was a humiliation that Kyle Swan had never forgotten or forgiven. And now the man who'd perpetrated the outrage was standing right in front of him.

"I've been looking for you, Bertrand," Swan said. He said it loud, challenging, a killer on the prod.

As Western men, everyone drew back, realizing this was shaping up to be a duelo between shootists, and even Kellerman didn't interfere.

"Howdy, Kyle, it's been a while," Bertrand said, smiling.

"I've waited a long time for this, Bertrand," Swan said, his reptilian eyes cold, staring.

"Don't even try it, Kyle," Bertrand said. "You were always fast with the blade but slow on the draw."

"I've learned a lot since then," Swan said. "I can shade you, Bertrand, any day of the week, any week of the year."

"And I got a feeling you're about to try."

Swan's mouth stretched into the pitiless grin of an alligator. "Now take your last breath as a living man and get to your work."

Swan's hand, a brown claw with stubby, broken fingernails, dropped to his gun. He was still leveling the revolver when Bertrand's bullet crashed into his chest . . . then he took another, a half-inch to the right of the first. The gun dropped from Swan's hand, and he looked at Bertrand in open-mouthed surprise and whispered, "My God, that was sudden."

Bertrand nodded. "I told you so, Kyle."

Swan never heard that last. He died a split second too soon.

CHAPTER 52

Lieutenant Atticus Cranston didn't witness the Bertrand shootout. He'd been with his Mexicans chasing down the few Comancheros who were still alive. But he did see Roscoe Wolfe run in the direction of a big-bellied man sitting a silver saddle who held the reins of Wolfe's mount. Cranston realized that the fat man astride a flashy palomino could only be Santiago Lozado, and the running man one of his captains. He saw the pair flee the field and decided that he could not let them escape—not after the carnage and destruction they'd caused.

Cranston caught up a loose horse and went after them.

Lozado and the other man seemed to be heading directly for their camp, no doubt to pick up water and some of their ill-gotten gains. His guess was they'd then turn south for Sonora and safety.

Cranston wasn't about to let that happen. It was a foolhardy play on the lieutenant's part, but he didn't give the consequences a second thought. It was his duty, just as West Point had taught him, and he had it to do.

After a few minutes Lozado turned in the saddle to check his back trail and saw a lone pursuer coming after him. He drew his gun and fired through a haze of dust, a shot that went nowhere. The other man glanced over his shoulder but held his fire. Around them were no hills, not even sand dunes—just endless flat, tawny desert under the bleached blue sky. Cranston had his Colt in his hand but didn't shoot, distance and a laboring horse guaranteeing bad marksmanship. Not so the possibly panicking Lozado, who fired again and again, his shots having not the slightest effect.

Then, for Santiago Lozado, tragedy.

His horse, for no apparent reason, stumbled and, head down, pitched forward, throwing its rider from the saddle. As a stunned Lozado lay on his back in the sand, the other rider saw what had happened and drew rein. He turned and saw Cranston coming on at a gallop and quickly swung out of the saddle. The tall, bearded man wearing an old Confederate greatcoat and gray top hat, advanced to meet Cranston, drawing a pair of Walker Colts.

The young officer reined in his mount and fired, kicking up an abrupt V of sand about three feet from Wolfe's left boot. The man came on, seemingly unconcerned, closing the distance, guaranteeing a kill.

BLAM!

Cranston saw Wolfe's surprise as his back arched and he raised up on his toes after the bullet hit him squarely between the shoulder blades. All the life went out of the man's face, and he fell forward and slammed into the sand, his top hat rolling away from him.

"Don't shoot, soldier," Lozado yelled. "I killed him for you." He pointed his gun at the sky and pulled the trigger. Click! "See, no more bullets, soldier. I surrender."

"Drop the pistol," Cranston said. "Now get to your feet."

"Soldier, I have money. Let me go and it's yours."

The lieutenant looked down at Wolfe. The man was

dead. The side of Lozado's beautiful horse was covered in blood; it looked as though the palomino had taken a bullet at Fort Misery but had managed to run for a couple of miles before it dropped dead. Cranston used the back of his gun hand to wipe sweat from his eyes and then trained the Colt on Lozado. The man was ugly, coarse, and cringing.

"I have enough in gold to make you rich, soldier," he said. "I'll show you the way."

Cranston said nothing.

"Ah, my friend, soldier, I see you think about it. We can come to an agreement, you and me. Such a simple solution to our little problem. I go free, and you get rich."

"I'm deciding whether I should shoot you or take you back to the fort to hang."

"No, soldier, have mercy on poor Lozado. I saved your life. Roscoe Wolfe would've killed you."

"Maybe. Now catch up his horse. You're coming with me."

Lozado shuffled toward Cranston. "Gold, soldier. As much as you can carry."

The lieutenant shook his head. "I'd rather see you hang."

"All right, friend soldier, then I can't persuade you to take my offer. I'll come with you."

But Lozado didn't turn. He sidled toward the standing horse like a bloated crab. An odd way of walking. . . .

He didn't want to turn his back!

The significance of that was almost lost on Cranston, and it very nearly cost him his life.

Lozado's right arm moved behind him with lightning speed and he came up with a Remington .41 caliber derringer. His presentation was good, smooth, and practiced, but at a range of ten yards the derringer didn't perform like a target pistol. Both men fired at the same time. Lozado missed, but Cranston scored a hit, and the Mexican went down, clutching at his belly, his face contorted with pain.

"Oh, mother of God, you've killed don Santiago," he said, through clenched teeth.

"You're not a hidalgo, you're a raggedy-assed Mexican peasant," Cranston said, suddenly angry. "My bullet was for a girl named Maria, remember her?"

Lozado screeched in agony. "I don't remember. Help me. Help me, soldier."

"You're beyond help. You'll die like a dog in a few hours, maybe a few days, I don't know," Cranston said. He picked up the dropped derringer, checked the remaining live round, and then threw the little pistol as far as he could into the desert. "When the pain gets really bad, maybe you can find that and end yourself."

Cranston leaned from the saddle and gathered up the reins of Wolfe's horse.

"You can't leave me here, soldier," Lozado said. "Take me to the fort. I need a doctor."

"Her name was Maria. Now do you remember her?"

Lozado's breath came in short gasps, and he was gripped by intense, scorching pain as his belly dumped bile into the peritoneal cavity. "She was a slut. . . ."

"She was a virgin, looking forward to getting married. Because of you, Lozado, she hanged herself."

"Kill me! Kill me! Don't leave me here, soldier. The pain is unbearable."

"So was Maria's pain, unbearable."

"Mercy! Mercy for poor don Santiago."

Cranston shook his head. "I have none to give, Lozado. All you can do now is die."

The lieutenant rode away, leaving a shrieking, screaming man behind him.

He glanced at the sky, where a few cumulus clouds had begun their drift to the west, looking like great sailing ships urged on by a fair wind, eager to reach port. Ahead of him a gray pall of smoke hung in the air, a dark shroud for the burning infirmary. The morning was hot and as clear as glass.

CHAPTER 53

Lieutenant Atticus Cranston rode into a scene of devastation.

The infirmary burned and dead Comancheros and Apache still littered the ground. The bodies of eleven soldiers and eight Mexican hussars had been laid out on the headquarters building porch, and nearby Mrs. Zimmermann and Sara Lark did their best to attend to the wounded. For all intents and purposes, Fort Misery's garrison had ceased to exist as a fighting unit.

Captain Joe Kellerman and Sergeant Major Olinger stood talking on the parade ground, watching the infirmary burn, when Cranston dismounted and reported.

"Where the hell were you, Lieutenant?" Kellerman said. His blouse was stained with the blood of his soldiers, and he looked strained, his eyes staring as though into a great distance. "I figured you were dead for sure."

"Sir, Lozado and a man named Wolfe escaped," Cranston said. "I went after them."

"And?" Kellerman said.

"Lozado killed Wolfe, and I shot Lozado."

"Is Lozado dead?"

"Not yet. But he will be." And then choosing the most

offensive words he could find, "I gut shot him, sir. He'll die out there in the desert . . . eventually."

"One for Maria," Kellerman said, as though reading the younger man's mind.

"Yes, sir. And I told him so."

"Well done, Lieutenant," Olinger said. "And you handled your cavalry unit perfectly."

"Thank you, Sergeant Major. How many did I lose?"

"Eight dead and the same number wounded."

"More than half my command."

Kellerman nodded. "They performed well, every one of them."

"A high butcher's bill, sir," Cranston said.

"It was a hard-fought battle," Olinger said. "Your charge saved the day."

Cranston nodded but said nothing.

"Come to my office, Lieutenant," Kellerman said. "You look like you could use a drink. Lieutenant Hall is already there, telling everybody how he won the Battle of Fort Misery."

"I could use a drink, sir," Cranston said. "I feel all in."

"Every soldier on this post is exhausted, me included," Kellerman said. "It was a long night and a bitter fight."

"How many of Lozado's men were killed?"

"Including Apache, we count forty, and a number fled the field. There were no wounded."

"There never are, sir," Cranston said.

"No, Lieutenant, there never are. Now, a drink with you and we'll listen to Lieutenant Hall's tales of his derring-do. He figures he should be promoted to major after all this."

"What the deuce! Lieutenant Cranston, you're still alive," Lieutenant Hall said.

"He killed Santiago Lozado," Captain Kellerman said.

"Well he's not quite dead yet, but he will be fairly soon," Cranston said.

"Then bully for you, dear fellow!" Hall said. "Have a pinch."

"Lieutenant, he's here for a drink, not snuff," Kellerman said.

"Ah well, your loss Lieutenant Cranston," Hall said.

Kellerman poured whiskey and said, "Sergeant Major Olinger, we've barely enough men to bury the dead."

"The soldiers are exhausted, sir. With your permission, we'll climb that hurdle tomorrow."

"Drag the enemy bodies far into the desert is my advice," Hall said. "We bury only our own dead at Fort Misery." Then, revealing how the high casualties had shaken him, "Damn that Lozado cur to hell."

"I imagine he's already there, sir," Cranston said. He downed his whiskey and held out his glass for another."

"Me too, sir, if you please," Hall said. Then, "Watch your drinking, Atticus."

Mrs. Zimmermann knocked on the door and came inside. She looked tired, older. "Captain Kellerman, my food supplies are very low," she said. "And the Mexicans have gone, leaving their dead behind."

"They've what?" Kellerman said. He stepped to the window and looked outside. "You're right, they've pulled out."

"They say they're going home to Sonora," Mrs. Zimmermann said.

"Across the desert without water?" Cranston said,

"They filled the canteens they took from Lozado's dead," Mrs. Zimmermann said.

"I'd say they earned the water," Kellerman said. "But it's a long walk to Sonora."

"Yes, and some of them are wounded or sick and will die

on the way," Mrs. Zimmermann said. "But they'll die as free men and women."

"God help them," Hall said.

"Mrs. Zimmermann, I'll send a wagon to Devil's Rock early tomorrow," Kellerman said. "But don't get your hopes up."

The woman's smile was slight, there and gone. "Fort Misery is the death of hope, Captain. I never get my hopes up about anything."

"Now Lozado is gone, it will get better," Kellerman said.

"Then I'll pray that it does. If God still listens to me."

Buck Bowman found Jim Bertrand grooming a tall American sorrel in the stables. "Going somewhere?"

"Not yet."

"Maybe not ever," Bowman said.

"Maybe."

"I heard you killed a man in a gunfight this morning."

"You heard right," Bertrand said, looking over the horse's back, brush in hand.

"You got a name for him? He might be kin of mine."

"He was a no-account out of Bisbee by the name of Kyle Swan. He favored a blade but was handy with a Colt's gun."

"One of Lozado's boys, of course."

"Yeah, he rode for Lozado. But Swan and I went back a ways."

"He needed killing, huh?"

"Few men need killing, Marshal, but if anyone deserved it, Kyle Swan was his name."

"Answer me this: What will I do with you, Bertrand?"

"I won't let you take me back to Yuma."

"You'd kill me."

"I don't know. What happened to your hand?"

"Thumb blown clean off. Thanks to Mrs. Zimmermann I'm full of laudanum."

"Your right thumb. Is that your gun hand?"

"Sure is."

"Maybe you can learn to shoot with your left."

"I heard in a gun store in Yuma there's a rumor going around that pretty soon Colt will come out with a self-cocker. But I don't know if it's true or not."

Bertrand smiled. "A self-cocking revolver? That's never going to happen."

"No, I guess not. Well, let's keep in touch, Bertrand. Don't be a stranger."

CHAPTER 54

"You have flecks of green in your eyes," Sara Lark said. "I never noticed that before."

As she'd done before, the woman sat on the corner of Lieutenant Atticus Cranston's bed while he occupied the tub chair.

He smiled. "I'm glad you came by. I didn't feel like reading tonight."

"Mrs. Zimmermann told me you killed Santiago Lozado."

"Yes, I did. The world is a better place without him."

"You really helped me last night, Lieutenant . . ."

"Atticus."

"You shared your strength with me. I'm glad it was you who killed Lozado, my West Pointer. Till the day I die, you'll always be my knight in shining armor."

"In tarnished armor, Sara. I shot Lozado in the belly and left him to die in the desert."

"He inflicted a lot of suffering on others, including myself. He got what he deserved."

"Sara, you really didn't come here to pass time with me, did you?"

"I like being with you, Atticus."

"But that's not the reason."

"No, it's not."

"So tell me."

"Jim Bertrand wants me to leave here with him."

"Do you want to?"

"I'm a whore."

"You're not a whore now. Does Bertrand know?"

"Yes, I told him. He says it makes no difference. He says he's a gambler, so we're a king and queen from the same grubby deck."

Cranston smiled. "Do you love him?"

"No."

"Does he love you?"

"I don't know."

"Given time you could learn to love one another. Just don't give up today, Sara, because it could all work out tomorrow."

"I'd like to take a chance on him, but I'm afraid."

"Of what?"

"Failure I guess."

"Jim Bertrand is a brave man, and as far as I can tell, an honorable one. I think you and he could make that a possibility."

A smile lightly touched Sara's lips. "The gambler and the whore growing old together. What are the chances?"

"Better than no chance at all."

"And then there's Buck Bowman to consider. He wants to take Jim back to Yuma."

"Bertrand fought bravely for this fort, so Captain Kellerman will have a say in that matter."

"I don't want Marshal Bowman to get hurt. He's already wounded, and he can't match Jim in a gunfight. If Jim killed him, it would be a terrible way to start a new life together. I can't let that happen."

"I'll talk to Marshal Bowman and sound him out,"

Cranston said. "I can't promise anything, but I'll tell you what he has to say."

"You'll do that for me?"

"Of course. For the both of you."

"Atticus, can a former whore find happiness with the man like Jim Bertrand?"

"Yes, I'm sure of it. Maybe one day I'll dance at your wedding."

To Lieutenant Cranston's surprise, just minutes after Sara Lark left his now bullet-riddled quarters, Marshal Buck Bowman knocked on his door.

"I just saw Sara Lark leave," Bowman said.

"Come in," Cranston said. "You're visiting late."

Taking up a lot of space in the cramped room, the marshal consulted his watch. "It's only eight thirty, not so late, Lieutenant. I guess you West Pointers go to bed early, huh?"

Cranston ignored that and said, "I've only got one chair, but you're welcome to sit in it."

"What I have to say, I'll say standing up."

"Is it about Sara and Jim Bertrand?"

"It is."

"Maybe you should talk to Captain Kellerman."

"Has the girl spoken with him?"

"I don't think so."

"Then you'll do for the time being."

"What do you want to talk about, Marshal?"

"Duty, Lieutenant Cranston, duty. The lawman who neglects his duty is not entitled to his rights as a lawman or a citizen. Do you understand me?"

"Perfectly. This is about Jim Bertrand, isn't it?"

"It is."

"You want to take him back to Yuma?"

"Did I say that?"

"No, you didn't—not so far."

Bowman took a sharp intake of breath and said, "The stump of my thumb hurts. Mrs. Zimmermann's laudanum is wearing off."

"You should be resting, Marshal."

"Plenty of time to rest later. Now listen to this, Lieutenant. I'll tell you a story."

"Marshal, I'm dog tired," Cranston said. "Tell me the story some other time."

"It won't take long. Are you ready?"

"I guess so."

"Suppose there is this lawman whose sworn duty is to take an escaped convicted felon back to the penitentiary. Now this lawman is conflicted because the felon, let's call him Tom, is a brave man who saved lives by fighting honorably in a great battle. Are you with me so far?"

"Yes, Marshal. Tell away."

"Now Tom meets this woman, and they plan to run away together and start a new life together. Ah, do we see what the lawman's dilemma is? If he does his sworn duty and takes Tom back to the pen, he destroys not one, but two lives, the other being that of the innocent woman of course. So, Lieutenant, what course does the lawman take? He must do what's right or lose his honor. Is that not so?"

"Yes, Marshal Bowman, I think it is."

"Now here's the rub: Let's suppose the lawman seeks out the advice of a young army officer he respects . . ."

"Thank you," Cranston said.

". . . and asks him where his duty lies."

"I expect the army officer would say that he must do his duty as a human being, not as a lawman."

"Then the lawman would need to ponder that answer before he decides on a course of action."

"And the army officer would hope he makes the right decision."

Bowman nodded. "Well, it's been a pleasure talking to you, Lieutenant Cranston. "Now I have to go in search of Mrs. Zimmermann." He smiled. "The fact is, I'm in a great deal of pain."

"External and internal, I imagine."

"Yes, Lieutenant. Both."

CHAPTER 55

It was still a couple of hours shy of noon when Corporal Lockhart returned to Fort Misery with an empty wagon and a long face.

"No supplies at Devil's Rock, Captain," he told Joe Kellerman, who stood with Sergeant Major Olinger on the body-littered parade ground.

"Damn it, now is the army trying to starve us to death?" Kellerman said.

"It would solve a lot of problems for them," Sergeant Major Saul Olinger said.

"I have one more thing to report, sir," Lockhart said.

"Then out with it, man," Kellerman said, his irritation with the army showing.

"Sir, big dust cloud to the west," Lockhart said. "It seems to be heading this way."

"Damn it, not more Comancheros or Apache?" Kellerman said.

"I wouldn't know, sir," the corporal said.

"Sergeant Major, where is the Navajo?"

"He's among the walking wounded, sir," Olinger said. "I'll get him."

Ahiga showed up with a bandage on his left arm,

sharing space with the barrel of his Henry. He answered Kellerman's unasked question. "Apache lance. It's not a serious wound."

"Ahiga, there's a dust cloud headed this way. Take a scout that way and find out what's causing it."

The Navajo nodded and left to get his horse.

"What now, sir?" Olinger said.

"Hell if I know," Kellerman said. He turned and stared at the officer's quarters, a flat-roofed adobe building, the same color as the surrounding desert. It had three adjoining rooms of unequal size, but each had a small, rectangular window front and back and a door overhung by a blue-painted, timber portico substituting for a porch. "We'll defend from there," Kellerman said, pointing. "Get Mr. Zimmermann and a few men to knock holes in the adjoining walls so we can come and go."

"What about the wounded and the two women?"

"We'll take them with us, and the priest, Father Stazc . . . Stac . . ."

"Staszczyk," Olinger supplied.

"Yes, him. He did well with dying soldiers during the battle."

"It's going to be crowded in there, sir," the sergeant major said.

"Saul, it's going to be mighty hot and mighty dangerous, like wading in quicksand over the fires of hell. What do you think of that, Corporal Lockhart?"

"Sir, I don't like it one bit."

"Neither do I, Corporal. Neither do I."

But the Navajo returned with good news. The dust cloud was raised by a troop of buffalo soldiers and a couple of wagons, not an enemy.

The officer in command was Major William Stone. His tanned face looked like it had been cast in bronze and then polished almost free of wrinkles, and his eyes were large and dark, crowned by heavy white brows that matched the color of the hair showing under his campaign hat. Heavy sideburns framed a large, Roman nose and a wide, expressive mouth. He looked around him with some distaste, as though someone held a rotted fish to his nostrils, and he sat his horse with the arrogant air of a medieval grandee.

"Captain Kellerman, I presume," he said. "Major William Stone, Tenth Cavalry, at your service." He looked around at the still-unburied dead and said, "You've been through it, Captain."

Kellerman nodded, "Yes, sir, you could say that."

He told Stone about his ongoing fights with the slave-trader Santiago Lozado and the culminating battle when he attacked the fort.

"You did well, Captain," the major said. "Believe me, I'll make sure General Sherman knows about it. That will make him wake up and take notice."

"Thank you, sir. You can tell him it was a close-run thing."

"Yes, I can see that," Stone said. "On a happier note, I've brought you supplies and reinforcements. Only ten men, I'm afraid. We're stretched pretty thin on the frontier."

"So I believe, sir."

"Can we talk in your office?" Stone's eyes moved to the shot-up headquarters. "That is, if you still have an office."

"A few bullet holes in the walls, Major. But it will serve."

"Excellent." He turned in the saddle, and said, "Captain Rising."

A youngish officer with a full beard to rival that of

Lieutenant Hall's, drew rein next to the major and saluted, "Yes, sir?"

"Dismount the men and have them prepare their noon meal. And Captain, you might want to distance the troop from this place. It stinks of dead Apache."

"Yes, sir. And what about the prisoners?"

"They're now Captain Kellerman's responsibility. He can feed them."

"Prisoners, sir?" Kellerman said. "I thought you said reinforcements."

"The prisoners are your reinforcements, Captain."

"I'll see to them, Captain Kellerman," Sergeant Major Olinger said.

"Be careful, Sergeant Major," Stone said. "Some of those men are desperate, dangerous characters."

"We had a few of those, sir. They died defending this post."

Kellerman introduced his officers to Major Stone who was quite solicitous about Lieutenant Hall's wound. "You're very pale. Are you fit for duty, Lieutenant?"

"Not quite, sir. But I'll be as fit as a fiddle in a couple of weeks."

"Despite his wound, Lieutenant Hall fought bravely in defense of Fort Benjamin Grierson against Santiago Lozado," Kellerman said. "He is to be commended."

"That's first rate, Lieutenant," Stone said. "I hadn't thought to find . . ."

Suddenly he looked confused. "I mean . . ."

"You hadn't thought to find an officer of Lieutenant Hall's caliber at Fort Misery," Kellerman said. He said it flat, without emotion.

"Please let me unsay that, Captain," Stone said. "It was thoughtless and unprofessional of me."

"Think nothing of it, Major," Hall said. "Water under the bridge. Gammon and spinach, as Mr. Dickens is wont to say. Of course, one likes to hear that one's bravery is being recognized. Would you care for a pinch of snuff?"

"I don't mind if I do," Stone said. "Clears the head, I always say."

Surprised, Hall passed his box, and the major placed a dip in both nostrils, sneezed, and then said, "Good stuff, Lieutenant."

"Thank you, sir. It's Garrett's best, you know, made in the great city of Philadelphia."

"I'm shocked that you can get it all the way out here in the desert."

"One's fond mama will always find a way, sir."

"Ah, quite. And if I'm not mistaken, here is a lady with coffee."

"I thought you might enjoy a cup after your long ride . . ." Mrs. Zimmermann glanced at Stone's shoulder straps ". . . Major."

As the woman poured coffee, Stone said, "You've gone through a harrowing experience, dear lady."

"We all have," Mrs. Zimmermann said, "Soldiers and civilians alike."

"Yes, indeed. The bodies on the ground attest to that. There should be a medal for brave civilians."

"Major, God will present all good Christians with shining medals after we enter the gates of heaven."

"Yes, I'm sure He will, and bully for Him, I say."

After Mrs. Zimmermann left, Major Stone tried his coffee, grimaced, and then opened the folder he'd carried in with him. He passed a sealed envelope to Kellerman and said, "Your orders from General Sherman, Captain. You may want to read them aloud for the benefits of your officers. . . . And you are?" This to Cranston.

"Second Lieutenant Atticus Cranston, sir."

"Lieutenant Cranston distinguished himself in a cavalry action during the battle," Kellerman, said, thumbing the envelope open.

Stone said, "Ah, yes, Cranston, I heard about you in Yuma, Lieutenant, a West Pointer mistakenly sent to the wrong post. Well, no matter, you may return to Yuma with me, and we'll get it all sorted out. Your orders, Captain Kellerman? I was ordered to make sure they were understood."

Kellerman opened a single sheet of paper and read aloud:

"'To Captain Peter Joseph Kellerman.

You are hereby requested and required to end the conditions of banditry, rapine, and murder along the river between the Arizona Territory south of Yuma and the Mexican state of Sonora. When caught, these people must be dealt with severely.' Then, written in a different hand, 'Joe, I want something done to stop this lawlessness. Go ahead on your own plan of action and your authority and backing will be myself and President Grant.' And it's signed William T. Sherman, General of the Army."

Kellerman leaned back in his chair. "Short, sweet, and to the point."

"Captain, do you understand your orders?" Major Stone said.

"Yes, sir, I do. But isn't that what we've been doing for the last couple of years?"

"It seems the trouble is now centered on the Rio Bravo. Mexican and American outlaws coming and going, raising hell on each side of the border," Stone said.

"I'll patrol that way, sir," Kellerman said.

"And now you have more men to do it," Stone said. "Here is a list of your reinforcements." He passed a sheet of paper to Kellerman. "Read 'em and weep, Captain."

The list didn't make inspiring reading for Kellerman.

> Connor Johnstone. Desertion
> Daniel Williamson. Desertion
> Michael Harper. Robbery with violence
> Martin Harris. Embezzlement
> Bill Clarke. Rape
> Jack Floyd. Cowardice
> Frank Katz. Nuisance
> Nelson Hare. Desertion
> Stuart White. Insubordination
> Howard Westcott. Habitual drunkenness

"Do with them what you can, Captain," Stone said. "They're all volunteers in that they chose a posting to Fort Benjamin Grierson."

"Instead of the penitentiary," Kellerman said.

"Quite so," Stone said. "Now that our business is concluded, I'll help you bury your honored dead. We'll let the desert deal with the others."

"I'd appreciate that, Major," Kellerman said. "Digging a mass grave in sand is a chore for the two men I have on that detail."

"Yes, I understand," Stone said. "Then, Lieutenant Cranston, be ready to leave after the burying is done."

"Sir, I'd rather stay where I am," Cranston said.

Stone was shocked. "Stay here, the back end of nowhere? Lieutenant, you're a graduate of the Point, as I am."

"And me," Lieutenant Hall said. "I quite distinguished

myself when I was there. But Lieutenant Cranston must make his own decision."

"There's no room for promotion at this post, Lieutenant Cranston," Stone said. "Captain Kellerman, talk some sense into your subordinate."

"Major, Lieutenant Cranston is a grown man and an excellent officer," Kellerman said. "I can't make his decisions for him."

"Advice, then, surely?" Stone said.

"Advice? Lieutenant Cranston, shake the dust of Fort Misery off your feet and run, don't walk, to your original posting at Fort Concho."

"Sir, I've thought about it, and my duty is to remain here until the Rio Bravo bandits are dealt with. To turn tail and run away now would impugn my honor."

Major Stone shook his head. "Can I believe what I'm hearing? You're ruining your career, young man."

"I'll take that chance, sir."

Stone sighed. "Then it's up to you. Lieutenant Hall, as a West Point graduate, do you have an opinion on this?"

"Sir, I taught this young officer everything he knows about soldiering, and I've much still to teach him. He may not grow in rank at Fort Misery, but right now as a cavalryman he stands head and shoulders above any second lieutenant you'd care to name. Let the boy reach full manhood here and then you can take him to Fort Concho. In a few years he'll outrank us all. Another pinch, sir?"

"Yes, thank you, I will," Stone said. "It's very good for the brain, you know."

"Indeed, it is, sir. I owe much of my superior intelligence to Garrett's best."

Stone sneezed and then said, "One last appeal, Lieutenant Cranston: Will you return to Yuma with me?"

"No, sir, I prefer to remain where I am."

"Then on your head be it. Captain Kellerman, shall we organize the burial detail? Unfortunately I have no chaplain with me."

Kellerman said, "Sir, we have a Catholic priest right here on the post, Father Stac . . . Father Stazc . . ."

"Father Staszczyk," Lieutenant Hall supplied.

"Yes," Kellerman said, "him."

"And Mrs. Zimmermann, a living saint," Hall said.

Stone nodded. "Well, Mrs. Zimmermann and Father Stazc . . . Stac . . ."

"Father Staszczyk," Hall supplied again.

"Can say the prayers for the dead," the major said.

The mass grave for the dead soldiers and Mexicans was deep, reaching slabs of bedrock in a few places. When it was covered up again with desert sand, it looked like no one was buried there. The priest and Mrs. Zimmermann said prayers for the dead, and Tobias Zimmermann marked the place with a large wooden cross he'd painted white. Since Major Stone had brought food supplies but no ammunition there was no salute. Soldiers like Joe Kellerman and Sergeant Major Olinger, who'd fought in the War Between the States and had seen huge mass graves before, thought the ceremony well done, but the younger men, including Lieutenant Atticus Cranston, were badly affected and stood grim and silent as shadows at the graveside, an expression of that-could've-been-me on their faces. But before the mourners dispersed an eagle flew over the grave, and the Navajo told everyone it was a bird of good omen and meant the dead were now one with their god. And that seemed to make everyone feel better, even Mrs. Zimmermann who usually didn't hold with such heathen notions.

* * *

Major William Stone stuck out a gauntleted hand. "Captain Kellerman, it was a pleasure meeting you. You have my admiration."

Kellerman shook his hand. "Thank you, sir."

Captain Rising drew rein beside Kellerman and said, "Captain, we dragged your enemy dead a good distance. You won't be troubled by them."

Kellerman nodded. "The desert will take care of them."

"Mummify them, I should imagine," Rising said.

"What the animals and the buzzards don't eat," Kellerman said.

"Harsh country, Captain," Stone said.

"The desert is unforgiving, Major."

"Well, we'll be on our way, Captain Kellerman. Take care."

Kellerman and Sergeant Major Olinger watched the troop ride away in column of twos under a Third Cavalry guidon. The sky was lemon yellow, free of cloud, the sands hot under the declining sun. There was dust in the air, kicked up by the troop, carried on faint puffs of a breeze coming from the west—that and the lingering, acrid tang of burned black powder.

"I got to admit, buffalo soldiers have style," Olinger said.

"A fine-looking troop. I wish I'd had them yesterday morning."

"Joe, Lieutenant Cranston's hussars would've put them to shame."

"Damn right they would," Kellerman said, smiling for the first time that day. "Now, shall we sample the whiskey that's just arrived?"

"Sir, I thought you'd never ask," Olinger said.

CHAPTER 56

At the laid plates on the table in the officers' mess, Mrs. Zimmermann beamed. "Gentlemen, salt beef, potatoes, and peas for starters, and plum duff with molasses for dessert. Duff with plenty of raisins, let me add."

"Mrs. Zimmermann, this is a veritable feast, a spread that Cleopatra might once have laid in front of Caesar. Despite my terrible wounds, I plan to do it justice," Lieutenant Hall said.

"It does look good, Mrs. Zimmermann," Lieutenant Cranston said.

"Atticus, you've lost weight since you arrived at Fort Misery," Captain Joe Kellerman said. "So eat hearty."

"Indeed, he has, sir," Hall said around a mouthful of beef. "But I must say that Lieutenant Cranston's mustache is coming along nicely. I've watched its progress with a fatherly eye."

"I noticed that too," Kellerman said. He stroked his own cavalry mustache with the back of his forefinger. "I swear, it will soon rival this beauty."

Cranston smiled. "I have a long way to go, sir."

Hall said. "Ah, yes, modesty. I like that in a man. I'd say that modesty is one of my own finer attributes. I never boast of my courage, my intelligence, or my fine beard, though I could. As an impartial observer, isn't that right, Sergeant Major Olinger?"

"Yes, sir, I've never heard you utter a boastful word," Olinger said, his face straight.

"Bully! You hit the nail right on the head," Hall said. "You will never hear a boastful utterance leave these lips of mine. Please pass the potatoes, Atticus. And once again learn from my great wisdom."

Kellerman dropped words into the following silence. "As you can see, we have guests in the mess tonight."

"Yes, Marshal Bowman and Mr. Bertrand, welcome to the officers' mess," Hall said. "Please try the peas, they're tip-top."

"You'll be leaving us soon, Marshal," Kellerman said.

"And you, too, Mr. Bertrand," Hall said.

"Yes, very soon," the gambler said.

"I'm very glad you were here, both you and Marshal Bowman," Kellerman said. "You both played a major part in our victory over Lozado and his rabble."

"Glad to be of help," Bowman said. He was a very neat eater, not a morsel of food soiling his mustache.

"And like me, the marshal suffered a grievous wound," Hall said.

"Lost my right thumb," Bowman said. "That's why I'm eating with my left."

"Unless Colt comes up with a self-cocker, I'd say your days as a lawman are over, Buck," Bertrand said.

"Then I'll enter politics. I'll be right at home among rogues."

That last made Bertrand smile.

"I haven't heard anything about a Colt self-cocker," Kellerman said.

"It's a rumor making the rounds in Yuma," Bowman

said. "All you'd have to do is pull the trigger, and the pistol does the rest."

"Handy, I suppose," Hall said. "But it's not a revolver I'd use." He chewed pensively. "Still, I could do great execution with a brace of those."

"Yes, I suspect it would get shots off faster," Lieutenant Cranston said.

"And you, Mr. Bertrand—what will you do when you leave here?" Kellerman said.

"As of now, I don't know," Bertrand said.

It was Hall who asked the question that was on everyone's mind. "I rather fancy your future depends on Marshal Bowman," he said.

It was a conversation stopper . . . until the lawman said, "We'll see."

Mrs. Zimmermann's plum duff was deemed a great success, and after everyone had eaten, Lieutenant Hall was prevailed upon to sing "Pat Murphy of the Irish Brigade," and afterward everyone, soldiers, and civilians alike, dog tired, sought their cots.

But Captain Joe Kellerman lingered after Sergeant Major Olinger asked if he could have a word.

"What's on your mind, Saul?" Kellerman said.

"Jim Bertrand."

"What about him? No, don't tell me, I know. Do we let Marshal Bowman take him to Yuma or not?"

"He fought bravely for us, Joe."

"I know he did." He poured whiskey into glasses. "But so did every other man of my command, some of them now laying out there under sand. Bertrand knew he was fighting for his life."

"I think he deserves a better fate than Yuma penitentiary."

"And we deserved a better fate than Fort Misery. Saul, he murdered a man."

"No, sir, he killed a man in a saloon fight. It wasn't murder."

"Saul, what do you want me to do? I can't usurp Buck Bowman's authority and free his prisoner. Hell, I could end up in Yuma myself."

"I talked to Bowman."

"And what did he say?"

"He wouldn't give me a straight answer. You know Sara Lark wants to leave with Bertrand."

"Yes, I heard that." Kellerman took a sip from his glass. "Talking about better fates . . . she doesn't deserve Fort Misery."

"No she doesn't, and Bertrand wants to take her away from here."

"And be his woman?"

"That's the straight of it."

Kellerman shook his head. "Saul, she could be trading one hell for another."

"I don't think so. I believe Bertrand would treat her right."

"Marshal Bowman is pulling out tomorrow. He urgently needs treatment for his hand. We'll wait and see what happens."

"Yeah, I guess that's all we can do," Olinger said.

"How are the new men settling in?"

"They've been quiet so far—a bunch of hard cases who know they've fallen in with another bunch of hard cases, except our hard cases fought to save this fort."

"Well, there's logic in there someplace," Kellerman said. He smiled. "Turn in, old warhorse, and get some sleep."

"And you too, sir. You too."

CHAPTER 57

The dawn made a spectacle of itself. It bannered the
sky with streaks of red, stained a few clouds deep
purple, and changed the light from black to tarnished silver.
The air held onto some of the night's coolness, and there
was no breeze, the rampant rooster on top of the stables
motionless.

Lieutenant Atticus Cranston was officer of the day,
and as he drank a cup of coffee in the kitchen he saw that
Sara Lark, instead of going barefoot as she often did, wore
her ankle boots and a battered campaign hat, probably supplied by Mrs. Zimmermann. Cranston thought that Sara
looked both excited and apprehensive. She was not a pretty
woman, the blue-and-gold kind a man took home to meet
the folks, but she had a certain worldly attractiveness.
There were a few wrinkles around her eyes and arcs formed
at each side of her mouth when she smiled. She walked
well, hips swaying just a little like a reformed harlot, and
her hair, not luxuriant but amber-colored and clean, was
brushed over her shoulders so it hung at either side of her
neck like bear paws. Her flowered dress, a castoff, was old
and worn but fitted her slender body quite well and was
high enough to reveal a couple of inches of white petticoat.

Sara Lark was all ready to go traveling, and to Lieutenant Cranston that meant trouble.

His suspicions were confirmed when Mrs. Zimmermann hugged her close and said, "Good luck, my dear. I'll pray for you to Saint Vitalis of Gaza. He's the patron saint of prostitutes and day laborers, and he'll give you his love and protection."

"Thank you, Mrs. Zimmermann, and extra thanks for everything you've done for me," Sara said. She brushed away a tear. "I'll never forget you."

"Nor I, you, Sara. Now be off with you. Your beau is waiting."

"Allow me to walk you to the stables, Miss Lark," Cranston said.

"Of course, Lieutenant," Sara said. "Between you and Saint Vitalis, I'm sure no harm will come to me."

"That is my intention," Cranston said.

The woman smiled. "Will you give me your arm?"

"Of course, I will."

When Lieutenant Cranston reached the stables, Jim Bertrand had two horses saddled, a gift from Captain Kellerman. He was dressed in a faded army blouse, a campaign hat, and wide canvas suspenders. He also wore his gun.

"Here to see us off, Lieutenant Cranston?" he said.

"I'm officer of the day, Mr. Bertrand. Seeing off guests is part of my job."

"I was a guest?" Bertrand said.

Cranston smiled. "I couldn't think of a better word."

"And you're here to protect me from Marshal Bowman?"

"Part of my job."

"Where is he?"

"I'm sure he'll be here."

"Well, he better be here soon. Sara and I are leaving. My regards to Captain Kellerman for his hospitality."

"You earned it, Mr. Bertrand, many times over."

"Going somewhere?"

Buck Bowman stepped into the stable, a new white bandage on his hand. He wore pants, shirt, boots, and his hat, and he'd swung around his gun belt so that the holstered Colt was butt-forward on his left hip.

"We're leaving, Marshal," Bertrand said. "I won't draw down on a man who's lost his gun hand, but you're not taking me to Yuma."

"Is that a fact?" Bowman said.

"Marshal, just let us go," Sara Lark said. "Jim has never done anything to harm you."

"I know. But the brave man inattentive to his duty is worth little more to his country than the coward who deserts in the hour of danger. Andrew Jackson said that, and it still holds true today."

"Stirring words, Marshal," Bertrand said. "Now, will you give us the road?"

"Lieutenant Cranston, who is this man?" Bowman said.

The young officer looked confused. "He's . . . he's Jim Bertrand, Marshal."

"No, he's not. Jim Bertrand was killed during the battle of Fort Misery. If there's any doubt about that, I'll tell the prison authorities in Yuma to come here, dig him up, and see for themselves. Lieutenant Cranston, am I right about Bertrand dying a hero's death?"

Conflicted, his honor as an officer and gentleman at stake, Lieutenant Cranston pondered the right and wrong of answering that question with a lie. Three people stared at him: Marshal Bowman was bemused, Sara Lark's eyes brimmed with anxiety, and Jim Bertrand showed no emotion, willing to accept whatever might come.

Finally, Cranston swallowed hard and said, "Yes, Marshal, that is my understanding."

Sara smiled, ran to the young officer, and planted a kiss on his cheek. "Thank you, Atticus," she said. "After so much death around me, you've given me life. A new life."

Bowman coughed politely and said, "Then where are you nice folks headed?" he said.

"East," Bertrand said. "There's lots of settlements that way."

"Take plenty of water," the marshal said.

"I've filled up canteens," Bertrand said. "We'll manage."

"Then be on your way, and good luck," Bowman said. "And stranger, if we ever see each other again, there's no need to say howdy."

Bertrand nodded. "I catch your drift, Marshal."

"Then so long, you two. Now I got to be going myself."

Bertrand touched his hat brim. "Adios, Lieutenant. Sara and I are much obliged to you."

With mixed emotions, Cranston watched the pair leave, but Fort Misery wasn't quite finished with Jim Bertrand yet.

Tobias Zimmermann hailed them, and Bertrand drew rein.

"You can't leave here penniless," Zimmermann said. "He held up a small leather pouch. "There's four double eagles in there to help you on your way."

"Why are you doing this?" Bertrand said.

"Call it professional courtesy. And when you do reach a settlement, your lady will need a place to lay her head." He touched his hat. "Miss Lark."

"Zimmermann, I can't take your money," Bertrand said.

"If you don't, Mrs. Zimmermann will be very cross with me. She says it's the Christian thing to do."

"Yes it is, Mr. Zimmermann," Sara said. She extended

her hand. "And you're right, I'll need a bath and a soft bed when we reach civilization."

Sara took the money, and then she and Bertrand rode on, but the gambler turned his head and called out over his shoulder, "Tobias, thank you."

Zimmermann kept on walking, but he raised a hand and waved.

Lieutenant Cranston watched Bertrand and Sara Lark ride into the vast, blazing desert until they were lost in the heat shimmer.

"Good luck, you two," he said. "I hope you make it."

CHAPTER 58

Over the next couple of months, during which time Christmas came and went, Captain Joe Kellerman sent out patrols, some as far south as the Rio Bravo. But apart from a minor brush with Mexican bandidos fleeing across the river from the Territory, they passed without incident.

Then two events happened that impacted Fort Misery directly and were destined to cause Kellerman and his motley command a world of grief and danger.

Lieutenant James Hall was officer of the day when the sentries reported that two mule-drawn wagons were coming in—one covered, the other open, with a driver at the reins and three men behind him.

"Graybeards by the look of them, sir," the sentry said.

"By the Lord Harry, graybeards," Hall said. "Not generals I hope."

"Sir, they don't look like generals, more like them perfessers that are always talking about strange stuff."

"Professors! Well, show them in," Hall said. "It will be a nice change to talk to my intellectual equals. And be respectful, you ruffian."

The drivers, not graybeards but a couple of rough-looking mule skinners, parked the wagons on the parade ground, and the occupants, three skinny older men in broadcloth and top hats, alighted and staggered toward Lieutenant Hall.

The oldest of the three was a tall, cadaverous man with long gray hair, rough-cut beard, staring hazel eyes that Hall at once decided were half-mad, and a sharp, pointed nose that was red in color, very sunburned.

"Officer, oh, officer," the man said in a gating, whiny voice. "What a dreadful journey, what an ordeal. Sun . . . heat . . . little water . . . and only disgusting dried meat to eat. I swear, we are almost dead."

The wagon driver, a rough-hewn character whose expression bordered on the villainous, said, "Which it is no fault of mine. I only drive the wagon. I don't control the weather. Which, it was all explained to you afore we left Yuma."

"And what is your name, and why are you here?" Hall said.

"My name is Paul Fernsby, Professor Paul Fernsby, and these are my associates, Professors Julius Dankworth and Oliver Berryman. Oh, listen to my voice. My throat's as dry as dust in a mummy's pocket."

"And why are you here, sir?"

"Young man, I'm here to uncover the remains of the lost army of the Spanish conquistador don Esteban de Toro and, if it's of any interest, his rumored treasure chest."

"Where is all this?" Hall said.

"Where is all this?" Fernsby parroted. "Do you hear that, Professor Berryman? Professor Dankworth?" He smiled and said, "Why, young man, if my map is correct, and I'm sure it is, we may be standing on it."

"So where do you want us to dump your stuff, Perfesser? Which if it isn't too much to ask," the driver said.

"Right here, my man," Fernsby said.

"I can't allow you to do that until I speak to my commanding officer," Hall said.

"Which it is of no concern of mine," the driver said. He turned in his seat and said, "Bob, get that stuff unloaded, if it isn't too much to ask." He shook his head and said, "Which he's the laziest of my sons."

"Halt!" Lieutenant Hall said. "You need the permission of Captain Kellerman."

Fernsby reached into his coat and produced a sweat-damp, lank envelope. "Right here is all the permission I need. It gives me and my archaeologist colleagues permission to dig at Fort Benjamin Grierson." He held up the letter inside as though it was a scroll. "Look at the signature, young man."

Hall read and then, shocked, said, "It's signed by President Grant."

"Indeed, it is. The president is a close personal friend of mine. One of his cousins is wed to my cousin Gertrude, and that makes us family."

"Close enough for me," Hall said. "I'll take you to Captain Kellerman."

"Julius, Oliver, stay with the equipment," Fernsby said. "I'll be right back."

The president's letter in mind, Lieutenant Hall decided to be ingratiating. He said to Berryman, a man as gaunt as his boss with hollow eyes and temples to match. "During the war I served with a captain named Oliver. We called him Ollie." He smiled. "Does anyone call you that?"

Berryman spaced out the words, stressing their severity, "No. One. Ever. Calls. Me. That."

Deflated, Hall said, "Ah . . . then Oliver it is."

"No, Oliver it isn't. You will address me as Professor Berryman. Do I make myself clear?"

"Clear as a bell, sir," Hall said. "Would you care for a pinch of snuff?"

"And what did he say when you offered him snuff?" Captain Joe Kellerman said.

"He said it was a barbarous substance used only by barbarians," Lieutenant Hall said. "I must say, it hurt my pride a little."

"You'll get over it. The boss feller changed his mind and decided to stay outside. Any idea why?"

"He wants to show you where he'll dig his trench."

"His what?"

"His trench. Apparently, it's what archaeologists call a hole in the ground."

"You can't dig a trench in sand."

"Begging the captain's pardon, but I think you should tell him that."

"All right," Kellerman said. "I'll go talk to him. What's the name again?"

"Professor Fernsby."

"Professor Frenzy . . ."

"Ah, that's Fernsby, Captain."

"You want to dig a hole in the middle of my parade ground." He looked at a pile of shovels, picks, and mattocks and pointed. "With those, Captain. According to my map . . ."

Kellerman lost it a little. "Damn it, man, what map?"

"Two years ago a parchment map was discovered in a hidden vault in the ruined castle of Vozmediano, situated halfway between Castile and Aragon in Spain."

"And X marks the spot of my parade ground?"

"Ah, you make a little joke," Fernsby said. "Since the map is dated 1540 it could hardly show Fort Benjamin Grierson. After adventures in Mexico, in 1538 the conquistador don Esteban de Toro marched this way, and his army, suffering from thirst, starvation, and exhaustion, was wiped out by local savages. But one man escaped, and he later returned to Spain and drew up the map, secreting it in the castle vault. Perhaps he died before he could return and search for the treasure chest that don Esteban was rumored to carry with him."

"Professor, this is a desert," Kellerman said. "Mile after mile of flat sand and dunes. A map needs coordinates and landmarks, and there are none."

"There is a rock shelf to the west of us that's clearly marked on the map."

"Yes, I know that shelf very well, but they come and go in the desert. Here sandstorms can be miles long and thousands of feet high, and they cover everything. Rocks you see today might not be there tomorrow." Kellerman shook his head. "Professor, your map is worthless."

"Ah, but that's where you're wrong, Captain. I spoke to a gathering of Yuma Indians who know the desert and remembered the rock shelf. Apparently there is a trickle of water atop the shelf that flows from an aquifer and collects in a rock tank. That's why the savages know it so well."

The two wagon drivers laid three trunks and tan canvas pants, shirts, and pith helmets beside the tools. The older one said, "That's it, Perfesser. Which is everything we brung." He'd lit a clay pipe that belched black smoke.

"Thank you, my good man," Fernsby said. "Come back for us in two months, mind."

"Which I will do," the man said. He nodded to Kellerman, gave him a wink, and climbed into the driver's seat.

"Two months?" Kellerman said, agitated. "You can't stay here that long."

"Oh, yes I can." He again pulled the limp envelope out of his coat and said, "Read it, Captain. Last paragraph." Then after a few moments, "Well?"

"It says I am to render you all possible assistance because the uncovering of don Esteban's treasure could be one of the most important archaeological finds in our nation's history," Kellerman said. He ran his fingers through his hair, a sure sign of his disquiet. He watched the wagons leave and then said, "How did the map lead you here?"

"Because the mapmaker wrote that the site of the massacre was a league to the east of the shelf. And then there is the matter of the bones and artifacts."

"What bones and artifacts?" Kellerman almost yelled that.

"It's common knowledge in Yuma that human bones and iron antiques were dug up when the foundations of Fort Benjamin Grierson were laid. It's the opinion of myself and my colleagues that these were relics of our lost Spanish army."

"I never heard anything like that," Kellerman said. "It's nonsense."

Lieutenant Hall spoke for the first time. "Sir, Tobias Zimmermann was here around the time the fort was constructed. I know he worked as a carpenter on the headquarters building and officer's quarters. Maybe he knows something about the artifacts."

"Then bring him here, Lieutenant. Tell Mr. Zimmermann I want to ask about digging up bones."

"And iron antiquities," Fernsby said.

"Yes, and those too," Kellerman said. "And Lieutenant Hall, be quick about it."

"Yes, Captain, we did dig up what we took to be human bones. It was hard to tell, since there were no skulls found," Tobias Zimmermann said.

"And iron artifacts?" Fernsby said.

"We came across a knife blade and an iron buckle, both badly corroded."

Fernsby said, his creaky voice hopeful. "A buckle from a sword belt?"

"From some kind of belt. Probably the bones were Yuma Indian, and the knife and buckle were trade goods."

"More likely the bones were Spanish," Fernsby said.

"I couldn't say," Zimmermann said. "One human leg bone looks like any other human leg bone." Then to Kellerman, "I'd like to return to my duties, Captain."

"Still patching up bullet holes?" Kellerman said.

"No, I'm repairing Mrs. Zimmermann's stove that was badly shot up."

"Then don't let me detain you. Right now the stove is more important than old bones."

"Quite so, sir," Lieutenant Hall said. "We can't take any chances on Mrs. Zimmermann's stove, or her entire kitchen, come to that."

"It is also Mrs. Zimmermann's opinion," her husband said.

"So what is the upshot of all this?" Sergeant Major Olinger said as he sat in Captain Joe Kellerman's office.

"The upshot is that the professors dig a trench in my parade ground," Kellerman said. "The president of the United States is backing them and has even supplied taxpayers' money to finance what Fernsby calls . . ." he made quote marks in the air. . .'his expedition.' "

Olinger sipped his whiskey, shook his head, and said, "Bad news, Joe."

Kellerman's smile came and went. "Saul, Fort Misery is the bad news capital of the world. Don't you know that?"

CHAPTER 59

Since Fort Misery had no telegraph, the news was sent by courier from Yuma, and it was bad.

The young trooper, aware of Fort Misery's reputation, stood uneasily in front of Captain Joe Kellerman's desk, his eyes darting here and there as though he expected at any moment a madman would spring at him with an ax.

"Is there any answer, sir?" the young soldier asked, his voice whisper quiet.

"What's your name, son?" Kellerman asked.

"Private Wilson, sir."

Kellerman sighed and said, "There's no answer. My orderly will point the way to the kitchen. Mrs. Kellerman will show you where to fill your canteen and tell her I asked that she give you something to eat before you leave."

"Yes, sir."

"You're dismissed."

The young man saluted and left. Kellerman waited a few minutes and then called for his orderly, Nelson Hare, one of the new men. "Did you show Private Wilson how to reach the kitchen?"

"I did, sir, but he scampered out the door, got on his horse, and fogged it out of here. I don't think he was at ease in Fort Misery."

"Fort Benjamin Grierson, Private Hare."

"Yes, sir."

"You've got your bugle handy?"

"Yes, sir."

"Officer's call."

"The dispatch makes for some depressing news," Lieutenant James Hall said to Kellerman. "Don't Apache ever stay home with their wives and children?"

"Apparently not," Captain Joe Kellerman said. "Two separate bands, Mescalero and Chiricahua, left the San Carlos a week ago and are headed our way. The dispatch says they probably intend to raid into Sonora."

"It doesn't give a number, but there's enough that elements of the Tenth Cavalry and several infantry companies is in hot pursuit—or will be in hot pursuit once they're mobilized."

"And when will that be?" Lieutenant Hall said.

"When the army is good and ready."

"And in the meantime?" Hall said.

"In the meantime we are to slow the progress toward Sonora of both Apache bands and at the same time ensure that . . ." he read from the dispatch ". . . Mexican troops make no unwarranted, armed incursions across the Rio Bravo."

"And we're expected to do all that with barely a cavalry troop? Hall said.

"Yes, we are. And let me remind you, Lieutenant, that we're considered expendable."

Olinger, a perceptive man, said, "Captain, you're holding back something. Is there more bad news?"

"I'm afraid there is," Kellerman said. He pinched the bridge of his nose and head bowed, said, after several false starts, "I was keeping this to the last." He drew a deep breath and continued, "The gallant Custer is dead."

The officers looked as though they each had been slapped by a steel gauntlet, and even the normally stoical Olinger was shaken to the core. "Sir, how? I mean . . ."

Kellerman read from the dispatch again. "On June twenty-five and twenty-six of this year, near the Little Bighorn River in the Montana Territory, five of the Seventh Cavalry's twelve companies were annihilated by a combined force of Sioux, Northern Cheyenne, and Arapaho. Among the dead were Lieutenant Colonel George Armstrong Custer along with his brother-in-law, First Lieutenant James Calhoun, and Captain Myles Keogh. Total casualties were 268 dead including four Crow Indian scouts and at least two Arikara. The regiment suffered 55 severely wounded, six of whom later died from their wounds."

The stunned silence that followed this news seemed to stretch forever, until Hall said, "Myles Keogh was one of the bravest men I have ever known, and his soldierly bearing was admired by all. He was par excellence a cavalry officer."

And Kellerman said, "Jimmie Calhoun was a fine soldier too, and so handsome he was known as the Adonis of the Seventh. He was married to Custer's sister Margaret— Maggie as we called her, a beautiful lady. Now, I think we all need a drink."

Kellerman poured the whiskey, stood, and raised his glass. "Gentlemen, to Custer and the gallant Seventh."

"To Custer and the gallant Seventh," the others said in unison. And then Hall added. "May they all be happy in Valhalla."

"Now you gentlemen understand why the army is slow in sending the Tenth after the Apache," Kellerman said.

"They may need every soldier they have in the Montana Territory."

Kellerman stepped to his window where he could see Professor Fernsby and his colleagues using whitewash to lay out a trench across the parade ground. Right on cue, Mrs. Zimmermann tapped on the door and walked inside.

"Captain Kellerman, what are those men doing?" she said. "I spoke to them, and they were very rude. They had the audacity to tell me to mind my own business."

"They're archaeologists and they plan to dig a big hole," Kellerman said.

"Why, may I ask?"

"They're looking for treasure, dear lady," Hall said.

"Treasure at Fort Misery? That'll be the day," Mrs. Zimmermann said. "And now I have three more mouths to feed. The only supplies those treasure-hunters brought are beef jerky, some crackers, and cheese, and mustard."

"Do the best you can," Kellerman said. "The professors will dine in the officers' mess."

"Mrs. Zimmermann, did you hear the news?" Hall said.

"What news? Good or bad?" the woman said.

"All bad, I'm afraid. The gallant Custer is dead, killed by Indians in the Montana Territory, and most of the Seventh Cavalry with him."

"Oh, dear God," Mrs. Zimmermann said. She swayed on her feet. "I feel faint."

"A chair for Mrs. Zimmermann," Hall said.

Sergeant Major Olinger placed a chair under her, and she sat.

"Here, drink this," Kellerman said, handing her a glass of whiskey. "It will do you good."

Mrs. Zimmermann downed the drink in one gulp, gasped for breath, and then said, her voice husky, "Jesus, Mary, and Joseph, and all the saints in heaven, what is to become of us, Captain Kellerman?"

"Talking as a soldier, the battle was a tactical victory for the Sioux and Cheyenne but a strategic defeat." Kellerman said. "Now the government will bring the full force of the army to bear, and the Indians, those that survive, will be penned up in reservations for years. It's a pity because the Indian way was a good way, but now they've signed their own death warrant."

"Yes, they'll follow the buffalo into extinction," Hall said. "In the meantime, the Montana Territory is far from here, and you have nothing to fear, Mrs. Zimmermann. Care for a pinch?"

"Disgusting," Mrs. Zimmermann said, making a face.

Kellerman said, "I should tell you that the Apache are out."

"Again?" the woman said. "Are they headed this way?"

"Yes, they are, but a dispatch I received from Yuma says two war bands intend to raid into Sonora. It will be our job to stop them."

"More bloodshed," Mrs. Zimmermann said. "Will it never end?"

Kellerman said, "I think the end is in sight. The Indians and their way of life can't last much longer."

"I hope I'm here to see it," the woman said.

"I hope we're all here to see it," Kellerman said.

Mrs. Zimmermann rose to her feet. "My poor heart is broken over General Custer, but now I must get back to my chores. I do wish Sara Lark was still here. She was such a help."

CHAPTER 60

The day after the news of Custer's death reached Fort Misery. Second Lieutenant Atticus Cranston led the Navajo and an eight-man scouting patrol west and got an unpleasant surprise: smoke rose from a fire at Santiago Lozado's old campground.

"Lieutenant, is he back?" Corporal John Lockhart said.

"No, Corporal, he's not back. He's dead."

Cranston halted the column of twos and used his field glasses to scan the area. After a while he said, "Looks like six men and a wagon."

"White men?" Lockhart said.

"Yes, white men wearing guns. What do you think, Ahiga?"

"Not Comancheros. Hunters maybe."

The young officer nodded, let the glasses hang, and said, "Form line and forward at walk. Let's get acquainted."

As he and his men advanced on the camp, the six men ahead of him grouped around a tall man who seemed to be their leader. The morning was clear, the sun rising, casting moving shadows of the troopers and their horses.

The men watched the soldiers come without any appearance of alarm and seemed to offer no threat. But a group of armed men in this wilderness had to be investigated.

When he was within talking distance, Cranston halted his men, saluted, and said, "Lieutenant Atticus Cranston. And you are?"

The tall man, half smiling, glanced over the soldiers, lingered on the Navajo, and then said, "Name's Lucas Dean, and these men are my associates."

"Why are you here, Mr. Dean?" Cranston said.

"Is that any business of yours, soldier boy?"

It was then Dean realized that this youthful officer had more sand than he thought. "I'm making it my business," Cranston said.

To emphasize that statement the Navajo adjusted the position of his hands on the Henry, a small movement but significant, and Dean knew it. The man said quickly, "We're hunters out of Yuma."

Cranston's gaze moved beyond Dean to the picketed horses. Six grade mounts of obvious quality and a Morgan to pull the wagon. The six men were dressed in shirts, pants, boots, and wide-brimmed hats. The clothing was dusty and nondescript, but their boots and gun leather looked custom-made and expensive.

"Hunting what?" the lieutenant asked.

The reply returned fast enough. "Mule deer and maybe a bighorn sheep."

"Why have you camped in this place?"

Dean jerked a thumb over his shoulder at the rock shelf. "Water up there. Not a lot but it drips into a tank. We figured we'd camp here, since it seems there have been plenty of hunters here before us."

"Mind if I take a look in the wagon?" Cranston said.

"Not at all," Dean said. "Look away, Lieutenant."

Cranston rode to the wagon and raised the canvas. Inside he saw food supplies, flour, baking powder, sugar, cornmeal, coffee in sacks, canned peaches, salt pork, and a side of bacon. It was basically chuckwagon grub and not suspicious.

"You gentlemen staying long?" Cranston asked when he returned to the others.

"Depends on the hunting, I guess," Dean said. "We thought maybe two or three weeks. If we sight bighorn, maybe longer."

"I'm sorry to tell you this," Cranston said, "but . . ."

"The Apache are out," Dean said. "Yeah, we heard that in Yuma. As far as I know, they're still to the northeast of us, playing hob. Maybe them young bucks will stay there."

Cranston shook his head. "No. Two separate bands are headed for Sonora. They'll pass this way, or close, so be on the lookout."

"We sure will," Dean said. "Won't we, boys?"

The man's smile didn't become him. His face was hardboned, his features blunt and coarse, lips wide and thin, the skin around them uncreased. A man unused to smiling. Only his eyes saved his features from the nondescript—startling green and almond-shaped, eyes that would be the envy of a beautiful woman. The five men with him were unremarkable—medium height, medium build, big mustaches—but they shared a cold-eyed, feral look, as though they'd been born outdoors and raised rough. Unfamiliar with the run of Texas draw fighters, Cranston didn't peg them as especially dangerous, but they were, and among them had notched up forty kills, most of them named men.

Unlike his new-to-the-West young officer, Captain Joe Kellerman, and certainly Tobias Zimmermann, would perhaps have marked them as men not to be ignored.

"Oh, you won't have heard the bad news, Mr. Dean," Cranston said.

"Well, you've already told me about the Apache. What else is there?" Dean said.

"Lieutenant Colonel Custer is dead, with most of the Seventh Cavalry."

The news appeared to have little impact on Dean or his men.

"Sorry to hear that," Dean said. "What happened?"

"The Seventh was attacked by a large force of Sioux and Cheyenne in the Montana Territory at a place called the Little Bighorn. Custer died in the field with his men around him."

"A hero's death," Dean said.

"Could the gallant Custer die any other kind?" Cranston said. "Well, good luck with your hunting. From time to time, patrols will be back this way to check up on you."

"We appreciate that, Lieutenant," Dean said. "It sets my mind at ease to know the army is close at hand. Sorry about Custer."

CHAPTER 61

"There's six of them you say?" Captain Joe Kellerman said, sitting behind his office desk, a whiskey in his hand.

"Yes, sir," Lieutenant Atticus Cranston said. "They say they're hunting."

"It sounds fishy to me, Lieutenant. Why camp on Lozado's old ground?"

"Because there's water, sir."

"And what's that man's name again? Bean?"

"Lucas Dean, sir."

"What's your impression of him?"

"Impression, sir?"

"Yes, his dress and demeanor."

"He's dressed in shirt and pants, and he seemed friendly enough, but he seemed to be a bit wary of the Navajo."

"A lot of people are wary of the Navajo. Orderly!"

Private Nelson stepped inside, and Kellerman said, "My compliments to Mr. Zimmermann and ask him to come to my office."

When Tobias Zimmermann arrived, sooty from his forge, Kellerman said, "You're familiar with these shady characters, does the name Lucas Bean . . ."

"Ah, that's Dean, sir," Cranston said.

"Lucas Dean. Does the name mean anything to you, Mr. Zimmermann?"

"I've heard of him."

"Tell me," Kellerman said.

"He's a badman and shootist out of Fort Worth, but he never works west of the Colorado."

"It seems he does now. He's holed in Santiago Lozado's old campground. Tell me more."

"For a while Dean was just a small-time crook who worked a kidnapping scheme, grabbing some rube's wife or kid and demanding money for their return. But Luke Short ran him out of Fort Worth, and for a while he took up the train-robbing profession. He soon tired of that and turned his hand to banks. But he got shot by some hick-town sheriff and was like to die until a whore nursed him back to health. Dean later married her. I heard she died of consumption a couple of years ago."

"Damn it, Mr. Zimmermann, you know a lot about outlaws," Kellerman said.

"Well, for a time, before I started selling my gun, I was more or less in the same profession. Outlawry is an excellent career if a man keeps his head and his gunplay to a minimum. Wes Hardin never learned that lesson, and that's why he's in jail today."

"So, tell me more about Bean."

"That's Dean, sir," Cranston said.

"Thank you, Lieutenant Cranston. Mr. Zimmermann, tell me more about Dean."

"Well, I'm a bit hazy on this, but Lucas Dean never hit his stride as an outlaw, so he recruited five guns who formed a gang they called the Trey-Treys, since, including himself, there were six of them. Seems like he rolled dice and came up with two threes and decided lady luck wanted him to keep his numbers to six."

"Hence the Trey-Treys," Kellerman said. "Clever. What's he doing now and why is he camped on my doorstep?"

"As to why he's here, I don't know. But he rents the Trey-Treys out to anybody who will pay big money for top-class gun work—ranchers and businessmen and the like. Why, he and his boys even tamed a Texas cow town once, signed on as lawmen. After they took care of the resident toughs, twenty of them, they robbed the bank and set fire to the town. The name of the burg was Ruby Point, but you won't find it on the map. All that's left is foundations and an overgrown boot hill. They say there's an actress by the name of Connie Cobain buried there, that she burned up when the hotel caught fire. But I don't know if that's true or not."

"True or not, you're a mine of information, Mr. Zimmermann," Kellerman said. "I know I've asked you this already, but why is Lucas Dean here?"

"Not to hunt mule deer, that's for sure," Zimmermann said.

"He says he came down from Yuma," Lieutenant Cranston said. "Is it possible the professors talked about treasure and somebody overheard and wired Dean?"

"You mean his being here and the professors digging up my parade ground are linked?" Kellerman said.

"It's possible, sir," Cranston said.

"Mr. Zimmermann, what do you think?" Kellerman said.

"A treasure chest is something that might interest the Trey-Treys," Zimmermann said.

"Let's have a greater mind than ours figure this out,"

Kellerman said. "Orderly!" Hare stepped into the office. "Officers' call."

"Yes, definitely the two are linked, and that's my considered opinion," Lieutenant James Hall said. "In Yuma, the professors ran off at the mouth about treasure, and somehow this Dean fellow heard about it. There it is, Captain, clear as mother's milk. As always, you can depend on my advice."

"So, there we have it," Kellerman said. "We have two Apache war bands heading straight for us, six dangerous gunmen camped on our doorstep, three professors digging up Fort Misery in search of dead Spaniards, and the ever-present threat that Mexican troops will cross the Rio Bravo into the territory and play hob. What does all that add up to?"

"Sir, a heap of trouble, I daresay," Lieutenant Hall said, opening his snuffbox.

"Exactly, a heap of trouble," Kellerman said. "Gentlemen, the storm clouds are gathering."

"We can handle it, sir," Lieutenant Cranston said.

"Bully, young Atticus!" Hall said, his face alight. "Damn it all, I've taught you well. Here, have a pinch."

HISTORICAL NOTE

Fort Misery is loosely based on an 1865 log house built by the army in Prescott to provide quarters for Governor John N. Goodwin in the newly created Arizona Territory. Though never a fort, the house's second occupant, Judge Howard, by all accounts a tyrant, delivered rough justice to felon and soldiers alike, and the place became such a punishment posting the troops gave it the name Fort Misery. Legend says the building was later converted into a boardinghouse and that the woman who ran the house, called the *Virgin Mary* because of her many charities, cooked barely edible meals for fifty men. If she ever existed, her real name was Mary Brown.

MRS. ZIMMERMANN'S PLUM DUFF

Plum Duff was a treat for the soldiers exiled to Fort Misery, but the steamed pudding's quality varied depending on supplies dropped off at Devil's Rock. There are no plums in the pudding, just raisins.

Her basic recipe was:

- 2 cups flour blended with 1 teaspoon of baking soda and a pinch of salt
- ¼ cup suet, chopped fine (you can substitute melted shortening)
- ¼ to 1 cup raisins
- ¼ to 1 cup sugar

Mix the ingredients and add a cup of cold water. The dough should be stiff.

To steam the pudding Mrs. Zimmermann would then place it on a floured cloth, wrap the cloth around the dough, and tie it at the top with a string, leaving a loop at the top. The duff expands when cooked.

Then she'd would fill a large pot with water about two-thirds full and bring it to a boil. She'd suspend the pudding in the pot by placing a wooden spoon through the kitchen string. Don't let the cloth touch the bottom of the pot! Steam for three to four hours.

After it finished steaming Mrs. Zimmermann would turn out the pudding onto a platter and slice it into servings. If the men were lucky and supplies plentiful, she might serve the dessert with molasses.

A taste of the nineteenth century . . . try it, you might like it.

Keep reading for a special excerpt!
PREACHER'S PURGE
William W. and J.A. Johnstone

**When greed overtakes men's souls,
it falls to the righteous mountaineer known as
Preacher to rain fire and brimstone upon them
from the barrels of his guns . . .**

Preacher has agreed to escort Barnaby Cooper through
Dakota Territory's hills to establish a trading post.
Accompanied by his friends Lorenzo and Tall Dog, the
mountain man hopes they'll be able to protect Cooper
from Sioux warriors, who don't want any white man
trespassing on their sacred grounds.

But the Sioux aren't the only hostiles staking their claim
in the region. Englishman Albion Shaw knows there's
gold in the hills. And with a band of cutthroat killers to
do his bidding, Shaw has enough manpower and
firepower to keep both trappers and tribes from settling
on the land where he can build an empire.

But Shaw didn't reckon on crossing a man like Preacher.
A man who not only knows what it takes to survive
in the wilderness, but a man who will fight for
freedom and justice to his very last breath—and
his very last bullet . . .

Look for **Preacher's Purge,** *on sale now!*

CHAPTER 1

"Them soldier boys are studyin' on us mighty hard, an' in an unfriendly manner, Preacher. So hard an' unfriendly my neck hair's standin' on end."

"I know it." Preacher sopped up the dregs of his stew with his last biscuit and devoured it.

The seven blue-uniformed soldiers his friend Lorenzo referred to had already caught Preacher's attention with their furtive glances and cold intensity. The tension had been building, and Preacher supposed he knew why that might be.

The soldiers sat around their table in the back corner of the Scalded Beaver Tavern. There were seven of them now, all wearing blue uniforms and all hard-looking men who looked like they'd been on both sides of the mountain. They drank heavily, but they'd been drinking before they came in. A couple of them had stumbled pretty good.

The time was just an hour or two past dark, and the meal was sitting well with Preacher. Or it had been. Most decent folk were back in their homes and only the night owls, gamblers, and those who had a taste for alcohol and soiled doves were out and about.

At another table on the other side of the tavern, a small

group of men peered at a map and talked quietly among themselves. In their own way, the men seemed just as intense as the watchful soldiers. Preacher didn't know if these men would be considered "decent," but the men didn't pay attention to much outside themselves.

One of them wore a tall, brown D'Orsay hat. Although the hat had been obviously cared for, the distinctive curved brim was wilted in a couple places and showed a few scuffed spots. The hat had been through some tough times. Preacher supposed the young man sitting under it had too because he had a knocked-about look that showed in his rough clothing and wind-burned face.

An air of desperation clung to the man and his group that wouldn't be found in most folks in Fort Pierre.

The mountain man looked away from the group and focused on the soldiers. Their grumbling had gotten hotter and louder. Those men weren't decent or quiet men. The scars and haphazard attention to their uniforms advertised that.

They were trouble. Or were soon to be trouble.

Preacher wouldn't claim to be decent, but he could be a bad man for those who had wronged him or others he decided to protect. He didn't hesitate when push came to shove, or when it was time to root, hog, or die. Tonight, he had no wish for aggravation.

He chased the last swallow of stew with a sip of beer and glanced over again at the group Lorenzo had called his attention to.

"They came in about an hour ago and have been watchin' us ever since," Preacher agreed. "I think they're workin' their nerve up to somethin'."

Across the table from Preacher, Tall Dog cut another bite of his steak with one of the knives he carried. The young

Crow warrior was a walking armory, and that was only one of the things Preacher respected about him.

Like Preacher and Tall Dog, Lorenzo wore buckskin pants and a shirt, all of them recently made and in good shape. He carried two pistols shoved through the sash at his waist. His Hawken rifle leaned against the wall close to hand just as Preacher's did.

"We could go ask what they find so interesting about us," Tall Dog suggested. "I would be happy to do that."

He popped the bite of steak into his mouth and chewed like he had all the time in the world.

Preacher pushed his empty plate away. "No. I don't want to go on the prod. The major over the army here doesn't much cotton to folks disturbin' the peace. We'll lie low and give 'em leeway to figure out their own path. They can't surprise us. If those varmints are dead-set on confrontin' us, they'll come back later when we ain't expectin' it."

Lorenzo grinned mirthlessly. His skin was dark, but his hair was going gray these days, not black like it had been when Preacher had first met him years back. He was slimmer now than he'd been, wiry and tough. Time was creeping up on him and had worn away at any spare flesh he'd carried. Until he and Preacher had gotten reunited a couple months ago at a Crow camp on the Snake River, Lorenzo had been talking about seeking the easy life. Boredom had settled in pretty quickly and he'd wandered West again.

"Now that you know they're lookin' at us lookin' at them," Lorenzo said, "any chance of you not expectin' them?"

Preacher grinned back. "Nope. But I'm not going to look at them too hard. I'd rather get this over with now if anything's gonna come of it. Before they talk themselves out of doing something now."

"You afraid of scarin' them off?"

"There are seven of them. Seems like if they were really feelin' froggy, they'd have jumped by now. I'd rather see it comin' than be lookin' over my shoulder the whole time we're here."

Lorenzo pulled a face. "You're bored, spoilin' for a fight, an' we only got in late last evenin'."

"After all the excitement recoverin' those rifles and fightin' Diller and his men, the trip back to Fort Pierre was just a mosey. A fracas in this tavern might take the edge off of bein' back in civilization."

"All of these people constantly around has that effect on someone used to living in the mountains," Tall Dog said. "Their presence is most . . . irritating. I find myself weary of it as well."

Lorenzo shook his head. "My oh my, but the bloom fades quick, don't it? An' here you was all excited to see a big town."

"I still want to see it," the young Crow warrior said. "I have heard many stories about large places such as this one. I just do not find the experience as relaxing or as informative as I believed I would."

"This ain't even big." Lorenzo snorted. "Fort Pierre don't hold a candle to the likes of St. Louis. An' if you really have a hankerin' to see somethin' of civilization an' society, why you should get yourself on down to New Orleans. Now that there is a big city, but it's got food the likes of which you ain't ever seen. Take you weeks to sample it all, an' there's a lot more to see."

"I think I shall have to limit my exposure to small portions," Tall Dog admitted ruefully. "I did not get much sleep last night."

"Them beds is soft," Lorenzo observed. "I found mine

mighty welcome after campin' out along the trail gettin' here."

"The bed is too soft," Tall Dog said. "I slept on the floor, but all the noise from the tavern on the first floor and out in the street kept me awake."

The broad-shouldered young man was tall with dark blond hair shaved to the scalp on the sides and left long enough on top to make a braid that hung down his back. His heavily bronzed skin marked him as an Indian, and that made him an outcast in several places within the fort.

He wore a sword with a looped hilt sheathed in a scabbard down his back. A short dark blond beard covered his strong chin. He'd gotten the hair color and the steel-gray eyes from his Swedish father. His bronze skin and polite ways came from his Crow mother. She was soft-spoken and had insisted on good behavior from her only son. His Christian name was Bjorn Gunnarsson, but he generally introduced himself as Tall Dog, a Crow warrior, because that was more believable.

When Preacher had headed north from the Crow village beside the Snake River, Tall Dog had, with the blessing of his parents, accompanied the mountain man to return the lost rifles they'd taken back from the rogue army captain Diller. The young Crow warrior had wanted to see more of the white man's world, though his father Olaf had promised him the visit would be disenchanting because he'd had enough of it himself.

Still, a young man tended to wander. Preacher knew that for a fact. He'd left home early himself because the mountains had captured his heart and imagination with their mystery and majesty. He'd never regretted going into the wilderness.

"If a bed is troublin' you," Lorenzo declared, "I can't

promise you're gonna get on much better with anythin' else you're gonna find here."

Tall Dog considered his empty plate. "The food is good."

"Are you certain?"

The Crow warrior regarded Lorenzo suspiciously before answering. "I am."

"I only ask 'cause it took you two plates' worth to make up your mind. From the way you wolfed it down, I figured you never bothered to taste any of it."

"Well," Tall Dog said, "from my continued observation, which was necessary, I now know that the food here is both good *and* plentiful."

Lorenzo shot a sour look at Preacher, who laughed aloud because the older man knew he'd been one-upped.

"Why don't you make yourself useful an' get us another round of beers," Lorenzo suggested to Preacher.

"I can do that," Preacher replied. "Need to stretch my legs anyway."

"I'll watch your rifle."

Preacher stood and adjusted the gun belt he wore. Even though he'd worn it every day for a few months, it was still a new thing to him. Normally he'd carried his flintlock pistols in a sash at his back. He still carried those there, but the new Colt Paterson revolvers he'd been given by the Texas Rangers rode in holsters on his hips. Those weapons had caught the eye of every man in the fort who knew armament. The repeating pistols were still new out West.

Tall and powerful from years spent living in the mountains and fighting Blackfeet Indians and outlaws, Preacher drew the attention of the men sitting around the Scalded Beaver. Some of them he'd met in passing while doing business at the fort. Others knew him by suspicion and reputation. He had a fresh haircut and shave, courtesy of the local barber, and his mustache was in fine fettle. With winter coming, he'd grow out his beard again soon, but for now being clean-shaven suited him.

The stout, red-bearded bartender was mostly bald on top. What was left of his hair was oiled into place and looked like a dead jellyfish spread out over his pink scalp. He dressed neat, though, with an apron and gartered sleeves. He spoke with a Gaelic lilt.

"You'll be having another three beers?" the bartender asked. "Or would you be wishing for something a little more powerful?"

"The beer's good. A man can't always get good beer."

"Beer it is, then."

Preacher glanced at the mirror on the wall behind the counter as the bartender stepped over to the tapped beer keg sitting on the long shelf beneath the mirror.

Three of the soldiers got up from the group at the back of the tavern and approached the bar through the scattered tables. One of the soldiers wore a fringed yellow epaulette on his left shoulder that marked him as a subaltern, probably a lieutenant.

"You got company coming, mate," the bartender said softly so his voice didn't carry any farther than Preacher.

"I see them," the mountain man replied. "No idea what they want."

Warm excitement filled him. Since the soldiers had come in, he'd weathered the threat they had presented with their covert, at first, attentions, then their downright brash brassiness.

"You know the leftenant?" the bartender asked.

"Nope."

"That's Judd Finlay." The bartender placed a full glass

of beer down and reached for another glass. "He can be a bad bloke."

Preacher nodded. "Thanks for the warnin'."

The lieutenant was broad and heavy-faced with high cheekbones. His nose sat askew from its proper position. His brown hair was combed back from his high forehead, but a few unruly strands hung down over his bushy brows. His mouth looked small on that wide expanse of face, only a little broader than his nose. Dark brown whiskers covered his square chin. He was about Preacher's age.

The bartender filled the third glass. "He's a southpaw. Catches folks off-guard with that. Hits hard enough most opponents don't recover."

"I'll keep that in mind."

The bartender placed the three glasses of beer in front of Preacher. The mountain man dropped enough coins on the counter to cover the beer, and added a nice tip.

"Thanks, mate." The bartender disappeared the coins and turned to Finlay and his two cohorts with a practiced smile that revealed nothing of the conversation he'd had with Preacher. "Something I can get for you, Leftenant?"

"Shot of whiskey," Finlay growled. He tucked into the bar to Preacher's left only inches away. The man smelled like a brewery. "The good stuff."

"All right then." The bartender turned back to the neat rows of bottles. "Coming right up. Shots for your mates, too?"

Preacher picked up the three glasses of beer. Lorenzo and Tall Dog watched him from their table. The four soldiers in the back moved toward the center of the tavern.

"Them, too," Finlay agreed and nodded to the men. He turned and focused his dark green eyes on Preacher. "Say, ain't you the one they call Preacher?"

Preacher returned Finlay's gaze full measure. "I am."

Finlay ran a finger alongside his crooked nose. "Story goes that you came in talkin' ill of Captain Diller."

"You're talkin' about the same Captain Diller who robbed Pierre Chouteau's shipment of rifles a few months ago," Preacher said evenly and loud enough to be heard around the tavern, "and blamed that robbery on Blackfeet warriors? That the varmint you're talkin' about?"

Everyone in the tavern stilled. Conversations stopped. Glasses quietly returned to tabletops. The man in the D'Orsay hat turned to watch with bright interest.

Finlay's face suffused with blood and he opened his mouth.

Before the man could speak, Preacher continued. Maybe he was on the prod. A little.

"You're askin' about the same Captain Diller who also murdered the Army's replacement for the major in command of the soldiers here? And all the soldiers who rode with him? Is that the Diller you're talkin' about?"

Finlay's eyes narrowed. "They say you killed him."

"I did. Shot that varmint right between the eyes while he was drawin' down on me. He knew what he was gettin' into."

"He was my friend."

"I gave Diller a Christian burial out there in Colter's Hell. He didn't deserve it, but I try not to leave a man without buryin' him. Especially if I killed him. I marked the grave so he'll be easy enough to find if you're of a mind to visit and pay your respects."

"If you killed him, you backshot him!" Finlay roared. "Ain't no other way you could take Diller head-on! An' then you spun that story about rescuin' Chouteau's rifles just so you could lay your own claim to part of them! I heard all about that! You're a liar an' a thief!"

Preacher spoke coldly, the only warning he was willing to give. "Maybe you need to learn to pick your friends better."

Finlay spun and fired his big left hand straight off his shoulder at Preacher's face. The lieutenant masked the blow with his body till the last minute. If Preacher hadn't been forewarned by the bartender and his own observation of the soldiers' heightened interest in him and his friends, he might have gotten caught looking.

CHAPTER 2

The mountain man swayed back just enough to be out of range of his opponent's fist, then he set the three beer glasses on the bar. He spun to face Finlay.

"Hey!" the bartender yelled. He reached below the counter and came up with a wooden club. "No fighting in here! Get out of my—!"

Finlay threw another left-handed punch. Preacher caught the blow on his right forearm and turned it aside. The impact partially numbed his arm. The lieutenant was strong as a mule.

Moving quickly because both of Finlay's cohorts closed in, and one of them had somehow gotten the bartender's club, Preacher took a half-step forward and jabbed Finlay in the face with his left hand hard enough to drive the man back, then pummeled him with a roundhouse right that caught him on the jaw and sent him stumbling backward in a rush.

The man behind Finlay attempted to catch the lieutenant and became tangled with him.

The third man circled them. Lantern light glinted dully off the brass knuckles on his fists as he stepped toward Preacher. Before the man's lead foot planted solidly on the sawdust-strewn and beer-stained floor, Preacher kicked the man's ankle and knocked him off balance. As the man tried to recover his stance, the mountain man caught his opponent's left wrist in one hand and gripped the man's elbow in the other. When the man tried to yank free, Preacher used the motion to violently crank the captured hand down and back. He drew his hand from the man's elbow, then drove it back down as hard as he could.

Something snapped in the man's elbow or shoulder, possibly both, and he squalled in pain. He dropped to the floor and cradled his injured arm.

Preacher didn't care. He'd intended to break at least one of those joints to reduce the odds and let the brawlers know how far he was willing to go. Finlay and his men outnumbered Preacher and his companions, and this wasn't just a barroom brawl. The surprise attack and the brass knuckles proved that.

Beyond the fallen man, Lorenzo and Tall Dog squared off against the other four soldiers. Patrons of the Scalded Beaver, including the man in the D'Orsay hat and his friends, were vacating the premises, but several of them crowded the windows to peer inside. They were backlit by the scattered lanterns that kept the night at bay along the cross streets where the tavern sat.

"Don't kill them unless you have to!" Preacher bellowed.

He wasn't wishful for any trouble with the current Army major or Pierre Chouteau. Fighting was one thing, but killing a man would bring more problems. He'd only intended a couple days of respite before returning to the mountains he loved. Profits in the fur trade were growing thin, and it was too late in the season to find a wagon train to guide. Preacher would make do living off the land for the winter.

Returning the captured rifles after claiming two dozen of them as his own hadn't left Preacher in any good graces with Pierre Chouteau, but it had given him a small poke after selling those rifles. Losing those weapons had deeply cut into the French trader's profit margin.

Preacher turned his attention to Finlay and the other soldier as they closed on him. He considered drawing one of the Colt Patersons and putting an end to the fracas. He might have done it if he weren't sure he would have had to kill one or both the men facing him to stop them. They were just mean-drunk enough to be stupid and stubborn.

Then again, if they'd tried to ambush Preacher in an alley, he'd have killed them straight off.

Finlay and the other soldier wore pistols and knives but so far hadn't seemed inclined to go for them. Evidently, they had been intent on just delivering a beating.

Growling an oath through his bloody lips, Finlay grabbed a chair and swung it at Preacher. The mountain man stepped toward his opponent to use him as a shield against the other man carrying the club, took the brunt of the chair across the thick muscles of his back, and slammed his right fist into Finlay's face.

The big lieutenant dropped the pieces of the broken chair and thudded to his knees with glazed eyes. Slowly, Finlay toppled onto his face and didn't move.

The soldier with the club swung over Finlay, but Preacher ducked, avoided most of the blow, and caught a glancing blow on his left cheek and temple. Even though he was a little dazed, he came up with a throat punch that temporarily shut off the man's wind.

Panicked because he suddenly couldn't breathe, the soldier stumbled back with both his hands wrapped protectively around his neck. His eyes were wide with fear.

Preacher grabbed the man by the hair, yanked him to the side, and kicked his feet out from under him.

"You're going to be all right," the mountain man told his opponent lying on the floor. "If you stay down."

The man rolled over onto his back and struggled to get his wind back. He made no effort to get up.

Tall Dog stood with folded arms in the middle of three unconscious men, two of whom had, at first glance, at least one broken limb. At six and a half feet tall, the Crow warrior towered over his vanquished foes.

Lorenzo struggled with one overweight soldier who was big as a bear and fought like a banshee. Despite the fat man's struggles, Lorenzo kept him corralled against the wall beside the tavern entrance. Lorenzo cursed like a mule skinner and sounded frustrated to boot as he huffed and puffed and swung his knobby fists.

The fat man hit Lorenzo in the ribs with a hard right that took the air out of the smaller man. Lorenzo responded with two hooks, a left and a right, that smashed into the soldier's face and caused his head to thump against the wall.

Preacher stood beside Tall Dog. "You ask him if he needs help?"

"I did. He told me he did not require assistance."

Preacher folded his arms over his chest and waited.

Lorenzo grabbed the man's ears and hammered his opponent's massive head against the wall with the stubborn intensity of a woodpecker working a new tree.

Preacher raised his voice over the thudding. "Lorenzo? You need a hand?"

"No, I don't need no help!" Lorenzo yelled and wheezed for breath. "I ain't some two-bit, wet-behind-the-ears greenhorn! This man is just too stupid an' onery to know when he's outhorsed!"

"You might need to blow for a minute," Preacher suggested.

"I'm fine," Lorenzo growled. "Leave me be. I've almost got him whupped."

"I think the man is mostly unconscious," Tall Dog said.

Looking at the ineffectual way the soldier swung his arms, Preacher agreed. "Hey, Lorenzo, just step back a minute."

Reluctantly, panting, Lorenzo stepped back with his balled fists in front of him. His opponent stood for a moment and jerked his arms. He never blinked. Then, slowly, he fell forward to the floor with a massive, meaty thump and remained still.

Lorenzo bent over and rested his hands on his knees. He drew in deep breaths.

"Told you I had him," Lorenzo said.

"You did," Preacher agreed.

"That's a big ol' boy," Lorenzo gasped and glanced at Tall Dog. "Wasn't no pantywaist like them you three were fighting." He shifted his gaze to Preacher. "Or them three you fought."

"I reckon not," Preacher replied agreeably. "You did fight the biggest one."

"I hope to shout," Lorenzo agreed.

"Maybe we should get out of here while the gettin's good," Preacher suggested.

"Lemme find my hat."

Movement out in front of the tavern caught Preacher's eye. Blue Army uniforms cut through the crowd and headed for the tavern.

"Might not get out of here after all," Preacher said and nodded toward the window.

Lorenzo glanced up and frowned. "Damnation." He bent down again and retrieved his hat. "You wouldn't think pole-cats like these would have friends." He shrugged and took a breath. "Takes all kinds, I suppose."

The front door banged open and a dozen soldiers ran into the room with their rifles raised.

Lorenzo waved a hand at them. "Preacher, you and Tall

Dog go ahead an' dig in. When I catch my breath, I'll be along. Save me a few."

The soldiers leveled their rifles at Finlay and his men lying scattered on the floor. A few of those rifles covered Preacher and his companions.

A whip-smart young officer walked into the bar and stood in front of his troops. One of his gloved hands rested on the hilt of his military saber. A neatly-trimmed blond mustache covered his upper lip. His blue eyes were hard.

"This fracas is at an end," the officer declared in a clear voice. "I am Lieutenant Kraft. I'm here to sort this mess out. Any continued hostilities on your part will result in you getting shot."

"Well," Lorenzo said like he was disappointed, "that plumb puts an end to things, don't it?"